THE BRINGER
OF OLD AGE

THE BRINGER OF OLD AGE

ZEMPEL

Published by GZworks
zempelbrothersmedia@gmail.com
instagram.com/thebringerofoldage

ISBN: 979-8-9903575-0-1

First Edition

Design by
Peter Bennett
Bennett Book Design
St. Louis, Missouri
www.bennettbookdesign.com

Acknowledgements

by Graham Zempel

To Michael "Mando" Kerper, who saved this book. In the years I've known you, you've proven yourself to be one of the strongest, most interesting people on the planet. Our countless conversations on the patio at Boogaloo were fuel to the fire that brought this novel to fruition. Thank you for being supportive when I was in the darkest point of my life. I love you like a brother, and I won't hold my breath waiting for you to finish reading this turd.

To Beau Diamond, a force to be reckoned with. I didn't know you liked us this much! I kid. You're a good friend to have, and I love your band and your music. The shows we've played together over the years will live on not only for us, but for everyone you've touched with your voice. Thank you for your support, and I look forward to both our futures.

To Dalton Webb, the diamond in the rough. In the short time we've known each other we've become best friends, and you're a great roommate. Whether we're talking anime and video games, venting about our jobs, or building something in the basement—there's never a dull moment. You stood by me and helped me during the darkest time of my life. Thank you for being you and being a part of this.

To Peter Bennett, simply, the man. This was the perfect scenario. When Joe and I finished writing this thing, we wanted to support local groups wherever we could within the publishing process. You've been honest, patient, and a beacon of knowledge and comfort for Joe and I as we venture into this new medium. We couldn't be more grateful for your work, and I'm proud to call you a friend.

To Michael Boyd, the Drunk and Nerdy. We had to plug your podcast—couldn't resist. It was our first impression of you, in fact. We look up to you as an icon of knowledge and good taste in the realms of fantasy and science fiction, and we're so happy to include you in this. This letter was written by both of us. Thank you for your encouragement, your kindness, and for trusting us with this mantle. Your support means worlds to us.

TABLE OF CONTENTS

Making an Exit

PEOPLE all around quake with a sudden and present insecurity. The young and ambitious Solar System, defined by expansion, staggers beneath the weight of tragedy and can only turn inward for answers. Hundreds of years after the Last War the people of Sol find themselves confronted with a forgotten yet familiar darkness.

United Frontier interplanetary biologists scramble inside a highly advanced greenhouse and botany lab located atop a skyscraper in the utopian metropolis of Shanghai. Jiang Laboratories is the United Frontier Center for Interplanetary Environmental Research. White and chrome architecture cradles immense glass panes, shaping a towering icon for interplanetary botany. The equipment and technology are the most advanced available, and the plant life is healthy and vivacious. However, morale is forgotten in this once comfortable, routine-driven symbol of agricultural sustainability for Earth and every planetary colony in Sol. The operations of the laboratory have been thrown into a tailspin. Those involved, whose careers have gone from cakewalk to cleanup, are on their feet shouting at one another.

Doctor Ezra Pierce stands outside watching the stars disappear into the summer morning sky. He takes a slow, deep breath, uses the backs of his fingers to stretch the dry, aging skin away from his tired, brown eyes. Ezra celebrated his forty-fifth birthday over the summer, and his age is finally beginning to show as he stumbles into the autumn months. He speaks firmly into a quaint, outdated recording device in his hand.

"New log … date, eight point one-seven. I've had it. The arrogance … it'll destroy us. Titan's research corps is a joke, who suspiciously claims to fear the unknown. All this, while investments pour in? The same who call themselves scientists — who commit themselves to sustainability and growth in genetics — refuse to share sufficient data with Earth. How long has UF on Earth known about the starvation toll?

"… And my suspicions grow ever further. Our political leaders are quiet while the Yellow-Sectors have begun pouring trillions into 'UF Research and Excavation.' All of this, at a time when it seems the population is losing faith in humanity, and the division between sectors has never been greater. UF's *Sol Media* tried to keep it quiet! Our golden age has ended, and those who could've prevented this crisis, or rather those who *would* have, were completely unaware.

"Food shortages have rendered nearly 500,000 in the Green Sectors dead of starvation just this year. At the current rate, it is estimated that Earth will lose millions to starvation as well as violence. The public and media toss their own ideas around as to the cause of this horror. Speculation begets misinformation and we are left with the greatest preventable tragedy ever to embarrass our species." His voice begins to tighten as hearing his own words feeds his anger. Other doctors and employees begin to notice his intensity.

"All the media's sudden and conflicting theories have done nothing but strengthen the animosity between sectors, dredging up outdated, century-old prejudices toward things such as race, and ethnicity. One thing I truly believe in, is humans' unrelenting determination to survive." Sunlight begins climbing down the skyscrapers of Shanghai. The city was always beautiful from on high, but now it feels as if the tall buildings, with their ergonomic structures and exterior gardens, are hiding a painful truth. He continues, "Which is also scary, given the circumstances... But another thing I truly believe in, is the scores of trials and research, along with our advancements in tech and synthetics. Our research has brought myself, and my scientists, to a profoundly simple theory." The doctor clutches a fistful of healthy soil from a nearby plot and briefly studies it, then resentfully throws it back. Car horns begin to chirp like distant birds as the city below comes to life. The overworked doctor turns to the interior of the lab. His path indoors is wreathed with rows of greenery. Ardent shrubs and dancing vines hug the warm, lit computer terminals at each plot. He continues ranting, and crosses the enormous greenhouse. Other scientists stop what they're doing and listen.

"We were adapting... learning from the changes in our climate and overcoming them, but something changed. The United Frontier found something they're not telling us about... I know it. Why else would UF's media hide the starvation toll?" His voice steadily increases in volume as his employees listen. He reaches one plot set apart by its verdant health and tremendous growth.

Ezra holds a bright green leaf in his hand, and admires the sheer strength of the plant as he pets and tugs it. Bittersweet Nightshade — an uncultivated weed — five times its normal size. The terminal screen at this enriched plot of soil reads, "Titan Synthetic Trial 001." This plot in particular is testing a nutrient recipe sent from an unspecified source on Titan. This mineral has penetrated and enhanced every plant it's touched. Very little was sent, and it was sent anonymously, but it's enough to raise questions, especially now.

He continues speaking to his recording device, walking toward the exit. "I've done all I can do here, and I have no choice but to make a drastic decision. A decision which I owe not only to my team, but to my father. The theory is corruption."

He quickly enters the elevator while the other scientists are left to murmur, confused by his sudden departure. He shuts off his recording device and shoves it back into his pocket.

"I *will* find out what's happening on Titan..."

The elevator moves slowly. Ezra Pierce knows this will be the last time he leaves this laboratory and the truth is sinking fast. He needs to hurry. People will talk about the little scene he's made and it will raise suspicions. His team is a gaggle of complacent fools who strive only to look busy and collect a check. It used to be a common saying that "there are no secrets in Sol," but times have changed. He remembers what his father, Bryndon Pierce, told him at his untimely death:

"Be what we couldn't."

Ezra had heard him say it many times, but it meant more now than ever.

Bryndon Pierce was a prominent scientist and explorer —Ezra's greatest teacher and only hero. Bryndon was a doctor and biologist, like Ezra, but also a ranking United Frontier (UF) Interplanetary Specialist. He was eventually elected Ambassador of Sol after the death of Harlan Cain, then named himself sole Ambassador of Titan after his own executive order, which abolished the naming of a single ambassador of Sol. Bryndon Pierce is credited with some of Sol's greatest achievements — much for Ezra to live up to. Ezra was never afraid of the challenge, and after Bryndon's death, he vowed to continue in his father's path. Ezra moved his family from New England to Shanghai, the epicenter of UF operations, and enrolled his son in the Mars Program, but his years spent working on Earth have since become stagnant. The divorce happened not long after. He'd lost every catalyst and the aftermath left him in a quiet, routine madness. It seems to Ezra that he is only now making the greatest decision of his own life. He's going to act, because it's what his father would do.

The elevator doors open to an extravagant, empty lobby with glass and marble stretching high into darkness. Time is already slipping away from him. He didn't even feel the elevator moving, but he can't think about what the fear may be doing to him, the extra weight in his feet as he hurries to the exit. He's eager, yet still he struggles with the thought of leaving his comfortable life behind. He hails a cab. He has a driver, but knows UF traces his private vehicle's location, so he keeps it in the garage at Jiang Labs. Through the sea of people and corporate-advertisement pollution that blankets the sidewalks of Shanghai, he sits in the back seat of a clean taxi, and is immediately identified by the automated vehicle.

"Welcome, Doctor, where to?" The empty interior of the taxi asks.

"Suzhou Park, no freeways."

Ezra begins to feel his identity stripping from him. He knows it's only the beginning of a much larger transformation. He can't just sit on his wealth, collect interest and retire only to live in ambiguity while the less fortunate suffer and die. The thing is, if only hearing about it on the news is causing this much anxiety, what will taking action do? What will it do for others? What will it do *to* others?

After a long meditative ride through the city, he arrives at a park overlooking a river beneath the golden Shanghai skyline to speak to his ex-wife, Aire. She sits at a park bench watching the sun crawl beneath the skyline. Ezra approaches her, catching early wind of her powerful perfume. She still works hard to remain physically attractive after remarrying, which is surprising to Ezra. Her olive skin and soft, shimmering black hair still dizzy his words.

"I was hoping you would understand," he mumbles, "and thank you for meeting me here." His past with her is troubled, but their distant friendship remains stable.

"I completely understand, honestly. I heard about your exit from work today. It's time, huh?" She says, knowing how strongly Ezra feels about Titan, and his father's connection to it.

Ezra is surprised that she would know about his departure from work so soon, but they do still share some mutual friends — though they are more like acquaintances to Ezra. "You must know what this means to me, Aire...but it's still only scratching the surface. This could change all of our lives — and not slowly." A tear fires down Ezra's face. Aire uses her thumb to dry the shining trail from his cheek. He continues, "Millions more will die if I don't act...but when

I do act, the United Frontier will make sure the road behind me is bloody. I have to choose the lesser of two evils, it seems." He hates how he sounds — political. He sees a group of children tackling and tagging one another playfully in the grass, and imagines a world torn apart by desperation. Men and women trapped in a life stained by blood and greed. He begins to grow hysterical.

"I've done all I can on Earth. My plants are better than they've ever been, but it's not enough anymore!" His voice intensifies, "We — "

"Ezra, please!" Aire interrupts, "Spare yourself." She looks directly into his eyes and says, "You have to fight, and our son will stand with you when the time is right. Send word to him. He will be happy to hear from you." She holds Ezra's hands together with hers. "And Ezra, you chose your path a long time ago. I chose mine. You know I can't help you."

"You're right, and I know." Ezra recoils, "I only asked you here to say goodbye. I don't expect to come back." The golden skyline turns to black as the sun creeps below. Stars begin to shine through the fading light of the evening. They share a moment of silence as Ezra takes a deep breath and asks, "How are Donnen — and Casey?" He struggles to remember the name of Aire's daughter.

"Donnen is Donnen. A good father, and a good husband. Casey's off to school, but right here in town, so we're excited about that," she says, "and I suppose I'll just tell you — I'm pregnant again," she says, nervously.

Ezra is taken aback. He shakes his head and says, "That is wild! And at your age? I didn't expect you to want something like that."

"Spoken like an ex-husband. Don't congratulate me."

Ezra is still marveled by her. He was a great scientist and neglectful husband, while she was perfect at everything she did, including raising their son with hardly any help.

Aire continues, "I could always tell you felt you didn't deserve what we had. Your true fight was always going to take you outside yourself, and away from all this. I only hope you remain as determined in your work as I've known you, and you stick to your strengths." She begins to sob. Ezra returns her favor by then pushing the tears from her face.

"I am happy for you, Aire. You always deserved more than I could give you. I have a lot to do, and I have to do it quickly. It was nice seeing you again."

Aire doesn't say a word, and can only muster tears as she stands and turns away from Ezra for what he feels may be the last time.

Ezra remains at the bench while street lamps begin lighting the pathways through the park. He turns to the nearest road, and begins down a wealthy, dimly-lit street deep within inner Shanghai. He needs a plan. Well, he has a plan, but it's in broad strokes: Get Support. Lay Siege to Titan. Fix Sol. It's not an easy plan to write, morally, much less repeat in your head as some childish hypothetical dream, but the tools are there for him to make a difference. There's a dark feeling of comfort in — or perhaps a warm disdain for — being right when you don't want to be.

Ezra's time in the UF hasn't been some archeological space camp. The UF is in the business of sustainability on other planets. Military, Agriculture, Engineering, and much more. He has the resources. He pulls his recording device from his pocket and speaks to it. He feels the need to hear his own words aloud, for clarity in potential madness.

"Personal log. This is likely the last time I leave this planet. If I'm to find out what's happening on Titan, I'll need help I can trust."

The single homes turn to shops and apartments as Ezra continues deeper into the city. He enters a dark and dirty, hole-in-the-wall bar, finding the air to be thick with the smell of overworked kitchen appliances and overused dishwater. The walls behind the strategically-placed decor are stained and eroding. He takes a deep, comfortable breath and sits at the bar. A young bartender looks away from the only television screen in the small dining room and scrambles to greet Ezra. "Eddy! How are ya? I've never seen you sit. Can I get you something?"

"I'm well. It's been awhile. Your worst bourbon."

"Ha, sure."

A dark silhouette slides into the seat next to Ezra, and speaks in a deep, raspy voice, "That shit bourbon pairs well with your shit personality, huh?" As the silhouette turns to the bartender, "I'll have a bourbon too, with bitters." The bartender rolls their eyes and fixes the drink.

The cloudy figure turns back to Ezra and playfully whispers, "It *has* been a while, hasn't it?"

Ezra remains stoic, and says, "I already said that... you must be the talent."

The silhouette turns into the light, revealing himself to be a rather goofy-looking, old soldier. His large nose is thick and pore-ridden from years of drinking. Teal eyes. He adjusts his posture to fluff his long, gray mane of hair and tie it behind his head. His militant-punk clothing style would raise attention just about anywhere. "I've missed your demeanor, Eddy… Never liked your clothes, but your words… they always have their dicks out." The man coughs and wheezes.

"Great, thanks Popp… I can see you and smoking are still happily together."

Popp retorts, "Ha! Smoking… and I already know why you're here…"

"Oh yeah? You bugging me, old man?"

"Hahaha… bo-ring, I can do better, fancy pants… and you're here… because… you're in over your head!" Popp says, as he slams his hand against the bar so loudly that it would startle the other patrons, if there were any. Ezra can only assume that Popp too has caught word of his outburst at work.

Ezra smiles, "I've missed you, too. And I need your help. All of Sol does, really, and we'll be completely outside UF this time."

Paulo Thiago Russo, or "Popp," moved to Shanghai from New England more than a decade before Ezra, already a trained UF Military Specialist, and has been a friend since Ezra's employment. Popp owned and operated an orbital security company at a young age, and he spent years working with Ezra's father, Bryndon Pierce, on Mars. During the First Manifest of Titan, his company, *Comrade*, was relieved of its services after a mining accident took Bryndon's life. After that fatal accident on Titan, Popp and Ezra's friendship was strengthened. Popp became a link for Ezra into his father's final years, years which Ezra spent reluctantly working on Earth.

Popp lost his orbital security license, and now runs an orbital salvage business, cleaning debris and garbage between Earth and Luna. Through a glitch in UF's systems he still has access to the United Frontier's "Obsolete or Unused Technology." He's used these privileges for years to build an armada of trained and armed employees. It's the most powerful private armada in the solar system, and Ezra is one of the few who knows about it.

Popp smirks and says, "Outside the chain — Sounds cheesy, but I like it."

"Well, strap in, because in order for my plan to work, Orbital Militant on Earth can't know we're leaving until it's too late, and we're, uhh, firing through space, to *Titan*." Ezra says before he covers his face with his hand.

Popp laughs, "So you need an entire armada —"

"And two carriers."

Popp rolls his eyes, and says, "Two carriers! To leave orbit *before* O.M. catches on. You realize, we're going to need the *Comrade*."

Popp is sounding more and more excited by the proposition.

Ezra carelessly lets his empty glass fall just a few centimeters onto the bar. He slides his hand downward from his face in despair. "Yeah. A bigger boat. I get it," he says, "And I think what I need is medication. You're right, Popp. I am in *way* over my head…" He shakes his head and addresses the bartender, whose attention is not easily taken away from the television screen.

"Another bourbon, please."

"Eddy, I have everything you need," Popp says, grinning,

"and I know you have the money."

"Go on."

"I have the soldiers, equipment, and the heavy shit. Titan would frankly be a piece of cake, with the right timing. I need to know *you* are ready for what you're about to do."

"I'm ready, Popp. And you sound confident, maybe a little too confident, but I seriously feel I need a miracle."

As the bartender sets Ezra's new drink in front of him, Popp continues, "What you need is a distraction, sweetheart. And your tab is on the house… I bought the place a few years ago…"

Ezra, baffled, says, "Seriously? What, are you staying well-off these days?"

Popp laughs, "Just follow me, sweetheart." Popp leaves his seat and walks toward the back of the room.

Ezra follows and murmurs, "Stop calling me sweetheart…"

Popp opens a poorly hidden door behind some dusty decor and crappy lighting. Ezra looks around the room, analyzing the unkempt walls and molding corners, and remarks sarcastically, "Did I read about this place in a magazine?"

Popp responds sternly, "You just watch your step, funny guy."

They reach the bottom of the stairs. The air is thick with dust. Popp shoves a large piece of covered furniture aside to reveal another doorway. Ezra follows Popp into a fairly large arsenal and map room. In the center shines a holographic map of Shanghai. Popp begins working the map's interface while Ezra looks at the weapons and tools lining the walls of the dirty, neglected room.

Ezra stands mesmerized by an old, tattered paper map

of the Solar System. The map is familiar. A very primitive depiction, as if it were copied from the wall of a cave. A picture he hasn't seen in more than ten years screams at him from across the room. These symbols left behind by ancient visitors to Sol are millions of years old, and have many religious interpretations, but nothing that Ezra, being a man of science, would take seriously. Two worlds, or perhaps two stars, orbit each other. Perhaps they fight for orbit. Another cave drawing displays only one star, with three worlds in orbit. The star in the center shines beams of light at all three, while one of the three worlds appears to be shattered.

The hologram in the center of the room shines bright and catches Ezra's attention. It changes to display a very large, very advanced space vessel. Ezra yawns, and Popp regains his attention, saying, "Hey sleepy-head, I know you've seen the *Comrade* before, but I wanted to let you in on some of the upgrades I've made. And don't worry — after this, you'll definitely need your beauty rest." Ezra is taken aback by the hologram in the center of the room. He says, "I'll be okay, but what the hell am I looking at here? I know what the *Comrade* is, but this..." Popp smirks, and continues, "Beautiful, yeah? She can do all the normal stuff — travel, Ship-Housing, Recon — but here's what I changed."

The display shifts to a digital library of large weapons and machinery. "Now pay attention, because this will probably come up later. The *Comrade* can now attach carriers to its port and starboard sides, giving us a little extra speed, and a little extra mobility. The *Comrade* can also house my entire fleet of fighters, so it looks like a damned space movie when *all* my Goons come out of the hangars to play..."

"Well, I'm impressed." Ezra says, before yawning again.

Popp shifts the display once more to show a large, interplanetary reconnaissance outpost, "This is what the best part looks like, Eddy. The *Comrade* could always land to establish recon on *any* planet, but now it can be the first step toward a new planetary colony! The *Comrade* lands, and immediately after grounding, tunnels and waterways are mechanically heated and pushed through the rock and ice. Once they link, they are cooled, and we have our sewer system. There's plenty more going on, but the entire process ends with a magnetically-charged and heated atmosphere around the newly-established reconnaissance outpost. Weapons are armed, the AIs — however annoying — take care of whatever I choose, and you're sleeping standing up."

Popp claps his hands and wakes Ezra. Ezra shakes his head and slides his hand down his face. "Sorry, Popp, I gotta get going," he says. "We have a launch window in five days."

Popp laughs as they leave the map room and begin making their way to the front of the bar. Popp opens the front door for Ezra and checks his watch, saying, "Yeah, it's nearly morning. So much for that beauty rest. I'll see you in five days. Shame that Lune won't be in that window, but Ceres is. We meeting on top of Jiang? Like the old days?"

Ezra knew Popp would be willing to join him in his plan, but didn't expect him to be so eager.

"That'll work. I'll be at a conference. Bring a team at seven hundred and I'll have my location turned on."

Ezra stumbles a short distance home. The streets are empty and the summer fog is thick. He falls against his door and sighs. This isn't the sort of thing you grow used to, because you never get used to failure. His home means nothing now. His belongings — they all mean nothing. It represents a lie. A lie he will not accept.

He enters his home, and slumps into a large chair in his extravagant living room. He knows he needs to hurry. He leans back, closes his eyes and whispers to himself, "Too many people already know I'm not long for this world." As quickly as the words can bounce from the walls and back to his ears, he snaps awake and realizes the sun is already coming up.

Launch day.

The morning sun lights the tops of the skyscrapers in downtown Shanghai like candles. Five days never happened so fast. Now realizing he also hasn't spoken to Popp for five days, he grows skeptical, but he heads back into Jiang Labs. His tunnel vision is beginning to clear in anticipation for today's conference.

The crowded lobby at Jiang Labs immediately falls silent upon Ezra's entering. He walks casually to the elevators, ignoring the fact that every single person in the lobby is staring at him. He moves quickly once he passes around the first corner, and enters the closest open elevator. Have the last five days been like this? He could only ask himself, realizing he hasn't spoken to *anybody* for five days.

Ezra reflects on his history within Jiang Labs. During Mars' Second Manifest, he was finishing school just down the street at the UF Space Academy. At the same time, Bryndon Pierce was leading the agricultural expansion on Mars. Bryndon was a charismatic, strategic, and truly brilliant scientist who accomplished much, with little to no resistance.

He was lucky for that. Ezra can't think about the petty comparisons between his and Bryndon's lives. Times change. His father came from a time of peace, and even then, people died. Even the good ones. Ezra has the resources, and he has to act. Now more than ever, he has to act.

As the elevator reaches the highest floor of the building, the doors open to a shimmering corridor of glass walls, crystal statues and electric light. Ezra can't help but cringe. He looks upon the wondrous interior in disgust, resenting the gluttonous extravagance of rooms that are so often empty.

The conference room at the far end of the hall is occupied by silhouettes: Fellow UF Scientists, Lead Engineers and Investors. These men and women are coworkers, acquaintances, and some of them are superiors. Jessica Barnes, UF's Ambassador of Earth, presides over this meeting. This is a time when communication between Earth, Mars and Titan is optimal, so several officials from all over Sol will also be present at this meeting. Ezra knew this meeting would be happening today; in fact, he's late to it.

Ezra can't just politely ask these people for help in his inquisition. Most of them are already corrupt. He knows he must inspire the ones who may join, and scare the ones who may resist. Those who intend to stop him won't have time. He's made sure of that. Ezra makes his way through the hallway and grabs a conveniently-placed crystal swan statue, slightly larger than a basketball. He takes a deep breath, and heaves the expensive statue from his shoulder and through the glass wall of the conference room. Everyone in the room leaps from their chairs as Ezra steps over the shattered glass to enter the room. He makes himself comfortable at the podium at the head of the room where everyone can see him.

The board members scramble and scurry to the other end of the room in fear, and they shout.

"Pierce, have you lost your mind?"

"Pierce, don't do this! It's too late!"

Ezra pauses to scan the room. He is surrounded by coworkers and supposedly like-minded scientists, whom he can only hope will share in his motivation. He announces in response to their clamor, "I've lost only my patience, fellow board members, but the loss is menial in comparison to the loss of dignity we are experiencing here, today. I'll be taking mine with me."

Jessica Barnes steps forward. "Okay, Doctor Pierce, and where are you going? An island, maybe?" Barnes says sarcastically. She stands firmly against Ezra; both are respected scientists. Barnes is young, attractive and savvy to UF politics. Her mysterious wealth stirs only greater suspicion within Ezra.

"I'm going to Titan, Ambassador Barnes. They've held back their research far too long, and — "

Jessica Barnes interrupts, "Call security. Everybody please move toward the screen, and away from this maniac." The board members move to one side of the room. They stand beneath a giant screen displaying busts and silhouettes of remote meeting attendees.

Ezra Pierce says to the room, "Do you even realize we're on the brink of tragedy!? The lower and middle sectors are running out of resources, and will revolt! You must help me. Come with me to Titan, and take the United Frontier back."

Jessica Barnes responds ferociously, "We already know what's happening on Titan! It's a terrible mess, and at this point, it's also a waiting game. If you don't want to wait, then I would tell you to donate, but it seems you don't want your job! Is this some kind of political move?"

As Barnes rants, Ezra sees a room full of frightened board members. He sees scared, complacent products of privilege who will likely not join him, and would prefer to collect their checks. He decides if they will not join him, then they will fear him. He gently lays his hand on a broken piece of glass on the conference table, as if preparing to wield it. He glares at Jessica Barnes and shouts, "A waiting game!? Barnes, you are naive, or corrupt, or both, and I will not sit on a dying ant farm while personal agendas are fed. I'm going to Titan, and I'm bringing back the near-score of data owed to us. You are lost."

Barnes calls out to the audial receivers in the room, "Security, where are you!? We need the *works*, top floor."

"Security won't be coming, Ambassador Barnes." Ezra says as Popp's militants burst from the roof's emergency exit and quickly occupy the glass maze. They carry magnet rifles and wear rustic, pale red armor. "*Inquisition Fleet* leaves within the hour. We are expediting Titan research, and Ambassador, if you get in our way, I'll arrest you myself, which means you'll be coming with us."

Ezra looks away just long enough for Jessica Barnes to disappear into the crowd of scientists, and out of his sight. He continues addressing the room, "Fellow scientists, join me. Titan is hiding something from us, and it's no longer a waiting game. You have until right now to choose your side of history."

The room is silent for a few seconds. One young male voice chimes in from the back of the group, "I'm in." The group parts in the middle to reveal one remote doctor's silhouette on the giant screen.

"And who are you?"

The silhouette replies, "My name is Delores. I will promptly meet you on Titan by my own means." The feed disconnects, and the screen goes black.

Ezra stammers, "Wait — "

One of Popp's soldiers leans to him and says, "Sir, launch."

Ezra turns to the frightened, murmuring board members. He drops the piece of broken glass to the floor, discovering cuts on his hand from gripping it so tight. He says to the group of board members, "The rest of you wouldn't last," before leaving the floor.

Ezra and Popp's militants exit the building from the roof, filing into a small fleet of airships. Ezra enters the cabin of the nearest ship. Popp is driving. Ezra sits in a passenger seat behind Popp's co-pilot, and they share a moment of silence. Ezra looks to Popp and sighs in disappointment. "We only have one board member joining us, and not right away," he says. Popp smiles and replies, "That would sound suspicious, if you hadn't started your little performance by throwing a damned statue into the room." Ezra is shocked that Popp would already know what happened inside. He asks, "You saw that?"

The ships lift off from the top of Jiang Laboratories and blaze toward the launch site. Popp scoffs and says, "It was broadcasted! You didn't think some clown in there would open a camera? You may be coming back to a different kind of Earth… at least one that sees you differently." He pauses, "Is this like, a political thing?"

"That's the question of the day! I never planned on coming back, Popp. No politics."

"Good to hear, Eddy. This old man needed to go out with a bang. And thank you."

"For what?"

"For giving me purpose! My family is gone. I don't have anything but my work, and this is the job of a lifetime. I really thought my greatest days were behind me, and I'm honored to call this job my last. And you're not much younger than me, old man!"

Ezra smirks.

"Which is crazy — not you, but," Popp continues, "Why are you doing this, anyway?" They share another moment of silence.

"*For Sol* sounds contrived, but the death rate in the Green Sectors is increasing, and with politicians giving hollow promises… and the media blatantly distracting — "

"Yawn!" Popp interrupts. "What are you talking about? I know all about what's happening on Earth. I'm asking *you* why *you* are doing this. I thought you would retire to a Red Sector somewhere. You're Yellow, right? Top of the food chain, as they say?"

"Yes."

"You could've hired somebody. You could've sued."

"I hired you, didn't I?"

"You know what I mean, Eddy. Seriously. Why you?"

"Boredom, Popp." Ezra says, blatantly sarcastic. "I'm just so bored with all my riches, my cars, my games — and my constituents have grown very needy. I need to recharge my batteries, and I heard a *military coup* is a great way to open the pores."

Popp is unamused. "We've arrived," he says. The ships slow to hover over a large air strip and launchpad. "Two carriers and *almost* my entire armada — your 'Inquisition Fleet.'" Popp says pompously, gazing upon his vast collection of hardware and soldiers as he lands.

"Hello, *Comrade…*"

An anomaly stands at the center: a magnificent ship, like a skyscraper, and several kilometers in width. Popp says, confidently, "The only thing they could do is surprise us…and I don't see that happening." Ezra gazes at the towering vessel, with two carriers attached at each side, dwarfed in comparison to the size of Popp's mothership. "Popp, this doesn't look like the hologram I saw. I had no idea the ship was so… aerodynamic! It looks like something out of a movie. This is an absolute wonder!" Popp scoffs, "Ha, You better believe it. The hologram was a cross section, so you were seeing a lot of the guts. It's gotta look pretty, right?" The small fleet of ships touches down at the top of the launch tower adjacent to the *Comrade*.

Popp and Ezra exit their ships, followed by Popp's employees. They hastily cross the bridge hundreds of feet high toward the enormous space vessel. Popp shouts to Ezra, "I gotta say, Eddy — this video from the meeting is gold! And 'Inquisition Fleet' *is* catchy. Thanks for keeping my name out of it."

Ezra, hardly listening to Popp's rambling, discovers a hole torn in the shoulder of his lab coat. He slows down and slides the coat from his shoulders. "My coat," he mutters, "I must have cut it on the glass."

Popp stops just a few steps ahead. "Huh? Your lab coat?" He says as he approaches Ezra, "I'm surprised you're still wearing it. No more chain of command, right?"

Ezra ignores Popp's reasoning. He remains silent. He holds the tattered coat over the side of the bridge with his bloodied hand, and lets the wind gently lift it away. He sighs and looks at Popp in such mania, Popp recoils. Ezra, trembling, says, "Those colors gave me everything I have. But I realize now, all that matters, truly, is what we take with us when it all inevitably burns." Popp looks in confusion at Ezra as the soldiers march around them and into the *Comrade*. Popp nears Ezra and says, "Eddy, believe me — I know what it's like to toe the line. And do you want to know what you're taking with you? What we're taking with us? You want to know what perseveres; what crawls from the ashes of the person you dreamt of being?" Popp turns and begins walking to the *Comrade*. Ezra catches up, and Popp continues, emphatically, "Change, Eddy. Violent change is the only constant, and the only true variable is the depth at which you decide you've had enough." He pauses, coughing, "You remember what happened between me and Melena, Eddy." He takes another breath, calming his throat. "The sacrifices we make when enduring swift, relentless change are what shape us. Tempering the mind like a steel sword. You'll never find the tenacity for change if the armor on your back isn't even yours."

Popp and Ezra enter the *Comrade*. Ezra is taken aback by Popp's harsh wisdom. Ezra's own words barely escape his breath. "You're right, Popp. Change is coming. Hopefully after today, I can still call Melena. She's deep in UF Diplomacy, but she'll help us." Ezra begins to dress himself for space. "I never asked, Popp, but you mentioned you had a distraction for our launch. What is it, exactly?"

"Heh," Popp scoffs. He enters the bridge of the *Comrade*, followed by Ezra. He sits comfortably in his plush Captain's seat, "My own personal arsenal of *distractions* — about sixty decommissioned satellites. I'm going to activate ten of these suckers simultaneously. They're about four hundred kilometers north of our position, and each one is packed full of paint and explosives. Once the fire burns through the hull, Orbital Militant will be on the case, and before they know it —

"Boom! A painted sky! And then," Popp says as he strikes the armrest of his chair repeatedly, "Boom, boom, boom! And so on! Nine more, simultaneously, *non-lethally* taking out patrols while we slide out. They'll think they're being attacked, until they see a giant rainbow falling from the sky!"

The launch sequence begins, and the *Comrade* eases from the ground by its starter jets before the launch magnets activate and push it into the sky. Just to the north, the luminous rainbow of debris glows in the evening, blinding and busying the nearby UF Orbital Militant ships as Popp had just explained. Ezra can see plainly the array of colors across the horizon from their launching ship, and is confused. It shouldn't be so close. "Popp, did you say four hundred kilometers? Or just meters?"

"Shit."

"Yeah, I concur."

In the distance, just north of Inquisition Fleet's launch, a squadron of eight Orbital Militant airships is investigating the mess of falling paint and machinery. One of these pilots easily spots Inquisition Fleet's launch happening to the south.

"Be advised," the pilot says, "all available units — we have an unregistered carrier making its way off-planet as we speak! Five hundred meters directly south of our position! The falling debris was a distraction! I repeat: All available units — "

Back inside the *Comrade*, the Orbital Militant's communications can be heard from Popp's console.

"Set weapons to lethal," says an unknown OM pilot.

Popp immediately addresses his own fleet via their intercom, "You heard the little dog! They're gonna bite! Prepare for an early mach-jump! Goons F-3 and F-4, move to defense. F-3 takes lead!"

Eight Inquisition fighters burst from the sides of the launching ship and fall behind it. The squad acknowledges, *"Roger that, Godspeed…"*

Ezra leans to Popp and asks, "Did that pilot say, '*Godspeed?*' What are they going to do?"

Popp explains, "Eight ships are falling back. I anticipated we might run into some trouble on the way out, and honestly, this isn't bad. One or two of them might actually make it out — "

Popp's fighter pilot's voice interrupts from the console, *"Sir, you're still on our channel…"*

"Whoops," Popp chuckles as he kills the connection and takes another drink, "I was saying, all my soldiers know the price of the mission, and my Goons don't mess around."

Inside a Goon fighter ship, a female pilot with a name tag reading, "Bella" removes her helmet and lowers a large, transparent head-visor with a tactical head-unit display. She is one of eight pilots falling back to defend the *Comrade* during launch. The eight fighter ships face perfectly downward, in the direct path of eight Orbital Militant fighters. The two teams of ships open fire, the crossfire creating a luminous cloud of smoke and brightly burning bullets.

Back inside the *Comrade*, Popp says to Ezra, "They will decide their own defensive strategy once they analyze the threat, and they will do whatever it takes to keep Orbital Militant away from us."

From the crossfire below, only half the ships remain — four UF Orbital Militant, and four Inquisition Fighters. The smoke hinders the pilots' vision. Bella is still alive and struggling to read a broken tactical display. Sparks fly inside her burning cockpit as she frantically flips switches to redirect air and fuel throughout her collapsing ship. Sweat rolls like machine gun bullets from her chin and nose, evaporating into the air around her.

Popp continues, "They'll likely die down there."

Through the smoke and electrical fire, Bella sees the remaining pieces of her broken display suddenly turn bright red. She takes a deep breath, and screams as she violently throws a lever downward from the ceiling of her cockpit. Her ship rocks and releases a sonic pulse from the rear into the billowing black clouds. A bright, white light breaks through the dissipating smoke, and the explosion creates an anomalous sound and vibration, which can be heard from the bridge of the *Comrade* above.

Ezra is startled by the strange sound. "What was that? Some kind of explosion? That sound was haunting."

Popp replies calmly, "Reactors. Orbital Militant prefers to strip their fighters for speed. It makes them weaker, but easier to fly."

Bella below struggles to regain control of her ship and reattach her helmet after the explosion. As she raises her fractured tactical visor in front of her eyes, she discovers that she is the last of Popp's Goon fighters. She scans the falling debris, and discovers one last OM fighter directly below her position. The OM ship fires into the bottom of her ship. Bullets rip upward through the floor of her cockpit. She quickly attaches a multi-tool — a UF-issued maintenance tool equipped with a lethal laser cutter — to her chest, and ejects into the air from her ill-fated ship.

Popp begins brewing coffee. He sighs, "There are two outcomes here…"

The Milky Way fills the sky above the atmosphere as the ejected Goon pilot is in free-fall, directly in front of the ascending Orbital Militant fighter.

She releases her parachute.

The OM ship's nose catches the open parachute, and the nose and cockpit are now completely covered. They move at an intense speed as the dangling Goon pilot secures herself to the side of the blinded ship using her magnetic boots.

Popp continues, "One outcome is — my Goons win, and maybe there are survivors. If so, then great! Outcome two, however, is their sacrifice to the fleet, and making sure the *Comrade* moves forward unharmed. Coincidentally, it's exactly what they signed up for. Their loyalty is unmeasured.

All orbital threats get the same treatment."

Bella's helmet is broken. She strips the pieces from her head and shoulders, cutting her face and neck. The cuts immediately scab and burn from the friction of the high wind. She locks the barrel of her multi-tool to the side of the ship, right on top of a small, painted warning reading, "Danger: Combustible." She activates her multi-tool, and cuts into the ship with a bright, white laser. The Goon pilot screams, and her eyes widen, wind burning. She slams her watering eyes shut and her tears form icicles before breaking away. The white light of her multi-tool cuts into the hull, and her laser changes to a vibrant pink, indicating a chemical reaction. She opens her frozen eyes as much as she can. Witnessing the changing colors, she smiles with relief. The last OM fighter bursts into flaming pieces around her, and at the very edge of the atmosphere, a bud of fire blooms atop a dying stem of smoke and debris.

"Sure did make an exit, huh, Eddy?"

Ezra is silent. He didn't imagine his actions killing anybody — at least not so quickly — and especially on Earth. For now, he'll piggy-back Popp's confidence.

Ezra drinks from a coffee pouch and peers with confusion at a computer terminal reading, "Priority Transmission — R. Pierce." A message from his son, Ronan. Popp grabs himself a coffee pouch and sits comfortably. "Like I said, my Goons don't mess around. If they didn't make it, then nobody down there made it," he rants, "and I can guarantee it was a spectacle," he pauses to take a drink. "Now hey, go call Melena. No way I'm doing it." Ezra's eyes grow wide, and he spits his coffee onto a computer screen reading "TITANKNOWS."

Popp simultaneously switches to the intercom to address his fleet, not noticing Ezra's reaction. Popp says, "I'm reading a full house on the *Comrade*. F-3 and F-4, we appreciate your sacrifice and we may be seeing you real soon. Mach-jump in four, three, two — "

ONE

The Promotion

THE young, gaunt Ronan Pierce awakens at a crowded train station. The short brown hair atop his head rustles as he shakes himself awake. He answers a phone call on his cybernetic earpiece — a common neural component for the newer generation of United Frontier employees, all of them made by the Delores corporation and aptly named "Wyg." The ocular interface allows him to answer by simple cognition.

"Hey, love," Ronan says as he leaves his seat and throws his backpack over his shoulder. He unnecessarily holds his hand to his earpiece as he speaks remotely. "I should be back soon. I'm leaving the station now."

Ronan boards the train with many others, leaving the station empty. Arcadia is a thriving colony, and a center of trade on Mars. Every single person works toward its betterment and expansion, and the colony is nearing the fiftieth anniversary of its establishment. The train is not on the red surface long before descending into a tunnel deep beneath the Arcadia Plain.

The tunnel opens into a vast, well-lit cave system. Abandoned mining operations left behind by ancient visitors to Sol, far below the surface of Mars, created a pliable, sustainable habitat for humans. The floor of this enormous cave system is painted with rows of synthetic soil below bright green and thriving vegetation. Uniformed workers tend the crops with peculiarly primitive hand tools, and no breathing assistance. Man-made structures, bridges and vehicles weave throughout these gigantic cave systems, and the underground city of Arcadia is now home to more than one million people.

The cavern begins to narrow as the train arrives at First Station. From the belly of a deep, misty crevasse, lit windows and bridges accentuate the dripping, blood-red rock walls hundreds of feet high.

As the young man exits the train, a colleague catches up with him. Sato Song's attire is barely distinguishable — while they both wear the standard UF employee jumpsuit, Ronan's is tinted red to indicate his status as a programmer. Sato's jumpsuit is gray to indicate that he is an engineer. His face sits under a tousled mess of thin black hair and shines with a cheerfully plucky disposition.

"Ronan!" Sato says as he runs to Ronan's side and hangs his arm over Ronan's shoulders.

"I have a double weekend starting right now," Sato says. "Was there something you wanted me to talk you out of doing?"

Ronan gently shrugs his friend's arm away and says, "You're funny, but no. I'm spending my break with Kitta."

They walk through a corridor lit with screens and holograms, a white and blue finished hallway decked with visual renderings of charming Earthly nostalgia.

Sato smirks, and says, "Ah, I remember, Mr. Fancy Programmer gets a bit of weekly freedom with his shifts."

Ronan eagerly retorts, "Yes, and I've earned it! You're welcome, by the way, for the perfect feed from — how many was it?" He directs Sato's attention to the advertisements and other visual entertainment surrounding them. Many of these renderings are visible only to those wearing the cybernetic Wygs. "*Ten* of the top ISPs from Earth? And there's more…" Ronan says, as Sato stirs with excitement. They both slow down, allowing the last few people to dissipate from their path.

"I was about to start clearing a path for your growing head," Sato says, "but you're serious? What can you get?"

Ronan whispers, "I'm linking more dark servers as we speak."

"What?! Wow!" Sato says, urgently wrapping his hands over his mouth to stifle his outburst. Ronan whispers, "They should be fully linked by the time I get home. It'll be nice to see some Red and Yellow Sector news. We'll have to catch up on it tomorrow." They arrive at Ronan's door, while Sato continues walking.

Sato turns and shouts from afar, "I'll see you next shift!"

Ronan enters his extravagant apartment. An entire wall digitally displays a sunset over the Shanghai skyline. He removes his backpack and hangs it on the wall, walks into his living room and picks up a digital tablet.

"Ronan!" A young woman prances into the living room and jumps into Ronan's arms. Ronan stammers, "Kitta, how are you, love?"

Kitta takes a few steps back from Ronan and smiles. "*Somebody* got promoted today! This is my new uniform!" She says with excitement as she strikes a playful pose. She's wearing the standard fiber jumpsuit, but with a blue tint and patches indicating an administrative status within UF.

"I love it!" Ronan says.

Kitta scurries to the bedroom to change out of her uniform. Ronan puts his tablet on the living room table, and moves to the bar to pour two neat whiskeys, hers with a dash of bitters. He sits, and Kitta walks into the living room in her nightgown. Her long, dark hair is sloppily tied up on the back of her head. She wields her sunken, teal eyes like swinging swords from behind her large, sharp nose. Ronan warmly ponders her plans and her schemes. She's a leader; not conventionally beautiful, but strong and radiant in her natural prowess and gaiety. To Ronan, there is no one more beautiful. The children she teaches on Mars are fortunate to be in her care. Though she doesn't care too much to socialize, and has few she can call friends, her peers would be lost without her tactful intelligence and playful charisma. She takes the bittered whiskey from Ronan and smiles at him.

"Congratulations," Ronan says, smiling back. Kitta pauses.

"You know, I still want to try to have a baby. I only want enhancers to be a last resort."

Ronan chokes on his whiskey, "You never mince words. And what about adopting?"

"If enhancers don't work, I'm open to adopting," she says, knowing enhancers would give them their child, "but of course I want it to be completely natural! I love you Ronan, and — "

Ronan interrupts, "You don't have to explain to me, Kitta. I appreciate your patience with me." He takes another drink and sits on the sofa, lamenting his impotence. The year they've spent attempting to overcome it feels fruitless to Ronan, though Kitta reflects his feelings only with confidence. Ronan comes from a high-society family of doctors with the means to alter DNA while a child is in the embryo. However, the process is not perfect and Ronan has discovered his reproductive impotence at age twenty. Kitta sits at Ronan's side and comforts him. "Ronan, the child we create will allow us to live forever!" She says with excitement, "You just need a little more faith."

Ronan laughs, "You're funny. My faith in *you* is enough for me, Kitta. Anything supernatural would just be a bonus," respectfully poking fun at her theistic beliefs, "as it has been since I've known you," but even the sweetened words are beginning to wear. Kitta comes from a lower class family, and joined the United Frontier's Mars Program in an attempt to escape a life of emotional abuse. Kitta pulls Ronan's wrist from her, and pivots from the couch. She walks hastily toward the bedroom, and says, "I have to be up early tomorrow, but we'll have our chance."

"But you barely touched your whiskey," Ronan says rhetorically.

The next morning, Ronan awakens in his empty bed to someone repeatedly banging his doorbell. An annoying, rhythmic beating sounds from the front door of his apartment.

"Okay, okay . . ." he murmurs to himself. Castle, the home AI, speaks, *Identity unknown.* Ronan rolls over in his bed. "Castle, show me the stoop." He turns his attention to a nearby surveillance monitor. "I suppose I deserve this," he says to himself as he sees Sato's cartoonish grin occupying the entire screen, thus disabling the AI's facial recognition. "Castle, open the front door," Ronan says as he lifts himself out of bed and drags himself into the living room to meet Sato.

Sato anxiously taps his steepled fingertips from pinky to

thumb. "Oh boy, this is exciting!" he says, "I haven't said a thing about this, by the way."

Ronan squints and stretches his arms to the ceiling. He yawns, and says, "That's okay. I should show this to UF first, but I still have some debugging to do. We'll be able to see some interesting stuff today." Ronan and Sato move to a terminal reading, *"Servers Linking @ 10EB/sec"* and a rapid countdown.

"Cool. You know I love you, man, but I need some new shows to watch." Sato looks upon the screen in amazement, "And that's crazy fast! How's Kitta, by the way?"

"She's great; not a cloud in her sky. She received a promotion — Admin, I'm guessing, based on her new uniform. I'm not even sure what her job title is now, but she left before I woke up."

The giant screen on Ronan's wall shows a completion of the server link. The first rendered news article shows a news story reading, *"Starvation Toll @ 10M by 2250? Who is the real Ezra Pierce?"* Sato shakes his head in confusion and says, "Pierce?"

Ronan is speechless. He begins to panic. He opens a leaked recording of his father standing in a conference room surrounded by broken glass. The video is shaky, obviously taken from someone's shaky hand-held or retinal camera. They hear Ezra in the video, saying, *"The lower and middle sectors are running out of resources, and will revolt! All you have to do is help me. Come with me to Titan…"*

Sato looks at Ronan, who remains stoic, and says "Ezra's your dad, right?" Ronan takes a deep breath, and says, "This is blowing my mind. He always talked about finishing my grandfather's work on Titan, but this…" Ronan begins playing another video, this one titled *"LIVE COVERAGE: EXPLOSIONS IN THE SKY."*

The video feed shows a tower of smoke and falling debris in the Chinese sky. The description reads:

"Dr. Ezra Pierce, son of the late Bryndon Pierce, is leading a private armada to Saturn's orbit. What is he looking for? What has been happening on Titan? All that we know about Dr. Pierce is that he has lived on Earth, working in the United Frontier's...."

Ronan quickly leaves the terminal and crosses the room in a fit of disbelief. He puts his hand to his earpiece and says, "Call Dad." Sato turns and says, "He's in the middle of a launch, right? Or still moving pretty fast." Ronan stops and says, "Shit, you're right," as he addresses his home AI, "Castle — Cancel call, prioritize signals, and try again without video." A loading screen appears on the wall in Ronan's living area, reading, *"Calling DAD..."* Ronan takes a seat in the living area and faces the giant screen; he anxiously rubs his hands together with such force that it burns him. Sato continues to scroll through news stories. "Ronan, you may want to see this," he says.

"What is it?" Ronan says. Sato's voice trembles, "I just searched 'Titan,' and look — "

Ronan interrupts and says to his AI, "Castle — Sync tablet to main screen."

The wall displays another video from a shaky mobile camera — A large armada of starships and several carriers underneath Titan's orange, misty sky. Sato says, "This is a leaked video from Titan... It just happened," he reads. "The Mayor of First City has mobilized his own defenses. You have to warn your dad!" he declares.

Ronan moves back to the terminal. "Sato, I like how you're thinking," he says. "Stay on that tablet and keep me updated. I think my dad is already traveling at 800K, which means we'll be lucky to even hear his voice." Ronan looks over to Sato and says, "I found the ship he's on... checking their launch coordinates... damn." Ronan says. "Castle, I want a new command sent to that ship. Strongest we can send. I want to change their destination coordinates." He says, "I'm sending them to Ceres. It'll be a good stopping point and it won't slow them down by much. I have to send a message. He's gotta know he's not under attack when I do this..." He begins typing. "I only have the bandwidth left to render about ten visible letters."

Sato pours himself a whiskey at Ronan's bar and says, "Titan..." before he pours a new one for Ronan, then says, "... knows." Sato sets the bottle down and walks to Ronan. "Damn, that's perfect," Ronan says. Sato hands him his drink, and Ronan continues typing.

"T, I, T, A..."

The front door opens, and Kitta enters a living room lit with screens. Every wall of their apartment is displaying news stories, videos, headlines and surveillance data. Kitta throws her tote bag to the floor. Puzzled, she says, "Hi, Sato!" and hugs him.

"Kitta, congratulations! I heard about your promotion," Sato says as he heads to their kitchen. "Can I get you any water? Juice?"

"Thank you, Sato. Just water." Kitta sees Ronan, who remains focused on his tablet, and she sneakily approaches him from behind, pouncing her arms around his waist. Kitta says softly in his ear, "You look busy — can't say hi?"

"Sent! Yes! Hopefully it gets to him in time." Ronan shouts as he throws his tablet to the sofa, and turns around and kisses Kitta. Ronan backs away, "Kitta, I seem to remember you only saying hi to *Sato*…"

Sato returns to the living room and says, "He's right!" Sato tosses a water bottle to Kitta. "Thanks, Sato," she says with a dash of sarcasm. "So what brings you here for first-shift?"

"Sato is here checking out some of the new network capabilities. We found something pretty urgent." Kitta sits on the sofa, looking back and forth at the walls surrounding them; screens displaying news articles with Ezra Pierce's name.

"It looks like Eddy needs help," she says. "And you plan on helping him. Do you have a plan?"

"We're just now learning this," he says before taking a deep breath and closing his eyes. "So far, there is no plan. We know that people on Earth are dying, and it's only been mentioned in Yellow Sector news." Ronan shakes his head and picks up his tablet. He sits on the sofa next to Kitta and says, "I hacked their destination coordinates and they're going to stop in a safe place…well, *safer*. My message also made it, so we'll have to see what he says. The best we can do right now is give the floor to you, Kitta."

Kitta smiles and asks, "What do you mean by that?"

Ronan hands the tablet to Sato and turns to Kitta, saying, "I mean, *how are you?* I was just telling Sato how little I know about your recent promotion." Kitta smiles and says, "Oh my! Yes, we didn't talk very much last night, did we?" She pauses, and stands proudly. "Well, the kids had a little farewell celebration ready for me today, so that was sweet.

But Ronan, if you want to hear about my new gig, you'll have to walk me back to work. My break is almost over. Sato, it was nice seeing you, and I'll have to catch you up later."

"That's okay. Nice seeing you too." Sato says, unable to divert his attention from the news.

Ronan leaves his seat to follow Kitta out of their apartment. He notices Kitta has left her tote bag behind. He turns inward and says, "You should stay here, Sato, if you can. Keep an eye on the news for me. Thanks again."

"There's plenty of whiskey," Sato japes.

Ronan and Kitta walk through the red rock corridor outside their apartment. Ronan stumbles behind Kitta, who appears to be in a hurry. "I apologize if your blood is a little thin…bad timing?" Kitta says, teasing him for drinking in the middle of the day. Ronan catches up as they reach the main corridor. "I'm fine, just a little on-edge with my dad's situation…" he says, "Kitta?"

Ronan turns in confusion when he discovers he and Kitta parted ways at the main corridor. Kitta yells to him from a new extension of the corridor; it is poorly lit, and cluttered with construction equipment. Ronan heads into the mysterious tunnel. "This way!" Kitta's echoes disappear past Ronan as he blends into the twilight.

"Kitta, is this safe?" Ronan says as he follows the curve of the tunnel. Light returns to his path, bringing color to an inactive construction site within a tall, red cavern. Rows of seating in lecture-hall form encompass the enormous room.

"Of course it's safe!" Kitta shouts and echoes to Ronan from the center of the room, at which an ornate podium has been carved from the red rock. Ronan meets her there.

"Kitta, where are we?" Ronan says. Kitta smiles and says, "For now, we jokingly call it 'Town Hall,' but I've been selected for the Governance, Ronan. I've been working directly with Ambassador Melena Horn herself!" Kitta holds Ronan's hands. "She's an amazing woman, and this could be huge for us, Ronan — for everyone. With your — " Kitta is interrupted by a dark, draped silhouette entering the cavern.

"Ronan Pierce..." the mysterious figure says softly. "Thank you for bringing him, Kitta."

Ronan is shocked. He responds, "I'm sorry?"

Kitta moves to Ronan's side. Clutching his hand, she says, "Ambassador! I arrived early so I could — "

Ronan mutters, "You're kidding..."

The silhouette reveals itself to be a beautiful, elderly woman. Dark hair and light brown skin, in elaborate garments; a dark-blue velvet robe, cuffed with shimmering, ornate patterns in gold, draping nearly to the floor. "It's okay, love. I'm happy you've brought Ronan here," the woman says. Ambassador Horn extends her hand, and Ronan shows respect by bowing, and holding her hand in both of his.

Melena Horn was a household name to Ronan as a child. She has served the United Frontier for over thirty years. She worked on Mars with Bryndon Pierce during the first Great Manifest of Sol, and they were both renowned for their work. Together, they revolutionized expansion methods on Mars, pioneering a new generation of growth. She also is equipped with neural-link cybernetics. Both Ronan and Kitta know much about Melena Horn and her accomplishments. She's a political celebrity.

"Ambassador, it's an honor." Ronan says, "You and my grandfather Bryndon — "

"We mustn't waste time," Ambassador Horn interrupts. "You've heard about your father?"

Ronan stammers, "Yes. Yes, I have. I sent him a message, and gave him a safer place to land. The Mayor of First City knows they're coming, and I have no idea what my father is bringing to the table. Ambassador Horn — I plan to help him."

The Ambassador scoffs, "Ha, Ronan — would you have told me, if we weren't standing here now? How long have you had privileged server access?"

Ronan chuckles nervously, "Ambassador Horn, I can promise you my intentions are purely in the interest of UF, and I did plan to show UF, once I — "

"No need to explain," says Ambassador Horn. "Call me Melena. I'd like to talk to you about how I can help you and your father on Titan, for the good of Sol. Follow me this way."

Melena Horn crosses the chamber, passing a few pieces of construction equipment before she enters a well-lit, finished service tunnel. Ronan and Kitta follow.

"Melena, thank you," Ronan says. "Do you know what my dad is planning, or what he wants with Titan?"

Melena Horn says nothing. They reach the end of the hallway, and enter a classically decorated lounge, a vibrant, Victorian library like nothing else on Mars. Ronan is stunned by the warmly lit, glowing wooden interior, and the refreshing smell of cedar and oak. He catches his breath and says, "Ambassador…I mean, Melena…What is this room?" Kitta stands at Ronan's side and holds his hand. Melena walks along the tall, ornate bookshelves lining the walls of the lounge and says, "Every book on every shelf is historic and authentic. It's an oasis among the red rock and sand… and frankly, it's disgusting."

"Melena?" Kitta says, concerned. She notices Melena struggling somehow, physically.

"We can't even grow trees on Mars big enough to build a room like this." Melena Horn coughs, and continues pacing around the room. Her voice intensifying, she says, "These untouched books… the extravagance and ambition of the UF is going to ruin us, if it hasn't already." Melena coughs again, but this time she doesn't come back to full posture. She slouches and begins to limp. She begins pulling books from the shelves, and letting them fall to the floor. She rants, "The people of Earth are suffering, while politicians are labeled pioneers, living in luxury… no matter their planet, no matter the cost." Kitta listens intently, worried for Melena but remaining calm. Melena turns to Ronan and continues, "Ronan, I don't have a lot of time. Your father knows better than anybody alive, and your grandfather, Bryndon knew better than anyone in my life — This frontier does not belong to us, and we must fear it. The Ancients we too often forget, the magi of our golden age, and the harbingers of our great mystery, have answered the eternal question." Melena stops to rest against a mighty wooden pillar. She struggles to breathe, but continues, "It's a warning — spelled out in their handprints, their fossils, and in what little they left behind… it was as if the Ancients ran out of time. Maybe they hoped we would understand, or maybe they didn't care." Kitta climbs beneath Melena's arm to support her. Melena continues with a rasping, weakening voice, "It's simple.

Everything we found here and on Titan had been abandoned by the Ancients!"

Kitta eases Melena into the nearest chair. Ronan and Kitta tend to her, but are speechless. She is somehow deteriorating rapidly.

She lies motionless before them. Not dead, but absent; not struggling, but incomplete somehow. She creaks and moans and leans to the small table next to her, opening a small decorative coffer. The coffer contains a mechanical device the size of a cigar. She squeezes the device in her hand, holds it to her mouth, and inhales. Ronan and Kitta watch with amazement as the color returns to Melena's skin. It glistens; filling its own cracks and promptly rejuvenating as her voice returns to its soft, reassuring form. Melena exhales, and closes her eyes.

Ronan approaches her and crouches to whisper. "Melena… what just happened?"

"You're thinking too small. You can see now that I'm not alright. You can see the danger." Melena snaps upright in her seat. Her eyes open wide. "I need you to promise me something, before we go any further. I *need* you to promise. You will help your father, Ronan, and you will share with him the information I am giving you today," Melena says emphatically.

Kitta holds Melena's hand, discovering Melena is tightly gripping the armrest of her chair with the other. Kitta massages the top of Melena's hand with her thumb, and says softly, "Melena, we promise. All of it. Do you need us to call for someone?" Melena begins to slouch and grows weary once again. The medicine she took seems to be wearing off already. She looks at Kitta, and releases the armrest to stroke Kitta's face with the backs of her trembling fingers.

Melena says calmly, "No, sweetheart. I've run from the truth long enough." Ronan remains speechless. Kitta begins to sob. Melena closes her eyes, sighs, and says to them, "The United Frontier found what your grandfather feared, Ronan. What the Ancients ran from. The same Jollitium magnets we use to power our cars, our weapons, the clothing you wear…it contains the power to enhance human metabolism. On Titan, they're using it to reprogram the human genome. It's the ultimate temptation. It can be broken down, processed…" she coughs and her voice grows weaker. "I gave my life to it — grew addicted to it, and the only price was my dignity. Only these treatments, no surgery, could help. I'd forgotten what it all really meant."

Ronan says with intent, "So for the Ancients, Titan *was* a paradise — "

"They tried to warn us!" Melena interjects, struggling to stand from the armchair, "Help me over to the lounge." Melena coughs and wheezes as Ronan and Kitta take her arms and lay her down on the lounge chair. The color in Melena's skin pales once again.

"Melena, is the Jollitium coming from Titan?" Kitta asks.

Melena takes a deep breath. Her arms and shoulders grow tense, and she struggles to speak, "Your father knows it could help the crisis on Earth, and I agree with him. Most of us agree with him, but the direct human applications are worth so much more to investors." Melena sighs, relaxing her shoulders and widening her eyes. "There's so much power. I flew too close, too early, and now my body is flipping every switch," she says. "I am ready." Melena grabs Kitta's hand and whispers to her, "Ronan, you must help your father." She can't see that she's holding Kitta's hand, but Kitta lets her continue. "Kitta is perfect. She will make a great leader if she trusts in herself, and you trust in her." Melena coughs, and her breaths slow greatly, "The future of the United Frontier is counting on you. Both of you…"

"Ambassador —"

Melena Horn is unresponsive. Kitta lifts Melena's limp wrist, checking for a pulse. "She's alive, but I don't know if she'll make it to Medical."

Ronan hangs his head, and Kitta grits her teeth. "Something needs to be done, Ronan." She picks up Ronans head. Their watering eyes meet. "And now we know where to start." Kitta says as she grabs Ronan's hand, "I'm going to call for Medical. You should go, Ronan. Find out what Eddy's doing." She kisses him, and he bolts from the room.

His footsteps fade as he shouts from the hallway, "I love you!"

Ronan calls Sato from his earpiece as he runs back through the narrow hallways, "Sato, you have anything for me?" He says as he continues into the construction zone, "Great! Keep him on. I'm on my way back." He makes his way into the larger corridors, pushing his way past other workers and citizens of Mars. The bystanders are confused by his urgency, and many of them know who he is.

He enters his apartment quickly. "Where are we?" He says as he discovers Sato talking to a live feed of Ezra Pierce on the main screen. Ezra sees Ronan and smiles, "Ronan, my son, I received your message." Ezra is dressed in a pale red, custom military-issued armor, and Ronan looks with confusion. "Dad! I…" he stammers. He's never seen his father in such armor before. "You seem calm. Where are you?"

"This is one of the carriers I hired. I'm just getting fitted. Inquisition Fleet is on the new route, and your ever-elaborate message appeared on every screen inside the ship just two seconds before mach-jump. It was to my surprise, but I'm glad you did it. Stopping at Ceres may prove useful," Ezra says.

Ronan sighs with relief, and Ezra continues, "I'm not only impressed, Ronan, I'm in your debt! I'm hoping you can help me further with a private link between myself and Ambassador Melena Horn."

Ronan falls silent, and takes a deep breath before walking toward his bar.

"Ronan?"

"That's not possible, Dad," Ronan says as he pulls the cork from a bottle of bourbon.

"Wait. What's that mean?" Sato says. "Reaching her should be easy."

"Ronan…what happened?"

The room shares a brief silence. Ronan struggles to throw back a finger of whiskey, and pours himself another. Sato moves next to him and sets an empty glass on the bar. "Hey man, take your time. Pour me another," Sato continues, trying to refresh Ronan's memory. "You walked with Kitta to her new job, yeah? You weren't gone too long…"

"You're right. I can't waste time. Kitta and I were with Melena in the council chambers…talking about you, Dad."

Ezra sighs, "So she knew I was doing this."

"Yes, and she told Kitta and me to help you, before we called for Medical. It didn't look good."

"Damn. She is a wonderful woman, Ronan. I really could have used somebody on the inside on Mars. Lymphoma?"

Ronan turns to Ezra, saying, "You knew she was sick?"

"Yeah, genetic. I'd guessed she had a purist parent or grandparent."

Ronan interrupts, "Dad — I don't think it was lymphoma. She was addicted to something that made her sick. Something they found on Titan."

"I certainly believed her," Ezra sighs.

"It blows my mind. One minute she's awake and attentive, telling Kitta and me about Grandpa Bryndon; the next minute she's pale and unconscious."

"And she told you she knows *why* I'm doing this? Did she tell you anything about Titan?" Ezra asks intently.

"Yes, and vaguely. They're using the Jollitium magnets, or something. We saw Ambassador Horn inhale from some device, right in front of us, and told us it made her sick. She also said they're reprogramming the human genome with it. Sounds crazy, but somehow it helped her." Ronan takes another sip. "If she is still alive, then Kitta will have plenty of questions for her."

"Whatever this is, it could have kept her lymphoma at bay. But hold on- you called for Medical from the council chamber? From one of your ear-things?"

"Yes."

"Ronan, in all my years, I have never been authorized in an Ambassador's council chamber."

"And if they find Kitta…" Ronan fails to complete his sentence. He throws the rest of his bourbon back, and drops the empty glass into a cushioned chair with great haste. Ronan has found a new fear in the UF's power and what could happen to Kitta if she's arrested. He bolts from his apartment without saying another word.

Kitta sits in the extravagant council chamber beside Melena Horn, who is laid across the chaise lounge. "Don't worry, Melena, I signaled for medical attention. You've been so sweet, and so kind to me, I just want you to know that I —"

Melena opens her eyes and grips Kitta's arm, struggling to speak, "Kitta… Security…" She coughs violently, her words barely escaping her breath. "You must hide. Smash your Wyg. Take mine. Hide!"

Melena Horn removes the data stick from her own earpiece, and thrusts it into Kitta's hands. She points to a piece of vintage furniture in the center of the room: an ornate sofa with tasseled floor skirts covering a space just large enough for Kitta to hide underneath.

Kitta tucks herself beneath the old sofa. Sweat breaks as she removes her own Wyg's data stick and crushes it between her teeth, having no idea if the data sticks or cybernetic earpieces are traceable by proximity. She hears footsteps approaching from the hallway. The rug scratches her face and belly. The springs of the couch dig into her back, pressing and piercing with each slow, controlled breath.

The chamber door opens, and footsteps quickly fill the room. At least ten people surround Kitta and Melena. A few seconds pass before Kitta hears a deep, raspy, yet powerful voice say, "Melena Horn… you called?" Kitta recognizes this male voice, but she can't remember whose it is. There's a hint of sarcasm. Several more seconds of silence pass before the same ominous voice addresses the room, "Doctor, have the Ambassador taken to Medical. This may be it."

A younger voice comments, "You know what this could mean, Dr. Feiser. Have we any reason to interrupt Ambassador Horn here?"

Kitta can see only footwear through the sofa's skirt tassels, and it's not Medical. These are heavy boots, and they're stationary. Medical would be tending to Melena. They must be Security. Kitta listens as the springs from the sofa continue to dig into her back. She knows the name Feiser, but does not recognize the younger voice. The younger voice continues after several seconds of silence, "Feiser?"

"Have some respect. Somebody called for Medical, and it wasn't her. And now she's here, but without her Jym? Find out *who* called for Medical, and find out where Melena Horn's data is. Security, take her to be treated."

The two voices leave the room with the rest of their security detail and Melena Horn in tow, but Kitta continues to listen to the low rumble of Dr. Feiser as they drift into silence. "Doctor, before we depart, I would like for you to delay the announcement of Melena Horn's death. I'll move forward with a search. Her data must be recovered before — "

As their conversation fades, Kitta waits for several minutes until the room is absolutely silent. She crawls from underneath the chamber sofa. The room is dark, and the only door is locked. She studies Melena's data stick. *Jym* — a different model than the Wyg she's used to, but still created by the Delores corporation. She attaches it to her earpiece, activates it, and the door instantly unlocks. The Jym's user interface appears to have greater security access and more tools than the Wyg, but Kitta doesn't have time to explore it. She bolts through the narrow hallway, and on to the vast, dark cavern of Town Hall, past the podium, and into the construction site. She discovers a newly-installed tactical security door blocking her path.

Ronan sprints through the empty corridors on his way back to Kitta. He rounds and jumps hastily through the inactive equipment toward the Ambassador's council chamber, only to be thwarted by the same tactical security door, and a pair of UF security personnel. Ronan shows the security officers the yellow patch on the breast of his red-tinted uniform. He says confidently, "I'm a Tech Officer, Level Three."

One security guard scoffs and says, "Level One access only." Ronan immediately calls Kitta from his earpiece and walks slowly away from the security door.

"Kitta, can you hear me?"

He doesn't hear anything. Kitta normally answers promptly. Suddenly, he receives a call from an unknown, Level One source. He answers.

"Ronan? Ronan, are you there?" It's Kitta.

"Yes, I'm here. Can you hear me?"

"I can. I'm stuck in Town Hall. There's nobody here, and a new security door's been set up," she says.

Ronan moves further from the security personnel and lowers his voice to a whisper, "I know about the door. I'm on the other side. It's a Level One clearance."

"Well, with Melena Horn's access levels, I think I can walk right out of here."

"There are two guards. Sit tight," Ronan looks at the surrounding construction equipment, and sees a dumpster full of dry red rock and dust. "Kitta, I can distract these guards," he says. "I need you to walk through the door in ten seconds, and keep your eyes closed. I'll grab your hand once you walk through." Ronan makes a suspicious eye contact with the security guards, and begins to playfully stride through the room, fondling and carelessly examining the construction equipment. He picks up a pair of construction goggles and puts them over his eyes.

The guards move toward Ronan. "Hey nerd, who the fuck are you, anyway? Get out of here, before we lock you up." Ronan smiles, grabbing the release lever on the door of the large dumpster.

"Sorry about the mess, boys."

He pulls the lever and releases red debris into the room. The billowing cloud of pink dust fills the hallway. Ronan holds his breath. He hears the security door open, and hugs the wall to move past the blinded security guards. They cough and stumble over one another as Ronan grabs Kitta's hand. "What the hell is happening here? Security, have this cleaned up immediately!" Kitta shouts, coughs, struggling to hold back her laughter. Ronan pulls Kitta from the billowing cloud, and they race ahead of it, into the red corridor toward their apartment. Ronan stops, gently swinging Kitta into his arms.

"Are you okay?" He says as he removes the construction goggles and tosses them to the ground. Kitta pulls him closer and they share a long, chalky kiss. Kitta takes a deep breath as they part, "I'm okay." She laughs at how dirty they've become and at the clean, goggle-shaped imprint on Ronan's face. "We have to get home, Ronan. This whole thing runs so deep."

Ronan and Kitta race back to their apartment to find Ezra and Sato in conversation.

"You guys look like shit," Ezra says, then pauses to look at Kitta. "Kitta, why is my screen's interface unable to identify you?"

Kitta catches her breath and says, "My Wyg is crushed. I have Ambassador Horn's data stick in my earpiece. She gave it to me before Security arrived."

Ezra is taken aback. He says, "And how is she? How did you make it out? Please take a second, if you need."

Kitta sits on the sofa and sighs, "Melena's not going to make it, Eddy. *Jameson Feiser* just ordered a delayed announcement of her death."

The room falls into an uncomfortable silence. Sato chokes on his whiskey.

Ronan squints his eyes in suspicion, and turns to Kitta. "Feiser…*Ambassador* Feiser?"

Ezra says firmly, "Kitta, I'm sure you know Jameson Feiser has been dead more than a year now, so if you're absolutely certain —"

"I'm sure of it. He showed up with Security, not Medical. There was one Medical with him, though…some young doctor. He said Feiser's name. His voice sounded familiar." Kitta takes a drink and shudders.

Ronan takes a seat next to her and comforts her. "Kitta, I love you, and you've done great. Ambassador Horn's Wyg will be useful."

Ronan turns to his father and says, "That's our inside source, right?"

Ezra nods.

Kitta takes the data stick from her earpiece, and hands it to Ronan. "It's not a Wyg," she says. "It's a different name. Have you seen this before?"

"*Jym*… interesting," Ronan says, "Some new brand? It looks the same, maybe a little more advanced?"

"I know it has full security clearance, and more tools, but I never saw. Again, Melena told me to crush my Wyg."

Ronan looks with confusion and says, "That's strange. Nobody would've been able to track you, if that's what she was thinking." He attaches the Jym to his tablet. "Thank you, Kitta," Ronan looks to Ezra on screen. "I'm accessing Melena Horn's data. I'll copy you everything I find," he says.

A few seconds of silence pass.

"Shit," Ronan says.

"What is it?"

"Jameson Feiser is definitely alive. His name is redacted from classified travel logs, along with other anonymous board members, but these redactions are useless if you know who you're looking for," Ronan says as he scrolls his tablet.

"Kitta, what else did Melena tell you?" Ezra asks.

"She said to help you, and…" She pauses.

Ronan turns to Kitta and says, "I can't hold on to this *Jym* for long. It may take UF some time, but they're going to track it. I'm copying all the data before I destroy it."

"But my Wyg is crushed!" Kitta says.

"Do you still have it? How badly is it damaged?" Ronan says as he moves to Kitta. She stands from the sofa and pulls the tiny, shattered plastic earpiece from her pocket. She hands it to Ronan, and he analyzes it.

"Ambassador Horn wanted me to help you," Ronan says to

Ezra, peering at the broken Wyg. "She was adamant. I told her I would, but I want to know Kitta is safe."

"Well, I certainly don't feel very safe here anymore," Kitta says, and pauses. She has little time to think before saying, "So, why don't I take the Jym, and go to Titan myself?"

Ronan turns and looks at Kitta in marveled confusion, and Kitta continues, "Ronan, think about it — you'll be so much more useful here. No Admin other than Melena would notice I'm gone."

"And crushing your Wyg was Melena's way of sending you," Ronan says to Kitta's surprise.

Ezra addresses the room, "I didn't intend to drag you three into this. I hope you can forgive me. This will change all of our lives, but for the better of Sol."

"We understand, Eddy. We're with you." Kitta affirms.

"There's a carrier leaving on Harlan's Tether in two shifts," Ronan says. "Dad, do you know anything about this?"

"A carrier? No."

"Well, it's UF registered, and it's loaded with weapons, ground vessels, medical supplies, Contractors with more than five hundred employees. Listed under a J. Delores."

Ezra scoffs. He remembers the name Delores from the UF boardroom in Shanghai, but refrains from mentioning it to Ronan.

Sato moves to the bar and begins filling another drink. He says optimistically, "That sounds like Kitta's ride, right? I can head to Harlan's now to secure her room, so when it comes time she can walk right in."

"Sato, we're lucky to have you helping us," Ezra says. "Be careful."

Sato drinks the last of his whiskey, and puts his empty glass on the table. Moving hastily toward the exit, he says, "I got this. Ronan, I'll see you again soon. Dr. Pierce, Godspeed." Sato lazily salutes the room and makes his exit. Ronan smirks, then sighs.

"He had quite a few of those whiskeys," Ezra says.

"He'll be fine. Once Kitta's on that carrier, I can hack into their servers and find out what they're up to. I'm sure it's easy," Ronan says sarcastically.

"Ronan, I'm proud of you. You too, Kitta. I'll see you both again soon."

"See you soon, Eddy."

Ezra disconnects, and Ronan stands alone in the room with Kitta. Kitta walks to the bedroom and begins to undress. She digs deep into Ronan's eyes with her own and jests, "It's going to have to work this time, right?" Ronan follows, seduced. He stands behind her and holds her close, subtly taking in the scent of her hair. Kitta shuts her eyes and breathes deep. He whispers, "You make it sound like we'll never have another chance."

Kitta turns and says, "I'm just scared, I guess. I'm realizing, we only ever hear great things about Titan. Melena said it would complete the 'old UF's vision of prosperity,' or something, but I never knew what she meant by the 'old UF.' I never questioned it, and now it has me more terrified than I've been since, well, ever."

"I know what you mean. We have a good life here, and it's all very suddenly being turned upside down."

Kitta's suit drifts to the floor, and she lifts her eyes to meet Ronan's. She hangs her arms around his neck, unfastening the back of his suit. She pulls the suit from his shoulders and lets it fall to the floor, firmly pressing her lips and nose to his. They kick their suits aside, and spend an extra moment standing in a warm, bare embrace. They simultaneously shout, "Castle, lights!" and share a chuckle as the room turns black.

Sato exits the monorail train at Harlan's Tether. He calmly makes his way through the crowded lobby, and toward the shipping yard. The exterior platform of this station is a paved runway, long and wide, concealed by a transparent dome. Several large ships prepare for launch outside the dome. At the end of the runway, one United Frontier carrier sits at the base of the kilometers-thick tether, stretching high to the moon Phobos. The attached carrier is surrounded by a garden of shipping containers, vehicles and personnel.

Sato blends into the foot traffic, and is met with a security checkpoint. The signage says, "J. Delores - Titan - 9:08." Sato casually approaches the checkpoint and points to the red badge on the breast of his uniform. "Hey guys, level three," he says to the security officers on duty. They're very relaxed, and say nothing, but barely have time to greet Sato with a nod before he passes through the checkpoint. He calls Ronan, but Ronan doesn't answer. He leaves a voice message —

"Ronan, I'm in. They have security checkpoints down here, but Kitta shouldn't have a problem getting in. I'll set up a sleeping pod for her. The ship leaves in nine hours."

Sato enters the lobby of the carrier. The shining chrome and navy blue walls stretch high, and the interior design curves toward the elevators in the center of the room. He struts through the crowded lobby, calm and confident, when a random person catches up with him. A Contractor. Sato notices most of the people on this carrier don't have badges on their suits; this is a ship full of privateer contractors and their employees.

"Are you lost? Red badges don't use the lobby."

Sato doesn't say a word, and hops over to the closest service door. He sweats and rushes into the bright white maintenance corridors. The walls are stained by red dirt smudges, scuffs and fingerprints. The air is noticeably thin. He races through the hallways, following the Loading Dock signage.

The hallway ends, and through an enormous gate Sato bears witness to the stress of these workers, and the pressure they are under. They struggle to move past one another; some of them carrying everything they own in one box, others carrying boxes with their employer's supplies. Not one person lingers.

Sato waits for an empty freight elevator and a break in the sea of employees. Before long he finds his chance, and strides to the empty elevator. The amount of alcohol in his blood is made apparent to him by his profuse sweating. He quickly shuts himself inside the elevator, and not quietly. Adrenaline racing, he quickly selects "Sleeping Corridors," on the elevator's interface. Sato cringes when the elevator bell roars across the Loading Dock, forgetting that this detail could also be attributed to the alcohol in his system. The elevator ascends, but not fast enough. Sato watches as the small window on the elevator door is occupied by the face of a curious employee. He can only hope this suspicious stranger doesn't alert Security, but speed is more important than discretion now.

The elevator reaches the Sleeping Corridors. The door opens

to an empty hall, lined with numbered hatches. Sato, panicking, rushes to a hatch around the first corner, and opens it. He uses the stationary tablet on the wall inside the pod to set the lock. Level One clearance. It's a half-assed version of what he planned, but ensuring Kitta can get inside the pod is all he can do if Security is on his trail. He leaves the pod and bursts toward the lobby elevators, rather than the way he came.

The elevator door is almost close enough to touch when it opens. Sato is confronted by two large, menacing Contractors, accompanied by the curious employee from the Loading Dock. A UF Carrier using Contractors as their security staff is strange and frightening. He runs toward the freight elevator, though he knows he won't be escaping this ship. "Good luck!" one of the men shouts as Sato sprints around the corner.

He activates his earpiece and calls Kitta, "Hey, your pod is ready. I'm going to be arrested. I set your pod to a Level One clearance. Please, both of you, be careful."

Sato turns around to face his pursuers. He falls to his knees with his hands in the air, and his Wyg between his teeth. He crushes it into pieces before the security guards reach him. "Be careful, boys!" He shouts sarcastically, coughing and gagging in a dramatic fashion. He looks up at the approaching Contractors just in time for one of their fists to swiftly meet his cheekbone, knocking him unconscious.

TWO

Old Friends

THE *Comrade* burns within a bright red laser beam, hauling the Inquisition Fleet through the vacuum of space at such a velocity. The electromagnetic engines have completed their final gravitational adjustment sequence, and Ceres orbit is one week away. Popp and Ezra sit alone on the bridge of the *Comrade* over whiskey and a bowl of untouched protein snacks.

"I don't like talking about it," Popp says, lazily.

"Exactly why I asked," Ezra retorts with a sarcastic, yet impatient tone.

Popp grows annoyed. "And it's a childish, dead-end curiosity! Of course I'm tired of cleaning up UF's and everybody else's space trash. I had dreams once, but I'm old now. Will you tell me why you're acting out like this? Maybe, you'll tell me why you've paid me *double* what I asked for this job!" Popp says sternly, "I know you're a doctor, but that's *deathbed* money. Tell me you're okay, man."

Ezra rolls his whiskey round and round in his glass. This ship's artificial gravity is last-generation; imperfect, and oddly nostalgic. Since the discovery of a magnetic superconductor in Jupiter's soft mantle, the ships powered by them, including the *Comrade*, contain engines which run through the center of the cylindrical structures. The engines draw gravity inward, allowing the passengers to experience

Earth-like gravity on the convex floors of the ship.

Ezra's skin tightens at his squinting brow, and he notices his longer than normal, unkempt hair. There's more gray than five days ago.

"I wouldn't know where to begin if I'm being honest," he says. "I remember getting the call from Titan. I was Ronan's age. Melena was with him at the time, and right at the start of a Trade Week, she called me. It was only minutes before Bryndon spoke his last words to me." Ezra pauses to shoot his whiskey. "Whatever they found out there — it's creating something I think my father warned me about."

"Ah. I remember that day. I didn't make it to Medical in time to say goodbye, but I wish I had," Popp adds, sulking. "He was my best friend, your dad, and I missed him after the blast; when they brought him in…I'm glad you two spoke." Popp is restless as he sits. He ties the long, gray bush of hair on his head into a sprawling, spongy tail of split ends. He shoots the whiskey in his glass, and pours another for Ezra, then himself.

"Right," Ezra pauses, "And the timing of it all. If Melena was sick during that call, had this new mineral been found? Used? Impossible."

"I never heard about it." Popp says, "I came back to Earth right after Bryndon passed, and that Bio shit was not my specialty anyway. It was a Trade Week, you said?"

"It was!" Ezra forces a joyful expression, "I enjoyed Trade Weeks *so* much before that day. I know you remember the Tweek back in the day — you had to greet new recruits on Mars, and —"

"And you switched my teleprompter to an old speech. That

was such a shit-eating, brilliant move!" Popp interrupts, both laughing and choking on his whiskey. "The names…" he scoffs through his speech, "oh-ho, those kids had no idea what was happening, and neither did I, until I read your name. That was a bigger moment for me than you think!"

"Well, in her memory, I'll confess to you — that prank was entirely Melena Horn's idea."

"Really…" Popp says, now deadpan, but hinting at a hidden smirk.

"Yes. Melena insisted I claim it, not sure why. The speech with my name in it was my only contribution, though I think she led me to it. Why was it such a big moment for you?" They pause to sip.

"I was complacent," Popp says, grunting and squirming in his chair. He yawns. "When I read your name instead of Ronan's I thought, *Really, man? Even the new Pierce kid didn't deserve a speech that was…*" he pauses to think of the correct word, "*distinguishable?* It lit a fire under my ass to refocus. And this whole time — Melena Horn — she wasn't speaking to me at the time. Not much at all after Bryndon."

Ezra sighs. "She really cared about you."

"Heh…" Popp chuckles, but only to keep from sobbing. He catches the tear early. "Well, she had quite a way of showing it," he says. "Kitta is probably tougher, never knowing her."

Popp and Melena's daughter had been conceived in Saturn territory, and born on Earth in secret. Kitta's conception and Bryndon's death happened nearly simultaneously and violently drove Popp and Melena apart. Melena would continue her work on Titan, and become the Ambassador of

Titan, however brief before her transfer to Mars. Popp would raise their daughter on Earth alone, operating his orbital salvage company, whose most common task was cleaning up wrecked or abandoned satellite stations among other forms of obstructive litter between Earth and Mars.

"I never knew *Melena* was Kitta's mother," Ezra says, dismayed. He'd never known Kitta's age, but the timing makes sense. The chances of Ronan's partnership with her seem amazingly slim, but not so farfetched considering how well Ezra and Popp get along.

"She came around just after I was removed from Titan," Popp says. Ezra can tell Popp is not comfortable talking about this. "Left for school at fourteen. She couldn't wait. I don't know where she is. She and Melena never met, and Kitta never knew who her mother was."

"She may have known Melena better than you think," Ezra says. "She was an inspiration long before she was an Ambassador."

"You're right, and Kitta would've known the better version. Melena knew that too, I'm sure." Popp fuels his aggressive sarcasm with more whiskey. "I just let it all happen. I didn't want to complicate either of their lives. It felt right at the time, you know?"

"Well, I don't think you did anything wrong. It felt right, because it was right. Do you miss her?"

"I miss it all, Eddy. I miss them both. Only time I saw them together was in dreams," Popp says, "but I was a terrible father, and Kitta deserved better. I felt like I deserved better too, but I've always been selfish. Melena would have been a good mother."

"I didn't know Melena personally, but she was a mother to many. Don't beat yourself up," Ezra says before he takes another sip. "My father did talk about how amazing your team was. You, Feiser, Melena, the others…" Ezra notices Popp pouring *another* new drink.

"Don was the fuckin' man," Popp says with a drunken slur. "*The others*," he repeats Ezra's words with resentment. *Don* was Popp's nickname for Bryndon when they worked together. "That's what's different about you now, man," Popp says. "You always looked like him. But now, I don't know. Before everything happened, we had plans, Bryndon and I. You should've been there."

"Don't say that," Ezra says sternly. He never liked being compared to Bryndon, and Popp knows it. Ezra can tell Popp's getting testy, maybe even belligerent with his unfinished and sporadic points.

"Okay, okay," Popp slurs and hiccups as he cozily readjusts in his seat. He's beginning to fall asleep. He continues, slurring his words, "You're right, *is* different. Don's only enemy was… stopping… think *stopping* killed him…"

"What do you mean by that?"

"I mean you stopping *soon?*" Popp mumbles. He can't keep his eyes open.

"What? You're speaking gibberish," Ezra says, knowing he couldn't get Popp to move to a bed by now if he tried.

"I'm stoppin' this," Popp says as his consciousness wavers.

Darkness squeezes Popp's peripheral vision. His eyes sink inward. The architecture of the room begins to blur and shift back in time. The blank taste of the sanitized cabin air cuts through his reinforced whiskey breath. Ezra's voice begins to grow deeper, more faded and ambient as it becomes less present and impossible for Popp to understand. Now feeling weightless, Popp reaches and stretches in all directions around him, both hands and feet, but touches nothing.

"Stop this! Get me outta here!" In his chest he feels himself shouting, but cannot hear himself.

Popp finds a plexiglass wall with his left hand. He knows this glass, and he knows why it's so thick. He's suspended in a low-gravity chamber. His clothes have changed, but are familiar — the old UF sparring jumper. Ezra has disappeared but the distant, ominous humming of a voice remains. Popp's vision begins to render a room beyond the glass wall of the chamber. Bodies and silhouettes move and blur about the large, incomplete room, and one figure stands just outside the glass chamber, looking in at Popp. Hands on their hips, perturbed... the height, the posture... Popp recognizes the figure immediately — Bryndon Pierce.

The low, muffled voice filling Popp's ears regains clarity, but is no longer Ezra's. It's Bryndon's, saying, "Alright, alright, let's get you out of there," over a speaker.

Gravity is restored to the chamber. Popp feels refreshed as he finds his feet. The usual aches accompanying his stiffened limbs, joints, and back have all been forgotten. His breaths are full and his eyes are wide. He opens the chamber door, and is reunited with an old friend. Bryndon Pierce stands before him, tall and smiling like always. "Don't be such a baby," Bryndon says, sarcastically.

"Don, I — I'm sorry." Popp says to Bryndon, struggling.

Bryndon's eyes squint, as if confused. He smiles. "Don't hate me, Pauly, it's just protocol," he says, seemingly ignoring

Popp's apology, "and Titan is half a day away, so you'll be glad we did this before peak hours." *Pauly* is Bryndon's nickname for Popp. And his voice — as soothing as it is commanding. It feels good hearing Bryndon speak again.

"I've been trained in all essential degrees of gravity," Popp says, confident and committed, "so you just worry about your own ass."

"Hey," Bryndon snaps back. "You're perfectly capable. It's just nice putting you in your place sometimes." Bryndon smirks at Popp, and Popp chuckles.

What a wonderful man he is, and what a magnificent time this is. By now, Bryndon Pierce has revolutionized agriculture on Mars, and is now going for the hat trick — Saturn. Saturn's moons are riddled with minerals, and they've barely been touched. The United Frontier has launched a large-scale Colony-grade carrier to Saturn's most attractive moon, Titan, to do three things- Build a sustainable, commercial mining operation, begin the construction of a habitat for humans, and complete a functioning tether in Saturn's orbit. Bryndon, now Ambassador of Sol, is Route Captain and Surface Foreman, while Popp is Bryndon's Route Co-Captain and Orbital Security Captain.

The United Frontier aren't the first humans to commercially travel to Saturn, however. The Lordes Company, or TLC, built Jupiter's first tether, where FeiserCorp began mining helium from the gas giant, and eventually, superconductor magnets from the planet's mantle. They would share the cost of their trip to Saturn, and would share in the spoils. FeiserCorp's is the true first-ever commercial mining mission to Saturn. The United Frontier is only one month behind them. TLC and FeiserCorp — Jameson Feiser's company — have representatives traveling with UF, and a care package in tow for their early birds.

Popp and Bryndon begin walking through the crowded carrier. Faceless figures pass and murmur in swelling streaks of blue and gray. This place is bustling, and very familiar. Popp suddenly finds himself unable to speak, but remains at Bryndon's side. This doesn't feel like a good time to show weakness.

Bryndon breaks the silence by saying, "Pauly, after you saved us from catastrophe on Mars, I wouldn't trust anyone else with the safety of this excavation. Hopefully James's people don't get in the way, but I think Melena can keep him at bay," And Popp is immediately distracted by the names Bryndon mentioned. Jameson Feiser, or *James,* and Melena Horn; old friends and UF coworkers. Bryndon says, "Here he comes now. Let's mess with him."

The blurry interior of the crowded UF carrier begins to consume the passing figures, and shrink around Popp and Bryndon. They continue walking forward and toward Jameson Feiser as the closing walls around them come into focus.

Popp recognizes it as the interior of the very first surface station on Titan.

Jameson Feiser, a short and stocky man with receding salt and pepper hair, stands before them in a cold sweat. He isn't well liked by his peers, and is often found in Bryndon's path, like a conspiring shadow. Jameson Feiser is in charge of Communications and Public Relations for UF, which means he can hear everything that everyone in UF says to each other, and he determines which of UF's accomplishments make the news. He quietly inserted FeiserCorp to begin working on Titan under contract with UF, so it didn't look like UF was beaten to Saturn. Two great launches, one goal — and that's the way the news goes.

Feiser begins barking and slurring incoherently at a stoic Bryndon, and the little man Feiser is clearly angry about something. Listening to him is always a drag. Popp begins looking around the room behind Feiser. He tries to make sense of his surroundings, but Feiser — the twerp. He's hiding something. He's considered a friend, but he's always had his own agenda, and this mission to Titan was his chance to make a greater profit and set up his own stations apart from his work on Io, in Jupiter's orbit, where the magnetic superconductor was discovered and named "Jollitium" by Jameson Feiser.

Popp feels present; quite healthy, in fact, but is still unable to speak. He's only able to let the oddly familiar, mundane moments play out in front of him, until he feels a deep ache in his belly. His senses begin to fall out of sync, and he realizes this pain is from a vision — a vision of shipping containers packed with weapons, on route to Titan. Weapons are prohibited on United Frontier groundbreaking missions where there are no hostile entities, but these shipping crates are labeled differently, falsely. Only with the name *FeiserCorp*. Popp knows the difference, but says nothing. These containers, particularly those carrying explosives, are too familiar for Popp's military education not to recognize.

Suddenly the room is devoid of light, pitch black, and Popp can hear only the sound of his own racing heartbeat. A blank, reactionless Jameson Feiser is the only other person remaining in the warm void. The pain in Popp's belly grows stronger. His senses realign just long enough for him to harness energy into his lungs and draw breath. He closes his eyes, and briefly catches the scent of whiskey. He squints and reopens his eyes to Feiser, and exhales.

Popp grunts as he thrusts his hands into Feiser's chest. The air feels as dense as water as he pushes Feiser, who drifts gently into a chair as if choosing to do so himself, into a chair Popp must not have seen. In the brief moment of confusion and embarrassment, Popp notices a smirk on Jameson Feiser's face as he sits casually.

Popp falls backward into a chair of his own, and the two now share a table. This chair is very uncomfortable — definitely a UF rec chair from Titan. A sleeping tablet sits on the table in front of Jameson Feiser, who sits across from Popp, who is still unable to speak or to hear the noises he can make. Feiser is stoic, with his usual conspiring facade.

"You're a hero, man. Just don't let it go to your head," Fieser says, in that oddly deep voice for his size. Popp can easily read the sarcastic tone. "*Glory* was always a mystery to me. When you make yourself known, you make yourself weak."

He's impossible.

"I've noticed you and Pierce getting along *very* well. How long after their Tether is finished, do you figure, before our business with *Lordes* turns sour?" This all sounds so familiar. It's always so hard to listen to him, but the way he talks about the Lordes Tether project has always been suspicious. "Tell me, Paul — I want to know you'll put Lordes' name alone in the dig's liability clause. If anything goes wrong here, it's important FeiserCorp and UF avoid the legalities." His low, conniving whisper makes his underhandedness louder than any sense cares to experience. Feiser is protective of those close to him until they outlive their use to him. "Pierce will be disappointed if he wants to treat this like some archeological vacation. And I know Lordes will be in Pierce's corner, politically speaking," he continues. "The future of this place will be a heavy burden for whoever is in charge," Feiser says, "and I know Lordes will also throw their name in the ring for Ambassador of Titan. I know Andrew wants it."

Popp notices the faintest details returning to his surroundings. The room is dark and small, and one faintly lit doorway flickers with the shadows of workers passing. The distant chatter is calming, until a short, stifled giggle grips Popp's attention. Melena Horn — impossible for Popp to mistake. In the doorway, Popp can see her right eye peeking into the room. A minute silhouette, but definitely her. She's not looking at Popp, though.

Jameson Feiser stands, his speech muffled into obscurity, and he turns his back to Popp. He walks to the door. Jameson Feiser and Melena Horn share a long gaze as he crosses the flickering light and leaves the room with her. Chattering, laughing.

Popp jumps from his chair. He pushes the table aside, and shadows close around him. What feels like crowded bodies pass him, push him, and pull at him as he trudges and reaches through the twilight for Melena. Popp finds the strength to speak as he loses sight of them, but he holds it down. Like vomit. He wants to call out to her, but speaking has become such a rarity in such a short time, it's best not to waste it. Melena's safe. Feiser's still a friend.

He feels a cold metal door handle ease into his right hand. The door opens into another crowded room. The shadows wash away, and the lights blind at first, but after adjustment appear to be great chandeliers radiating with a warm nostalgia, bringing color and shape to this vast, yet familiar ballroom. He takes a deep breath, and sighs.

"You make yourself known, you make yourself weak," he says softly.

Shit.

Popp takes a deep breath, hoping he hasn't missed his only chance to speak. He looks down at the formal suit and tie he's wearing. This doesn't seem right. A suit? The faces in this room are impossible to make out, but they're all in formal dress. The classical piano echoing from an unknown location; the sounds of laughter, champagne popping and glasses ringing.

This is the Titan Groundbreaking Party of '75.

"Pauly! Come sit with us!"

That voice again. A beacon. Bryndon Pierce sits at a long, seemingly endless dinner table with Melena Horn, Jameson Feiser, Andrew and Patricia Lordes, and somehow Ezra Pierce is there listening intently with his little recording device. They all sit opposite Popp. Popp can't help but look at Melena. Her charisma is unmatched. She will definitely go far in her UF career. One could only hope the best for such a beautiful soul. Popp sits at the only open seat, unsure of and unconcerned with the vague figures beside him.

The others seem to ignore Popp's arrival and continue their conversation.

"You truly are one of a kind, Miss Horn," the overweight Andrew Lordes says to Melena.

"I appreciate that, *Mister*… Lordes? *Lord* Lordes?" She looks to the couple with confusion, "Is there a formal title for you two?" She's trying very hard to keep from laughing at them. Melena Horn has little respect for her fellow Yellow Sector authorities, but is subtle with her insults. Her beauty is so certain to Popp. In this time and place, she excels in her field, and herds the dipshit diplomats she works with like cattle. Even when she isn't being obvious with her sarcasm, Popp can see it. It's one of many reasons he loves her, and won't miss her until long after.

"No, no. No silly titles!" Lordes says as he wheezes with laughter. "Royalty is purely your surroundings, and we come from the States, where *money* has always been king."

"And with all your wealth," Bryndon interjects, "you wouldn't be considered royalty? Culturally, it must be close."

Andrew is about to speak, but Patricia cuts in, "We're slaves, dear," her voice as sharp as razors, "slaves to the almighty dollar, and those who deny it, are doomed to lose it!" She pauses, and looks seductively into Andrew's sunken, brown eyes. It is truly amazing, how someone as beautiful as she is comfortable with a man so physically unhealthy. "My master beckons," she jokes, referring to their wealth as she and Andrew share the only laughs at the table.

"Well, without you, it certainly would have been very different out here," Bryndon says, trying to hide his distaste for The Lordes Company and their presence, "I say the more the merrier, and cheers to the Lordes Tethers! You'll pave the way for commerce between the outer colonies." Bryndon was no pretender, and even he was terrible at faking adoration for Andrew Lordes. The tether is definitely a large part of this operation, but those in control of it are not scientists. They're the elite rich, and wanna-be politicians. Bryndon toasts, "Congratulations on your conquest, and I can only hope to bring such glory to my own name." He takes a drink.

"I have no doubts, Ambassador, and you have already made quite the name for yourself, and your family," Andrew Lordes toasts. "I know your son Ezra is following in your footsteps on Mars, and his son will certainly be a frontiersman. A true dynasty of explorers you're creating, within Sol!"

"Thank you, Andrew, and I hope my son can take my place here within the year."

Popp toasts as well, but doesn't say a word, and doesn't take a drink. A hidden curiosity, maybe fear, has rendered his mouth and throat useless. Nothing in, nothing out. He remembers working with Ezra Pierce on Mars, and that Ezra never made it to Titan. It's strange and unnerving seeing him here. He instead traveled back to Earth — out of fear, depression, Popp assumes — but complacency is the word that fills his mind. UF shoveled riches at him in order to keep him on Earth, and away from his father's work. Popp is sure of it.

Jameson Feiser scoffs. Suspicious timing. Nobody else at the table notices but Ezra Pierce, who glares at Jameson Feiser like he wants to kill him. Never mind how Ezra got here.

Bryndon's voice cuts through. "I believe Ezra understands as well as I do — if these Ancients wanted us to find something, they would want us to treat it with care." Such wisdom among animals; he, *and* Ezra.

"Care?" Feiser says, entertained. "Please, Doctor, I hope you're not one of those who paint superstition over the Ancients' messy operation leftovers. What we found on Mars is glorious, truly, but my concern is sustainability. How long do you plan on being out here, Bryndon?" He's a pragmatic one, Feiser. He's also known Bryndon long enough to call him by his first name.

"I only speak of caution, James," Bryndon answers, intently. "Our operations on Mars were far from perfect. Ambition got the best of us." He turns to look at Popp, then back to Feiser. "And we were prepared for it, thanks to Pauly here. Caution, James."

Suddenly Popp feels a hand on his right leg, and turns to look at Andrew Lordes- who would never be able to sneak up on him, but is now seated next to him. The details in his face are too much not to be distracted. The shimmer of status is visible in the essential oils membraning his thick, olive skin. The acne he suffers from has left small scars about his bushy browline. Andrew looks at him directly and says softly, "I look forward to our surveillance outing, Captain Russo. I know you'll be very busy, but I hope I can acquire you fully."

He must be drunk. Tether construction is paid for and overseen by TLC, and now suddenly he needs help? Something must have gone wrong. If they plan to launch that thing into Saturn's orbit in time to send the first payload back to Earth, then they cannot afford for something to go wrong. That tether is the only way back for many of us.

Popp struggles to swallow in a dry throat, hoping to drum up the slightest bit of hydration. Words fall from his mouth, completely out of his control.

"Andrew, our future here depends on that tether," Popp says with a suspicion obvious to Andrew Lordes. "I'll be busy, alright. But if something's wrong — "

"Oh, nonsense!" Andrew's words crash like thunder, shocking Popp into his previous muted state. Even the words from Popp's mouth are out of his control, but they feel natural; old, even. There is comfort in them. The tense exchange retains a vague familiarity hidden within the discord, though Popp can tell his questioning has angered Andrew. Popp's blood in turn rises to boil.

"Everything is on schedule and the Company is tip-top, as always." Andrew says.

"Then why are you and FeiserCorp bringing explosives!?"

Popp stands and screams into Andrew's face, his hand gripping the fat man's shirt. Popp's entirety is shaken. He feels an aching in his liver, and a shortness of breath. His teeth and joints ring. The soreness is separated by time, like a long-forgotten fear. Popp is struck by an omen of what he could become. A version of himself who never followed through on his plans to build a business between Saturn and Jupiter. A version of himself retreating to Earth, having failed his friend, his love, and himself. A version of himself that would go on to fail his only daughter, who would abandon him at first chance.

This pain — it comes from a place where Bryndon could have been saved, but died in agony. It comes from a place where Melena Horn was forced to put their daughter into embryonic suspension to be born on the other side of Sol with no mother. A place where Popp saw the signs and the corruption, and when he could have acted, he fled. A loneliness weighs on his mind; a bitter old man had been cursed to his own vices, hated by what little family he had, coping with loss by collecting old war machines and keeping himself busy behind the curtain of work. This path, clouded in regret, familiar by pain, could not be allowed.

The conversations at the table continue uninterrupted. Andrew Lordes sits below Popp and continues bobbing his head and socializing, laughing with others as if nothing has happened, even with Popp's hands clenched at his chest. The faces sitting at the table begin to blur and fade with echoes of laughter as Popp notices Melena standing across from him, staring into him. Her details remain copacetic. He releases his grip to follow her as she prowls opposite him along an endless, altering table. The room begins to drain itself of color and shape, contracts and expands with every breath as Popp focuses entirely on her.

The old furniture, the old friends, the commotion fades. Only she remains, on a large stage. She turns her back to Popp, facing a bright light and clutching a podium. Popp shields his eyes and shuffles to the side, finding himself backstage behind a long, thick curtain. The room stretches far beyond her now, and an ocean of seated onlookers examine her with great intent, and listening ears.

She's campaigning. She wants to be Ambassador of Titan after Bryndon Pierce. Her countless followers surely see the unfettered grace Popp sees in her, but nobody else knows her so deeply. Not even Bryndon Pierce nor Jameson Feiser know the true Melena Horn, her at her darkest. It's in front of them now, and only Popp can see it. The political facade, the scientific agenda, the ebb and flow of resource funding in

UF all do well to distract her, but her home is burning. The ticking clock has begun to melt.

Her lymphoma is in remission, albeit replaced with something intangible. Whatever stews in the cancer's wake is suffocating her.

Their child grew inside her for ten weeks — small enough for no one to notice, and large enough to be extracted without Popp having to change the suspension tube before full maturity. Embryonic suspension has its moral implications, but it's certainly the best move for her career. Hard for UF to hold bias against something they're funding.

Popp can feel she's close; the reeling lavender in her soft, statuesque hair. The warm curtains in his hands dress and dance from her shoulders to her waist. He stands at the podium with her, and she wears the familiar show-worthy attire, but these public settings were never comfortable, at least for him. She trembles. The discomfort is uncharacteristic of her, but for Popp to share in it felt uncommon in a selfish way.

He holds her closer and nestles her ear. "I'm here," he hums.

She exhales, and smooths her nerves. She leans into his neck. "I'm afraid," she says. "You should have stayed. We could have stayed together."

"But I'm right here," Popp says, confused. "It's not too late. Come with me. Kitta needs you."

"It's not too late," Melena mimics his words.

Popp is surprised by Melena's mirrored complicity. She repeats again, louder, "It's not too late!" Popp squints until his eyes hurt. He clutches the now cold, detached curtains, realizing his body has snapped backstage, forced to watch Melena from afar as she enthralls the UF voters in the audience.

This is Earth.

"It's not too late to make Saturn work for us! We will build upon our Titan colony, and invest in Saturn! Radiation storms and other natural disasters will be met with sound preparation, and the preventive measures I've proposed for Saturn's expanding rings will be paid for by the mining operations in Saturn's orbit!"

She's just beaten Andrew Lordes in an election for UF Planetary Ambassador. It was the hardest she had worked in her entire life. She appealed to the UF with her persistence in securing and investing in the first Titan colony. In the year leading up to the election she had grown so distant from Popp that it feels she's forgotten her daughter, who is now a few months old. The fear returns. Some hidden fact, a realization beneath the familiar words and this vibrant atmosphere. This should be exciting, but somehow it's only foreboding.

She continues, "The late, wonderful Ambassador Bryndon Pierce knew the value of human presence within Sol, and I knew him well." There it is. The hidden truth of this bittersweet time is his own failure.

Bryndon Pierce is dead.

"It's not too late," he desperately murmurs to himself.

Another echo from the rear steals Popp's attention. "It's not too late!" But it's not an echo from before. Melena's voice shouts from afar, now stricken with adrenaline and hysteria. Popp turns to face a bright light. He reverts his eyes briefly to notice the abandoned curtains have smoothed and retracted into hanging, white plastic sheets. The entire room around him has turned small and bright white. Medical. Popp begins to fear; for what, he doesn't know, but the fear is familiar. The high hum of the medical equipment grips him only tighter. He remains composed, but suddenly this is no longer Earth. This is the surface of Titan once again, and these separations in time share only a hollow gut sense, an ache of loss.

The double doors at the other end of the room burst open with several doctors and nurses, Jameson Feiser and Melena Horn frantically bearing a heavy hospital bed. The bed coasts to Popp in the center of the room, and the doctors scatter to their positions. On the bed below lies Bryndon Pierce — burned, bloody, and unresponsive. He's barely recognizable. The room is familiar, but the situation isn't. Popp didn't make it to see Bryndon before he passed, only after.

"There's neural activity," Feiser says. "Doctors say he's in a state of comatose, so we can communicate with him, but he doesn't have long."

The doctors begin placing small transmitters about Bryndon's skull, and activate a neural processor to determine either Bryndon's final thoughts, or any potential message or request he may be holding in his subconscious. The monitor screen flickers and shakes from the activity picked up from Bryndon's brain.

"Bryndon, there's been an accident. If you can hear us, say something," Melena Horn articulates to a motionless Bryndon Pierce.

Words appear on screen, slowly. One letter appears every ten or so seconds to display Bryndon's thoughts.

The first two letters are E and Z.

"I need to prepare a message for his son right now. We should have a window," Melena directs a nearby security guard. "Doctor Ezra Pierce is with UF on Mars. Go, now!"

The guard scurries away briefly to return with a planetary receiver. The statement being generated from the neural processor stops, meaning one of two things: the thought or message has completely rendered, which is uncommon, or the machine is no longer picking up any activity, and Bryndon is truly leaving us. In this case, it's both. It's characteristic of him, to say the least, to complete his final transmission against all odds and statistics. And to Popp, to do it within minutes of death is poetic, if nothing else. Melena picks up the video-phone and holds it in front of her while she peers into a camera lens.

"Ezra. You must sit down to hear this. There has been an accident. Your father suffered critical injuries. He doesn't have long. He had a message for you. A short one I'll send as soon as I can."

The worst has happened.

"How?" Melena insists.

"There was an explosion," Feiser says. A heavy guilt weighs suddenly on Popp. The eyes of others in the room take to him simultaneously. Feiser continues, "Orbital scanners missed a pressure pocket in the mines and Bryndon was down there." Jameson Feiser's statement was simple, but his eyes told a different story. The look in his eyes told Popp to hold back, not to interject and expose the lie that the scanners don't miss gas pockets. Ever. Melena's hand sneaks into his. He finds her eyes commanding in the same manner as Feiser. Don't speak up, the eyes say. There are more important things.

Melena pulls him aside. The bustling of the emergency room fades, and turns quiet. "I have to tell you something, Paul," she whispers. "You have to promise you won't speak a word of it to anyone." She's shaking.

But what could she possibly have to say? It's all so predictable by now. She'll inevitably ask for Popp to return to Earth, not only for their unborn daughter, but now for political reasons as well. As head of UF security for this operation, he is the first to blame. He is considered lucky to have shared the blame with Andrew Lordes and TLC, who were also held accountable due to their name being on the security's liability clause, which Feiser had orchestrated. It ended up causing, or already caused, Andrew Lordes to lose the election to Melena Horn. The shifts in time and location rack the mind, and it's taken long enough to admit the cause.

This is a dream.

The truth is, Popp has already failed the late Bryndon Pierce. He has already abandoned Melena Horn, Titan and the entire UF operation on Saturn and Jupiter. All the expensive equipment and the enduring faith of the soldiers of his company; everything he'd built in the following decades of hollow depression meant nothing knowing the true reason he left, and why he came back to Earth in the first place. Melena didn't feel safe after Bryndon's death and wouldn't subject their daughter to a life of such risk. He returned to Earth with a daughter he believed he was saving, but who would grow only to despise him and abandon his protection. He could blame only himself.

How much of this trip to Saturn was controlled by Feiser

is unknown, but nonetheless, there could be more answers hidden within the subconscious. The fear and naiveté of the past are no longer an object, however annoying it may be to have traded this truth for the happily forgotten damages of age. The effects of habitual drinking and drug abuse are a harsh reminder of not only his failures, but of the less productive ways he chose to cope. Little can be done here to rectify what this particular expedition to Saturn has created, but if reliving this trauma can help explain what's happening to Sol in real time, then so be it.

Suddenly he hears Bryndon's voice. "You alright?" But he's nowhere to be seen. He tries to follow it, but the directionless echoes only further expose this environment corrupted by lucidity. Everyone has disappeared. He hears the voice again. "Popp, get up." It's Ezra, not Bryndon. Popp opens his eyes and the bridge of the *Comrade* is revealed to him. The pain in his body becomes real again. The soreness and depression of the mind returned in full force. Ezra stands over him with one hand on his shoulder.

"Popp, you were talking in your sleep. Sweating profusely. Everything okay?" Popp has grown accustomed to these haunting reprisals of the loss of his friends, his career, and Melena, and he promptly regains his composure. He then notices Ezra's other hand slipping his recording device into his pants pocket.

THREE

Commands

I'M jealous, really," Ronan says through a garbled, lo-fi filter. The personal tablet he buzzes from displays a selected photo of him as Kitta listens. "But it blows my mind," he says, "officials have access to this tech. Wyg is the only cybernetic equipment that employees use out here, and it never occurred to me that the Admins were set up to use these Jyms against us. The Privateers and Contractors may have Jyms too. Is it full-staff cybernetics on that ship?"

"Yep, just about everybody. I've tested it," Kitta says, sitting quietly in her sleeping pod. "I'm surprised we can speak to each other. This ship is moving really fast."

"I downloaded some of the Jym software to my Wyg's data stick. Not all of it is compatible, but apparently these Admins can communicate with high-velocity space vessels in real time. I just hope you're careful. Past few days I've looked a little more into what you'll be able to do with your Jym. Augmented Reality Tools for Administrative Cybernetics was a hidden file in UF's servers. And you're right — Admins using a Jym like yours, or Ambassador Horn's," he pauses, taking every chance he can to grieve the late Melena Horn, "*They* can still see you when you activate your cloaking tool, so there isn't much of an edge over them. If you're put into lockup, there's very little I could do to — "

"Have you heard anything about Sato?" Kitta interrupts,

easily predicting Ronan's warnings.

"UF has been quiet about it, but so have I. His file says he's in the middle of a shift."

"Wow!"

"Yeah. It seems UF lies quite a bit," Ronan affirms. "The ship you're on is registered with UF, but the exec is private. A surgeon. He's pretty popular. Have you learned anything about this Jaco Delores?"

"The J doesn't stand for *Jack*? I've seen the young doctor. He's just a bit older than us, and has no cybernetics."

"The guy is a cyberneticist. Seriously?"

"Nothing suit-visible, at least. I haven't gotten too close. I overhear people talk about him like he's the only authority." Kitta pauses, and Ronan waits for her to continue. "This ship is very peculiar — very lax, not many security personnel," Kitta says, having tested the Augmented Reality's cloaking tool on her Jym, allowing her to remove herself from the vision of Wyg users.

"There's a lot of laughter and conversation here," Kitta adds. Leaving her pod for food has shown her much of the carrier's interior commute.

"Well, don't go having too much fun," Ronan warns, "but I found that Jym has more useful tools, too. It's just a matter of copying the enabled code back to you, which you can download from a terminal on that ship."

"What other tools do you mean?"

"I'm sending you the manual for them. I also made *you* the primary user, rather than Melena Horn."

There is a brief silence. The many people on this carrier are either part of a Company, or a Contractor of some sort — all looking to take part in the commerce of the outer planets. If their business were to be disrupted, then they would fight to keep it. Jaco Delores seems to know this, and has brought the weapons to equip the different companies and their staffs. Kitta asks, "These employees — they don't know about what's happening on Titan, do they? On Earth?"

"They may not."

"Well, most of them don't seem like bad people," Kitta says. "I hope they're not forced to fight… for Eddy's sake too."

"Once you're in that server room and you've sent me that ship's data, we'll find out what they're doing," Ronan says.

"Okay," Kitta says. "Ronan, I'm so sorry about Sato. When you find him, and I find Eddy, we'll find our way back together."

"I look forward to it, and I'm sorry too. I have to go. If you see a security drone following you around, and it's labeled with a capital R, it's me." Ronan hangs up.

Kitta senses Ronan's coldness — the emotionally distant tendencies to which he has a right. He searches for Sato. Without anyone to watch his back on Mars, Kitta can only hope UF won't catch on to what he's doing. All of this new information about UF, and Ezra Pierce's call to action have inspired Kitta, but it's all sending her on a path away from Ronan. It seems her love for Ronan and her commitment to the people of Sol have come into conflict.

Titan is one week away, and Kitta has spent most of her first week on Jaco Delores's carrier in solitude, rummaging through the limited memory data in Melena Horn's Jym. Much of Melena's personal data was corrupted during the abrupt transfer in Arcadia, but Kitta finds what little she's listened to fascinating.

In the beginning, Melena threw herself headfirst into the difficulties UF experienced during expansion. She was excited to do this, and is the reason Titan had progressed so much in mere decades. She worked as UF's Intercommunications Director, controlling the ebb and flow of commerce in a newborn off-world colony. She was excited for the future and gave herself entirely to UF's cause. The later writings and recordings grew depressing, however. Melena eventually sounded trapped. Her love for Sol had turned to fear in spite of the progress she had achieved.

Kitta lost her greatest teacher, but through the few recordings she has, she feels closer to Melena Horn than ever.

Kitta wonders about Ezra Pierce and his connection to it all. Even during the short years Ronan shared with his father on Mars, he didn't speak much of Ezra, mostly of his grandfather, Bryndon. Bryndon was always painted as a hero while Ezra apparently had little worthy feats or stories. Now, the people of Earth are suffering, and Ezra seems to be the only person doing something about it. Ambassador Feiser, the Mayor of Titan, whoever these people are — to Kitta they had been poisoned by the outdated incentive of fiscal profits over human prosperity. The corruption has reached a tipping point to the dismay of many, and Kitta must understand it before it can be stopped.

This new mineral which had apparently kept Melena Horn alive was the true landmark in her recordings. Bryndon Pierce died in a terrible tragedy not long after. Melena Horn privately alleged in her recordings that Bryndon's death was conspired by Jameson Feiser. She lamented at her complacency throughout the ordeal. She had an ultimatum that would kill her if she didn't go against her own integrity, toeing the UF diplomatic line. The work it took to secure her new medicine drained her of her conviction. This ultimatum would eventually send her to Mars, where her career and influence beyond the Belt would fade into obscurity.

Oddly enough, this young Doctor Jaco Delores, or "Jack," sounds similar in his speech to Melena's more inspiring, earlier recordings. His dreams of expanding within Saturn's orbit are very public, and his prowess as a public speaker makes his political grooming obvious, but not off-putting. On screen he is profusely charming and downright handsome, but the repetition of his sentiments, whether played in videos or on intercoms throughout his carrier, feels like propaganda.

Kitta receives a message from Ronan. It's titled, "Jym Accessories Manual." Ronan left a note with the attached file reading, "I've sent the Jym Accessories installation file in a message that you can open at a regular comms terminal. Whenever you're ready, find that server room, connect your tablet directly, and I'll take it from there."

The manual she's received is divided into three sections: Augmented Reality, Commands, and Warnings. Kitta skims the manual. The Augmented Reality tools allow for basic visual renderings like ads, directions, etc., on top of digitally removing herself from the vision of the employees using the less-advanced Wyg. The Augmented Reality tool also gives her an image copying option, allowing the user to select a nearby object and copy it in position. The largest object that can be copied is a person, including the user themself. The copied objects are visible to Wyg users as well as Jym users, giving Kitta a potential edge over other Jym users.

The Commands tool would allow Kitta direct access to applicable AI within the ship, from simple electronics such as lights, cooking and plumbing appliances to piloting and power controls from inside the carrier. The Commands tool also gives the user a backdoor into a Wyg user's neural-link and can even subdue a Wyg user by rendering them unconscious.

The manual warns of privacy, and the moral obligations of a Jym user, but the Commands tool has the potential to seriously injure or kill a Wyg user if used improperly. The warnings feel like a joke. The device now seems more like a weapon than anything, and the UF symbols peppered throughout the official pages of the manual only feed Kitta's distrust in the UF Admins who have been using them.

An alarm sounds from the wall-tablet in her sleeping pod. A shift has just ended, and the majority of employees on the ship will be resting or in leisure for the next few hours.

The carrier is enormous, and Kitta would need an administrative map to find the server room — another use for the ominous yet necessary Commands tool. Both the moral implications of this device and the power it enables frighten Kitta, but it's her only form of protection. A comms terminal should be easy for her to find so she can download them.

She shoves her tablet into the outer-arm pocket of her suit. She opens the door of her pod slowly while listening for any potential passersby, however unlikely. Kitta notices several employees loitering throughout the long corridor, but none are close enough to notice her exit the pod. She activates her

Augmented Reality tool, instantly becoming invisible to the Wyg-equipped employees of the carrier. She closes her pod and uses the nearest ladder. The upper service walkways are seldom used and more discreet.

She walks softly toward the closest junction, only a few meters above the heads of two loiterers. The interface on her Jym selects and identifies them as G. Rudek and B. Veranda — both Contractors, like many of the people Kitta has been able to scan. They cannot see her, further confirming that the Jym is limited to United Frontier Admins. Kitta doesn't stop to eavesdrop, but listens to their conversation in passing —

"I have to get back to my pod. Don't wanna miss touchdown."

"Do what you like. I heard we aren't touching down right away. Weather."

The two Contractors chuckle before separating and leaving the corridor.

A jungle of wires and mechanical equipment surrounds her, until the upper walkway comes to an end at the next intersection. Kitta is forced to the main walkway. Signage ahead directs her to an Information Center — a likely place to find a computer terminal. She rounds the corner to an empty hall with a hatch at the far end. A small security drone springs from a hidden corner ahead and stalks her. The drone is close enough to be scanned, labeled "Security Drone- R," and the fear she felt for Ronan's potential arrest, along with the appreciation of his skill as a programmer, strengthens her resolve. Even from afar, Ronan can still protect her in ways she may not anticipate.

The Information Center sits at the junction directly ahead of her. The frosted port window in the center of the door blinks with a blurred, gray shadow. Then another. There are surely at least two people among the terminals. Kitta has been in space for one week without so much as being seen by anybody here — much less having to interact. She may not have a choice now.

The drone zips away. Kitta looks down at her jumpsuit, and ponders the promotion she left behind on Mars. It's obvious to her the promotion is gone, along with many other things back on Mars, but Kitta still has the indigo-tinted suit. Indigo being indicative of an administrative status could prove useful now.

Another gift from Melena Horn.

As Kitta reaches the hatch, she checks her surroundings. The paths to her left and right are barren, and the only sound is the faint, rhythmic hum of conversation from within the Information Center. She deactivates her cloaking tool. She decides her best approach is improvised. She knows she'd fail if she were to allow herself time to second-guess her actions.

Kitta slides the handle and slowly opens the hatch. She hears the conversation cease as the air within the room shifts. Kitta studies the room. There are rows of available terminals, UF medical and military signage, a second hatch on the opposite side, and a group of four loiterers. They stare awkwardly at Kitta as she walks toward the closest terminal. She smiles and nods in their direction, noticing their clothing. Three men wear standard gray employee suits, with different badges indicating the companies they work for, but they're too small for Kitta to read. The fourth person in the group brightly stands out, sporting casual clothing. Kitta can't scan the three employees in their gray suits before they move to the hatch opposite whence Kitta came. They've clearly been made uncomfortable by her presence, leaving the room and neglecting to close the hatch in their haste. The young casual remaining wears a bright, flowery button-up shirt and khaki chino pants. The clothing, heavy-framed glasses and tousled hair could mean this person is a high-ranking admin, or from the private sector. They're of a slender, but masculine build, and wear a casual layer of mascara and eye makeup, including brightly colored fingernails. This person is also equipped with Wyg cybernetics.

Kitta activates a terminal, opens her inbox and begins downloading the new Jym software. She can feel this stranger looking at her, but she continues working, keeping the mysterious figure within her periphery.

The installation finishes in seconds.

"Getting some extra credits in?" The ambiguous loiterer asks in a soft voice, approaching Kitta.

"Might as well, if Titan's weather is gonna hold us in orbit."

"Yeah, hopefully the radiation passes quickly," the young character says calmly, peering around the room casually, yet nervously. The golden, cinema-quality hair and light makeup are oddly comforting; a very clean and free spirit denying mainstream cultural conformities. Their heavy-framed glasses hide their eyes well.

"You don't look familiar…Mars-hire?"

"I go back and forth pretty often these days," Kitta says with a confident facade. "I'm a trade graduate."

"Okay, so that explains the blue," the stranger laughs.

"Those other guys thought they were in trouble."

Kitta wonders, if this individual is from the private sector, then why would the other employees leave? Are they working for UF? She also wonders why an executive on a UF carrier would be here talking to employees and wearing such attire, but it seems like a waste of energy attempting to analyze an operation so unorthodox.

"You couldn't *pay* me to walk around telling people to go to bed," Kitta says sarcastically, "But you — you look nice, if not familiar. You on vacation?"

"Ha! *Vacation*. My name is Sam. Sam Levin, and thank you. I'm Jack's favorite journalist," Sam jests, "far from the fiscal superiority of him and our other overlords." Of course — journalists often wear casual attire to distinguish themselves. It could be a strange coincidence, but Kitta won't allow herself to be fooled. Kitta notices small things about the way Sam speaks; the warm eye contact and cushioning chuckles would feel flirtatious if Kitta weren't so nervous.

"I have family on Titan, too. I haven't seen them since I was a kid. If I'm being honest I'm nervous about what I might find. I know Titan is pitched as some kind of paradise, but if I'm being honest, Earth is my favorite. I like being outside."

"Well, that's quite a take, Sam." Kitta conspires, "So are you here working as well? Are you investigating this whole thing, or fluffing it? I hear the man in charge of this ship has it suspiciously good." She hopes Sam's response may provide information, or answers to questions Kitta hasn't thought to ask herself.

Sam begins with excitement, "Oh, I'm no fluffer, but there's something wild and amazing happening outside the

Belt. The work never stops." This person's comfort and confidence is intriguing. "I know enough about Jack. He's kind of an old friend. Surgeon, cyberneticist, innovator, and he's what, twenty-three years old? But he's going to Titan! Why!? I'm sure you're in too deep to say anything about it." Sam looks at Kitta with anticipation. Kitta looks back, expressionless. She seems to have this stranger fooled for now. She reinforces her impromptu alibi: "I don't know anything wild and amazing about Titan. Private trade logistics tends to bore most." She hopes using the word "private" will help ease Sam's trust — the notion being they're both outside UF.

"So you aren't contracted by Delores, and you don't work for UF at all," Sam says suspiciously. Kitta seems to be losing control of her alibi. Regardless of Sam's informational value, Kitta has to find the quickest way out of this room and back to her pod. Sam's expression grows dark, and greatly suspicious. Kitta feels Sam's trust fading.

"A trade graduate…" Sam repeats Kitta's alibi with a lackadaisical tone.

A light buzzing sound from behind reminds Kitta of the open hatch behind them. A drone just entered the room through it. She accesses the ocular interface on her new Jym software. Her new tools should have something to help her out of the Information Center. She selects "Commands," then looks for the safest option she can. "Proximity," then, "Lights."

"So you're with FeiserCorp's shady skeleton crew, or you're lying and you're a stow — "

Sam is interrupted by the Information Center and adjacent halls turning black. Only the blinking mechanical and safety indicator lights throughout the room remain. Like constellations they guide Kitta as she lifts herself from the terminal and prances on light feet to the open hatch. She slips through on her toes, leaving the hatch ajar, and Sam in the dark.

"Hello? What happened? Who are you!?"

Kitta moves quickly to the first corner. Color and light slowly return to the tunnels as she races through them and into yet another unknown area of the ship. She has time only to activate her cloaking tool and vanish. She looks behind to see if Sam followed — nothing. After rounding several junctions, she finds time to slow down and catch her breath. Sam said something about a FeiserCorp skeleton crew, who must be the Contractors who are distinguished by their outdated space uniforms and large stature. They're only seen walking with Admins, including Delores, indicating that they're working for the ghost Jameson Feiser.

This new Jym software has greatly expanded Kitta's applicable options. She accesses the Jym's interface and opens the Commands file. She selects "Ranged AI (*Delores I*)", and chuckles at the young doctor "Jack" Delores naming the ship after himself. From there, she selects "Interior," then "Map."

The environment is immediately lit with holographic, navigational signage cybernetically rendered only to Kitta's vision. She waits for the AI to speak.

"Hello! My name is Carter. Where would you like to go?"

Intrigued by the advanced AI of the ship, Kitta remembers the grueling hours Ronan put into programming such systems for UF carriers. The Interior and all other automated systems within these carriers have highly advanced personalities. Some of them can also be very sensitive, for they spend their idle hours conversing with one another; challenging themselves with hypothetical user interactions and crisis predictions.

"Sleeping Corridors," Kitta says. Centered on the path behind her stretches a glowing, thin green line. It rounds the corner whence she came — toward the Information Center, which is out of the question.

"Sleeping Corridors are right this way," Carter says.

"Find me a different path, Carter."

"Is there something to report?"

This must be a new ship. Many of the conversations these AI systems use to improve their functioning are in their programming, but eventually most AI personalities are built from user interactions. This one may be new or neglected, and unfamiliar with the mundane- recreation, unwinding — the things humans do for no reason. Carter is young and curious.

"No, nothing to report," Kitta says. "This is recreational. No reason."

There is a pause.

"Is there something to report?"

Kitta grows nervous. These AI's might alert Admins of suspicious activity within their systems if it consistently inquires to report. Kitta wonders if Carter has somehow been affected by Ronan's tampering with the security systems on *Delores-I*.

"No, nothing to report," she repeats.

Kitta bitterly deactivates her Commands tool, deciding to find her own way. The signage at the junction ahead shows the Server Room isn't too far, and she already has the tools she needs to get the ship's data to Ronan. Hopefully he's ready. What Kitta doesn't have is enough time to get back to her pod before the next shift begins.

Kitta sneaks around the next corner. A long, tight corridor stretches ahead of her, with doors staggering to the far end. She remains invisible and completely silent, moving slowly. An alarm sounds over the ship's speaker system. A shift is beginning. The Server Room is at the end of the corridor.

A low voice rumbles from the path ahead. The hallway is too tight to sneak past another person. She climbs faster. The voice stops. Suddenly a young man bolts from an open door, colliding with Kitta's invisible body. He writhes in shock. His hand grips Kitta's arm. She's still cloaked, but her form is absolutely clear to the young employee.

"What the... who?"

Kitta doesn't speak. She places her feet before the man's chest, and pushes away from him in the only direction she can — toward the Server Room door. The man's head strikes a corner, causing him to bleed. Kitta clings to the handle of the door as the man approaches angrily, glaring in her direction.

"Show yourself! You may as well. You're at a dead-end here."

Kitta opens the door to the Server Room. The man in pursuit isn't far behind. He's unaware he would be able to see Kitta if he were to take the Wyg out of his earpiece — which to Kitta means this person may not be very intelligent, or perhaps he is simply distracted by the adrenaline and confusion.

The Server Room is large, but the long server racks stretch in tight rows intended only for maintenance drones. The only way out of this room is through the same door, and there's no place to hide.

Kitta throws the door shut, but doesn't latch it. She backs into the room, accesses the Commands Tool on her Jym and looks through the available options, hoping to somehow distract or escape the pursuing Employee and avoid using her cybernetics to subdue him. The door bursts open and rings loud like a bell when it hits the nearby railing. The Employee creeps slowly into the Server Room, and approaches Kitta, knowing to look only for the ripples in his vision created by the minute imperfections of her cloak. She's run out of options.

"Come on out…" he sings. "Don't be embarrassed, little spy."

Kitta uses her Jym to select him, then Options. The Employee spots her and lunges toward her. Kitta selects the Deactivate option and watches as the man falls limp and barrels to the ground. A violent crunch forebodes possible injury, but hopefully just broken equipment. Kitta stands, turning to investigate, and is surprised by the amount of blood on the floor of the server room. His head has split against an edge and he may not survive the blood loss.

Kitta shuts and latches the door. She pulls the tablet from her arm pocket, and attempts to activate it, but it's dead. No lights, just a blank screen. It must have been knocked or shaken during the struggle. She looks at the bleeding man. He's still alive. The med kit on the wall has temporary bandages, but this man will need medical attention. She accesses the ship's Map AI once again. "Carter, direct me to the closest med bay!"

"The med bay is right this way. Is there something to report?"

FOUR

Baby Bird

THE front door of Ronan's apartment opens to his surprise, though he thought UF would've caught on much sooner. Two UF Security personnel rush in and move toward him as he frantically finishes typing and shuts off his terminal. He removes his Wyg's data stick and tucks it under his lip, then raises his hands. The guards stretch a blindfold over his face, and drag him from the room. Not a word is spoken between them. UF is choosing to apprehend him between shifts, perhaps so the halls are empty, with nobody to witness his being arrested.

"You guys gonna kick my ass or something?"

The guards cradle Ronan's arms, and carry him toward the Town Hall construction site through the main corridor. He can't see but he knows the layout of the nearby corridors well enough to keep track of where they are. He hears a knocking sound, and an unfamiliar door opening in front of them. Something hidden.

"You don't speak," one guard grunts. "I don't know why we're here, or what you've been up to, but now you're *their* problem." The guards shove Ronan forward, and an enormous hand catches him, lifting him like a child by one arm. The door closes behind them and the UF guards who arrested him are gone. Ronan dances on the tips of his toes as this Behemoth moves quickly. His strength disturbs Ronan's arm.

"So are you the one who's going to tell me what I'm being charged with? Am I *technically* in UF custody right now?"

"UF…" the Behemoth scoffs.

Ronan's blood boils. He can hear the Behemoth's heavy breath. "You're breathing awful heavy for a dead man," Ronan threatens, not as if he has any recourse, but because he's desperate for a reaction from this mysterious figure. Ronan is answered by the Behemoth slamming Ronan's head through a service door. Ronan's head had turned in such a way while being thrusted that his Wyg experienced the brunt of the impact. The door latch rips from the wall. Ronan's Wyg is damaged, and his ear bleeds beneath his blindfold.

A man shouts from across the room they've entered, "Hey! Easy, you ape! Get him in there, and then come back here to fix that door!"

Ronan doesn't recognize the voice. The pain is too distracting. Ronan scoffs and snorts through the running blood of a few broken teeth. With his mouth exposed, he sprays blood into the space ahead of him.

He hears another voice, a younger man's voice from below. "Are you kidding me?" The young man rants, "Hey, Pierce — you should know we've been watching you and your girlfriend ever since we caught your drunk buddy. You're going to stay here until you give us the encryption to end your broadcast."

Ronan spits again before he's dragged across a wide, echoing space, and can hear a few workers murmuring. He's then slammed through another door, nose first. He stumbles and falls onto the hard floor of a holding cell. The blindfold is ripped from his head. The sudden brightness of the room brings only more pain to his already throbbing head. Ronan screams as the door shuts behind him. Ronan can't even open his eyes to adjust to the brightness. His head rings. Every hard plastic surface of the cell is intensely lit, but a silhouette can be seen slumped in the corner, along with a toilet and sink. Ronan digs his Wyg's data stick from his bloodied gum and dries it on his shirt. He attempts to shove it into his earpiece but recoils from the jolting pain of doing so. His Wyg has been damaged at the nerve.

"Rough week?" A weakened Sato rasps from the far corner of the bright cell. Ronan recognizes his voice immediately.

"Sato? What's happening? Are you okay? These lights…"

"Yeah, they roughed me up pretty good. I think these cells are designed to keep us tired, but after a week I'm definitely going blind."

"Sato, I'm so sorry."

"Don't be. These bastards forgot about me. They've barely fed me. The faucet only drips."

"Sato… this is where you've been the last six days? I've been searching, and your UF status read that you were on shifts all week. Are those UF employees outside?"

"It was quiet here at first, but the past few days have been getting louder outside this cell. They seem angry, which is nice."

"I'll bet they are. The broadcasts of Kitta and my dad have gone viral on the UF servers. I'm pretty sure it's spilling over into the mainstream now," Ronan brags, only to distract himself from their situation. "It blows my mind, thinking of the shitshow that must be happening on Earth right now."

"Earth," Sato sulks, "I guess I'll never get to see it again."

"When was your last time?"

"Five, six years ago. I've only visited once since UF orientation."

"Orientation? You mean when we met? Wait — *visited?!*"

"I was born here."

"Stop. You're telling me you were born on Mars, came to Earth, and said 'no thanks.' How rare is that?" Ronan mocks.

Sato chuckles, "Well, it was the most fun I've had in my life, I'll admit; I enjoy being able to see everything from the simulations, and I had become such good friends with you and Kitta. I had to come back to Mars, for my family. Plus, by the time I could leave, I didn't really want to. Earth is loud, anyway."

"It is loud, isn't it?" Ronan laughs, "Especially now, I'm sure. Unbelievable. I thought I knew you better."

"It never came up," Sato grunts. "My parents wanted me to move to Earth and stay, but they got sick that year."

"Of course. But all your memories of them are here. Why stick around?"

"We became such good friends that I decided to save Earth for a better time. Retirement, maybe."

Ronan sighs, "You were only looking through the news with me when all of this started. My father, the reason all of this is happening," he declares.

"Hey man, *you* changed *his* coordinates, remember?"

"I saved him!"

"Just saying, you wanted to help him. We all did." Sato diverts to keep Ronan from raising his voice and wasting his energy, "Kitta's out there, huh?"

"She is. She was just getting ready to link that ship's

servers directly to me, but I think she's been caught. She's very resourceful, but I'll be honest, man — we didn't plan this very well. *One — Get to Titan, Two — Help my dad.* We've been high on excitement and adrenaline the past week, and we've forgotten that every tool we're using to subvert our enemy was given to us *by* our enemy."

"Our enemy?"

"UF, man."

"Shit," Sato says. "I've spent so much time thinking about it — to hear it out loud," Sato pauses to cough, worrying Ronan. He sounds sick, and weak. Sato continues, "UF is all I've ever known."

"Will you be okay?"

"I'm pretty confident I won't make it out of here."

There is a long pause. In spite of his own agony Ronan ponders ways to comfort Sato. "Sato — do you remember when my dad said to me, 'I'm in your debt,' and can you guess what I did in response?"

"What'd you do, send him a bill?"

"I did that, yeah."

"For what?"

"For lost income the past week. The time I've spent helping him instead of helping UF; but billing him isn't the whole thing."

"Okay, so you billed him. Is it a lot?"

"Technically, yes, but that's not important."

"Okay, so money is no object — even though there's a bill. Is it a failsafe of some sort?"

"Good question! It's set to be triggered after a certain amount of time has passed. So you've figured it out?"

"No. Did you find another way into the servers on Delores's ship? You're gonna blow the whistle on 'em?"

"You know, the more I think about it, the less necessary I'm realizing the info on that ship may be. The drones following Kitta have done so well to infatuate the public and spark further investigations into UF activities. All I've been doing is filling in the blanks for her audience. I don't think she has any idea — the millions of people cheering her on."

"So you've made them famous? Your dad too?"

"My dad's situation is slightly different. Drones are watching, but the people tuning in only see old men in old uniforms. They can read all about how my dad launched with his Inquisition Fleet from Shanghai to start this, but Kitta's live feed is much more popular."

"How's that for you? Have you and Kitta talked about how this ends?"

"We haven't. I've thought about it, and I've considered the worst. Truth is, I may never see her again. At this point, it's likely. I've tried blaming anyone but my father, but it's difficult." Ronan takes a deep breath, and hears Sato stifling his cruel heaving. "I was set," Ronan continues, "I had expectations. Kitta was being promoted. I never imagined I'd be helping my father overthrow his rotten bosses."

"*Our* rotten bosses."

"Yes, of course. But you get the point. I feel like I'm having trouble staying afloat mentally when things keep getting pulled from under me. In one week I lost my two best friends, my job, and now my earpiece is damaged."

There is a brief silence. Ronan's eyes still can't adjust, so he's bitterly relieved when he hears Sato cough again.

Ronan continues, "So the short answer is no. I never got into those servers. Whoever caught Kitta got hurt, and could be dead. It's not exactly Kitta's fault, but it's probably the reason I was also caught. It blows my mind how naive we've been. They grabbed you on the carrier, so of course they found the room you prepared for her. They were probably watching her the whole time, too."

"Sounds like I owe *you* an apology," Sato strains.

"Don't you dare!" Ronan smiles at Sato's sarcasm.

"So do you have any other secret weapons?"

Ronan laughs. "I was hoping Kitta and the servers would be a secret weapon, but it's not such a good prospect anymore."

Ronan's eyes are slowly adjusting to the light, but he wraps his shirt around his face to avoid long exposure. He wants to touch Sato, but it's hard to tell the size of this room and Sato's distance from him. Sato would have undoubtedly embraced Ronan, had he the strength. Sato may be too weak to be embraced at all.

"It sucks, huh?" Sato rasps.

"What does?" Ronan writhes. Tying the shirt around his head disturbs his broken earpiece.

"The light. I can hear you getting cozy, or whatever you're doing."

"Yeah, it sucks," Ronan shouts. "I'm not kidding when I tell you I'm — "

"Hey, take it easy, man," Sato coughs and catches his breath. He knows Ronan is about to start firing threats at UF or anybody listening outside the cell. "I got mad at first, too. Don't waste your energy."

"You're right. But I gotta get their attention somehow," Ronan grunts and analyzes his broken nose with his fingertips. The blood running from below his new blindfold and down his neck is as annoying as it is alarming. The earpiece has been bleeding internally as well, deafening his ear until he turns his head to empty the blood into the fabric of the blindfold.

A small slotted hatch slides open on the wall near Ronan, expelling two small objects to the floor in the center of the bright cell. Ronan blindly scans the floor with his fingertips and discovers two protein bars in plastic wrappers. He frantically opens one and crawls to Sato. "They gave us some food. Here," Ronan says as he extends the protein bar forward, wagging it from left to right. Shortly he feels the scratching of long fingernails and dry knuckles lifting the bar from his palm. The crinkling sound of the wrapper isn't loud enough to hide Sato's sobbing, or perhaps he's laughing.

"I can't chew," Sato says. Ronan climbs closer, promptly opening his own protein bar. "I can do it for you," he responds before taking a small bite. Ronan chews until the protein bar is consistent enough to swallow. He finds Sato's face. Using his tongue to push the mangled, nutty paste into Sato's mouth, he smells the rot and decay in Sato's breath. Sato has experienced this as a result of his neglectful captors. After several bites Sato says, "Thank you, Ronan. I think I can take it from here."

"It blows my mind they think they can get away with this." Ronan pauses. "I sued my dad, Sato. That was my big plan."

"You're mad!" Sato's voice buzzes with excitement, nearing its original tone, further reminding Ronan of how weak his friend has become. "I don't have such a mind for legal stuff. So the courts will look for you?"

"Theoretically yes, but we don't have time anymore. My earpiece is bleeding quite a bit. We have to find a different way out of here."

"So your Wyg doesn't work? I'm not —"

"Ahh!" Ronan screams. He has dried his bloodied earpiece with his shirt and forced the Wyg in, swift to disregard the potential damage it may do and the pain he may experience. He has been answered with an internal pressure at his ear so agonizing he can't help but rage. It hadn't occurred to him the pain he's in could be worse, but his Wyg is too important to lose now. Before Security showed up at his apartment, he was able to download the administrative options for his earpiece, like he'd enabled for Kitta. He huffs and sweats, struggling with the ceaseless aching. Sato responds but to Ronan it's only a distant hum buried beneath the ringing within his skull.

The software comes online. The damage from the interfering blood is apparent in the distorted, flickering interface. The Augmented Reality tools have been corrupted, and are not supported by Wyg hardware to the point where the options don't show, but the Commands are still effectively available.

"Ronan, you okay?" Sato wheezes.

"I need you to listen," Ronan grunts. "I have a new plan. I just need you to follow my lead and be silent when I start shouting. All I need is for them to send someone in here." Ronan sits at the cell door gently listening to the commotion outside. He can't discern their words. He waits only for silence, and for the room outside to clear. He knows he may still be concussed so he tries to avoid falling asleep, but the pain and the blood loss are tiring.

Ronan wakes from an unintentional slumber having no idea how long he's been unconscious. His blood-soaked shoulder peels from the wall he leaned against as he stands quickly. He continues listening but now with a greater anger and renewed sense of urgency. There is only silence for several seconds before he begins bashing on the cell door. "You killed my friend!" He screams and weeps, initiating his deceptive new plan. "You'll burn for this!" He continues bashing the door until he feels footsteps approaching.

Ronan activates his Commands tool. The Behemoth crashes into the room, knocking Ronan to the floor. The open door reveals the room outside, dampening the light of the holding cell. The Behemoth enters the room and Ronan promptly selects him with his Commands tool, aware the monster is equipped with cybernetics. Ronan selects the "Deactivate" option and watches the monster's now unconscious body slump into the corner of the cell next to Sato. Without second thought Ronan stands and speeds through the open door. He uses his Commands tool to shut off the lights around him. He knows the room is large, but has no clue what time of day it is, or who may be in the room with him. His eyes blur and adjust while the unrelenting pain in his ear makes him more and more nauseous. The brightness of the cell behind him and several computer terminals within the room create a soft twilight. The room is quiet and empty between shifts and the Behemoth was alone.

Ronan finds the closest terminal and quickly accesses the security system on Delores's ship, which he's left in shambles, but the few computers in this lab are powerful enough and fully capable of continuing his work for Kitta, wherever she may be. He finds that the hacked security drones on Delores's ship remain available to him, and his new access levels now include the various programmable weapons. He accesses the tablet Kitta took with her to discover she succeeded in connecting it to Delores's administrative servers. The data is immense. The amount of research technology Delores has in tow is uncharacteristic of a ship preparing to fight. The hired Contractors and their Employees would be fitting for a carrier on its way to a new world, were it not for the arsenal of weapons to accommodate them.

Ronan notices additional and unfamiliar options throughout the terminal's interface. The standard UF terminal has been unlocked to offer Ronan administrative access, due to the new software in his Wyg. The entirety of UF's undisclosed data is now at his fingertips, localized to servers on Mars. He rummages through officials' physical data, even searches among technology and innovation data hoping to find a list of individuals equipped with the same enhanced cybernetics. He finds a folder titled Quantum Travel Roster and checks the source: a mysterious program titled Quantum Elevator. Upon opening the program, a large domed machine in the center of the room whirs and pulses and comes to life. The spire of metal and fiber has a warmth to it; almost magnetic, as if it's generating its own gravitational pull. This great machine has a wire-caged facade and two separate doors, each leading into spacious chambers. The advanced machinery reaches into the ceiling of the cavern and toward the surface. The Quantum Elevator program has a menu which includes locations of other such machines, a startup sequence, and a schedule. Ronan opens the Travel Roster and sees what he had suspected but believed impossible, at least not in his life. The Quantum Elevator is a large quantum computer, used for long-distance teleportation. It's worked for decades, and the distance is vast. The names of UF officials, among others, have travel logs from recent months. Jameson Feiser and now Melena Horn are among the names of the deceased, with Jaco Delores among the living. The records stretch back far enough for Ronan to discover Ezra Pierce's name near the beginning of the list; one trip from Mars to Earth, just before Ronan was born. Some of the more recent logs go to First City on Titan, and plenty to Earth. Ronan closes the UF interface to reopen Delores's. This is not the time to be distracted from helping Kitta.

As Ronan continues, he uncovers a video file with his father's name in the title. The video is a week-old conference call with UF in China, and Ronan watches as a room full of frightened UF officials on the top floor of Jiang Laboratories declines his father's offer to join his inquisition and his over-the-top display of defiance. He then hears a young man's voice stand out as the source audio of the file; Jaco Delores — accepting Ezra's proposal and telling him that he would travel to Titan on his own. This information Ezra somehow felt necessary to keep from Ronan, Kitta and Sato.

Ronan suddenly catches a horrid scent, and remembers his friend in the holding cell, along with the unconscious Behemoth. He sprints toward the glowing light of the doorway.

The deathly aroma thickens. Ronan tilts his head to empty the pooling blood in his earpiece, grabs a pair of tinted goggles hanging outside the cell and slides them gently around his head. Sato lies in the corner of the cell with the still body of the Behemoth weighing on his legs. By the smell Ronan first assumes Sato is dead, but then Sato coughs.

"I hear you there, you bastard," Sato grunts. "Get him off me."

"What's that smell?" Ronan gags as he rolls the deadweight man from Sato's leg.

"He was on his back. I was close enough to suffocate him. I didn't know what else to do. He would've killed us." Sato shifts his legs from beneath the carcass. Sato's legs are unbroken by the fallen Behemoth, and his new-found energy allows him to stand, though shakily. Ronan attempts to help, but Sato rejects him. "Let me get up on my own. So we're the only ones around?"

"Yes, but I don't know how long it'll last. Can you walk?"

Ronan helps Sato from the cell and into the laboratory. "This room — it feels weird. What's that sound?" Sato asks, referring to the pulling and the buzzing of the Quantum Elevator. Ronan places a new protein bar in Sato's hands and turns to the nearby computer terminal. "It's a lot. I'm not sure where to begin, but with this new software I'll be able to do more than just watch Kitta. My dad, too."

FIVE

The Queen

EZRA has spent the past several days exploring the *Comrade* and making small talk with Popp's employees. Several of them are older than Ezra, nicknamed "'75ers," meaning they were present for Titan's groundbreaking and have been with Popp for decades. The '75ers witnessed Popp working with Bryndon Pierce in the earlier days of Solar migration. Their stories of lovers back on Earth who'd left them in the fallout of Popp's dismissal from UF having been led by promises of wealth, the families they were trapped from seeing for years, and the rumors of both Popp's heroics and corruption tell Ezra more than he would ever learn from Popp on his own, or from eavesdropping Popp's sleep-talking episodes. Some of the more seasoned employees have been hesitant to share their stories until learning Ezra is Bryndon's son.

"Good morning. You busy?" Ezra asks as he enters the bridge where Popp sits alone at a computer terminal. Popp turns to Ezra and sips his coffee. "Not busy. I've delegated everything. Just browsing my inventory."

Ezra sits, relieved to find Popp drinking something that will keep him awake. "I've been talking to your Goons, as you call them. There are entire families here working for you."

"I have them split up pretty good for when it comes to field stuff. Everyone here lives well," Popp says. He joins

Ezra at a holographic map of Sol. The luminous digital renderings of planets and their moons dance back and forth around the center — much faster than real time, highlighting the window in which Ceres and Titan will be closest in their respective orbits.

"I don't doubt your ethics, I'm just amazed by some of the crew — especially the guys who knew my dad."

"Linus and Vik would never tell you but they saved James Feiser, your dad and me from a gas pocket deep in Mars," Popp rambles, "We were so confident, and on our way to the site when we felt the explosion. They triggered the opening early because they knew it would kill us and the workers behind us. They took the blame for the damaged equipment and were fired instantly, making them my first hires; off the books, of course."

"Can't hire out of UF while you're still in bed with UF, eh?"

"I got away with a lot. I still do, even though UF knows they screwed me. Linus and Vik had nowhere to go. You remember them from F-Squadron's memorial."

"I've spoken to them since," Ezra responds, "and they told me a bit about the company you were planning."

"Lordes Road was perfect for the company, too," Popp declares, "and it never came to fruition! Lordes built their tethers at Jupiter and Saturn, and we were on the ground floor." Popp moves the map's orbiting planets to the ideal commercial distance between Jupiter and Saturn. He highlights the route between them.

"I don't pay attention to the Tweeks like I used to," Ezra's tone darkens. He recognizes the pattern of planets nearing one another on the same side of Sol. "Too many private companies and redactions nowadays."

"Ha, it's bittersweet for me. I wanted to go commercial outside the Belt more than anything, and would've been one of those redactions on the public servers, but the frontier was changing so fast. Still is. We weren't on Titan very long when the Jollitium surged again and those Tethers became obsolete. Patricia Lordes disappeared into retirement right after Andrew croaked."

"I had no idea about Lordes going broke. Isn't Harlan's still bustling?"

"Mars ain't Saturn. It was crazy when we started out here and I'm sure it's only gotten crazier. UF and Feiser led the way to the outer planets, but we weren't the only ones. The business became about the Jollitium after we were already out here and I would've settled down, using my fleet to move rocks between the planets, but Don — " Popp becomes silent.

"I never made it out this far. I always had work to do on Earth or Mars," Ezra adds.

"UF kept you busy."

"Mostly maintaining my dad's work, but yes."

"Paid well, too, huh?"

"It *did* pay well," Ezra notices Popp is leading him. "You think my dad's death wasn't an accident. That's where this is going."

"I always thought nobody else cared," Popp sulks.

"I was far away, and I certainly never had reason to suspect murder. You're saying someone wanted my father dead?" Ezra remains calm, to Popp's surprise.

"I hate myself for not seeking some kind of investigation. But it all happened so fast, and it all seemed so perfectly accidental. The progress with the Jollitium afterwards was extraordinary, and it wasn't my place to speak out. I was scared, I'll admit, but Feiser was playing a long game. It wasn't long after the second Jollitium surge that he unseated Melena in the next election, sent her to Mars, and had complete control of UF. He knew he had time to cover up Don's death *and* keep you out of the picture."

"Is that why you apologized to Bryndon in your sleep?"

"Could be," Popp grunts, knowing that is the reason. "Don wanted you to come out here, you know."

"He never told me that."

"And of course UF floods you with lucrative work inside the Belt to keep your name off the front lines."

"Why are you saying all this? Especially now?"

"You said your boy heard James's voice on Mars."

"That's right," Ezra lies, reaffirming to Popp that Ronan, not Kitta, reported the supposedly deceased Jameson Feiser's presence on Mars. If Popp knew his daughter was not only involved, but stowing away on Jaco Delores's ship, it would only distract him. Popp's still unaware of Kitta's life on Mars, and of Ronan's and her affinity for each other.

"But why would Feiser fake his death?" Ezra asks. "I thought he could do anything, how powerful he was back then — "

"How powerful he *is — now*," Popp emphasizes, "if he's alive like your boy says, he's still telling UF where to dig, and what to say. And why? Because he and Don disagreed about a lot, and Don had diplomatic power over him through UF. I can't believe I didn't see it before but FeiserCorp might have been in trouble when Don rolled back the Jupiter stuff. If he's presumed dead, then he has more time to work — time away from the press, diplomacy, etc."

"And what, this 'Mayor' is just him? I thought the Jovian Project already happened and boom, magnets everywhere."

"I'd believe it. The Mayor of Titan? I've already forgotten his name. He's hardly ever in the press. It could be a committee — FeiserCorp, or something. And Don halted the Jovian Project 'cause he wanted to expand colonization while Feiser wanted more magnets, even though there was already so much of it. When it came down to *why* Feiser thought we needed to expand Jovian mining, he simply didn't have a reason other than — well, profit. Old-world shit."

"So when UF lost my dad, they lost you and Lordes in the fallout, right? If Feiser wanted to ramp up mining between Saturn and Jupiter, then wouldn't that have slowed everything down?"

"Lordes was a privateer, and yes, the tethers were *it* until the magnet boom, but Don may have been naive in assuming FeiserCorp didn't have dirty tricks. FeiserCorp and UF had the first mining crews — the only ones at the time, and UF was definitely tapping Feiser to lead after they lost your dad. He died on their turf. Obviously not how they put it to me when they asked me to resign, but Orbital Security was easy to blame. *We should have seen the gas pocket*," Popp mocks, then realizes his coffee is cold. He notices Ezra has already taken a few steps to the machine and begun filling his own cup. "You're still light on your feet," Popp remarks. Ezra returns to the map with two cups. "You were a good teacher."

"You never took your combat training very far," Popp

conspires, sipping his new coffee. Ezra notices the topic of conversation wavering. "I felt obligated to continue my dad's work. I had more fun in the lab and in the dirt than I ever did in combat. The only real money in combat was in the competitions anyway."

"I'm the one who told you that, but you're remembering it wrong. There's a lot of money in public fighting, but it's certainly not the only way to make a good living. Saturn is a constant fight. Ask them," Popp says, indicating Linus Fogarty and Advik Anand entering the room. The two large men are barely distinguishable in size and stature, but while Linus is pale and red-headed, Advik is dark and swarthy. Both cultivate a very old-fashioned, high and tight swagger in a futile attempt to combat their age.

Ezra nods to greet the two men and continues to Popp, "You mean a fight for survival?" Ezra leans closer to confide, "Do you mean the mind?"

Popp scoffs, "In a way I do mean the mind. Eddy, I hear the Yellow Sector news talk about the end of our golden age and all that. I feel like you believe there was a golden age to begin with, and that worries me." Popp turns to his two soldiers who stand at ease, "Earth has experienced a golden age, sure. Mars too. But Linus has killed out here. Vik has killed out here." Popp nods to Linus and Advik, permitting them to sit. Ezra can't believe Popp's words. *Killed?* Popp continues, "Linus, how many have you killed?"

"G'morning, lads. And sir," Linus says in his thick Irish accent, firming his brow to address Popp, "forty, give or take. I'll say I stopped counting back then in '75." He forces a chuckle and has a scratchy high-pitched voice, apparent that he's versed in sarcasm, perhaps utilizing his sense of humor as a coping mechanism. The four get comfortable on waist-high stools surrounding the map. "Hasn't been a lot since then, but it felt like a lot then. Cannae remember exactly."

Nonchalant Linus Fogarty speaks of extinguishing human lives like Ezra speaks of seeds going into the dirt. Ezra remains speechless, quietly accepting, rather succumbing to these new truths while the combat-hardened fellows entertain Ezra's curiosity with their stories. It's far too late for Ezra to recalculate the risks of this mission, and he knows now he was far too ignorant to have considered the risks in the first place. Despite his embarrassment, he finds himself liberated and warm to the disregard of the risks to come.

"We're here to discuss Stinger, are we not?" Having spent little time talking, Advik refocuses the room with his rich and broad voice. "I know we've been delayed, but I need to know this team is legitimate."

"This is first-string, Vik. Our team is surely enough to accommodate your approval," Popp jests.

Advik glares at Popp with a joyous intellectual appetite. "How long has it been since you've led an away team?" Advik asks, aware from Popp's language that he would be leading the upcoming field operation on Titan. Popp sips his clinched coffee and attempts to squint away his brewing headache. "We're going back, Vik. I'm not going to miss out on that. And I'm sure you've heard about James Feiser by now."

"Sir, respectfully, Feiser's death always had rumors around it," Linus bashfully interjects, then begins working the map's interface. "So why are we going back now?"

"Because of me," Ezra says sternly. "'Stinger'?"

"Stinger is the code word I put in today's memo," Popp says, "and it's going to be the four of us, the Snare, and I'm using B-1."

"Bone Squad! Alright," Advik approves.

Linus navigates the map to display Saturn and Jupiter at their nearest in orbit. "This is important, lads. We're in the middle of a trade window between Titan and Jupiter. Now, it'd be unfortunate in normal times to be caught in a storm during a Trade Week, but it happens, right?" Linus asks rhetorically.

Popp responds, "We were just talking about Jupiter. Does missing one window hurt their trade so badly?"

"I think I'm with you Linus. If that window is expensive, then it would be a good reason to fake a storm — so we don't interrupt it," Ezra says.

"A storm is an easy thing for them to fake on Titan," Linus agrees, "and apparently those shipments are surging."

"More magnets?"

"I've heard of something more than magnets," Linus continues. "The Mayor of Titan is rumored to be playing with genetics, and something is giving Titan bigger trees, bigger food; apparently the livestock they have is — " Linus shudders. "Well, they're rumors anyway. It may have nothing to do with the shipment, and the storm could be completely real, but the rumors always start somewhere." Linus pauses to look at Popp, who is stoic.

The fear within Ezra now reaches deeper than he could have imagined, gripping him and pulling him further beneath the waves of truth and change; further from the bubble of privilege he so abruptly fled. The rumors Linus speaks of match Ezra's own experience with his plants, as well as a few of his suspicions, but never had he heard of genetic experiments on animals.

"A fake storm, yes," Advik grows impatient. "With no storm holding us back we need to debrief Stinger *now*."

Popp takes control of the map's interface and opens a topographical map of First City on Titan.

"When we land, the surface team has their orders, and they'll be ready to put on a show while Stinger goes underground," Popp says. "That's our quickest way to the Mayor." Popp opens a map of the tunnels beneath First City — more mines carved out by the Ancients and plenty more by humans in the last decade. Popp irons out the details of his plan, albeit shoddy due to potentially outdated information about Titan.

"And who's the snare?" Advik inquires.

"Well, since we're stopping at Ceres I thought I'd freelance it. It's Stella." The three of them look at one another in silence, all nod, and begin to depart from the table. Ezra doesn't bother to ask about Stella, figuring they'll meet shortly.

Ezra addresses Linus, "I believe there's truth to what you're saying. The rumors. I was sent a nutrient sample which did amazing things to a few plants in my lab, then the news broke that people had been dying. That's why we're here. Why I'm here."

"You know, when we first came out here, our enemies were so small," Linus says. "What we're facing now may be worse than anything Bryndon Pierce ever saw, but whenever something strange or terrible happened back then, Bryndon's greatest weapon was always the facts. You certainly sound like him, and I'll say, it makes me feel better about coming back out here."

Popp jumps from his seat at the map table at the sound of a soft alarm, and heads for the closest door. "We're entering Ceres' orbit. That means it's time to suit up. Full armor," He shouts from across the room. Ezra shouts back, "Full armor?"

"This is the Belt, Eddy. Gateway to the mess."

The *Comrade* rests in Ceres' orbit while Ezra, Popp, Linus and Advik glide in a small passenger ship toward the space station tethered to the dwarf planet. The traffic between Ceres Station and the surrounding asteroid belt is thick with carrier vessels hauling minerals. Ezra notices that none of these vessels have UF signage or indicators, but are of the same or similar design. A few have done little to hide that they were once UF ships, but now carry a different logo, reading, "TLC." He immediately checks his own clothing to make sure he's removed all of his official tags and emblems as a precaution.

Popp notices. "I would've said something if you had any UF logos on."

"I'm having trouble understanding where UF is. Are these stolen ships? And why are we passing the station?"

"The people we're meeting are on the surface. And I've heard UF never found their footing here, even though they've said that they're running the place. Probably a good thing not having UF around here, but we still gotta be careful," Popp says with the unshakable facade of confidence he musters so easily when there's potential danger.

Ezra continues to adjust emotionally, further stripping away his identity by first letting fear take reign in the absence of UF. Ezra's work was all he had left of Bryndon, and UF had taken that. He knows, however, how little his fear matters as innocent lives on Earth suffer.

The passenger ship nears the Ceres surface. The small structures dance and flow with the natural geography of the planet, looking natural and very well hidden. The ship lands in a discreet lot outside an abandoned UF docking station. There's clear evidence of violence at this shambled station. The four of them leave the ship slowly, fully armored with weapons not drawn, but close.

"Check this out," Popp says as he pulls a misshapen metal pebble from a small crater in a broken stone wall. "Bullets," he says, then lifts his magnet-pistol from his holster and sends a bullet of his own into the same wall. He analyzes the freshly-fired pebble and sighs, "Well, it's old, but it's the same stuff."

"Don't you use UF equipment?" Ezra asks, ever curious about whatever UF presence might exist on this dwarf planet.

"Yes," Popp boasts, "but that could mean anything. I'm not the only freelancer buying old UF equipment, though I'm really good at it." He pauses, "It could very well be stolen, too. Make sure you're all weapon-ready. Open-channel comms. The main road is up ahead."

The four trek a short way down a road between disheveled structures. During the day, the quiet gray and gloom of Ceres is somehow both comforting and ominous. The bullet-scarred walls are obvious to Popp. Ezra notices a scrawl on a nearby wall reading "Lordes." Advik also notices and addresses it to Popp. "The paint looks old," Advik says.

"This is where Patricia came after Andrew died," Popp responds.

As the structures they pass come to life, the people stroll about the main road in their magnetically-weighted boots, carrying out their daily routines. The nearby commuters and workers stop to stare at them while they march in their pale-red armor. Ezra becomes worried. The armor they're wearing is UF-issued, but the paint and extra details stripped that recognition even from Ezra until now, so it's not likely the reason they stare. Wherever Popp agreed to meet this "Stella," who Ezra is now aware works for Patricia Lordes, it's beginning to feel too far. They follow Popp to a mysterious hatch, low to the ground on the wall of a much larger building. Popp, seeming so far to know where he's going, opens the hatch door with haste, and is met with the short, firm barrel of a scatter-gun.

"Welcome," a spacesuit-filtered voice tings with a surly tone. "How can I help you today?"

"I'm here to see Patricia. I'm a client."

"She ain't here, so I guess you gotta go."

"Go where?" Popp asks with reflective gaiety. Ezra watches, wondering how such a ridiculous exchange between strangers could yield any progress. This stranger takes a second to look at the warriors, then at Ezra. "Try going East. Recreation."

Popp turns from the door, "She's at the East Building, move."

The stranger with the scatter gun keeps his airlock open and watches the Inquisition leaders walk away.

"We've already spent too much time here," Advik puts in.

"What schedule are you on? 'Titan knows,' remember? And this Delores joker is an entire day behind us."

The four hike and bounce along a road that grows cleaner, the onlookers peppered throughout meaning little to them at this point. One cheers, "Inquisition, ho!" on the open comms channel, and others follow with yelps and find whatever nearby objects they can to wave and make noise. Ezra knows immediately this is his son's work.

"It seems your boy is working hard," Popp says. Ezra can only hope Ronan is safe. The sun is out, but the sky is dark, and drones are scarce.

They enter the recreation building through an unguarded airlock. They walk the narrow hallway and pass the most ornamental militants the four have ever seen. Mostly females, and few others. The thin metal chains, carved gems and trinkets dance and sway across their chests in the light gravity. There are tags on the breasts of these soldiers reading "TLC." Some of these soldiers' ornaments look like bones of human fingers, further concerning Ezra. Popp, however, is entertained. "This is some retirement!" Popp removes his helmet and shouts down the hall into the next room.

They enter a tight lobby with few tables and many guards, and are greeted by a near-elderly, alluring woman; dark brown hair with bleached ends, and artificially tanned skin; doubtlessly Patricia Lordes.

Another woman, dark-skinned, intimidating and large in stature, inspects them. She wears a sleeveless shirt beneath her armored vest exposing her muscular, tattoo-painted arms. Her armor is dressed with trinkets as well as munitions, including grenades. Stella.

"Paulo Thiago Russo," Patricia says with a smooth and charming voice.

"Pat."

"So this is the son of Bryndon Pierce." Patricia's mannerisms toe the edge of insincerity as she welcomes Ezra, making for healthy sarcasm. She continues, "Sit down, boys. I know you're in a hurry. I've been watching you dear, sweet heroes on the *Comrade* and the young Delores boy's ship when I can. You intend to take on UF, Ezra? After everything the great Bryndon has done for them?"

Ezra grows nervous. Popp still doesn't know Kitta is on Delores's ship. Luckily, Popp isn't paying close enough attention, and appears to be looking Patricia up and down as if he's been reunited with an old flame. Ezra chimes in quickly to keep the conversation moving. "It's not the same UF."

Patricia's mouth kinks with intrigue. "That's what I was hoping you'd say."

"Jameson Feiser is still alive," Popp groans as he snatches a small pouch of drinking water from the table and sucks on it.

"Oh yes, I'm aware," Patricia says. "He came here with UF and his FeiserCorp cronies to build an outpost. UF's second attempt, but it was the first time he dared show his face here. He was already pronounced dead, but he made himself known to me. I guess he figured I liked him. My girls and I let him know — the hard way — he wouldn't be getting anywhere near me or the people here. He killed your father, Ezra."

Ezra is taken back by her succinct sincerity. "So I've heard," he says.

"Stella here is too young to remember Bryndon or the migration. She fought UF when they came here, and we won, but at a cost."

Stella holds a closed fist against her chest and hangs her head. The militants bordering the room follow her gesture in solidarity for their fallen.

"The people outside were cheering for us," Linus adds after a brief pause in the conversation.

"I believe it. They've been watching you too. And you'd like Stella to join you in your little Inquisition, yes?" Patricia says backhandedly. "You know she's my absolute best."

Stella smirks.

"We have many great warriors here," Stella says in a deep voice. Her golden-bleached dreadlocks are tied behind her head, and her dark brown skin is very new. She's very large and very beautiful, lacking scars or any other evidence of personal battle damage. "All thanks to you," she concludes, fondly looking at Patricia. The four men of the Inquisition look at Patricia curiously, so she indulges them.

"My dear Andrew died not long after Bryndon, and I came straight here because UF had mostly abandoned it for Jupiter. It was ripe for the taking, and the people here welcomed The Lordes Company with open arms. I don't think UF knew how many people they hurt by leaving them here; how many people starved, and even killed themselves to escape their pain; UF certainly knows now."

"And you kept his name, huh?" Popp asks.

"His name is still synonymous with money — power. Our tethers beyond the Belt may be a much slower form of travel than the precious Jollitium magnets, but they're still very useful to us. Changing the name of The Lordes Company would only cost money better spent on the people here."

Ezra can't help his confusion, knowing UF controls most of the trade and agriculture within Sol, but he likes how Patricia sounds — empathetic. Patricia notices the perturbed look on his face. "I'm wondering," Patricia says to Ezra, "what do you plan to do on Titan?"

"Take UF back from whoever or *whatever* corrupted it."

"Sounds vague," Patricia scoffs. "That's a big job. I would argue that UF is unsalvageable and it's better off burning."

"I'm not ruling that out."

Patricia pauses and studies Ezra with a Mona Lisa smile. "Well, consider Ceres and TLC friendly, and safe harbor if things go south. Take Stella with you, and if you can take down UF, then consider the price paid."

"What do you know about the genetic experiments on Titan?" Ezra asks, gripping the attention of the Inquisition as well as Patricia's nearby militants.

"They've been growing bigger food for over a decade, bigger livestock. We've hijacked and plundered many of their vessels traveling downstar from Titan. A few ships have had both amazing and scary things in tow, including the genetically-altered produce, fish, but also Jollitium. We have enough Jollitium now to catch almost every ship that comes by, but they've slowed their traffic when we align with Mars. FeiserCorp owns the rights to whatever method they're using for these genetic manipulations, and they're not sharing. They're trying to enhance anything they can — including people."

"They're experimenting on people?"

"Without a doubt. When UF came back here, we were prepared, and had good numbers, but they sent a monster to our surface..." she pauses. "They sent a soldier twice Stella's size, but it was... imperfect."

"What do you mean?"

Patricia benumbs. She shudders. After a heavy sigh, she clenches her fist repeatedly. "It was very tough, but it was disorganized — stupid. It took nearly forty of my soldiers before it fell. It was human. At least it used to be. This was ten years ago. They haven't been back, but when they do come back, we'll be full-tilt." Her mood and that of her warriors has entirely darkened remembering the terror of UF's mutant beast.

"Do you know what they're using to do this? What is so important to them that they can ignore the death toll on Earth?"

"I'm no scientist, Ezra, and I'm sure we on Ceres had only a glimpse of their — potential," Patricia quivers. "I never heard of a death toll on Earth."

"People are starving in the Green Sectors. It's all I'd heard about in the media before coming here."

"And if James is still alive, then it's still *his* media, yes?" Patricia asks expectantly, but continues before Ezra or anyone has a chance to answer. "Well, I can tell you, if you had waited any longer to do this, I wouldn't be helping you at all."

Popp looks to Linus and Advik and nods, "Get the ship ready," he says, then addresses Patricia, "Your operation here is very impressive, Pat."

"As is yours, Paul. I'd say we didn't stray too far from one another in our response to UF's shit-show in '75," Patricia says as she looks at Popp with seductive eyes.

"Well, it sounds like I've had it easy compared to you. When this is all over, I — "

"You'll be returning my Stella to me, that's what you'll be doing, *when this is all over,*" Patricia mocks, chuckling. "You're so confident. So young at heart."

Ezra interjects, "Pardon me, Patricia, but you haven't heard of the death toll on Earth?"

"We only get Green Sector media out here, and we have heard about the usual shortages, but nothing about death. And you said the deaths were in the Green Sectors. Sketchy."

Ezra doesn't respond, only ponders.

Feiser's Media.

"I'm not the only young heart between us, Pat. I know you're out there robbing UF trade carriers. You're the *Pirate Queen of Ceres,* and I trust you'll have something for any UF forces that may follow us upstar?"

"Nothing gets past the Belt without me knowing it. I can at least send word to your Inquisition if I can't stop them. Just bring Stella back to me, Paul. I've enjoyed seeing you, much more than I expected. The broadcasts haven't done your good looks any justice." Patricia winks at Popp and dismisses them.

The *Comrade* doesn't stay in Ceres' orbit long after they board with Stella. The Inquisition's time ahead of Jaco Delores cannot be abused.

SIX

Two Lifeforms

H IS name is Providence, and thanks for asking, but of all the heads that could have been damaged, that's an important one," Jaco Delores says as he sits on the bridge of his carrier with Kitta, who sits opposite the table, her hands tied together in her lap. She's been in holding for several days since the incident with Delores's Employee. One other young man with short, rusty hair and glasses sits next to Delores, and appears to be his assistant. With Delores also stand two gigantic soldiers, nearly three meters tall, fully suited for space in what must be specially-tailored suits for their size. Though they look identical, one of these giants is a robot. The subtleties in its movements make that much apparent to Kitta. It's not often androids are hidden by wearing human clothing, or used as personal security. Androids come in many different shapes and sizes, and the humanoid isn't typically used for fighting or protection, so why bother? Kitta wonders, attempting to dissect Delores's character.

Delores continues, his voice far from threatening, "So I do appreciate you bringing him in. He wouldn't have survived. And we were standing around the surveillance screen like idiots, freaking out when we saw the blood." He chuckles as he talks, nudging his brooding friend and taking his Employee's injury lightly while making it known to Kitta he's been watching her. "I must say, I'm very impressed by your man on Mars. He hacked into a number of my surveillance drones for your broadcast, and greatly limited my reach within my own ship. So you've sent all my data to him...what next?"

"I just needed a ride to Titan. Personally, I don't care about your data."

Delores scoffs. "Well, I would've thought you knew what I was doing — who I'm meeting. You sent my data to his son."

Jaco Delores is near Kitta's age, and a celebrity in the scientific field. He specializes in cybernetics, yet isn't equipped with any, which very well could be to preserve his clean-cut style. His dirty blond pompadour splashes from the top of his head, and a few hairs hang just above his strong brow, and his pale blue eyes rest cozily within his elegant complexion.

"Meeting him?" Kitta asks.

"I spoke to Doctor Ezra Pierce the day of his launch. I was in Arcadia, but I was at that meeting. He didn't tell you?"

"We spoke once, and you didn't come up," Kitta says, remembering Ezra scoffing when he heard Delores's carrier name. "Where are we?"

"Administrative quarters. Pretty nice, huh?"

Kitta scoffs at his arrogance. "So you're going there to help him," she says, "with all these Employees, all these Contractors? The weapons?"

"It's a lot, right? But it pales in comparison to what your Doctor Pierce enlisted. He hasn't told you much — has he told you whose ship he's on?"

By his question alone, Kitta deduces the answer. Her father's ship, the *Comrade*, was hired by Ezra to stage the coup on Titan. She remembers in her adolescence her father's prioritization of his working collection over raising her. She knows it's pointless to attempt understanding Ezra's reasoning behind omitting that information, for she realizes she would have traveled to Saturn anyway by Melena Horn's direction.

"It doesn't matter," she says. "Melena Horn sent me."

"Well, you have my condolences," Delores's voice becomes rigid. "Ambassador Horn was found dead on Mars the day before our launch. She died peacefully."

Kitta suddenly realizes she's heard this man's voice before.

"You know what this could mean, Dr. Feiser. Have we any reason to interrupt Ambassador Horn here?"

"I was there, in the council chamber. So were you," Kitta jabs, but only in defense of her own tears. She refuses to show weakness in front of Delores, who falls silent, momentarily. His assistant violently spins his head to look at him with surprise, awaiting his reaction. His assistant is a small, frail-looking man with short red hair and thick-framed glasses.

"So you have her data too, then. Her Jym?" Delores assumes.

"The data was corrupted. All I know is what she told us, and I've listened to some of her old audio logs. The new mineral from Titan keeping her alive… she had some sort of device for inhaling it."

"Ha! So you really don't know much at all." Delores laughs, then continues, "Ezra Pierce doesn't even know the real reason he's going to Titan. He's impulsive, and dangerous. I'd say he's in over his head if I wasn't afraid of his firepower, and your father's finger on the trigger."

Kitta looks around the room and notices there are no cameras, no drones. She worries for Ronan, but also wishes this conversation with Delores could be recorded. She then realizes she *can* record it, using her Jym, which was not confiscated. Unbeknownst to Delores, she opens her Commands Tool and begins recording their conversation.

Delores continues, "Pierce heard of the death toll on Earth and did what we assumed was impossible — he acted — and in a big way. Your father has quite a collection of soldiers and armaments, too. Very unexpected. I'll admit, UF has let a lot of simple things slip lately, but I can assure you I'm not going to Titan to fight. I was already going for business. I got lucky with the timing, to be honest."

"You keep saying 'we,' and I'm guessing you're referring to Jameson Feiser? Is he on this ship with you, with his Feiser-Corp goons?"

"FeiserCorp is here, yes," Delores detests, "those old bags — but Doctor Feiser is already on Titan."

"How? That doesn't make sense."

"It makes perfect sense when you take the Quantum."

"What are you talking about?"

He chuckles, "It's an instant transmission — relatively new technology. You enter a suspended space called the Quantum — so fast that time outside the vessel stops, until the engine is fired again from the suspended space, at which point you appear at the set coordinates."

"But how?"

"The same mineral which kept Ambassador Horn alive,

and the same mineral which increases organic growth and metabolism…Miss Russo, it is the same Jollitium which has powered our ships and their artificial gravity, our cars, and tools, weapons… for the past twenty-something years. We're simply finding new ways to refine and apply it organically."

"The magnets? From Jupiter?"

"Precisely. I plan to create a vaccine, so humans can live longer, eat less."

"Because the Green Sectors are starving? Aren't you a little behind?"

"I would be, if the death toll were real."

"The death toll is fake?"

"Well, people in the Green Sectors die all the time since the Jollitium came to Earth, but yes, the numbers are fluffed and there is no *real* food crisis. Yet. It was Doctor Feiser's idea to fake a death toll to get money from Yellow Sector investors, who had a vague idea of the potential of what we were doing out there. I'll say, I know for a fact it would all help to prevent any future crises, but it's strictly been *Yellow Sector* media. The Red, Blue and Green sectors probably hadn't heard about a death toll until your man, Ronan, started broadcasting it."

Kitta can hardly believe what she's hearing. She ponders the potential futility of her entire journey. Sato's arrest and Ronan's subversion from UF have put them in grave danger. However late it may be, she cannot allow her own reasons for being here to waver, for Melena's memory, and for the simple truth of this refined Jollitium and its purpose.

Suddenly she vomits on the floor next to her. So much for not showing weakness. Her skin crawls feverishly. Small maintenance robots scurry from the corners of the room and quickly clean up the mess.

"Are you sick?" Delores asks as he reaches into his pocket and finds a pair of eyeglasses, presumably used as a visor to substitute for cybernetics.

As Jaco Delores analyzes Kitta, the assistant chimes in. "Two lifeforms. You're pregnant," the assistant says, equipped with cybernetics himself.

Delores calls for a security escort. "We need to get you nourishment. We can accommodate."

"Thank you, Jack."

Kitta reels from the news. She's been on Delores's ship for nearly a month, but has been so preoccupied that she didn't realize she was late to bleed. Now Ronan's and her child grows inside her. The timing couldn't be more inconvenient, but Kitta is happy. Finally, they have their child.

"Well, this just means I have two stowaways to feed, so don't thank me," Jaco Delores says.

Delores orders the security escort to take Kitta to a holding area, which is more of a lounge — one designed to support and comfort those recovering from injuries and illnesses and, though not common, undergoing pregnancies.

A gilded cage for the pregnant stowaway.

Delores and his assistant follow them to the holding area, and Delores waits until Kitta sits to say, "You should consider working for me. I see your administrative colors, and I know you worked directly with Melena Horn on Mars. What we plan to accomplish on Titan would require your intellect and savvy, especially since you've incapacitated Providence. Lucky coincidence for you, having similar transcripts. Think about it," he says before shutting the door, leaving her alone and under surveillance. The human guard remains, and the robot leaves with Jaco Delores.

Delores climbs through the adjacent hall followed by his assistant, Spencer Gant.

"Spencer — "

"Yes?"

"Do you think I said too much?"

"Hard to say," Spencer ponders. "Kitta Russo is very beautiful, and I believe it may have fueled your confidence, rather your trust, in her. But you're the most careful person I know. I trust you not to let her facade distract you."

"You think she's beautiful? Not sure if I agree, but either way, she has potential, given she agrees to join us. I think she will."

"I would have left Doctor Feiser and the Quantum out of it. But that's only hindsight. The girl just learned she's with child."

"You don't think she already knew?" Delores asks.

"Maybe she didn't, but she knew about Ambassador Horn. She said she was *there*."

"Yes! I loved that. We didn't scour the room. Idiots."

"Not the sort of thing that normally gets past you, me, or Doctor Feiser. If not for this little hiccup I would say Ezra Pierce has lit a fire beneath us," Spencer applies his wisdom, which Delores values greatly.

"I would argue Doctor Feiser had no need to exaggerate the deaths on Earth. I would have done things much differently."

"It *is* a mess," Spencer concurs, "but this was Feiser's

operation, from the beginning. All we can do is adapt and hold true to our vision. *Your* vision."

They move through the empty corridors of the ship with their robotic guard. They enter the Lab and Observatory; a large wing of the ship with a crowded and busy lower level of employees wearing hazmat suits, and isolated human subjects in thick, plexiglass chambers. Some of these subjects are exercising, some of them are resting. All are larger than normal size, being examined for their physical and psychological conditions. Delores and Spencer stroll along the bridge above as their guard follows.

"I'm getting tired of it, Spence. I really am. I don't want to half-ass these experiments any longer. Feiser asked for cybernetics and I went above and beyond for their little admin shortcuts, as redundant and petty as they are. He asked me to use his Jollitium to create his abominable soldiers, but I can do so much more, if only I were given more — allowed to *see* more."

Some of the subjects below are engaged in combat training. The three-meter warriors are exhibiting unparalleled strength and fortitude. Military issue blades are thrusted at normal human strength only to find themselves mere centimeters into the muscle bound flesh. The humanoid training robots engaging these warriors are being violently dismantled. The scale of destruction which these altered humans are capable of is made possible by hormone treatments, protein manipulation, and minute doses concocted of the refined Jollitium induced via radiation treatment. The results are not perfect. Sometimes while sitting still, other times while in combat scenarios, these behemoths — though genetically engineered — can rapidly develop formidable brain tumors, giving these newly mutated beings a brief shelf life.

"I wish Feiser could be here, now," Delores says, shuddering. "Not because I *like* the guy, but because these serums are so far from complete, and I know he has no idea what he's doing. That much was obvious when he hired me to create these monsters. He took one to Ceres only to lose it."

"That wasn't your fault."

"But I read the reports," Delores retorts, "and that *thing* wasn't even cleared for space travel! He was desperate — in over his head."

"I agree," Spencer says.

"Now I'm no fool, and I realize how expensive it can be. But if UF and world governments would incentivize it, and give it back to the people, then we have greater volume. The vaccine has been done, you know this. I just need more material at my disposal. All that the politicians needed when Feiser brought them Jollitium-powered vehicles and weapons was to know where to sign. Animals."

"Hold on," Spencer says, stopping in his tracks. "Feiser sent a decrypted message. He's on Jupiter, not Titan."

"What? Why?"

"He hasn't said, but he's assured he'll be on Titan in time for the Inquisition's arrival. He intends to appeal to Ezra Pierce. A parlay, if you will."

"That means there's a Quantum Elevator in the Jovian System."

"That would make sense. It's Feiser's tech." After a pause, Spencer asks, "Was Miss Russo correct? Are you behind?"

"What kind of question is that?"

"Psychological. Do *you* feel you're behind?"

"Yes, Spencer. I do, and I'm tired of it. Kitta will come around. You watch."

"And if she doesn't?"

"Then we kill her, simple as that."

Kitta sits sobbing in the recovery lounge. Reeling from the multitude of new information, all she can think of is how she wants to hear Ronan's voice, and tell him that they've overcome the odds and produced a child. She can only hope that Delores's ship's data provided him some helpful information. She reaches the refrigerator and grabs some packaged vegetables and calcium pills.

A door opens on the other side of the room while she eats, and the journalist Sam Levin enters hastily, flying to the sink. Sam sweats and heaves over the running water.

"Are you okay?" Kitta asks.

"I was touring the garden, ate something bad," Sam groans. Kitta finds two bags of drinking water and hands one to Sam.

"Drink."

"Thanks."

They sip for a moment before Sam looks at Kitta and recognizes her immediately, also noticing her tied hands. "You got caught," Sam says with a smile.

"I did. Somebody got hurt because of me, so I took them to medical."

"That's sweet, I guess. So who are you?"

"My name is Kitta. I'm — "

"Oh my. I've heard of you," Sam interrupts, gently balking,

"I get limited news feed up here so I haven't been watching the broadcast, but it's you. Do you have any idea how many people have been watching your broadcast? I can't believe this is the ship!"

"My partner on Mars is broadcasting. My mission was to send him the ship's data and find out why they're going to Titan. Doctor Ezra Pierce is his father. We saw his launch on the news and decided to help him."

"I wish I could hack drones like that, so useful. And now what? Why are you here instead of a holding cell? You don't look sick."

"I'm pregnant. Jack and his assistant told me after scanning me."

"His assistant is Spencer. He's alright. But that's something! I'd say congratulations, but how do you feel about it?"

"Ronan and I have been trying to have a baby for years. I know it's a miracle, so I'm happy, but the timing isn't so good."

"How long has it been? If you really think it's dangerous for the baby then you can suspend it. The medical tech on this ship is amazing."

"Three weeks? Hard to say. *Suspend it?*"

"That should be long enough. And suspend like in a tube. It'll grow normally, just outside of you. It's a seamless surgery. Not a scratch. Ectogenesis is actually part of my research assignment here."

"Of course. My mother did that with me. I never met her, though."

"Was she a politician or something? It's expensive — must've been even worse back then."

"I don't know. My father raised me, if you want to call it that. He wouldn't talk about my mom. I just found out Ezra Pierce hired my father's armada for his Inquisition too. It's a lot."

"So you were talking to Jack. What else did he tell you? Anything about his objective on Titan? I know it's not part of my assignment but I'm naturally curious."

"If you help me out of here, I'll tell you everything."

"Deal. Do you want to suspend the baby?"

"I think I do," Kitta says, "but I don't want to just leave it in some lab."

"I know a doctor here who will help you out, and look after it. We've actually spoken about you already. She'll be happy to. I'll distract the guard here, and meet you at Medical. It's just around the other corner where I came from."

Sam leaves the room and begins talking to the guard outside the lounge. The guard watches a video on Sam's tablet as Kitta slips behind them and away. When Kitta arrives at the medical station she is greeted by a sleeping receptionist. Sam shows up only seconds behind her.

"Go left, there's an open room here," Sam whispers. "I don't know where my friend is, but I sent her a message."

They enter an empty laboratory with curtains and operating tables. Several embryonic suspension chambers are mounted against the far wall, and some of them are already occupied by fetuses. One of the embryos is labeled "Delores." Kitta begins to have second thoughts when a doctor enters the laboratory.

"Di!" Sam greets the doctor with a hug. "Kitta, this is Doctor Diana Archer, whom I told you about."

"I got your message, Sam," Diana says, then looks at Kitta, "Your name is Kitta?"

"Yes," Kitta says nervously.

"Russo," Sam says excitedly.

"You weren't kidding, Sam. I suppose my questions can wait. Right now we need a baby suspended, yes?"

Sam interjects, "Yes, and thank you, Di. Kitta has information she can share with us about Jack."

Kitta is led to an operating table and given painkillers. Diana gives Kitta the necessary physical examination and deems the extraction feasible, though the child is still very small after barely one month. A large machine hovers over her, and she feels the painkillers kicking in almost instantly. She breaks the silence while the machine begins operating.

"My partner, Ronan Pierce, found out about his dad's Inquisition. That day, I spoke with Melena Horn, and she told us to help him. There's a new mineral coming from Titan. It's dangerous. Jack said that it's just a refined version of the Jollitium magnets, and they're using it in genetic alterations on food, humans too. He wants to use it to make a vaccine for everyone. He says it can extend life, metabolism, people can eat less," Kitta begins to grow loopy, and the operation is finished before she knows it. She begins to slur her words.

Diana says to her, "You're doing great, hon. Just rest here. I'll make sure your baby gets everything he needs."

A boy.

SEVEN

Jollity

An Open Letter by Jameson Feiser

TO my species — *I write this with disciplinary intent. Much has gone unexplained in the latest generation of the United Frontier, and I hope to give credit where credit is due. Many have asked personal questions of me, many which I have declined due to their trivial nature. Whether my beliefs be theistic or cynical, conservative or progressive — no such sense would, or could guide my decisions as the United Frontier's President and Ambassador of Sol. My only counselor has been my own experience, and that of those before me. What I'm writing is not intended for those who know me now, or knew me in the beginning. It is not intended for those who ask questions of my children. It is for after I am gone. It is not an escape, but my right of passage to the next life. What I write is not what I would consider an answer, nor an apology, but admonition.*

The Jovian System was my home for many years, beginning at birth from a United Frontier embryonic chamber on Io. In my adolescence I counted my days by the great blue clock — our dear Earth. I could hardly imagine its intimate beauty at the time. I would see it only in pictures, and by the romantic pale-blue dot in the night sky. I was taught social skills by one human birther, while he was still alive. Gordon was a simple and old man. He was my first and only teacher before he died on Io and his task was continued by the contrived UF education programs. Negativity was discouraged, but the United Frontier's definition of positivity was simple — subservience. I was taught never to complain, never to idolize, never to assume that I was any more than a cog in the great machine. The only other humans I saw growing up were simulations. I truly had nobody else. As real as the holograms and AI seemed in the beginning, they weren't perfect, and would commit their suspicious repetitions, reminding me constantly that I was alone. Emotion was not a foreign concept, but certainly taboo. The pale blue light in the night sky would remain a gorgeous mystery, while Jupiter and its children were certain and handsome even before I knew that my future lay within.

My repertoire with the United Frontier was enough to secure my election, but my upbringing in the Jovian System is what brought me to where I am today; where I intend to remain until my death. The enlightenment of a primitive race and its inevitable transformation was my destiny. I feel the most thorough method of understanding the unanswered lies within the history of the United Frontier and my own predecessors.

When we broke ground on Titan in the '70s, the United Frontier had a great many things planned — to further commercialize minerals, and establish a human colony using tethers that orbit Saturn and Jupiter. Harlan's Tether on Mars made our conquest possible. It was the beginning of a great colonization of the planets beyond the Asteroid Belt. The robotic workers and AI ahead of us paved the way. Frankly, I was tired, hearing of Ceres and that it would be the farthest humans could live from Sol. How wrong they were.

I begin with Harlan Cain, the ignorant architect of our conquest. I was a child during his tenure, and as frivolous and inspiring as his vision was at the time, it is pure nostalgia now. I was told my entire life would take place in the Jovian System, and my only purpose was to serve; tend to the machines that would usher in a new era for my species. The machines were my only family on Io. Harlan Cain had a deluded vision of expansion, with an underlying hope, rather a goal, of being discovered by a more intelligent life. The ancient beings who visited Sol, many eons ago, were thought to be near. Harlan Cain was convinced he had sparked the fire that would signal their return. He believed they were watching, waiting for humans to achieve a form of galactic merit. In my education I witnessed the scale at which the Ancients operated and knew Harlan Cain was insane. The Ancients never showed. Harlan Cain committed suicide in a state of severe dementia, which the United Frontier held as classified information.

After Harlan Cain came Bryndon Pierce, the unadulterated. Bryndon Pierce's vision was purely conservative, and put the people first. He inherited the title, and hardly utilized it. He thought himself above no one. It was because of him I was brought to Ceres from the Jovian System and my purpose was redefined. We were the same age. We became friends. The colony on Mars was nearing tragedy when his agricultural initiative saved tens of thousands of lives at the cost of delaying upstar expansion. His election came easily. By Bryndon's inauguration, the United Frontier had thriving colonies on Luna, Mars, and Ceres. As transparent as he seemed, it became clear to me in our adventures that he wanted glory, and nothing else. The people's love for him was unmatched, and he basked in that power. Said power took him, myself and a great many others to the first colonization of the Saturnian System.

My beloved Jovian System had been abandoned, but only for a short time. With the power I had attained in the United Frontier's administrative division came the monetary resources to return home. I had hidden something there. It beckoned.

The Lordes Company was the perfect asset. They sought glory as Bryndon did, but only through their investment in the United Frontier's expansion — in me. I promised them a sound investment, and they did not disappoint, nor did I. The magnets on Io, my magnets, would prove to be humanity's next chapter. The key to our expansion beyond our solar system. It was the Lordes Company's tethers — one orbiting Saturn and one linking Io to Jupiter's rocky mantle — that made it all possible. However, their tethers and Andrew himself were short-lived beyond the Belt. They shared in the initial profits of our precious Jollitium magnets, but what happened on Titan in the '70s ruined The Lordes Company.

Bryndon Pierce was elected Ambassador of Sol, and immediately relinquished the title and named himself the Ambassador of Titan alone. His idea of presiding over Sol was one of shared powers, and decisions to be made by council between the Ambassadors of Mars, Titan, Ceres, and Earth. He had become somewhat of a conqueror; at least that is how some of our low-tier Administrators and Privateer Contractors on Titan referred to him. To be frank, it frightened me.

When we arrived on Titan, Jollitium was still my secret. The Lordes Company was oblivious. The iron and sulfide chemicals harvested from Io were more than enough for them at the time. I made sure of it. Meanwhile, the unnamed Jollitium lay in wait, stockpiled by the automated machines on Io. Bryndon Pierce succeeded in his mission to populate Titan, though he died tragically before he could see it to fruition. The Lordes Company, among others, was held accountable for the incompetent safety measures, and they were relieved of their involvement. It was then I decided to unveil my discovery.

Then came Melena Horn. It was not long after the Jollitium was incentivized for propulsion and space travel that we found what it did to the human body. Ambassador Melena Horn became the Drunken Queen, treating Jollitium like a drug. It wasn't long after the positive lab tests on human subjects that she began ingesting it. The refined Jollitium enhanced metabolism, and it could be manipulated to feel euphoric. Living upstar for so long extended life in token, but Melena Horn longed for more. Though she was undeniably adored by the public, it didn't go unnoticed by UF officials that her short but prosperous term as UF President and Titan's Ambassador was on the back of Bryndon Pierce's accomplishments. She had a love affair with a Security Contractor which rendered a child, and she abandoned it. Her new coping mechanism within the refined Jollitium proved effective. Any long-term effects of ingesting the Jollitium wouldn't be known until she was relieved and sent to Mars, by my direction. Though I didn't have high hopes at first, my election to the United Frontier Presidency proved effortless. She remained Ambassador of Mars, nothing more, nothing less. Her dependency on Jollitium allowed us to discover another important property, perhaps the most important.

The magnetic attribute of the unrefined mineral grew stronger, heavier as it moved downstar. It allowed us more variety in our experiments, and more funding. This heaven-sent magnetic superconductor was a doorway into a greater future for humankind. The name "Jollitium" came shortly after this particular discovery. The name was in front of me the entire time. "Jupiter — The Bringer of Jollity." A perfect name, for a perfect element, after a perfect song.

"What are you reading?" Sato Song asks as he jogs the circumference of Arcadia's hidden Quantum Laboratory. He's moved the excess chairs and tables to clear a path, and his fingertips brush the red rock walls. Though he's lost much weight and is now mostly blind, he has regained his energy by shoveling protein bars and other supplements from the laboratory's vending machine. Ronan Pierce sits at a terminal skimming through any relevant data he can find on UF's classified servers, including Jameson Feiser's available data, though much of it appears to be localized to servers on Io and Titan, thus are inaccessible.

Ronan's been taking painkillers to suppress the agony of his damaged cybernetics. "I'm reading about Jameson Feiser. He wrote an open letter explaining, well — his mentality, and his plans on Titan. His history on Io, where the Jollitium comes from. Looks like there's another Quantum Elevator there, too." Ronan explains to Sato that these elevators are large enough to store crates of Jollitium and instantly transport them to Titan, Mars and Earth.

"So what's our plan now? We use this machine to get to Kitta and your dad? There's an elevator on Titan, right?" Sato stops at the vending machine and dispenses a pouch of drinking water.

"There are elevators on Titan. I just don't think Titan is our smartest move right now. UF is on high alert."

"You're probably right. So where do we go?"

"Well, I've programmed a failsafe in Delores's AI and Robotics, disabling them from harming anything organic. So if Delores decides to attack, he won't have any drones to help him. It's a good start, but I can't see exactly what weapons Titan has. Even with the new access levels, Titan is still blocked. So is Io."

"That's rough. I would say let's go to Titan and see what we can find there, but my eyes — I really can't see much anything."

"Do you still have your Wyg?"

"Yeah, why?"

"The hardware should be able to handle the Augmented Reality tools. I tried to download the software, but my Wyg only gave me the Commands tool. If it can handle just one of the two, then there's a visual assistant for blindness and deteriorating vision in the AR tools. I'd say it's worth a shot."

Sato hands Ronan his Wyg. Ronan uploads a tailored version of the administrative Jym software to it, which solely includes the Augmented Reality tools, hoping the program won't suffer the same fate that rendered it useless to Ronan, though it could very well be due to his damaged cybernetics. He turns his head once again to empty the pooling blood from his ear, but it drains more slowly after having time to coagulate. He urgently needs medical attention, but the cost would be to turn himself in. Helping Kitta is more important right now.

"It's odd, but I think I can make this work," Sato says after inserting his updated Wyg and activating the Augmented Reality tool. His central vision has become a dark pit bordered by a colorful, blurred periphery, but the Wyg's interface is visible to him, and the visual assistant tool cleanly and accurately outlines the corners and edges of the room he's in with glowing bluish-gray lines, and labels the doorways with directory signs. The chairs, tables and other smaller objects in the room are visible, but more obscure and difficult to make out. It's an odd visual, but an improvement nonetheless.

"Are you able to see this stuff too?"

"My earpiece was damaged," Ronan says. "My tools are limited to Commands, which I'm still not sure the hardware can handle properly, but I was able to knock the big guy out." Ronan says, referring to the now dead Behemoth in the nearby holding cell.

"Well, I feel like we've been here a little too long. Next shift should be starting soon, and I can definitely smell him now," Sato jests.

Ronan smirks, still amazed by Sato's formidable sense of humor. "I think this elevator is our best shot right now," Ronan says. "We need to go where we're harder to find, and where Titan's data is more accessible. Io covers both of those."

"I've never been past the Belt. The people there won't expect us, and probably won't be happy to see us. Should we take weapons?"

"Yes," Ronan hops to the lab's small arms station. A shoebox-sized wall apparatus contains one pistol and one multitool, equipped with a laser-cutter, which is a perfectly viable weapon at short range.

"Can you see me?" Ronan says as he holds the multitool at his side and takes a keen stance in front of Sato.

"You have an orange outline, a hazy filling, and I can even see your vitals." Sato says with enthusiasm. "This is actually pretty amazing."

"That blows my mind. I'm glad you're feeling better. I can't express how sorry I am for all of this."

"We don't have to talk about that. We're just getting started here. Jupiter, then?"

"Yeah, and the sooner the better." Ronan programs the buzzing Quantum Elevator to transport them to Io. The user warnings tell only of risks involving organics, and to spend no more than seven days in Quantum suspension due to mental health-related side effects including mania and addiction. Ronan looks inside the elevator's large departure chamber and notices an area containing empty shipping crates, divided from a small laboratory and recreational area. The individuals who travel using this machine are given access to data, the opportunity to exercise, and time remains still outside the chamber until they enter the landing code, and arrive instantly. The resistance machines used for exercise within the chamber imply that there is no artificial gravity while in transit.

"Okay, so no holding hands, got it," Sato says playfully after he and Ronan read the warnings. "So when they say time is frozen, will we age inside of the chamber?"

"Hard to say. I imagine so, but we can't be in there too long. The directions say to fire a switch, and not to be in there for more than a week."

"Okay, so we'll have time to prepare, right? Should we bring anything else? What's in this room that can help?" Sato asks.

The empty crates in the elevator chamber vary in size. Some of them are small enough to be carried by hand. Ronan paces through the Quantum Laboratory followed by Sato who holds one of the smaller crates, and they begin filling it with protein bars, calcium pills, carb and sugar snacks, and water pouches from the vendor. They round the room again with a second crate and load it with two mobile computer tablets, the magnet pistol, the multi-tool, and two extra UF Employee jumpsuits that are similar, but more generic than the career-designated jumpsuits they wear now. Ronan goes into the holding cell to check the body of the dead Behemoth, and removes the FeiserCorp tag from the breast of his jumpsuit. Ronan then closes the holding cell door to contain the corpse.

The first step in preparing the Quantum Elevator is sanitizing the air in the room. The fans and chemicals blast throughout the laboratory, removing any toxins, including the wicked scent of the rotting Behemoth. The next step is load preparation, which includes securing themselves.

"Can we trigger this thing from the inside?"

"No, but there is a countdown that I can set however I want," Ronan says. "One minute should be enough."

"Do we know who will be on Io? Are the shifts the same?"

"I would imagine so, but I can't even get a basic camera feed right now. What I'm hoping is that FeiserCorp is simply busy, and their Quantum Lab is just as empty as it is here. We're going in *blind*."

"That's not funny," Sato retorts, making fun of Ronan's choice of words. Sato's sense of humor is still well intact.

Ronan begins the countdown. Sato secures himself to one of the mounted seats within the chamber. Ronan uses his extra time to scan the room once more for anything useful. He reflects, realizing this may be the last time he sees this place, and the last time he leaves Arcadia. If he makes it to Titan, and Kitta succeeds in helping Ronan's father undo UF's corruption beyond the belt, then what will happen to her? It won't be long before it's discovered that she's Melena Horn's daughter; and not only that, but also that she was trained for governance by Melena Horn herself. She would be tapped to lead. She would deserve the chance.

Ten seconds remain as Ronan closes the door and fastens himself to the mounted seat next to Sato in the recreation chamber. The lights flicker once as the countdown ends, and Ronan feels nothing — no shaking, rumbling, or any characteristics of a typical launch sequence. The room simply becomes quiet, and the gravity vanishes.

A timer begins on the wall clock of the recreation chamber. Sato and Ronan unfasten themselves from their seats.

"Was that it?" Sato says, noticing the timer on the wall.

"I think so." Ronan studies the chamber's computer terminal, which contains the firing switch to stop their timer and their transport to Io. Not a physical switch, but an entered code.

Sato begins to weep. The adrenaline from the laboratory has subsided, and the calm of the Quantum Elevator provides a bitter but safe feeling. Ronan can't hold his tears but holds to his resolve.

"I killed that man," Sato laments. "I never thought I'd have to kill someone. What if he had a family? Kids?"

"Don't think about that. These giant FeiserCorp men are like drones, and nothing more. That monster killed me by damaging my earpiece, I'm sure of it." At that moment Ronan realizes he didn't bring any extra painkillers. It won't be long before his current dosage wears off.

"We can't be here long," Ronan says. "I swiped the Feiser-Corp tag from the big guy, so that's a potential disguise. If we run into people on Io, then we can at least look like them. We could pretend something happened on Mars, and we escaped."

Sato agrees.

Ronan changes into the more generic UF jumpsuit and sticks the Feisercorp tag on his breast. He tears the part of Sato's new jumpsuit that would hold a tag, including one entire sleeve, thus strengthening their disheveled alibi. Sato takes the pistol and tucks it under the damaged armpit of his suit. Ronan attaches the multi-tool to his side, and leaves the computer tablets in the crate, for now. They decide to lie down, where possible. Even in this suspended space and time, they keep their resolve. Ronan uses his multitool to blast a laser into one of the barren walls within the chamber as evidence of a struggle.

When they arrive on Io, anybody there could possibly be convinced of a revolt, or an uprising in Arcadia. Once they gain an advantage on Io, Ronan can access the localized FeiserCorp data.

"For consistency, let's keep our story simple. We were attacked, and didn't know where the Elevator would send us. You were blinded by the same explosion that damaged my earpiece, which is when we found shelter in the lab. The insurrection was about to break in, and the elevator was our only way out. You'll be able to shoot that thing?"

"Yes. I'm ready," Sato says.

Ronan enters the stop code for the elevator, and the timer

ends. The machine regains its idle hum. The gravity returns, and their magnetic boots compensate. Sato sits on the floor in a fetal position. Ronan exits the elevator and dramatically falls to his knees, now inside the Quantum Laboratory on Io. He accidentally drops his multitool, but has no time to pick it back up before hearing a deep, guttural voice cough and exclaim, "What is this? This is a restricted station!"

There is only one man here. A short, old man. His wrinkled skin is tainted an almost unnatural yellow-gold. His messy, strawberry blond hair has gray streaks, and his eyes are green and rheumy. He looks sick, but is emphatic in his speech.

"Where are we?" Ronan says.

"This is Io, you fool. Who are you? What happened?"

"Jupiter? Shit." Ronan grunts as he stands to get a better look at the lab. It's identical to the lab on Mars, but messy. The room is warm and muggy. Could this old man be here alone? Ronan continues. "There was some kind of revolt in Arcadia. We and other employees were attacked, and I barely made it into the elevator before they broke into the lab down there." The longer Ronan looks at this man, the sooner he realizes that it's Jameson Feiser. He looks different from memory, but similar enough, and his deep voice is recognizable, but weaker. Calmer. This man is home.

"There was an explosion. My earpiece was damaged, and it blinded our friend in there," Ronan says as Sato cautiously exits the elevator.

"Sit here," the old man says. "We'll get you situated and send you to Titan for medical attention. We have limited resources here."

Ronan's ear begins to sting. The painkillers are fading,

and coagulating blood impairs his hearing on his right side. He sits with Jameson Feiser as the old man programs the elevator with Titan as the destination. The pain is returning wholly and swiftly. The throbbing and the hollow weight of pooling blood become too much for Ronan to sit still. This old man is outnumbered if Ronan and Sato were to attack him right now. Sato moves closer, but imperfectly, pretending to be fully blinded.

"Who are you?" Ronan asks, knowing this man will attempt to lie to him.

"That's not your problem right now. Thirty seconds before Quantum launch. You're one of my programmers?"

Ronan doesn't answer. Jameson Feiser's very question has given him away. *My* programmers. He fakes a wavering consciousness as Feiser sits and programs the elevator, but the pain makes concentration a commodity. The compounding anger toward this man — the reason Kitta is gone and Ronan may never see her again — can't be answered with some silly trick.

"Hey, stay with me. What's your name, son?"

Ronan rushes the old man and pushes him from his chair. Ronan reaches for his multi-tool, already forgetting that he dropped it on the way out of the elevator. He tackles Jameson Feiser to the ground and grabs his head. The mounted old man fights from his back with flailing arms as Ronan shoves his thumbs into Jameson Feiser's eyes. He screams and kicks Ronan away.

"Shoot him!" Ronan shouts. "He's heading for the elevator!"

Sato, with limited sight, sends several bullets at Jameson Feiser's glowing silhouette as he crosses the room. Sato successfully hits him once before he enters the elevator and shuts the door. The machine goes quiet shortly after. Ronan reopens the door to the elevator and notices the splattered blood at the doorway. The elevator is empty, and a wounded Jameson Feiser has been forced to Titan.

EIGHT

ROUS

THE *Comrade* has landed vertically with a vicious shaking of the smooth surface outside First City on Titan, darting itself deep within the top-crust of the moon. The weather is hardly torrential, and the anticipated UF warships are nowhere to be seen, nowhere to be scanned. Popp has wasted no time wondering where they have gone, and he's given the order to assimilate the *Comrade* to the moon's surface. Great hot metal ducts burn and expand through the rock and ice of the moon's crust to complete the subsurface annex of a newly established base of operations.

Popp's cartographic information on Titan, though admittedly outdated, has proved correct in locating several smaller tunnels leading deep beneath First City, and the *Comrade* has landed accordingly among them. Popp's employees flood the newly-cooled subsurface annex to finalize the *Comrade*'s surface-adaptation by erecting turrets at multiple burrowed conduits, which have reached upward through the top-crust, and back to the surface. Each turret stretches ten meters high and is equipped with a rail gun. The *Comrade* base is not far from First City and sees no resistance upon landing.

The *Comrade*'s hangar doors at the surface open, and hundreds of four-wheeled, magnetically-weighted tactical military vehicles form their trained reconnaissance patterns surrounding the ship. Hundreds of foot soldiers march into formation, standing ready and face the external platform above First City.

The enormous surface platform above First City is the primary entrance, and the city lies entirely underground. The platform is surrounded by towers, tall and thin, stretching high into the orange and white opaque methane clouds. They are conductors, created to absorb the frequent lightning and convert it into auxiliary energy for the city below.

Operation Stinger has filed into two vehicles, and speeds through the subsurface base and into a rocky tunnel in the planet's crust. The two vehicles are each outfitted with a detachable rail gun, and reconnaissance equipment including flares, digital trackers, and sidearms.

Stinger consists of eight hardened soldiers, and Ezra Pierce. Popp is driving the leading vehicle with Ezra, Linus, Advik and Stella as passengers. The four members of Bone Squad travel behind them in the secondary vehicle. The cave tunnel ruggedly slopes and descends as Popp navigates using the holographic map on his dashboard. The rocky underground knocks the vehicles side to side as they rush through the tunnel. Dead lights and broken signage begin to line their path. Man-made equipment and formations in the rock become more common as they travel deeper. The ground begins to level when suddenly, the convoy stops. In front of them is a deep chasm, too wide and long for their vehicles to cross.

"Helmets on. This is where we get out," Popp says. "Grab supplies. Linus, get the big guns."

Ezra, Popp, Advik and Stella fasten their helmets, and climb carefully through the vehicle's airlock in their pale-red armor, except Stella, who is proudly set apart by her extravagant TLC armor. Linus detaches the two hefty rail guns from the outside of each vehicle, then quickly tosses them to the other side of the gap. The four members of Bone Squad exit their vehicle and rendezvous with them moments later. Ezra analyzes the broken technology surrounding them and throughout the tunnel.

"This is from the landing," Ezra observes.

"Huh?"

"This crevasse is new."

Bone Squad stands at ease, awaiting orders.

"Okay Goons, looks like we're on foot from here. Welcome to the First *Sewers* of Titan," Popp jokes. He then points to Danny Jelani and Houston Ives of Bone Squad. "We still have plenty of time to surprise them inside. I want Ives and Danny to stay with the vehicles."

The tunnel grows larger up ahead, past the abyss. Ezra looks at the humid walls and notices the glistening rock. The lights shine through the cave and reflect drops of water falling slowly from the soft and impotent stalactites. This area is very humid. Far too humid. Ezra has studied Titan his whole life, and not only is the humidity peculiar, but the unexpectedly ample gravity —

Suddenly, a wailing shriek is heard from the tunnels ahead.

"Did anyone else hear that?" Popp asks.

"I did," Linus says.

"Everybody else, make sure your external mic is on. Ives and Danny, I'll give word if we're compromised." Popp struggles to hide his discomfort. The foreign sounds from the tunnels ahead remain ominous, and grow louder. Popp looks to Ezra, then looks to members of his team before catching his breath. "And as I was saying… be on your toes, team. We can jump this hole, here."

The group takes turns deactivating their magnetic boots and leaping over, leaving Houston Ives and Danny Jelani behind with the vehicles. Linus and Advik each hoist a rail gun, being the largest *Comrade* employees in the group. Their boots are promptly reactivated upon crossing the crevasse.

Stella towers over everyone in the group, keeping her pistol drawn. As they make their way deeper into the caves, mining equipment becomes more and more frequent. Some of it looks damaged, but not from the *Comrade* landing. There is no electricity; however, it is inconsequential due to the abundance of floating, ornamental ice droplets reflecting the light from their guns.

"This looks abandoned," Popp says, choking nervously and stumbling over his words.

Ezra isn't used to Popp sounding nervous. Popp continues, his voice tightening with frustration. "These crystals would be pretty if they weren't crowding my damned vision." Popp begins to wave his hand through the air in front of him aggressively.

Ezra notices small patches of brown moss and mold becoming more frequent on the walls and equipment within the cave. "It's water," he says. The others halt out of curiosity and look at Ezra, waiting for him to elaborate.

"Well," Ezra says, "it's irregular, to say the least. Methane alone doesn't behave like this. It's mostly water. Also, the gravity down here is much greater than it should be. You deactivated your magnets for the jump. You felt it. Titan's gravity should be closer to Luna's, but it's greater. Closer to Mars'. I know I don't sound worried, but I'll be honest — this is terrifying."

Suddenly Popp hears the light hissing sound of a helmet being removed. "Goons!" Popp shouts, "Equipment check!" He looks at his team to see a member of Bone Squad, Tess Kovacs, removing her helmet. "Tess, what are you doing?!"

As she deeply inhales the air around them, "I just read the atmosphere," she says. "We're not far off nominal. It's a little icy-hot, but it works, right?" the young soldier says, confidently.

"We're hundreds of meters deep," Ezra says, "but that doesn't explain much. We have to find out what's doing this."

"Keep your fucking helmets on!"

As quickly as Tess can take a second deep breath, a violent rustling and tumbling of rocks catches everyone's attention from the tunnel head. Whatever it is, it's close. Everyone points their lights and guns in all directions, some trying and failing to follow a whisking shadow beyond the reflective droplets. Before Tess can reapply her helmet, she is violently tackled to the ground by a grumbling, wheezing creature. Light is cast on a feral animal the size of a person. Thin hair, gray and white, is in patches across this animal's lumpy, cyst-ridden back. The sores and scabbed lesions bleed and ooze puss in obscure patterns. Fluids trail between its growths and over its toned muscles.

The fourth member of Bone Squad, Charlie Gordon, aims his rifle. He splits and splashes the monster into pieces with his bullets. The beast falls limp over Tess Kovacs' corpse. Charlie pushes the meaty mass aside to see its face. Tess's knife is plunged deep into its chest. Her head has been reduced to a bloody stump.

"A rat — it's a rat, sir," Charlie Gordon whimpers.

"Is this what Lordes was talking about?" Popp asks Ezra, referring to the mutant soldiers on the surface, "Rats?" They shake their heads with confusion.

"I don't think Feiser planned this," Ezra puts in. "You said these were *sewers*, right? This thing was sick. Look at the cancers. They're affected by the radioactive runoff. It's residual. The disposal of this mineral from upstairs is sloppy."

Everyone is silent. Popp performs signs to the group, signaling them to maintain their silence as they continue into a wide and wet cave junction. The floor becomes smoother, paved, but still heavily cracked and unkempt. Dead and more ordinary-sized rats and formidable stones of feces disrupt the team's steps. Abandoned mechanical and construction equipment is nearly unrecognizable, and coated with molding organic grit and sediment dust. The phosphorescent floating drops of ice are now fewer, begetting a thicker humidity. The walls of the cave are glossy and dripping wet.

There are two open and rusted doors on opposite sides of the cave. A ladder between them, opposite the group's entrance, reaches high to a hatch on the ceiling. The chittering of scurrying animals can be heard beyond the rusty doors. More rats are nearby. Uproars of screeching are frequent, but any violence seems to be solely amongst themselves. The hatch at the top of the ladder has a small window lit by the room beyond.

Popp signals Linus Fogarty and Charlie Gordon to shut and guard the doors, and for Advik Anand to begin climbing the ladder. Advik hoists his heavy rail gun over his shoulder and moves quickly upward. Ezra follows close, tightly hugging the slick ladder. Each of the giant doors is hardly usable, groaning and echoing through the tunnels as Linus and Charlie ultimately fail to shut them. The noisy bustling of rodents grows louder, closer. Linus and Charlie quickly take point at the base of the ladder as Popp follows Ezra upward, followed by Stella.

As the commotion draws nearer, both of the ajar doors vomit swarms of small, panicking and bloody lab rats. Linus and Charlie hold their ground, weapons ready as the rats scamper about their feet. The abundance of rats hides the floor of the junction completely, climbing over and around their feet and ankles.

Both doors burst open by the force of a horde of giant, feral rodents. Some are the size of dogs, with full hair and even proportions, and are hesitant to attack the soldiers. Others, however, are as large as crawling humans, with blistering sores and cancerous abscesses rising from their hairless heads and backs. The beasts are ravenous and muscular, some of them choosing to bite and snap at their lesser competitors as they stumble over one another, but they are ultimately fixed on the human flesh before them. Linus and Charlie open fire. Linus' rail gun sends a lit stream of bullets through the room, severing the monsters like a glowing hot blade through soft fruit, but there are too many rats.

Popp, Advik and Stella do their best to fire their weapons from their positions on the ladder, but Charlie soon falls to the hungry rats. The rodents of unusual size rip and writhe through his suit and skin as he fires upward into the monsters with little score. The rats tear his arm from his body as he wails in agony. The small to medium-sized rats are eager to take part in feasting on the soldier who has fallen to the ground, and Linus's formidable rail gun cannot keep up with the hungry swarm.

Drenched in the blood of Charlie and other rats, the horde converges around Linus.

"Go!" Charlie screams.

Linus ascends the ladder. Charlie has no choice but to wrestle his pistol from his side and use it to throw a bullet through his own head.

As Linus ascends, he is gripped at his upper leg by razor teeth. He screams, holding the ladder and attempting to shake free from the beast. One of his hands slips from the ladder. Stella leans back, takes a deep breath to aim, and shoots the beast with her sidearm. The rodent's grip is quickly released. It falls to the ground, and Stella drops from her position on the ladder. She lands over the squirming mutant rat and violently stomps on its neck with her boot, killing it instantly. She then releases a blinding signal flare into the room, removes her helmet, and lets loose a deep, guttural roar. Her competitive cry and bright flare intimidate and disperse the remaining rats long enough for her to follow and help Linus to the top of the ladder.

Ezra frantically opens the rusted but accessible hatch and enters a bright and empty hallway. Popp and Advik help Linus and Stella from the hatch. Linus bleeds profusely, and doesn't waste his energy speaking. He calmly uses his tactical med kit to wrap his wound to stop the bleeding. The hallway is empty.

"Ives, come in! You need to get out of there!" Popp screams into his comm. He pauses for a response, but hears nothing. As the group finds their feet, Popp takes up the rear as they move toward the closest room, and away from the dead end in the other direction. Popp makes sure the hatch stays open.

"I'll kill him," Popp says.

"Who?"

"Feiser. I know he's here."

"Linus needs medical attention first," Ezra says. "We'll worry about what he's doing to this moon later. You noticed there was no airlock to get in here."

Popp opens a tactical map on his mobile tablet. "Medical is this way."

Advik joins Stella beneath Linus Fogarty's arms. The halls they stumble and hoist him through are lit, but unclean. The long-overdue maintenance shows in the few flickering lights and accumulated soot at the bottom of the walls. Popp removes his helmet and lifts it to let it hang on his back, prompting the others to follow suit. The smell of chemicals and cleaning agents is odd, considering the condition of this place, albeit comforting as an indication that it isn't *completely* abandoned.

Popp and Ezra enter a large, empty laboratory. While it is a medical laboratory, it appears to have been converted into something more. A multitude of embryonic suspension chambers contain unrecognizable, bird-like creatures smaller than human infants, resting in warm fluid and flecked with respiratory monitors. Some are tiny, even microscopic and are held in petri dishes inside large freezers.

One of these creatures is on display as an anatomical

diagram, highlighting its organs and adaptive appendages. The skin of this animal is dark and leathery like a rhinoceros. The elongated nose comes to a sharp, armored point above its mouth, and it doesn't have eyes, suggesting that it would use sonar to move, and possibly to communicate. Two arms, more like fins, shoulder the animal's legless, dynamic body, by which Ezra can only assume that these strange animals are some sort of marine or aerial wildlife. These creatures could also be completely synthetic, though the process is uncommon and expensive.

Advik and Stella place Linus on an operating table.

"Give me the tablet," Linus moans. He begins programming one of the medical appliances to disinfect his leg before operating.

"I'm not going to make it," Linus says.

"You're high. Let the machine do its thing," Popp says.

"It tested my blood," Linus says. "The infection is already spreading too fast. Best I can do is get this thing wrapped up and keep what blood I got left."

"What about a full detox?" Advik asks.

"That would knock me out for days, with this level of bacteria."

"Worth it. You're not dying here, buddy."

"I don't wanna wake up and find out you're dead. I can continue the mission. This surely isn't the only medical bay. I'll get wrapped up here, and detox later."

Linus lifts his leg into the air, as prompted by the great machine lingering over him, and the delicate mechanical arms weave and tighten fresh bandages around his wound. Linus sits upright, but is not ready to move to his feet.

Ezra continues to study the diagram of the strange foreign creature, but can find no literature other than the diagram — no history, no habitat details, no safety warnings other than the ordinary laboratory protocols. He locates a tablet — a simple city guide with a current map of First City — and hands it to Popp.

"I'll work that next medical bay into our path, yeah?" Popp says.

Stella performs her own analysis of the room, grunting and scoffing as she peers at the leather birds in their suspension chambers.

"These things…they are the true weapon." She says.

"How do you know that?"

"The effects. The rats, and the people — they were unrecognizable, but these things grow well, and a thousand fold. I've seen them before. Wherever they come from, they're more accepting of these…treatments."

"Where have you seen them before?"

Stella is silent.

Ezra nods in agreement as Popp and Advik look to him for approval, knowing Ezra has the highest degree of scientific knowledge among them. Ezra still continues to rack his brain for reasons behind the exponential increase in Titan's gravity.

"The news articles here are riddled with propaganda," Popp says, tablet in hand. "This is sick. 'Trust in the United Frontier,' they say. They're assuring these people that loss is a way of life, and those on Titan are 'born to serve… sacrifice for the good of our species.' Most of the people reading this were born here! This language is crafted to gaslight their suffering. What is Feiser doing to them?" Popp continues reading.

"This is madness," Advik interjects with his thick and commanding voice. "Where are the founders? The '75ers? This… *Mayor*? His fleet was nowhere to be seen, there was no storm, and this place is a mess!"

Linus can now stand from the operating table. He gives Popp a ready nod.

"I just know the longer we stay here, the closer we are to seeing those rats again. Let's go."

NINE

The Greenhouse

"ENERAL *Duval Kamasi of UFS* Pyxis, *this is your Mayor — your launch has been halted for a military emergency. I have activated all militants, and repurposed all others to defend our beloved First City from an incipient attack. A renegade faction has today launched from Earth, and will be here within weeks. Carrier* Pyxis *and all those involved in their mining expedition will be reassigned to military purposes. All of those with General Ren Tilson and UFS* Caelum, *currently in Saturn's inner orbit, have been ordered back and will be reassigned when they return in one week. Remember to trust in the United Frontier, and the fruit of our sacrifices will be reaped in the glorious protection of our beloved city, and our humanitarian right to expansion.*"

"*This is General Duval Kamasi of the UFS* Pyxis. *I will not mince words, my fellow miners and family — it is my belief that this is not our fight. I know of these attackers, and I know it is led by one Inquisitor. A man named Pierce, the son of our late, great Bryndon Pierce, has initiated this Inquisition to do what I believe is long overdue — to restore humanity to the United Frontier beyond the Belt. I say to you — think of your children. The United Frontier has taken them from so many of us. What will they take next? This carrier has the potential to maintain the hundreds of us in Saturn's inner orbit far longer than two*

167

years, and it is my intention to launch. We have the potential to sell the great mining spoils of UFS Caelum — who have elected not to return to Titan — to The Lordes Company on Ceres. Yes, it is against the Mayor's orders, and against the interest of the United Frontier of Saturn. It will be risky, but I believe it to be the ethical, the noble side of history beyond the Belt. Prepare to launch, or don't. I understand if you must stay and cannot leave your children behind, and I will not force you."

Few ships stayed on the surface of Titan that day. One week later, UFS *Caelum* and its workers did not return from their mission. The miners, security and carriers are required to return home, regardless of their mineral quota being fulfilled, after two years. UF learned early that any more than two years in working space could prove dangerous for mental health, especially to those working for privateers who operate outside of UF health regulations. However, UF mining carriers are built to remain in space in perpetuity, so the two carriers declined in protest. The hundreds of employees operating in UFS *Caelum*'s vicinity and those with UFS *Pyxis* would eventually turn to Ceres to sell their minerals.

UFS *Delores-I* coasts close in Titan's orbit and prepares to enter the dense atmosphere. Spencer Gant accompanies Jaco Delores on the bridge, where a small team of specialists navigate, and Delores struggles to establish communications with Jameson Feiser. *Delores I* reaches the surface and deploys its landing gear, making for a much softer, less permanent landing than Popp's *Comrade*.

"Pierce stopped at Ceres, did he not?" Spencer asks after a long silence.

"Yes." Jaco Delores replies, although preoccupied with reading the testimonies from the mining employees of UFS *Pyxis* who stayed; the UFS *Caelum* declined to return.

"That could be an issue," Spencer continues. "I can only assume they don't like Dr. Feiser, and Ceres is currently the closest outpost where *Pyxis* and *Caelum* could — "

"Could have taken their mineral quotas because yes — Who the hell would just stay in orbit?" Delores interrupts. "I understand your concern, but consider this — *Pyxis* had only just left Titan, so they don't have a quota. *Caelum* could very well have traveled to Ceres, but also consider: Ceres is disorganized. They're pirates. If a UF carrier shows up then it's unlikely they would 'team up,' or that the Lordes Widow would want anything to do with them. She may end up robbing them."

"How very optimistic," Spencer digresses.

"I'm just being pragmatic. *Pyxis* is probably doing their job. I'll hail them now. Feiser must be busy. *Pyxis* is close enough for us to talk live."

"You think they're going to answer?"

"I don't see why not." Delores activates a terminal and begins establishing a connection with UFS *Pyxis*.

"And what of *Caelum*?"

"They must have spoken with *Pyxis* by now, so I can find out. *Caelum* is least likely to answer my call."

The connection begins to load, but slowly due to the energy needed for their ship to land and integrate to the surface. The *Comrade* and First City's main entry platform are within sight. The three are of equal distance — just a few kilometers — from one another. The clouds have mostly dissipated, revealing an icy glacier plateau in the northern distance, with *Delores-I* nearest to it. Spencer notices the turrets surrounding the *Comrade*, and how deeply the Inquisition's ship has pierced the surface.

"I didn't expect the Inquisition to use that ship's colony protocols," Spencer comments.

Delores pays it no mind. "Damn, I wish this thing would hurry up. My programmers are still struggling to clean up the mess Kitta Russo's boyfriend made," Delores grunts.

The connection to UFS *Pyxis* is established, and Major Kamasi appears on the bridge's main screen. A tall and tan, tight-bearded man with black hair, and little facial expression.

"Major Kamasi, I hope I'm not interrupting. This is Dr. Jaco Delores."

"I know who you are. I answered out of curiosity. You must be near, if the connection could be made so quickly." Kamasi's voice demands respect. Low and raspy, but healthy nonetheless.

"We are, General. We've just touched down outside First City, and though I was hoping to speak with you in person, I'm hoping you can at least grace me with a status report."

"Our mission goes according to *our* plan. I'm sure you're aware of the Ambassador's predicament," he pauses. "Or perhaps you aren't and that's why you've called."

Delores is perturbed by Major Kamasi's lack of respect, but puzzled by his answer. "Well, *our* mission here has little to do with…the Ambassador? Do you mean your Mayor? There hasn't been an Ambassador since Jameson Feiser," Delores lies, but grows nervous.

"No, I mean Ambassador James Feiser. I'm aware he's

alive, boy, and I know he and our mayor are one and the same. There are no secrets in Sol."

Delores tries to remain calm. "I will say, we are skeptical, which is why we landed on the surface, rather than within the city itself."

"Very interesting. And your mission *is?*"

"Private. You, however, are disclosed. If your mission has changed, I would like to know how it has changed, as it could potentially affect the lives of my contractors and their employees. *Caelum*'s absence has already struck quite the commercial blow."

"We left the surface of Titan against the Ambassador's orders," which Jaco Delores already knows, but he lets Kamasi continue. "And we plan to follow Major Tilson and UFS *Caelum* to Ceres, where we intend to sell our minerals."

Delores recoils in confusion. "Pardon me, major, but what minerals? You've only just left the surface."

"Yes, and those who left with *Pyxis* know the risk. To answer your question, *Caelum* doubled their quota in a short amount of time, and what they have is more than enough for an audience with the Pirate Queen, Patricia Lordes. Our carriers and physical resources are potentially enough to allow new lives for those who choose, and safe passage for those who want to return," Kamasi smirks with a condescension intended to stir Delores.

"Ceres is a mud ball —"

"With a functioning command station, and reports of a people free from the clutches of the United Frontier... or what's left of it," Kamasi raises his voice. "I'm a '75er, boy! The UF you know and its authority are no longer recognized by me, Ren Tilson, or our crews."

Delores begins to sweat, and resorts to insults in his rage. "So what's the plan then, old man? You rescue your people and add it to your repertoire for a stab at Governance?"

"Listen to yourself. This is the new UF talking. A far-reaching and frankly childish attempt at manipulation over the people of Sol. I'm sorry, truly. It is clear to me you have chosen your side of history here beyond the Belt, and your greed will sooner than later catch up with you."

Delores ends the connection and stands quietly, eyes shut. He takes a deep breath and stifles his anger.

Spencer approaches and speaks softly. "The landing coordinates were correct, and the passage to the Greenhouse is nearby. I've made sure there's a vehicle ready for us, with an escort convoy. Has anybody found Miss Russo yet?" Spencer asks.

"I haven't heard anything. I didn't take her Jym. She probably slipped the guards." There is a pause. "I'm not afraid of her. If I had taken it, she'd be less likely to join us."

"She'll be far less likely to join us if she sees what you've been creating for Dr. Feiser."

"As I said earlier — she joins, or she dies."

Kitta hasn't made it back to her sleeping pod. Her personal tablet, which she uses to communicate with Ronan, is there. The halls of *Delores-I* are crowded, and she is completely visible to all; no time or private spaces to vanish. All she can do is blend into the ebb and flow of the ship's interior traffic. Luckily, the commotion of contractors and employees preparing to dismount *Delores-I* is enough to keep them uninterested in Kitta's presence. Certain eyes will lock onto her as she passes, whether to wonder at the new face or acknowledge her administrative colors is unclear to her. She's learned how to play the part by now and deter herself or others from lingering conversation.

She finds herself following signage to the armory out of pure curiosity. The hallways begin to clear as she nears. She takes a sigh of relief, warm to the feeling that these citizens may not likely be thrown into a fight. Upon entering the armory, she finds it is very small in comparison to the rest of the ship, and mostly empty, which concerns her. Are the weapons being stored somewhere else? Have certain members of the ship already been armed? She can only wonder. She overhears a conversation around the first corner, coming from a locker room.

"It's crazy that we didn't use the main entrance," a female voice says, calmly. "Why are we on the surface instead?"

Another soft voice answers, "We landed at a different entrance. I've been instructed by some UF Admin to be part of an escort. Jack wants to go in through First City's Greenhouse. Apparently that big colony vessel that landed here has scrambled the AI in First City, and on our carrier. I think we're stuck here."

As Kitta listens, she starts getting dressed in a surface outfit she's found on the wall nearby. She deliberately has her suit zipped only halfway up her torso, leaving her Admin colors visible for when the two voices make their way from the locker room. She stands from putting on her boots as they turn the corner and see her. The two are both in tight and black Delores uniforms, and one of them scurries past Kitta and out of the armory as if she isn't supposed to be there.

"Are you here for the escort?" The remaining employee asks, her eyes widening at the sight of Kitta.

"Yes, and it seems we're both running behind," Kitta answers.

"I apologize, we can head down there together. I'm Jan." Kitta can tell this innocent redhead is attracted to her, though intimidated by the circumstances. Her freckles pop from her face like firecrackers as she smiles and blushes in effervescent embarrassment.

Sam Levin bursts into the armory as Kitta and Jan finish applying their helmets. "Hi, girls," Sam says frantically. "I'll be right behind you. Escort, right?" Sam is unable to identify Kitta due to the tinted visor of her surface suit.

"Yes," Kitta says. "You go ahead, Jan. I'll help this one," referring to Sam.

Jan leaves the armory and Kitta removes her helmet. Sam coughs and laughs with surprise. "How the — "

"Don't make a thing of it! I gotta see what's happening down there, and meet Dr. Pierce. This ship isn't going to move."

"You're wild. I've never met anyone like you in my life. Have you talked to your boyfriend? Does he know about — you?" Sam looks at Kitta with eyes implying the condition of her suspended child.

"I haven't been able to speak to him. I haven't even been to my pod since I last saw you and Dr. Archer."

Sam suits up for surface travel, and doesn't bother changing from their casual attire, but simply bunches it into their suit; it doesn't seem comfortable at all. "You can join me in my vehicle. We'll be right behind Jack and his little posse."

"Thank you, Sam, I'm glad you're here." Kitta attaches a sidearm to her hip, then she and Sam enter an elevator just outside the armory and descend to the vehicle bay.

"I'm really excited to see First City; I just wish it were under better circumstances. My family has been asking questions I don't have answers to. Your friends have everybody here a little on edge, but I am excited to have a front-row seat to your antics. This is the story of a lifetime."

As Kitta and Sam leave the elevator, they are met with an airlock labeled Vehicle Bay Three. They enter, and the escort sits ready. Four vehicles — the two at the front and back of the convoy — carry large rail guns on top, and Delores's vehicle is just ahead of Sam's, outfitted with communication hardware. Every vehicle but Sam's has a bright green light shining from the bay beneath it, indicating that they're ready for departure. Kitta and Sam enter their vehicle and Sam starts it up. Immediately the dashboard monitor lights up with Delores's face.

"Sam, thank you for joining us," Delores says with a surly tone.

The airlock depressurizes. The outer bay door opens to a calm weathered, smooth orange surface. As the vehicles depart, their carriage magnets activate and secure them to the surface, compensating the moon's weaker gravity.

"This is strange," Sam says. "My info on Titan says the carriage magnets should be working nearly twice as hard. I can't believe UF would be wrong about the gravity here, but it's the same as Mars right now. Maybe greater."

Kitta remains silent, pondering.

Sam continues, "Keep your helmet on, I'm gonna call Jack back." Sam connects to Jaco Delores's cabin.

"Sam?" Delores says expectantly.

"Sir, you're seeing what I'm seeing with the carriage magnets? If not, then my car may be compromised."

"Yes, we are, Sam. Magnets are roughly at half power because the gravity here has changed. Spencer and I are discussing." Jaco Delores disconnects.

The vehicles travel on a little-used road for a short time before they encounter a small platform just large enough for their four vehicles at the base of the icy plateau. The vehicles align two-by-two, as outlined on the platform, and wait a few moments before the platform descends.

Deep below the plateau, the road ahead is lit and clean. The drones and robots throughout the tunnel and at each junction work to maintain the technology as well as the subterranean geography. The tunnel runs deeper as the convoy follows the signs labeled Greenhouse, and the crystals of ice and methane create a dreamy ambience.

The convoy slows to enter an airlock. The hatch behind them shuts, and the large airlock depressurizes almost instantly.

The bay doors ahead of them open to reveal a vast and bright garden kilometers long and wide. The icy plateau is hollow, and the glacier is its ceiling, creating a greenhouse effect supported by long bars of lighting stretching horizontally around the entirety of the underground farm. The pale orange and deep purple layers of sedimentary rock in the walls of the cavern travel in a parallel pattern, almost perfectly flat. The operation is similar to the farms on Mars, but much greater. Kitta is in awe of not only the scale of this operation, but its potential for the people of Sol. It's designed to feed much more than the population of Titan.

Kitta finds a comms tablet inside the vehicle and shoves it into her side pocket. She remains fully suited in her black Delores surface armor.

The convoy stops. "You should get out here, right now," Sam says. "Before everybody else. I don't see any other guards or a welcoming party, and you can escape the group. Go find Dr. Pierce and do what you gotta do."

"Thank you, Sam. Find your family. I'll find you later."

Kitta swiftly opens the door and notices the guards at the vehicle to their rear exiting their vehicle and removing their helmets. They're oblivious to her. She quickly finds the closest hiding spot behind some crates of synthetic soil. She notices the farm is mostly tended to by robots, and there are a few humans working these great indoor fields. She waits for Jaco Delores, Sam Levin and the other personnel to move on before emerging.

Kitta removes her helmet and ditches the black surface attire — keeping the comms tablet — and attempts to better blend in with the few field workers by keeping her distance. She takes time to meander along the rows of oversized vegetables and fruit. Potatoes and carrots too large for humans to carry are cradled from the ground by large, automated machines. Lemon trees with trunks thicker than oak produce lemons each bigger than a human head. A large aquarium opposite the Greenhouse's office annex is home to tuna fish as big as people. Kitta wonders how it could be possible — even with an over-exaggerated death toll on Earth — that people could possibly die of starvation when growing such food is possible. Could this cavern have been made by the Ancients? It renews her sense of urgency, an urgency to rid Sol of its petty secrets and restore the vision of prosperity she was taught by Melena. Luckily, as she draws close to the United Frontier employees of Titan's Greenhouse, they bear the same UF uniforms as the employees on Mars.

Finding Dr. Pierce shouldn't be difficult. And now that she has a capable comms tablet, Ronan should be reachable as well.

TEN

Beasts of Titan

THE desolation of Io weighs heavily on Ronan Pierce and Sato Song. On top of the very size of the puny station — no longer meant for prolonged human operation — the supplies are scarce. The protein bars they've brought with them are dwindling, and so are the few painkillers Ronan has found in the station's paltry medical bay. The air quality is less than ideal — lightly contaminated by radiation — prompting Ronan and Sato to make their time short.

The machines around them and outside the station continue to haul Jollitium ore from Jupiter's core and into the airlock. Unkempt, squeaking robotic machines then bring the crates of ore to the outward Quantum Elevator and prep them for transport. The commotion irritates Ronan, but he is unable to reprogram the heavily protected robots.

Ronan reads a message from his father. He learns of the monstrous rats the Inquisition's Stinger operation narrowly escaped; two soldiers were lost, with two missing and Popp's officer, Linus Fogarty, badly injured. Ronan is amazed by the experimental creatures they've found, all of these anomalies stemming from the processed Jollitium superconductor.

Ronan learns from Ezra that Melena Horn is, or was, Kitta's mother.

With access to Titan's localized servers, Ronan reads testimonies from mental health checkups of the fear-stricken citizens of Titan. Their miners have not returned. The minerals that directly stimulate Titan's economy are only yearned for now as Titan begins supplementing the losses by shipping large amounts of food to Mars and Earth using their Quantum Elevators. This has resulted in a sudden food drought for the people of Titan. They grow more and more anxious.

The media narratives begin to shift as the Inquisition is painted to be either a means to an end of the United Frontier's supposed corruption upstar, or to be a hot-blooded political gimmick by the son of Bryndon Pierce designed to usurp control. Meanwhile, the hundreds of workers on Titan find themselves without purpose, and a shrunken food supply.

The localized files on UF servers beyond the Asteroid Belt are far more accessible from Io, as Ronan predicted. He has done some digging of his own into the experimental animals on Titan. These Leatherbirds, as they've been nicknamed by those helming the study, originated on Enceladus. The southern hemisphere is teeming with organisms nearly microscopic, and their reaction to the Jollitium is the cleanest that scientists have witnessed in a living organism. Exponential growth with little-to-no mutations or cancers when a Jollitium compound is applied. The experiment is still in its early stages, with several of these strange birds having grown to the size of house cats, and the amount of collected microscopic organisms in refrigeration is staggering.

Ronan continues to scour through UF data on Titan, and discovers what is called the Titan Terraformation Project. Funded by Yellow Sector investors from both Earth and Mars, the United Frontier on Titan has been dumping Jollitium ore into Titan's core, increasing the mass of the satellite.

The Mayor of Titan has made a compelling case for this procedure as being the first essential step to making the surface of Titan habitable. Ronan has little time to read, so he copies the file and sends it to his father, who he correctly assumes is already experiencing the changes in Titan's gravity and atmosphere.

He turns away from UF's servers and breaks into Jaco Delores's classified data. Delores's plans for a human vaccine using a Jollitium compound seem to take precedence, based on the dates of use attached by both Jaco Delores and United Frontier officials. These plans have been presented to UF, but have been denied funding as well as public investment options.

One very well-hidden file in Jaco Delores's servers contains plans for a mining operation not sanctioned by the United Frontier, or funded by anybody but Jaco Delores himself. This operation includes blueprints for an entire station set to lie deep in Saturn's inner orbit, and a tether to be linked to Saturn's mantle deep within the gas giant. The tether is similar to Feisercorp's operation between Io and Jupiter, without the convenience of a moon. It seems to Ronan that Jaco Delores is attempting to find his own source of a superconductor similar or identical to Jollitium. It's already under construction. FeiserCorp and UF officials don't have access to these particular files, which means Delores is conducting it behind their backs. It appears that Jaco Delores is self-funding all of his operations.

Sato Song has spent his time mostly in silent meditation. He sits on the floor with his legs folded and his eyes closed. "What do we do about Kitta?" He asks softly.

"Well, we go to Titan next," Ronan says, his eyes fixed on the terminal in front of him. "I can't help but think it'll be heavily guarded, but I have one more thing I want to do while I'm here. That open letter Feiser wrote — it hasn't been released. Still classified. I'm going to write a letter of my own and publish it, making Feiser's letter redundant."

"That's a fun idea," Sato says. "It's been a few days since you heard from her, yeah?"

"Yes, not since she was captured. I know Delores's ship is about as useful as an apartment complex on Titan's surface now, and Kitta may still be there, but she's safe at least."

"And your dad?"

"He sent me an update. He and Kitta's dad, the rest of his Inquisition, landed on Titan, and they took a small party underground. I've found out this mineral my dad's been so hungry for is the Jollitium magnets we've been using for over a decade now."

"Seriously?" Sato looks at his own suit, where the Jollitium magnets have been applied to the boots he's been wearing, and the tools he's been using for so long. "I know so little about Jollitium. So it makes plants bigger too?"

"Much more. It does crazy things to humans and animals too. I'm barely keeping up with all of it right now. Blows my mind."

Sato sniffs short and hard, catching Ronan's attention. "You feeling okay?" He asks before discovering Sato is crying.

Sato regains his composure, conserving his energy and wiping the tears from his face. "What are we doing here?"

"Honestly, if I knew everything I do now, I would have just told my dad when he asked, that it was all just another slow-moving political thing. At least tried to talk him out of it all. But I know that wouldn't have been good enough for him. He was always so…" Ronan grunts and shudders. "I can't think about it. We've come this far already, and the damage he's caused has already killed me. What it's done to you, my friend; I can't stand it."

Sato nods in agreement. "I just *had* to check out those dark servers." He says sarcastically, chuckling, hoping to calm Ronan, and succeeds in making him laugh along.

Ronan abandons Jaco Delores's server data and reopens First City's. He discovers surveillance feeds from Titan's surface. The towers surrounding First City's surface platform are peppered with mounted remote-inspection cameras, giving Ronan multiple vantage points of Popp's *Comrade*, and *Delores-I*. The cameras are on tractable swivels, and provide high-resolution optics.

He sees the *Comrade* for the first time, planted in Titan's surface like a half-stricken railroad spike. Six spires surround it, each one equipped with a manned rail gun. Hundreds of foot soldiers stand in formation, clad in red armor, between the *Comrade* and First City's platform. *Delores-I* sits inactive, as Ronan could have predicted, with about fifty armed employees, dressed in black, securing the perimeter of its landing zone. First City's platform remains empty, but not for long.

Ronan watches as the hangar doors open at the base of each tower surrounding the city's platform, and hordes of soldiers begin sprinting and leaping toward the Inquisition troops. Flares are sent upward from the *Comrade*'s spires, high into the sky between them and First City's towers. The

Inquisition troops march to meet the horde, and as they draw closer, the difference in their size becomes clearer.

The horde is made up of more than one hundred of the three-meter giants — humans mutated by Jollitium compound applications. The Inquisition soldiers fire their weapons into the horde, but to little avail. The altered environment of Titan's surface and the giants' reinforced face-shields do well to protect the horde as the bullet holes in their suits are of little consequence. Once the Inquisition's bullets reach the skin of these giants, they do little damage.

When the horde and the Inquisition meet, Ronan can only sit and watch the unthinkable. The weaponless giants of the horde possess fantastic strength, removing limbs from Inquisition soldiers and tossing them aside, like children in a toy room. Ronan witnesses the rail guns at the *Comrade*'s spires ejecting larger ammunition into the horde — the rail ammunition is much more effective, but the beasts continue fighting even as they lose their own limbs. Many of the Inquisition soldiers retreat at the sight of these gargantuan human atrocities.

A small troop of non-mutated First City soldiers takes up the rear of Titan's horde. They have explosives and other tactical weapons towed by quadruped drones. As the Inquisition troops continue to fall back to the *Comrade*, it becomes clear to Ronan that the Inquisition is losing the fight.

Ronan takes action by breaking into Titan's tactical network. The secondary tactical squad behind the horde intends to sabotage the *Comrade* by using EMPs to disable the rail gun turrets, and explosives to destroy the tunnels between them. They also carry computer viruses in tactical drives, with the intention of dismantling the *Comrade*'s AI and computer system. This could do as much damage as cutting off oxygen for those inside, killing hundreds.

As he looks frantically for any means of stopping First City's progress, Ronan discovers programmable rail guns at different levels of the platform towers. The *Comrade* and its turrets are too far away to be effectively targeted, so Titan's rail guns have been programmed only to target heat signatures of a certain volume as a last measure. In case the Inquisition drew too close, First City would only have to flip a switch, and activate the rail guns. They were ready to extinguish their own fighters as well if the Inquisition soldiers got too close. Ronan decides it's now or never to turn the course of this battle.

He flips the switch. The rail guns immediately target the nearby heat signatures, which include not only the secondary tactical squad, but the horde of behemoths in range as well. With several rail guns at each of Titan's towers, the devastation is immense — but it's not enough. The secondary tactical team is no more, but enough of the horde has escaped the rail guns' targeting distance and continues to ravage the *Comrade*'s ground troops.

Many of the remaining Inquisition troops have noticed Titan's rail guns firing upon their own troops, and have fallen back into formation, but it is in vain. Even as the Inquisition troops dwindle, and the *Comrade*'s own rail guns along with their turrets have been bent and mangled by the horde's sheer strength, the beasts of Titan begin to fight amongst themselves and kill one another. These monsters seem to be in more pain than they can inflict, and many have killed themselves by throwing their entire bodies into the machinery of the *Comrade*'s turrets.

On the surface, it would seem that the battle is lost, though Ronan saved the *Comrade* from an ultimate sabotage. Few of the Inquisition troops have made it to safety within the ship, and now the remaining tens of giants wrestle amongst themselves like wild animals outside.

Ronan has trouble believing what has just happened. He knows now how serious the corruption on Titan really is. He finds the footage file from the cameras he used, and copies it. His open letter will contain the attachment for all to see.

He looks to the wall inside of Io's quantum lab and notices the medical kit has one respirator. He and Sato decide to split their usage of it in order to extend their time on Io and avoid radiation poisoning from the contaminated air. Ronan will keep his recent actions a secret from Sato for now. He's been through enough. Ronan begins working on his letter. All of his increasing pain, both physical and emotional, will be going into the text. He's a fairly popular programmer, especially on Mars, and anything he writes openly will make headlines when relevant to the biggest story of the decade, which his own father started. He will send it to Kitta as well, then find his way back to her on Titan.

Kitta has left Titan's Greenhouse. Without hearing from Ronan for so long, and with the tablet she carries not being sufficient enough to reach him, she can depend only on the access her Jym provides her throughout First City until she finds a terminal powerful enough to contact him. Her rendezvous with Ezra Pierce is top-priority. She remembers her father's involvement in their shared mission — a man she hasn't seen in more than five years. She wonders if Popp knows of her involvement. She searches her mind for reasons to forgive him, for when or if they do meet. Her father was always preoccupied, neglectful of her, and even mentally abusive when confronted about his habits. None of it can matter — the past — when so much is at stake. The United Frontier has been morally bankrupt, and must be taken back before the very name becomes synonymous with deceit, hypocrisy, and corruption. Kitta pushes forward.

"Hello! My name is Topher, where would you like to go?" First City's navigation AI asks her. It opened for her quickly — much quicker than the map AI in Arcadia, or even *Delores-I* — indicating that the AI is outdated, or simply not busy.

"Take me to the closest laboratory. Computer, Medical, doesn't matter."

"I'll need you to be more specific," the AI responds.

Seriously? The AI is an earlier generation than in Arcadia. Kitta can only wonder, with the amount of recent investments pouring into Titan, why the Mayor — or Jameson Feiser — wouldn't be investing in their digital infrastructure. She continues through the surprisingly unkempt tunnels of First City.

"Show me where the Medical Labs are," she says. The AI shows her the lowest floor is made up of six different medical labs, which seems like a lot for one floor, but a very likely place to find an open computer terminal or at least a more capable tablet than her own. It's also strange that these particular medical labs would be so distant, separated from the rest of the underground structure.

She checks the tablet she brought for any potential messages. One, from the primary medical bay on *Delores-I*. Doctor Diana Archer has graced Kitta with a vitality update on her child. He grows at a natural rate, and Diana inquires if Kitta would like to name him. Kitta responds with gratitude, but declines to give the boy a name. In the meantime, the machinery surrounding her child will be labeled "Russo."

Suddenly, the lights of the halls shift bright red, and an alarm sounds, indicating a city-wide red alert. Kitta increases her pace as she begins making her way toward the nearest elevator. There's one just around the corner. She uses her Jym's interface to access the alarm system, and shut off the sound, but she lets the lights continue.

"Hey there!" A hurried voice shouts from behind her. Kitta turns in confusion and says nothing, her face grimacing in administrative character until she notices this man wears administrative colors just like hers. "You're admin, right? I'm glad I'm not the only late one. It's faster this way," the young man says as he passes her and continues through the hallway. Kitta increases her pace to keep up with the stranger. This man has shaggy black hair, and his light brown skin tone is identical to hers. They hurry along past the elevators, and toward the central hub of the city.

"Late for what, I'm sorry?" Kitta asks.

"All admins and officers have been called to Tactical. How do you not know this?"

"I just left Medical, it was stressful. I go to the Greenhouse to clear my head," Kitta lies, thinking quickly. "They only discharged me a few minutes ago. What's going on?"

"There's a fight on the surface, not sure exactly," the

exasperated admin says.

The hallway ends at the deep-rooted, far-reaching centriole of First City. The enormous cylindrical underground is topped by the platform at Titan's surface, with landing platforms lining the inner walls above. The deep, seemingly endless bottom of the central structure is dark and misty, with large crates being hoisted from the lower levels on automated tracks, then below and beyond the haze. While the size of First City is a marvel and the colors in the sedimentary rock are mesmerizing, the unclean floors and the lack of digital finery, advertisements, and other Earthly niceties makes it very bleak. The entire place looks mostly empty due to the red alert. First City makes Arcadia look like a luxury resort.

Kitta is led to the elevators by the fellow admin. The architecture of First City curves outward following the circular frame of the deep centriole. "What's your name?" The Admin asks, "I don't know if I've ever seen you around."

"Yes. I'm Kitta," she says, caught off guard without time to think. It may not be a good idea to give her real name, but with this particular admin, it's too late. She continues, "You don't look familiar either, are you coming from the Greenhouse?"

"I was only surveying there," he says, noticeably sulking. Kitta follows him into an elevator. He selects Armory on the elevator's interface and the elevator trudges upward.

"Something wrong? Where were you surveying?" Kitta asks.

"I'm from Medical, but in the lower levels. It was just some surveying, that's it. I'm the only shift down there lately, and I wish clearing my head was as easy as visiting the

Greenhouse." He's protective, ashamed of something.

"You didn't tell me your name," Kitta averts.

"Quinn. Quinn Peña," he says.

The elevator stops and opens at one of the higher levels of the city.

They round the corner and soon arrive at the conference chamber in the Tactical wing of First City. The circular room is crowded with other admins and officers. There is a sunken lower level in the center of the room where Jaco Delores leads a tactical briefing, with his two large guards at his sides. Jaco Delores notices Kitta right away, but only smirks and continues speaking to the group of First City Admins. Sam Levin sits to the side and takes notes on an advanced tablet, unaware of Kitta's presence. Quinn Peña splits from Kitta and disappears across the room.

"Your Mayor has sent me to see that everything runs smoothly," Jaco Delores declares. "Given the circumstances, it would seem that our best course of action is to wait for this 'Inquisition' to enter the city and negotiate."

"What circumstances?" Somebody shouts from across the room. The Admins and Officers of First City are anxious and uneasy. Other voices shout angrily, things such as — "Where is our Mayor?"..."We never see him!"

"Watch this video," Delores says, and directs the group to the large, central monitors on the ceiling, displaying footage of the carnage on the surface — particularly of Titan's soldiers being ravaged by rail gun fire — but the vexed crowd of Admins and Officers refuse to be so gullible.

"Are those cameras from the towers? Why does it look like we're firing on our own staff?"..."What are we watching here?"

"I can explain, if you'll let me," Delores begins to lose control of the crowd when a silhouette appears on every monitor in the room, silencing everyone.

"This is your Mayor," the silhouette grumbles. "I need all of you to listen. Our rail cannons were hacked, and have been activated upon our own soldiers. We do not have time to grieve. Some of our soldiers were found out of range of the cannons and have laid siege to the foreign ship. We were winning, and still are."

Kitta recognizes the voice from the council chamber in Arcadia. The ominous, commanding voice that accompanied Jaco Delores. Jameson Feiser. The voice seems to be filtered slightly, but not enough for Kitta to not recognize it.

The voice continues as Kitta begins navigating the forest of UF officials to get closer to Sam. "Our cannons have been disabled, and will no longer fire. However, we have another weapon — below the city. Dr. Delores will lead an away team that will include select Officers. You will receive your summons momentarily. Never forget what our sacrifice means for the good of Sol. We will not be stopped."

The transmission ends. Kitta stands behind Sam, who attempts to follow Jaco Delores from the room until Kitta grabs Sam by the arm. She whispers, "Let me borrow your tablet. I'll find you later."

Sam turns and smiles at the sight of her, shoves the tablet to her, and scurries from the room behind Delores. On his way out of the room, Delores turns to address the room one last time. "I recommend we return to our stations and await further commands."

The room begins to empty. Kitta attempts to establish

contact with Ronan, and the connection is made immediately. No picture, only audio, but alarmingly fast.

"Kitta?"

"Ronan! Where are you?"

"I'm close to Titan. I can't talk now, but I'm happy to hear your voice. You need to be careful. Titan has these… monsters."

"I was just watching a video of their cannons being hacked; did you do that?" Kitta whispers.

"I can't hear you," Ronan says, lying to avoid explaining himself. "I'll find you when I get to Titan. I have something important I need you to read."

Ronan disconnects. He seems very troubled. How is he getting here so quickly? He could be taking one of those transports Delores was referring to. *The Quantum*, Delores called it. What could Ronan need her to read? Kitta can only wonder.

She notices the other Admin, Quinn Peña, is one of the last to leave the room. He walks with his head down. She catches up with him. "Those soldiers…" she says to him, "did you have some friends up there?"

"Those soldiers…" he echoes Kitta with malice. Quinn looks around suspiciously, then slows down. "Follow me," he says. He leads Kitta back through the hallways they came from, away from all the other admins and officers returning to their stations. Once the coast is clear, he continues, "Those soldiers are bred here, and experimented on, since before I was old enough to work. Past decade or so, they've extracted the children that couples, or whoever, didn't want — the surprise pregnancies, mostly. It eventually came to the point where families were allowed only one child, and any others were… confiscated. The rejected fetuses are given an experimental compound while in suspension. They grow fast, in a matter of a few months, and when they're born, they keep growing at wild rates. The stolen infants, however, are given the compound as they grow. It causes horrible mutations. Many of them don't survive. The ones that do are strong. Too strong. They get to be three meters in height most of the time. I'm a doctor. I'm a *good* doctor, but I didn't sign up for this. All I do is play damage control while being told I'm doing the right thing; that 'our sacrifices are the root of our progress,' but I'm sick of it. It feels wrong." Quinn is clearly against Titan's agenda, and can be very helpful to Kitta if he wants to make a difference, but he seems afraid.

"Is there no recourse for you?" She asks. "You can't report it to UF?"

"It *is* UF," he says. "UF is approving all of this, and the Mayor will show up on screen and tell us how much good we're doing."

"You mean Ambassador Feiser," Kitta says, assuming Quinn and the rest of Titan's population believes him dead.

"I've heard the rumors," Quinn says. "But these are human lives…not…rats."

Suddenly Kitta and Quinn are startled by a loud, inhuman screeching sound echoing from the deep central hub of First City.

"We need to find Sam," Kitta says.

"I've been called downstairs to assist Doctor Delores's away team."

"I'm coming with you."

ELEVEN

Agendas

JACO Delores waits at an elevator near the central hub of First City. His two guards stand firm, and Sam Levin arrives anxiously behind them. The elevator opens to reveal Delores's assistant, Spencer Gant.

"What did you find?" Delores asks as they enter the small elevator. Sam isn't able to fit.

"I'll catch up with you guys," Sam says as the elevator closes.

"Don't bother!" Delores shouts. "We should have left them on the ship," he murmurs to Spencer.

"I didn't get far," Spencer answers as the elevator descends, ignoring Delores's distaste with Sam's presence. "And we shouldn't go too deep. There's a rat problem downstairs. I found the armory — full of weapons, but no people. I trust you saw the fighting going on upstairs?"

"I saw it. Doctor Feiser is absolutely out of control. He wants me to lead a team to lure these rats through the underground and into the Inquisition's ship, but if the rats are here, we're in trouble. We need to recover Doctor Feiser's research as soon as possible."

"It's right here," Spencer says confidently as he brandishes a flash drive, then sticks it in his pocket.

"You're the man, Spence. Leatherbirds?"

"I didn't see any up close, but I have the data. They're not ready."

"Damn. I suppose the data's the best we can do for now. Great work." Delores sighs.

The elevator stops at the second-to-lowest level. Jollitium Processing. As they exit the elevator, they are met with one long, curving walkway, high above the processing plant, jammed with large shipping crates full of Jollitium ore. The crates are lifted onto tracks, which lead either to the centriole of First City, or to Titan's Quantum Laboratory where they are readied for transport throughout Sol. Technical service drones float and sputter through tight passageways spoking the inner curve above the walkway as Delores, Spencer, and their guards follow signage toward the Quantum Laboratory. Monitors throughout the processing plant display the tons of Jollitium ore being sent to Mars and Earth, as well as the staggering amounts of highly magnetic material being dumped into the core of Titan.

"This must be how Doctor Feiser plans to terraform this place. Amazing," Spencer says.

The door at the end of the walkway leads to the Quantum Laboratory, and the door sits ajar, which Delores finds unusual. He signals his guards to hold back while he and Spencer enter the Laboratory.

"Come in," Jameson Feiser says as they enter. Feiser sits shirtless on a mobile emergency medical bench within the lab, using a multi-tool to cauterize the wound in his side.

Titan's Quantum Lab is considerably larger and state-of-the-art compared to the labs on Mars and Io, even Earth. It's the cleanest wing in the entire city. Three Quantum Elevators sit at the other end of the room. The largest and most active is in the center — being efficiently loaded with crates of Jollitium and activated every several minutes. The two elevators flanking the center are smaller, and are used for personnel transport.

Feiser sits adjacent to an array of deactivated computer terminals. Grimacing to himself, he says, "Ezra Pierce's kid has really impressed me. I'm not sure which, but he, or a friend of his, shot me on Io. Now my cannons have fired on my own soldiers."

"Will you be okay?" Delores asks insincerely.

"The bullet went right through. I got out in time."

"And Ronan Pierce is on Io now? With a friend?"

"That's my guess, but they can't be there long, and these elevators don't give them very many options."

"So you think they'll be coming here next."

"I can't be sure. Honestly, I don't care. There isn't much more the kid can do. The cannons are off, Paul Russo's ship is quiet, and I trust you still have some soldiers on your carrier?"

"About twenty of the big guys," Delores says, knowing Feiser is referring to the mutated giants aboard *Delores-I*.

"Only twenty?" Feiser grunts and shakes his head, obviously disappointed. "Send them. We need more ground troops, and I don't know how long those apes will last before they start fighting each other. What we need to do is draw the rats from downstairs into Russo's ship through the passages underground."

"My *apes* are much smarter. They'll do just fine by you." Delores despises those awful experiments. He sits at a computer terminal and activates it, then sends a message to Delores-I instructing his militants to send the giants to the surface.

"What else do you have? Any more soldiers? Weapons?"

"Ronan Pierce did a number on my ship, too. It's stuck where it landed, and my external weapons are dead."

"I saw on surveillance, one of your guards is mechanical. Is the other one human, and that large?" Feiser asks.

"Yes. I've been trying to do better than your *apes*."

"You and your agendas," Feiser scoffs cheekily at Delores. "If you would only use what I gave you *as I instructed*, you would be a better, less wasteful asset. What are you really doing here, Jaco? Can I still trust you?"

Delores's blood rises. He's doing plenty here, and he's not just here to be somebody's asset, but everything he's doing must be kept secret until he has unfettered access to the Jollitium ore. "Yes, you can," he sneers, but submits, keeping his answer succinct.

"Send your guards up there too, since you're so capable. You won't need them down here anyway."

Delores leaves the room and quietly instructs his guards to find and protect the journalist. Sam may be of use if they're found in the right place, and at the right time.

Spencer has been anxious to interject, "Doctor Feiser, sir. We do have rats on the lower level amongst the medical labs."

"I've seen them, boy," Feiser says with distaste toward the dweeby young assistant. "Those few are fine where they are. They can't use elevators, and we have Russo's away team pinned down there. I believe both he and Ezra Pierce are down there."

Feiser finishes tending to his wound and redresses. His outdated prospector's garb has many pockets, most of which are empty now, but would be used to keep worthwhile mineral samples found deep within the mines when breaking ground on various moons. He pulls a small capsule from one of his pockets and ingests it quickly and casually, without thought.

Delores knows exactly what Jameson Feiser is doing —ingesting a Jollitium compound in order to extend his life by boosting his metabolism. Delores looks upon him in pity, and asks nothing of it. A man who is barely seventy years old, much older than most who grew up in as harsh an environment as he, relying on experimental medication to survive. Medication which Delores has already perfected, but has only enough to enhance fetuses. Feiser looks about, expecting Delores to react somehow, but the silence beckons.

"I have some tricks of my own," Feiser says. "Send your damned ground troops to Russo's ship and I'll handle the rest."

Sam Levin arrives at Jollitium Processing via the elevator and is immediately met by Delores's guards, who step into the elevator and trap the nervous journalist inside with them. One guard selects the Hangar level, per Delores's updated instructions. They are to take Sam to Jameson Feiser's rendezvous, where the select admins and officers were instructed to meet.

"Party's over? And the after-party is…" Sam quips rhetorically. The guards say nothing, as expected.

The elevator reaches the top floor, and opens to a control room with several computer terminals and windows separating them from the vehicle hangar. The few vehicles within the hangar include two jumpers, designed to exit the atmosphere with haste, and two surface carriers, each with the four-wheeled surface-crawlers in their holds. Sam recognizes some of the Admins in the control room, including Kitta. Sam slides out of the elevator, but the guards stay, leaving them on the hangar level. Sam then reunites with Kitta, who is talking to one of the young Admins.

"You have my tablet?"

"Right here," Kitta says, calmly handing Sam the tablet.

"How's the baby? Have you talked to Diana?"

"She's been kind enough to send me updates. Everything is normal — as it can be, I suppose."

Sam's curiosity is uncontrollable. "So do you have a plan? What are you doing here in the hangar?"

"I was hoping to get a hold of Ronan and meet him here. This place has been doing terrible things, and we need all of Sol to know, before UF destroys itself."

"So you're going to blow the whistle on UF, and hope the power goes to — who, someone better? A new Melena Horn?"

"Melena Horn taught me to lead. I worked under her on Mars as a teacher, then I was recruited and trained to govern before all of this happened. She sent me here."

"Isn't she dead?"

"I was there."

Sam reels, overwhelmed. "And what's happening here?"

Kitta goes on to explain what she's learned from Quinn Peña, in broad strokes, about the experiments being done on rejected and confiscated children using the same Jollitium compounds used in the Greenhouse — the same compounds that enhance organic growth in plants, fruits, and vegetables. Quinn finds his way to the group and stands idly as Kitta enlightens Sam.

"The soldiers from the video?" Sam asks, growing uneasy.

"Yes. They're mutated. Farmed and weaponized. It has to stop."

Quinn chimes in, "She's right. I've been working with them for years now. It's all I've ever known, and I knew something wasn't right. I could feel it." A brief silence passes, allowing Kitta to comfort Quinn by putting her hand on his shoulder. Quinn continues, "It may get worse, too. They've been experimenting with rapid growth on the marine life found on Enceladus. They begin nearly microscopic, but when introduced to a Jollitium compound involving the amino acids from Titan's surface, they undergo the fastest and cleanest growth rate seen yet."

"You're saying a multicellular organism, from Enceladus, is being experimented on here? For how long now?" Sam asks with frightened eyes.

"A couple of years. I could've guessed by now that UF was keeping the whole thing secret. The few of us involved live under non-disclosure. The penalty is unknown. Nobody's even tried talking about it."

"I can't believe what I'm hearing." Sam wipes a tear away. "How can I help?"

"There's plenty you can do to help us, Sam. Jameson Feiser is still in control of UF and has people like Quinn working in the dark, completely unaware of the moral implications, to turn humans into weapons — monsters."

"So what are we doing here in the hangar?" Sam asks Quinn.

"The programmers are here," Quinn says, beginning to sweat. "They're triggering something that's supposed to devastate the Inquisition's giant ship outside. I'm not sure exactly what they're doing. I'm interested to see what's happening on the surface right now, but I should get going. We'll meet up later."

"Sounds good, Quinn, and thank you," Kitta says. "Sam, let me see that tablet again."

Jaco Delores and Spencer Gant are in the Quantum Laboratory, alone. Jameson Feiser has departed in order to see his new plan to fruition. Delores has Spencer, who is a semi-experienced programmer, immediately go to work retrieving the blueprints to Titan's impressive Quantum Lab, so that they can replicate and improve upon it when erecting their own mining operation in Saturn's inner orbit.

"An *asset*," Delores murmurs, but loud enough for Spencer to hear.

"I didn't like that either," Spencer responds. "How long before Doctor Feiser's usefulness to *you* has run out?"

"I still need more data. The machines on Io, for one."

"I'm working on it. You'd think Kitta Russo's programmer boyfriend would have stopped the operation while on Io, but he may not have been able to."

Delores shakes his head in disinterest. "He tried to kill Feiser, which at first I thought, 'Okay, fine,' but I realize now it's too early. Most people still think Feiser's dead. He has to be exposed before he can take the fall for what's happened here."

"True," Spencer says.

"We still have Ezra Pierce, however," Delores ponders.

"What do you mean?"

"He and Kitta's father, Paul Russo, have created an absolute shitshow. Pierce is the biggest name in the media — in all four sectors by now, I'm sure. This whole thing could easily be twisted to look like his blundering. *The son of Sol's greatest ambassador*, right? How often is a son of such privilege a hero?"

"That would be tough." Spencer retorts.

"But not impossible. Another reason Sam could prove useful. We have to see how it plays out. Ezra Pierce's son, Kitta's elite programmer boyfriend, will need to be dealt with."

"Dealt with?"

"He's the most dangerous of them so far. He's likely already seen my data, and Feiser's. He could simply leak it, and we're all toast."

One of the smaller Quantum Elevators on the other side of the lab activates to Delores's and Spencer's surprise. The machine winds and whirs, and lights above the arrival chamber door blink yellow, then hold green, and the machine calms. The door remains closed.

"Where's that from?" Delores asks, but feels he may know the answer already.

"Io," Spencer says from his computer terminal, confirming Delores's suspicion.

Delores approaches the door. He lifts the heavy handle, and opens the door slowly. The door is suddenly thrust open from the inside, and Delores stumbles backward, now with the firing end of a multi-tool in his face. The young man holding the pistol looks rabid, feral. His bloodied and scabbed earpiece has stained his neck and shoulder. The multi-tool shakes in his hands. He blinks rapidly and is visibly in great pain.

"Don't you move," he says.

Delores looks at Spencer, who nods, affirming this must be Ronan Pierce. "Ronan? Ronan Pierce?" Delores asks, hands raised.

"I need painkillers," Ronan stammers, nearly sobbing. "Now!"

Spencer scurries to the medical kit on the wall and retrieves a bottle of painkillers. He approaches Ronan, but Ronan is surprised by him and fires a rock-cutting laser at Delores's assistant. He misses, prompting Delores to knock the multi-tool from Ronan's hand and across the floor.

"Hey!" Sato Song shouts from the doorway of the Quantum Elevator, pistol in hand. "Nobody move. You," he motions at Spencer, "give him the painkillers. He's sick."

"Who are you? What happened?" Delores asks, angrily.

"I'm with him," Sato says, "and his earpiece has been broken."

"Yeah, no shit," Delores responds vigorously. "Have you seen all this blood?" He asks rhetorically, pointing to Ronan's blood-stained bust as Ronan retrieves his multi-tool from the floor. Ronan points the multi-tool at Delores.

"I can't see much anymore," Sato says, "but I can see his vitals. I can see you both."

Delores is close enough to study Sato's eyes — the rapid movement. "You're blind," he says. "Are you using my AR option?" Delores asks in wonder.

"*Your* AR option?"

"I designed it. My company created it."

"You're Jaco Delores," Ronan says.

"You can call me Jack — and my friend, you need serious medical attention," Delores says as he signals Spencer to move to the side. Spencer begins inching his way out of Sato's line of sight. "That's internal bleeding," Delores says. "The scabs have clogged your head with rotting blood. I'll call a doctor and — "

"Don't you call anybody!" Ronan shouts. "Not yet. Where's Kitta?"

Spencer gets close enough to Sato to attempt to knock the pistol from his hand, but fails. Sato remains calm, and doesn't fire.

"Hey!" Sato shouts, steadily aiming the pistol at Spencer.

Spencer begins to back away. Ronan turns his head away from Delores, allowing Delores to take Ronan's multi-tool from his shaky hands.

"You both are hysterical," Delores says, pointing the multi-tool at Ronan. "I'm calling for medical right now. Put the pistol down," he says to Sato. "Give it to him," he motions to Spencer.

"He's right, Ronan. It's been too long," Sato says, feeling the weight of everything that has happened to them in such a short time. He's ready for the violence to end, and he hands the pistol to Spencer. As soon as the pistol leaves Sato's hands, Delores fires the multi-tool's laser in Ronan's chest, slicing into his ribcage with bright white heat. Ronan slumps to the floor.

"No!" Sato screams, thrusting toward Delores. The multi-tool needs to recharge, keeping Delores from firing again, and allowing Sato to tackle him. Sato mounts him and repeatedly punches and drops his elbows into Delores's face and neck. He breaks Delores's windpipe before two of Spencer's bullets find Sato's back. Sato falls. Spencer quickly pushes Sato aside to tend to Delores. He gasps and is unable to speak. He looks at Spencer with wide, desperate eyes.

"I'm sorry. I'm sorry," Spencer says. He activates the comm in his earpiece. "I need medical personnel in Jollitium Processing, now!"

TWELVE

Like a Father

STELLA has locked all the doors to the second, cleaner medical lab Stinger has found in the lower level of First City. Linus Fogarty is in a controlled coma on one of the many medical tables, undergoing a detoxification procedure. The group now waits for the few mutant rats that made it through the hatch Popp left open to disperse. No telling how many more rats may come.

Popp uses his tablet to communicate with his officers on the *Comrade*. Their reports from the surface are tragic. The gruesome footage from his soldiers' helmet-cameras makes Popp visibly sick, and angry.

"My Goons got torn apart up there. Some of them made it back inside the *Comrade*, but the giants Pat was talking about," he looks to Stella, who has met one of these Behemoths on Ceres, "there were nearly a hundred."

"Were?" Stella asks.

"Only a fraction of them are still out there, hanging around my broken turrets. Apparently First City's rail guns were hacked, or something, and fired on their own guys."

Ezra can only assume the turrets were Ronan's doing, but doesn't interject. He's only just learned of Ronan's legal suit against him, and wondered why, until now. Ronan must have left Arcadia and Mars altogether. Ronan filed suit against him in an attempt to protect himself from UF, if taken into custody. A clever move, but it doesn't protect him from FeiserCorp or any other privateers.

"I should be up there," Stella grunts.

"If you weren't with us, we'd be dead," Ezra says. "Time is precious right now. We need to find the elevator — *any* elevator — and get to Feiser." Ezra looks at Popp, who carries the map in his tablet.

"And then what?" Popp shouts in hysteria. "My Goons should have opened that platform by now, but instead, we have Linus sleeping in bandages, and the rats are in front of us. Again. Delores's ship is on the surface, too, by the way. Hasn't budged."

"You don't want to know why Feiser's done all of this? What his plan is with those…creatures? We didn't come here to kill, Popp. Remember? It was a side effect." Ezra adds.

"Yeah, well, we didn't come here to die, either."

"Did we not?" Ezra asks playfully, reminding Popp of their conversation back on Earth.

Popp is not entertained. "Not my fucking Goons. Those are my kids we're talking about."

"And what about Kitta?" Ezra asks, subtly calling out Popp's hypocrisy as a father figure.

"Don't you say her name, Eddy." Popp grows more annoyed.

Ezra decides it's time to stop withholding. "She's here, Popp. Kitta's been with UF on Mars, and she hitched a ride on *Delores-I*. If you — "

Before Ezra can finish the sentence, Popp grips Ezra's neck and pins him to a wall of inactive medical monitors. Ezra kicks and flails in futility, unable to speak. Stella sneaks up behind Popp and knocks him unconscious with the butt of her pistol.

"Hey!" Advik Anand shouts from across the room, pulling his sidearm and pointing it at Stella.

Stella remains calm, sets her weapon aside and raises her hands. "You're the one paying us, right?" She asks Ezra.

"Yes, but I've already paid him half," Ezra says, choking. He motions to Popp's unconscious body. "Will he be okay?"

"He's going to be fine," Stella says before looking at Advik. "Now get that gun out of my face, and let's get him onto one of the beds."

Advik grunts in disapproval, lowers his gun and helps Stella hoist Popp's unconscious body onto a medical table. Advik slides a machine down from the ceiling above the table to check Popp's vitals. "You're lucky," he says to Stella, after confirming Popp's stable condition.

"No, you're lucky. If you hadn't put your gun down you'd be in far worse shape than *Dad*, here." Stella retorts.

Ezra quickly steps in to mitigate. "Okay, now. If we fight each other, we won't make it out of here, right? Vik, how's Linus doing?"

"His decontamination is not complete, and it's going too slowly. I'm worried."

Gunfire sounds from outside the medical lab that Stinger came from. Bullets ricochet through the hallways and come to a sudden stop. Somebody knocks violently on the door. "Captain! Doctor Pierce! Open the door!"

Stella opens the door to Bone Squad's Houston Ives and Danny Jelani — -both covered in the blood of rats, caked with sediment dust, but neither of them injured.

"Boys! How did you find us?" Advik asks with excitement.

"Well, we lost our comms when the rats attacked us," Ives

says in a rush. He's obviously very mentally afflicted. "We waited in the damaged vehicles for the swarm to die down. They sniffed around the cars for a while, but it looked like they went back to…wherever they came from. What is happening on this moon?"

"Okay, slow down a bit. You're safe with us now. It's good to see you both," Advik says. "We've had some rat trouble as well. Tess and Charlie didn't make it."

Ives and Danny bow their heads in solidarity for their fallen team members, and Advik joins. So does Stella. Ives and Danny notice Popp on one of the operating tables, but wait to inquire. "We know. We found what was left of them," Danny says. "We got their tags."

"Good work. Is this level now secure?"

"Yes, and we closed the hatch. Sir," Ives addresses Advik as their commander. "We followed your path — the footprints — but there was an old map down there. The rats are coming from — and we believe they're nesting in — a trash dump below this level. It used to be an incinerator, but it was abandoned years ago. You can smell there's trash down there."

"I can *still* smell it," Danny says, and after a pause, he inquires about Popp. "So what happened to the boss?"

Stella and Advik immediately lock eyes.

"He's unconscious," Advik says, "but he's stable." He knows there's no time for any further animosity. He also knows Popp is more sensitive about his daughter than he previously knew. Knowing she's here, Advik makes what he feels is the best call. "I need you two to stay with him, and Linus," he says to Ives and Danny. "When the boss wakes up, get back to the *Comrade*. They'll need him. Linus is detoxifying after a rat bite. If he doesn't wake up in time, leave him. He'll be safe until I come back for him."

"Roger that," Danny says. "What's going on up there?"

"It's rough," Advik says, retrieving Popp's tablet. "They'll need him," he motions to Popp then to Ives and Danny, "and they'll need you. Bone Squad."

He salutes them both, and they both heartily salute back.

"Be careful getting back," Advik says. He looks at Ezra, then to Stella. "Let's get moving." Advik hands Popp's tablet to Ezra, gives Stella an unapproving look before handing her Linus's rail gun, then leaves Ives and Danny to look after Popp and Linus.

The already dirty halls of First City's lowest active level now reek of death. The floor is stained red and brown from the blood of the giant rats attacking one another. They arrive at an elevator and wait for the car to arrive. Ezra gags and struggles to hold back his vomit, while Stella appears unphased by the carnage. The elevator arrives.

"Where do we find Feiser?" Advik asks Ezra. Ezra, realizing Advik is now looking to him for leadership, looks at the many levels within First City: Residences, Recreation and Disposal, Greenhouse, Hangar and Armory, Medical-1, then Jollitium Processing. Advik's finger hovers over the Jollitium Processing button, as if expecting Ezra to want to go there. Ezra hesitates. Feiser may already know they're down here, and he may not. If he does, then he would expect them to go to the Jollitium.

"Greenhouse," Ezra says. "We can't go anywhere that Feiser may be ahead of us."

Advik and Stella agree, and the elevator ascends. Ezra

turns to Advik and Stella. He knows Popp's outburst was as troubling for them as it was for him, and he says, "I want to say — Popp, your boss, was like a father to me after Bryndon died. I don't want any bad blood within the group, and I recognize the part I've played in his current instability. I just need you both to know that I take full blame for what's happened, and you two working together is what's most important moving forward."

Stella takes a deep breath, and looks at Advik. Advik says to her, "You saved Linus's life. I'll never forget that. The Captain lost his cool and maybe you didn't do the *right* thing, but you were the only one close enough to do *anything*, and I respect that."

"Your boss is a good man. A good man, but a troubled one. I hope your friend Linus is okay."

"So do I."

THIRTEEN

First City Blues

I'M hungry," Kitta says as she and Sam Levin descend from the Hangar level in an elevator. She quickly strikes the Residence Level button, just in time for the elevator to stop. "But it can wait. Didn't you say you had family here? Can I meet them?"

Sam grunts, and apprehensively exits the elevator. "Yes, we can do that. I was just with them a little while ago. We'll get you fed, and I think it'll be important for you to meet them anyway."

"What's wrong?" Kitta asks, sensing Sam's melancholy. Sam leads her through the curving residence hallways.

"My older brother, his family," Sam shudders. "I found out earlier today when I first dropped by their place," Sam starts to weep, and stops, then hugs Kitta tight. "We'll talk about it when we meet him, but it really is something you should know about the people here, and UF's leadership here." Sam stirs with anger. Their makeup runs from their eyes, leaving little dark trails down their cheeks. "These people in charge — Feiser, whoever else — we have to stop them. Whatever it is you and Doctor Pierce are here to do, just know I'm with you now." Sam rubs the running makeup from their face after letting go of Kitta.

"And I'm with you, Sam." Kitta is confused, but keen. She rubs Sam's back to comfort them as they both continue walking through the winding residence corridors.

The halls are cleaner than most of the other levels. Not one other person is seen walking or loitering, and it's completely silent. Gray paint is wearing from the barren walls. The doors of each residence have the first initials and surnames of their occupants.

Sam and Kitta stop at a door reading "J. and M. Levin" and Sam knocks. Kitta notices the shared last name, which is unusual. Domestic partnerships where both last names are hyphenated are most common, but a shared surname is typically characteristic of matrimony, or a religious bond. She then notices a customized welcome mat at their feet with a circled, pagan-style cross.

"Are your family theists?" Kitta asks quietly.

"They are. Not me, though. Why do you ask?"

"Because I am," she says.

"You continue to surprise me."

The door to the apartment opens barely an inch with enough space for a man to peek out. A bald, blond-bearded, fair-skinned man, with eyes identical to Sam, opens the door wide when he sees Sam.

"Oh, you're back. That was quick," the man says. "Who is your friend?" The man looks at Kitta with a familiar smirk.

"John, this is Kitta. She arrived on the same ship with me. Could we come in?"

"You didn't tell me you arrived on Jaco Delores's ship," John Levin smiles at both of them as he turns his back and clears the doorway. He wears a pajama suit, which tells Kitta this man works from home, or is currently unemployed. He's also equipped with the standard Wyg cybernetics. Kitta looks at Sam, puzzled, wondering how this stranger knows who she is.

"Yeah, John, I'm sorry for not telling you. I was in a hurry earlier and didn't want to scare you," Sam says.

"It's alright. I don't like the guy, but I trust you. And it's nice to meet you, Kitta. I've been watching your broadcast, as well as the now famous Doctor Pierce." John begins pulling chairs away from the dining table centered in the minimal apartment. Although clean, this apartment is much smaller than the residences in Arcadia. It looks more like an office — no entertainment system, not even a central computer. The kitchen is small, tucked into the far corner next to a tight passage leading to bedrooms.

"So the setup I sent you still works? After all this time?" Sam asks, referring to an ISP box they sent to John a few years ago.

"It does. Would you both like some water? We don't have much else to drink."

"Yes, please," Sam says. "And some snacks too, if you can. We're both pretty hungry."

"I have enough food, sure," John says as he prepares bowls of protein and calcium snacks on the table. He takes a seat along with Sam and Kitta.

"Where's Maria? Joy?"

"They're both here, napping. The last week or so has been very exhausting for everyone. They've been scared. It feels like... well, it feels like last time."

"Last time?" Kitta asks.

John hesitates.

"Why are you here?" John asks Kitta. He lifts himself from

the table and walks to the counter to retrieve a hidden bottle of whiskey.

Kitta can tell this man is scared — sad, even. "Melena Horn sent me when she heard of Doctor Pierce's departure from Earth. It seems things have gotten out of control here, and people are suffering because of it." Kitta takes a handful of protein snacks and stuffs her mouth. She knows the death toll on Earth was falsified, but the people of Titan are citizens of Sol, no less than the people of Earth.

"Melena Horn, huh?"

Sam interjects, "Kitta knows by now, things are pretty messed up here," Sam turns to Kitta. "Most, if not all of the '75ers left with their mining parties or didn't return, and it's because they know too, that — "

Kitta interrupts, "Excuse me, Sam. John, can you tell me what you mean by 'last time'?"

"The last time Titan mobilized any military personnel was to lay siege to the Pirate colony on Ceres. From what I heard, UF won. I know about it because of my community status. I'm a wellness counselor for the people here."

"And how are the people?"

"Well, their sacrifices for the United Frontier surely haven't gone unnoticed by the Mayor, until recently. Lately, the people feel abandoned. The food shortages have hit everyone pretty hard. Every once in a while they'll lament a child that was given to the cause, and — "

"Hold on," Kitta interrupts. "Given?"

"Like last time, sort of," John says, his eyes growing red and wet. "After winning Ceres, the United Frontier demanded any child born after the first would be given to the cause and recruited to the expansion." John sits at the table once again, and fills a short glass of whiskey.

"I've never heard anything about Ceres. And UF *demanded*? That's not like any language I'm used to with UF on Mars. I worked for Ambassador Horn directly. Did something happen to you? The people?"

"Maria and I adopted a son back then," John says. He takes a drink of his whiskey. "About ten years ago, months before UF went to Ceres, we took part in First City's adoption program. Little Anthony was almost a year old, and had been with us for most of that time, when UF came to our door with a directive to 'recall' the adoptions. Maria and I were heartbroken. Joy was too young to remember, luckily."

Kitta can't believe what she's hearing. "I'm sorry, John. That sounds terrible. And did the people of First City vote for this?" She asks.

"There was a vote, and the Mayor said that across Sol, it was accepted. But there was a bit of unrest here, because even though the majority in First City voted it down, it was still implemented. It's been like that since then — one child per partnership. I didn't have access to all of Sol's news until Sam here sent me that ISP box years later. I haven't heard about it since, so I assume it's still happening. We were told it would help cut down on domestic inflation per colony as well."

"John, there's never been a directive like that on Earth or Mars, or anywhere else. I've never even heard of such a thing, outside of history books," Kitta says. Her eyes begin to grow soft with remorse. She feels anger toward the usage of these children, and knows why they're "recruited" as John said — what they're being turned into. Does John know? He couldn't.

"It's hit the population here pretty hard, emotionally speaking. Most of us came here when we were young, and the '75ers are all miners. We don't talk to them, and they're never around long before their next mission."

Kitta can clearly see the oppression these people are under, and it seems they have almost no idea. They feel that something isn't right about how they're being treated, but it's the only life they know. "How is there a food shortage here when the Greenhouse is growing food bigger than me?"

"You've seen the Greenhouse?" John asks rhetorically. "I've never been. I don't have the clearance for that level. Bigger food? We get rations, sometimes. But it's been less and less lately."

"I have level-one access through my cybernetics. Melena Horn gave it to me before she passed."

John takes another drink.

"Watch," Kitta says as she uses her Jym's retinal interface and Augmented Reality tool to select John's bottle of whiskey, and copy it. She grabs the whiskey, and moves just a few inches, displaying two whiskey bottles to everyone in the room.

John reaches for the original whiskey bottle, and his hand goes right through the copy. "What am I looking at, Kitta?" John asks.

Sam shakes their head in disbelief.

"Sabotage," Kitta says. "The cybernetics we've been equipped with by UF contain *Wyg* data sticks, and as far as I know, they are deliberately less advanced than what I have, which is called a *Jym*. The Jym could be newer, but I can do much more. All the UF elites are equipped with it. Not all the admins, but at least the Ambassadors have them. I haven't had this thing very long, so I'm still working to understand it."

Just then, a little girl enters the room from the far corner. Her blonde hair is tied into pigtails which have clearly been tussled from her nap. She rubs her sleepy eyes and stands halfway between John and the kitchen, waiting for someone to notice her.

"Joy, hi, sweetie," John says as he leaves his chair to hold her. "Is Mom still sleeping?"

"Yes," the little girl yawns. "I'm hungry."

"We have snacks on the table here, baby. Come sit up." John lifts Joy into an open chair at the table with Sam and Kitta. John grabs a couple of handfuls of snacks from each bowl and places them on the table in front of Joy, "That's all I can give you until dinner, now. We have guests. Say hi to Kitta."

Joy is shy, doesn't say a word, and is quick to fill her mouth with snacks. She gives Kitta a reserved look.

"Hi, Joy, it's nice to meet you." Kitta turns to John. "I saw your welcome mat, John. You're theists."

"Are you asking?" John begins to grow weary of Kitta's presence, having been through an emotional roller-coaster since she arrived. Kitta can sense he's overwhelmed.

"I would like to pray with you, if we could."

FOURTEEN

New Enemies

POPP shakes his head and checks his surroundings. The gravity feels lighter, but familiar. Bryndon Pierce lies dead before him on an operating table in Titan's first subterranean medical lab. Melena Horn stands across the table from him, but doesn't look at him. Her long, dark hair dances and sways along the sides of her face. She's attempting to hide that she's crying while she reads a tablet.

What could she be reading? Popp wonders. It may have to do with their child, but he can't think about that right now. He can't think about how different things could have been for both of them. *Time is precious.* Somebody grabs him by the arm and pulls him away from the table. He knows it's Andrew Lordes before he looks over, by how fat and soft his grip is. Somehow Popp is compelled to follow, feeling safety in the familiar motions.

"Don, I'm sorry," Popp says to Bryndon's lifeless body. Melena Horn and the medical room fade from vision as Popp turns to look at Andrew Lordes.

"Come on," Andrew says and they walk through the unfinished tunnels. Construction surrounds them and faceless workers pass and murmur. Their sounds are incoherent, but they seem confused. Suspicious of Popp. He concentrates on Andrew Lordes. The figures dissipate, and the hallways become darker and tighter. Popp notices the olive skin on the back of Andrew's neck perspiring. He's nervous about something.

"I'm screwed," he says. "He died on one of my sites. TLC is liable!"

Popp remains silent as they walk, but not by choice. He tries to open his mouth to speak to Andrew, but the words echo inward and die in his head. He wants to tell him to fight the case, to have the site investigated.

"It's going to kill you," Popp says in futility. "Losing your status out here is what killed you." He says — chuckling, even — but the guilt-ridden words continue to reverberate and drown within. Lordes keeps moving, no longer holding Popp's arm, but Popp is compelled to follow anyway. The halls shift around them, curving and bending for them as they walk.

Andrew continues, panicking. "How am I going to come back from this? You have to help me."

But Popp remembers his conversation with Jameson Feiser. The liability clause. FeiserCorp is tight with UF, and with The Lordes Company out of the way, FeiserCorp would have free reign over UF assets and could claim more land for privateers to purchase and contractors to work. Popp was promised immunity from any accidents happening on UF property, so how did Andrew's lawyers so successfully find fault in Popp's orbital security? He can't remember. It hasn't happened yet. He feels if he proceeds confidently, with the fear of the truth drowned by his ego, he may find more answers.

As the hallways around him continue to shift and turn,

he notices he's no longer following Andrew Lordes through Titan's subsurface. His heart rate becomes slow and heavy. He squints, coughs painfully, then looks up to realize he now follows Melena Horn, who escorts him through an unfamiliar darkness. Her dark, wagging hair and rigorous steps are all he can see of her. Popp struggles to keep up with her.

"I don't believe it," she says. "I know it's a terrible time to think about this, but somebody is going to make a political move. Fast. I need to be faster. I thought Bryndon would be Ambassador for at least another ten years. I want it, Paul."

"What about Kitta?" Popp says, painfully echoing Ezra's words.

Melena doesn't answer. Kitta hasn't been named yet. Popp's unstable words continue to fall on deaf ears, and thinking of Ezra Pierce causes his lungs and joints to ache. The questions he asks, the names he uses and ponders are out of place — out of time.

"What does this mean for us?" He tries again. He has to get through to Melena somehow, and in terms that his memory of her will understand.

It works this time.

"I'm sorry," she says. "I've decided to suspend our child so I can pursue taking Bryndon's place as Ambassador. I believe I can do it."

Popp shakes his head, confused. He feels the integrity of his psyche waning. He knows what Melena has to do — what she *feels* she has to do. But what is her hurry? Popp can only wonder. She would go on to become Ambassador, and loved by the people of Sol, but it feels now like she is protecting something: UF, or their daughter, or him — possibly.

"I know Lordes wanted it — to be Ambassador — but he wouldn't have killed Bryndon on his own dig site. It's ruined him. If he runs for Ambassador, he'll lose. He knows it now." She says as she turns to face Popp. Her face is smooth, indistinct — barely recognizable, he admits to himself, but her voice is unmistakable. They turn and sit at a table in a dark room, in those awful UF rec chairs. They even share a chuckle as they cringe from the discomfort. With nobody else in this unfamiliar room, he leans across the table with open hands, waiting for her to hold them, but she doesn't. She remains stoic.

"You know, dressing your employees in red is cute. I know you only started doing that when I was sent to Mars. Does it make you think of me?"

Popp only utters a smirk in response. She's right, even though she couldn't possibly have seen. He has always respected her wishes for discretion, and this seemed like a good time to show the slightest affection, but his hands have been rejected. She casually puts a pill in her mouth and swallows it. The action seems familiar to Popp, and he never questioned it. Between the calcium supplements and other vitamins everyone would take when away from Earth, he had no reason to question it. He only wonders now, when it feels too late. He wants to ask, but doesn't. Better to let her lead the conversation.

"The only candidate I can see making a serious move would be James," she refers to Feiser, "and he's explicitly told me he plans not to. If I'm being honest, it's more suspicious than if he *did* say he wants to make a move. He's planning something. Maybe he wants me to relax, which I certainly will not do. You can't relax either."

A door opens on the other side of the room, casting a dim light to Popp's surroundings, but the room is still unfamiliar. A vague silhouette in the doorway summons Melena, and she promptly leaves the room. Popp tries to follow, pushing away from the table and chairs, but he finds himself stumbling over unseen objects, and the air grows thick, as if the gravity were turned off, or they've entered a new realm. He can't keep up. Melena is gone again. The light blinds him as he passes through the doorway and into the next room. No gravity. Bryndon's funeral service is being held on a carrier in Titan's orbit. The ceremony is held in an observation chamber, with great windows providing a front-row seat to the cosmos. Per Bryndon's poetic request, in the event of his untimely death, he specified that his body be *sent to the stars*. His only family was his son, Ezra, who is stuck in school all the way on Mars.

Popp looks around the room, and notices Patricia and Andrew Lordes. Andrew is a nervous wreck, but Patricia Lordes seems calm, like she's somehow safe from the aftermath of Bryndon's death. She's wearing a great many jewels, some of them tribal. She stands with two guards who are in a similar, intimidating garb. Melena Horn is opposite in the room, weeping, and Jameson Feiser comforts her. Harlan Cain is also there, but he looks young, and prime. He stands proudly, as if he's cheated death by attending a ceremony more than a decade after he took his own life. Popp looks away as Harlan Cain begins to turn his head toward him. The mixed continuity of this strange yet familiar place is triggering a headache. The other figures in the room face Bryndon's closed casket as it sits on a track, being lifted into a small, tubular airlock. The airlock closes, and Bryndon Pierce — his best friend, maybe his only friend — is truly gone.

The room begins to clear, and Popp is left alone. He nears the display at the head of the chamber, where a portrait of Bryndon stands tall, and other pictures of him on Mars, some with Popp, and many others are strewn about a transparent display table. Ezra Pierce joins him at the table, standing to his left. Upon seeing him, Popp begins to feel sore. His joints ache worse and worse, and his stomach burns.

"Eddy. You made it," Popp toasts, realizing he now holds a flask of bourbon in his hand.

"No, but I wanted to," Ezra responds, sulking. "I would've given a lot to be here, but there's work to be done. UF is really putting me through the trenches. I hope they don't expect me to fill Bryndon's shoes anytime soon."

Popp closes his eyes and takes a pull of bourbon from his flask. No taste. He opens his eyes again to a reset chamber. The portrait, the pictures, and even Ezra are gone. Popp corrects his posture and shakes away the physical aching.

Jameson Feiser stands next to Popp in Ezra's stead.

"How long before you depart?" Feiser asks.

Popp says nothing. He feels lost without Bryndon. The wound feels too recent, and he doesn't want to leave.

"Understandable," Feiser says. "I know you two were buddy-buddy."

How dare he minimize Popp's feelings for Bryndon? What does this twerp know of friendship? Popp attempts to tell Feiser, "You don't know anything," but the words are weak, as if he's speaking through water. "You're only friends with those who are of use to you, until you cast them out."

He motions to the very space into which Bryndon's casket was jettisoned. *Cast out.* The words echo in his mind. He then remembers the suspicious amount of weapons labeled *FeiserCorp* in blast-proof crates that were in tow to Titan. He could've only wondered where they ended up, but it's all too clear now.

"You'll be receiving a hefty severance, courtesy of Feiser-Corp and UF," Jameson Feiser says. "It's set to be transferred to you once you and your crew are downstar from the Belt." Feiser continues, "A small but generous percentage of stock in my new mining operation, which goes public in just a few weeks. My discovery will revolutionize travel throughout Sol, and beyond."

Now Popp is being cast out. "What use was I to you?" He asks, but to dead air. He turns from the room and attempts to collect his thoughts, returning to the halls, wherever else he can go — away from Feiser is all that matters right now. Popp was grateful for the money, and his shares in Feiser-Corp would become his gateway to building his own fleet on Earth, but at what cost? These questions he continues to ask himself begin to wear on him physically. He turns the first corner and runs right into Melena Horn. She drops the tablet she was reading.

"You fool!" Melena shouts as she retrieves the tablet from the ground. "Your orbital security didn't pick up the gas pocket that killed Bryndon because there was no pocket! James had explosives. UF sanctioned it for use on Io, but not here. They never went to Io. Feiser used you, along with Lordes, to cover up Bryndon's death and make it look like an accident. You knew, and you did nothing! Wake up!"

"Wake up?" Popp asks. He doesn't want to, but he knows by now he's in another dream.

The pains in his abdomen, his joints, his throat — all triggered by the people, names and speech used out-of-time. The conflicts in the continuity of this place, including Harlan Cain, Ezra Pierce, and even the way Melena speaks to him now. It's all there to wake him up.

"Wake up!" A familiar voice shouts. The halls quake around him. He falls to one knee, and picks himself up to realize Melena is gone. Darkness closes around his shoulders, and he's alone once again. He hears the commanding voice once more.

"Sir, wake up!"

Popp feels gravity weigh upon him. He's on his back. His throat burns, and his joints ache once again. His head is throbbing. The smell is horrendous. Suddenly he recognizes Linus Fogarty's voice.

"We have to go, sir. We cannae stay here. Let's get you up," Linus Fogarty says in his thick Irish accent. Houston Ives and Danny Jelani also stand near Popp in the medical laboratory in the depths of First City.

"Where is everybody? Eddy?"

"Vik and Stella continued the mission with Dr. Pierce," Linus says. "Vik recommended we get back to base. I agree with him. They need us."

The feeling of failure weighs heavily on Popp's mind. He couldn't bear to look at Ezra right now, knowing that he was ignorant of, and practically complicit with Bryndon's death. He's never felt weaker.

"He's right," Popp says, finding his feet.

Popp knows the *Comrade* is now under siege by Feiser's mutant soldiers. Linus shows him surveillance footage of a group of twenty-something more mutant giants — reinforcements — leaving *Delores-I* to join Feiser's monsters at the base of the *Comrade*. Instead of fighting one another, the brutes from Delores's ship are more organized. They hold formation, and are able to render obedient the ravenous beasts Feiser let loose, as needed. Whatever Jaco Delores is doing to create such beasts, it appears to be cleaner and even more dangerous than Jameson Feiser's operation.

Popp is confident Ezra Pierce is in good hands with Advik Anand and Stella, and can complete his objective to find Jameson Feiser. He remembers Ezra's mentioning Kitta, and that she's here in First City. Why is she here? Popp can only wonder. He hasn't seen Kitta since she was fourteen. Five, maybe six years ago? He doesn't remember well, only that she enrolled in United Frontier's higher education program and left. He can't let her presence distract him from the hundreds of lives on the *Comrade*. Kitta has Popp's and Melena Horn's blood running through her. She'll be alright.

"What about you?" Popp asks Linus.

"Detoxed…mostly," he says. "I woke up and felt alright, so I cut the detox short. Not feeling one-hundred percent, but good enough to get back to base."

"You trust that old blood of yours?" Popp jests.

"I trust my body enough right now to help us come back from this. That's all that matters."

Popp agrees. He, Linus Fogarty, Houston Ives and Danny Jelani attach their helmets, and they leave the medical lab. They quietly retrace their steps through the bloodied hallways and to the hatch above the lower catacombs, where the rats can be heard rummaging through garbage and fighting one another in their nest. The group stays completely silent as they descend the ladder and hustle through the rocky tunnels, back over the ravine, and to the vehicles they left behind. The four pile into one crawler, leaving the other, in case it's needed by the rest of Stinger.

When driving through the tunnels, Popp considers bringing a larger party through the catacombs, and going back into First City. The rats are tough, but with enough artillery they could be wiped out easily, if confined to the tight, underground channels. He would have to get back to the *Comrade* first, and get an assessment of the damage from the fight at the surface, but he's confident it would work. The tunnels, some of them too small for vehicles, are usable by foot soldiers and lead back to the tunnels between his turrets. Linus accesses a three-dimensional map of the tunnels beneath the *Comrade* to find a path back into the ship. The surface is riddled with mutant soldiers who could easily take advantage of an open hangar door, if Stinger were to fully retrace their path. Popp hits the brakes, and the four of them abandon the vehicle, heading into a smaller passage.

The passage ends at the base of one of the *Comrade*'s turrets. Not far along the outer wall of the *Comrade*'s turret is an airlock. The door opens, but the inner airlock door is disabled. The terminal inside indicates that the turret has been structurally damaged. Popp knows they're still far below the surface, and remembers how easily Tess Kovacs removed her helmet before they were attacked by the mutant rats. He does a reading of the atmosphere within the turret and surrounding tunnels, and while the oxygen content isn't nominal, and methane concentration is still high, it's close enough for them to safely board the ship by overriding the airlock and skipping the depressurization process. Linus does just that, and they continue, still silent, through the *Comrade*'s lower tunnels. Soon they reach an entrance to the main ship.

Popp checks his tablet, and notices several messages from Ezra's son, Ronan. He opens the first message, titled *Titan Terraformation Project,* which contains information about First City and Jameson Feiser's plan to rapidly transform Titan's surface into an ideal habitat. He doesn't have time to read much, but at least some light has been shed upon the reason behind Titan's peculiar atmospheric conditions.

The doors to the next airlock are transparent, and also shut due to emergency protocols. Beyond them Popp can see bright lights and many plants in long planters hanging from the ceilings and placed high on the walls. This is another emergency protocol in case the oxygen in the lower decks of the ship becomes compromised. He enters the airlock, and has Linus step in to override the second door. As they enter, the air readings improve, and Popp removes his helmet.

"Why do you think this is?" Linus says, referring to the strange atmosphere. He removes his helmet.

"It's Feiser. He's changing the moon." Popp says. "We have to move."

"Hold on. I'm getting a sonic reading," Linus says. "It's high — like a dog whistle, but it's there. I can hear it a little bit naturally, but my sensor just went nuts." He turns to Ives and Danny. "You guys getting this?"

"Yes sir," the two say simultaneously, frantically removing their helmets. "It's disrupting the audio in our helmets," Danny says as he digs into his ear with his pinky finger, obviously annoyed by the frequency.

Popp walks faster to the nearest elevator. "We have to move!" he shouts.

FIFTEEN

Space and Time

JACO Delores awakens in First City's upper medical lab to Spencer Gant standing over him. The machines surrounding Delores are silent apart from the hissing of nearby oxygen pumps. He can't speak, and can only breathe very slowly. His neck is held in place by a large mechanical brace, and the hissing machines attached assist him in taking full breaths. His upper body is numb and his head feels lighter than air.

"Don't try to talk, it'll only slow the healing," Spencer says softly. "The doctor will come back after the shift gap, and you'll have a few exercises for them to approve you."

Delores points to the tablet attached to Spencer's side. Spencer hands it to him, and Delores opens a text document in order to communicate.

"Approved for what, discharge?" Delores' text reads.

"Yes. Ronan Pierce is dead, and his friend — Sato Song is his name — did some serious damage. From what I hear your voice won't return to normal, but cybernetic surgery can assist you."

"No."

"I'm not sure if you'll have a choice in the matter. And again, I'm sorry. What you did took me very much by surprise."

"Is Sato Song alive?"

"He's comatose, here in the same room," Spencer says. *"Don't lose him."*

"He's not going anywhere. We'll talk to him when you're discharged. Doctor Feiser has begun his plan to swarm the Inquisition's ship from underground. I will update you fully once you're rested."

Sato lies on another medical bed across the room, not comatose, but listening. His anger overwhelms him. His best friend is dead. His muscles in his back ache through his torso and his skin stings all around. He's been shot. He can tell from the context of Spencer's words that it's too dangerous for him to stay under Jaco Delores's watch. He has to find a way out before a doctor comes back to release Delores. His Augmented Reality hack is still functional, so he can still see the vague shapes of the equipment and people in the lab in his central vision. He watches in his lasting peripherals as Spencer sits in the chair beside Delores's bed. He knows they're between shifts now, and he has until the next shift to make a getaway. The clock on the wall tells Sato he has two hours.

He waits one hour for Spencer to doze off in his chair beside Delores's bed. He looks down at his chest to find two bandaged exit wounds — one at his right side and another at his right shoulder. He leans forward and tries to sit up, and discovers a plastic zip-tie fastening his right arm — now his weaker arm — to the crib bar. He is still able to reach his patient record from the foot of his bed, and he learns he was shot twice. Both bullets exited his body without striking any organs. He then looks around at the machines keeping track of his vitals. He knows if he disconnects any of the receptors, the noise would wake the entire room or alert any nurses nearby.

He sees a nearby operating tray, and a cauterizer which must have been used to seal his wounds. He reaches the cauterizer, and uses it to burn through the zip-tie and free his right hand. With both hands free he sits up, and looks over the vitality monitor for a power source. He swivels the machine around and finds the power cord, which is mounted securely to the back. He carefully uses the cauterizer to cut through the power cable, unaware of what alarms it may set off, if any. The monitor goes dark, and nothing happens. The room is still quiet.

Sato slowly lifts himself from the bed, closely watching the sleeping Jaco Delores and Spencer Gant. Wearing nothing but a hospital gown, he tiptoes from the medical lab and into the hallway. The only thing he can think to do is find Kitta, and tell her what happened: that her partner — his best friend — is dead. He knows Ronan sent the open letter to her, at least, before coming to Titan, but did he go public with it? Sato doesn't know. He hasn't even read it, but he has to make sure it makes the news before Jaco Delores or Jameson Feiser can catch up with him.

Sato heads for the closest lab with a computer terminal. There's another medical lab nearby which should have a capable terminal. He scurries down the hall toward the next room, and at the end of the hall a short, round figure turns the corner and faces him. Two large, glowing figures stand behind him.

"You!"

Sato can tell by the old, grumbling and raspy voice that

it's Jameson Feiser. He hurries to the next lab and shuts the door. The lab is empty, and he quickly accesses the computer terminal. He hears yelling from down the hall, but can't make out the words. He opens his own inbox and finds Ronan's open letter has been sent to many addresses — to Sato Song, Ezra Pierce, Kitta Russo, Jaco Delores, Paulo Thiago Russo, and Aire Keng — Ronan's mother. He doesn't have time to read the letter before the door opens to Feiser and his two guards, who promptly apprehend Sato and drag him from the room.

"This isn't going to end the way you want," Feiser says as Sato is choked by his gown, heels dragging through the halls to the closest elevator.

As soon as they stop, Sato attempts to wriggle free of his hospital gown, and fails. One of the guards strikes the back of Sato's head and stuns him. He slumps to the floor, now being held by his left arm. His consciousness wavers and what's left of his vision is blurry and irritating. Feiser and his guards drag him into the elevator and Feiser says, "Jollitium Processing. It's time to tie this loose end."

Sato chuckles, "You've already lost."

"You don't know what you're talking about, boy. You think you know of loss, because of your parents? Your friend?"

Sato remains silent.

Feiser continues, "The only thing I've lost is time, which is no commodity of mine. My life is defined by loss." The elevator descends. "Bryndon Pierce took my life from me when I was your age, and dragged me into the stink of the inner Solar System. The people, their ideals- it's a cesspool, murky and persistent with nepotism. Complacency. I've hated it. I always have. What I plan abandons all emotion, and paves the way for humanity to realize their only true purpose, and the only true mark possible for our species, millions of years from now, when the next troubled race stumbles upon our fossils."

"A *mark*," Sato mocks.

"Yes, boy — a mark. A mark of unity through expansion. Those who resist this common goal will be erased from history, be it through war, or by accident. Those who are lost in the process are heroes. And when the dust is long settled, what will be left behind is a simple vision. *My vision.*"

"And what's that?"

"That we at least tried," Feiser's tone softens. "Harlan Cain thought the Ancients would return. They did not. Bryndon Pierce thought the Ancients fled in fear, but that was because he did not care to understand. He was shortsighted."

"And Melena Horn?" Sato interjects.

"Melena Horn was a placeholder. She was addicted to the Jollitium compound I gave her and was useful to me until it was time for me to assume control of the United Frontier. She made it easy. Now her ex-lover and the dead boy's father think they can stop the inevitable. It's embarrassing."

"You're selfish. A coward." Sato grows angry.

Feiser closes in on Sato as he lies on the floor of the descending elevator. "I'm doing this for all of us," he says.

"You know nothing of loss because you never had anything to begin with," Sato says. "You started with nothing, and Bryndon Pierce gave you everything. I remember when you died. Your magnets changed everything, and everyone was grateful. They celebrated your life and your gift to us.

Was that not enough? Did Bryndon not enable you to achieve that greatness?"

Jameson Feiser takes a deep, shaky breath. "It would have been my gift whether Bryndon enabled it, or anyone else. I suppose you're right when you say he enabled me, but Bryndon only delayed its potential by pausing upstar expansion. It cost him his life."

The elevator stops at the Jollitium Processing floor. Sato finds his feet and the guards pull him along the curving breezeway above the countless, moving crates of Jollitium ore. They enter the Quantum Laboratory, which Sato recognizes immediately.

"Where are you sending me?" Sato asks as Feiser signals the guards to put him inside one of the smaller Quantum Elevators. Feiser ignores Sato and begins programming the elevator.

"Out of the picture," Feiser says after a pause. The countdown begins, and the timer inside the elevator activates, reading zeros. The lights outside the elevator blink yellow. Feiser's guards throw Sato far inside. Feiser lifts a pistol from his guard's holster and aims it at Sato. "But first, I'll return your favor," Feiser says before shooting Sato in the stomach, then sending several bullets into the elevator's computer terminal before shutting the door. The countdown outside the elevator ends, and the light above the door briefly holds red before shutting off. Feiser opens the door to an empty elevator with a broken terminal.

"We're going to finish this," Feiser says into his comm. "Doctor Delores and Mr. Gant, meet me at Disposal."

Sato squirms and moans inside the elevator, breathing

heavily and attempting to slow the bleeding from his abdomen by applying pressure to the wound. The many blood droplets, both small and thick, float in the zero-gravity atmosphere of the chamber. He looks to the wall and sees the clock which would normally count up from the start of the trip, but it shows nothing. He activates his magnetic boots, stands up and limps to the door, and tries to open it, but it's locked. He tries shouting and screaming, banging on the inside of the elevator door, but knows he's trapped.

He sits against the door and lets go of his wound, letting the blood run into the air in front of him. He sighs with relief, knowing Ronan's letter made it to Kitta. That's all that matters. Even better that Ronan was smart enough to send it to so many others. Feiser wasn't wrong about everything, Sato ponders. Few people are wrong about everything, and even fewer may be right about everything. Ezra Pierce wasn't right about everything, and neither was Ronan. Was Ronan the end of the Pierce family? Sato can only wonder. He's been disconnected. *Out of the picture*, as Feiser referred to it. Sent into the Quantum with only his thoughts and predictions, but no regrets. It's not how he ever imagined dying, but at least it's finally quiet. A quiet resting place — a grave suspended in space and time.

Secrets of Sol

KITTA and Sam Levin have found Quinn Peña on the Hangar Level of First City. They follow him hastily through the halls to the closest elevator. Quinn, among many other admins, has been instructed to meet Jaco Delores at the Recreation and Disposal level. The lights of the alarms continue flashing. Quinn has no idea of Kitta's cybernetic capabilities, but Sam is fully aware now. The three of them arrive at the elevator, and Quinn presses the call button.

"What's wrong, friend?" Sam asks Quinn. Sam can sense Quinn's discontent.

"I have a feeling I know what's going to happen," Quinn says. "The experiments downstairs produce waste, like anything else, and the Mayor's plan may involve a way to clean up a mess they've created in the caves beneath the city. Lab rats have been running free down there to catalog how they adapt to the terraformation of the moon. Consequently, they've been exposed to the Jolitium waste, and mutated — ferocious things — and the Ancients' tunnels are all over the place. Even under that giant ship that landed here."

"How long do we have to — " Kitta asks before being interrupted by a notification in her Jym. A sonic disturbance is happening nearby, though barely perceptible to human ears. "I'm sorry," she says. "I think you're right, Quinn. My earpiece just picked it up."

Quinn and Sam both look at her, puzzled.

"Picked what up?" Sam asks.

Kitta admits to Quinn her cybernetic capabilities, but not that she obtained them from Melena Horn. Quinn can't be exposed to so much so soon. He's obviously been through a lot. Sam keeps quiet and doesn't add to what Kitta is comfortable sharing. The three of them stop and wait for an elevator to arrive.

"The ship outside belongs to my father, and I've been something of a spy for Doctor Ezra Pierce, just looking further into what's going on here. It appears Jaco Delores is — " Kitta is interrupted by the elevator door opening to Spencer Gant, alone. She notices a pistol at his side, and he looks nervous.

"Miss Russo! Sam! What are you two — " Spencer can't finish his question. He has too many questions, and can't decide how to begin. He pulls his thick glasses down from his bushy red hair and over his eyes. They share a moment of silence, which confuses Quinn further.

"Jaco Delores is what?" Quinn asks.

Before Kitta can answer, Spencer shouts, "He's injured! He's in the upper medical bay now, and he won't make it to the rendezvous on the recreation level. I've received word from the Mayor that his plan is already underway."

"How was Mister Delores injured?" Quinn asks.

"It's *Doctor* Delores," Spencer objects, "and he was injured by a spy who came in through the lower levels." Spencer glares at Kitta, hoping he hasn't said too much that alludes to Ronan Pierce, but based on her calm he assumes she doesn't know that Ronan and Sato made it to Titan. Spencer left Delores' side only minutes ago to search for Sato, so Kitta has no idea her lover has been killed. Spencer knows of her child, however.

"Was it Ezra Pierce? Have you seen him?" Kitta asks.

Before Spencer can answer, Quinn asks Kitta, "So you know Doctor Pierce?"

Spencer answers Kitta uninterrupted, "I have not seen Doctor Pierce or your father or anyone else from that ship. How are you feeling, by the way, Miss Russo?" Spencer asks. Kitta knows why he's asking, but he doesn't know the child has been suspended, and is still on *Delores-I*.

"Fine," she says as she holds her belly with her hand, attempting to mislead Spencer. Spencer then uses the vitality monitor in his glasses to see that Kitta is no longer carrying a second lifeform, but he says nothing. He correctly assumes that the child is in embryonic suspension, but doesn't know where. He makes room in the elevator for the three to enter with him.

"Has anyone from that ship tried to reach out to you?" Sam asks Spencer as the elevator descends toward the Recreation and Disposal Level.

"We assumed they would attempt to contact us, but they haven't."

"Well, that doesn't surprise me at all," Sam says.

"Excuse me?"

"You guys showed up here and immediately went to the Mayor, and Jack has only followed him around like a dog, taking commands." Sam grows angry, and so does Spencer as he listens. "Pierce has every reason to be suspicious of you,"

Sam continues, "and you've only bolstered it by not attempting to contact the Inquisition upon your arrival."

"Doctor Delores has his own plans. Jameson Feiser is still useful to him, but for how long, I don't know."

"So what's Jack planning now?" Kitta asks.

"Other than what he has already told you?" Spencer queries.

"I mean now that he's *here*. He can't play both sides forever, so what's his endgame?"

Spencer fumes at the audacity of Delores's plans being reduced to *playing both sides*. "His plans go beyond this fight between Pierce's Inquisition and Doctor Feiser," Sam raises his voice and wags his finger. "He very well could've fixed everything Doctor Pierce and your father came here to *fix*, only he would've done it quietly, rather than raise hell and cost lives."

Sam interjects, "And what about the lives you've taken, Spencer? Or at least the losses you've abided by Jack's side."

"Sam," Spencer says as the elevator reaches the recreation and disposal level. The door opens. "Come with me, Sam. Kitta, do what you like." Spencer briefly looks at Quinn but does not address him as he and Sam leave the elevator.

"No way," Kitta says as she holds the elevator door open. Spencer then unholsters his pistol and aims it at her and Quinn.

"This isn't your floor," Spencer growls. He then looks at Quinn. "Go back to the armory. I'll send the other admins to you. Delores's orders."

The elevator door closes, and Spencer and Sam walk the halls toward the disposal room.

"What's going on with you? Are those orders real?" Sam asks.

Spencer holsters his pistol. "Yes, it's real. I've sent the order. I'm next in command while Doctor Delores is in Medical. Whose side are you on anyway? After all we've given you, how generous we've been with our information, you're going to hold it against us in favor of the enemy?"

"Oh, so now *they're* the enemy too?"

"First of all, you're ignoring my question. And yes, they are *an* enemy. Jameson Feiser, Ezra Pierce and Captain Russo — they're all enemies; obstacles, Sam. Right now, I need to know you're with us. With Feiser out of the way, we can calm Pierce and Russo. You have to understand that we can only overcome one obstacle at a time!"

Sam reconsiders their position. As a journalist, if the real story is with Delores and his agenda, then they must commit to it — even if it means playing sides — a hypocrisy that isn't lost on Sam. "Okay, okay," Sam says. "What about Kitta Russo and Ronan Pierce? Ronan has been sabotaging your tech, all the while broadcasting the Inquisition and Kitta's progress. You and I both know the media is torn, if not in the Inquisition's favor."

"The problem with Ronan Pierce nearly took care of itself, but at a cost. I'm looking for his friend, Sato Song, now. He was in Medical with Doctor Delores, but escaped."

"What cost is that? Why was Sato Song in Medical? That must mean Ronan is here too."

"Ronan showed up on the Quantum Elevator downstairs. He and Sato attacked us. Doctor Delores and I were only defending ourselves when they were both shot."

Sam again notices the pistol at Spencer's side, never having seen Spencer carry one. Spencer must be desperate, and if Sato ran rather than help Ronan or attack them both, then what is Spencer hiding? Sam takes no time to wonder before pulling the pistol from Spencer's side.

"You need to start telling me the truth, right now," Sam says.

"Calm down, Sam." Spencer raises his hands and stares helplessly into the barrel of the pistol.

"I can't trust you to tell me what happened. I already know what Jack's agenda is here. No matter how magnificent or *worthy* his plans may be, he'll do terrible things to get there. He's already done terrible things. You're carrying this pistol, looking for Ronan's friend. I can see right through it. Ronan's dead, huh?"

"I've already told you, it was all in self-defense," Spencer lies. "You didn't see the man. He had lost his mind. His friend too. Ronan's earpiece had broken and the blood was pooling inside his head for days, maybe more than a week! He was dead already. Sato Song cannot live."

"You people and your secrets! No more!" Sam angrily strikes Spencer's head with the butt of the pistol, knocking him unconscious.

Whether or not Spencer told the truth about Delores's orders to go to the Armory doesn't matter. Kitta knows now that she's going to need a weapon. She and Quinn redirect the elevator whence it came.

"This is my fault," Quinn says quietly.

"What do you mean? How could any of this be your fault?"

"About two months ago I sent Doctor Pierce a soil sample

from the Greenhouse here. I stole it and sent it illegally. I'm sure that's why he's here. He's a botanist."

"We can't worry about that now, but trust me; none of this is your fault. You did a good thing. You were lied to, and you did the right thing in spite of Doctor Feiser's propaganda. Things will get better here because of you. Because of us."

The elevator doors open, and the Armory and Hangar level is crowded with the same admins from earlier, all headed for the Armory. Some of them recognize Quinn, and mostly ignore Kitta's presence.

"Quinn!" A young admin joins them. His skin is dark, and his hair curly and bouncing just above his shoulders. He seems excited until he reads the sadness in Quinn's expression. "I haven't seen you in a while! Who's your friend?"

"This is Kitta," Quinn says. "Kitta, this is Hassan Khalil- K, for short. K, how have you been, man?"

"I've been okay, just a bit confused lately," Khalil says. "Everything feels like it's been turned upside down. I was in programming, working on the Greenhouse drones just two weeks ago when I was reassigned to the Armory. They had me programming dog-drones for combat until today. Now we're running in circles following that hot programmer that just showed up from Mars — Delores. What about you?"

"Oddly, I feel better now than I did in the lower levels," Quinn says. "They had me working on their Jollitium experiments." Quinn informs Khalil of the Jollitium compounds used to mutate alien creatures, as well as humans, in the lower levels of First City, and their weaponization by UF. He warns Khalil of the potential in the Jollitium waste as well, and the mutation of the rats which also have been weaponized against the *Comrade* and the Inquisition forces. Khalil is perturbed. He is not surprised by the suspicious behavior of the Mayor, whose true identity as Jameson Feiser also comes as no surprise. Kitta listens as her trust in Quinn is strengthened, and her hope in UF is restored by the willingness of the Admins in her age group to listen and adapt to all the new information.

The group of nearly one hundred admins reaches the Armory. The Armory's foyer is large and has few doors stemming from it — one to the hangar, and another to the weapons depot. Another few hundred citizens of First City, not admins, but UF employees nonetheless, have been called to the Armory as well. Two large guards stand at the entrance to the weapons depot and hand a rifle to each person as they pass. Kitta can tell these guards are robots, and does her best to stay clear of them in case they can identify her and flag her. The guards look similar to Delores's guards, but one was a robot, while the other was human, which means these are different. As soon as Quinn obtains a rifle of his own, he hands it to Kitta with a sad look in his eyes, making it clear to her that there's no way he'd be able to use it.

"I programmed them, too," Khalil says, referring to the guards.

"How many of those things are there?" Kitta asks.

"About twenty."

The monitors in the Armory all come to life simultaneously. A silhouette on every screen addresses the room. Jameson Feiser, and to most of the room, the Mayor.

"Titans — the time has come to defend our legacy. Our assets in the underground have begun their assault on the foreign ship. It is my prediction, and all our hope, that this will finally end their interference in our great expansion. Ponder the wonderful things you've seen on this moon. The food and minerals; the health and strength of our people, the likes of which could never be achieved on Earth, are only the beginning of what we can accomplish. The weapons you have been given by my guards are only a final measure. I will do all I can in my power to make sure you don't find their use necessary. Thank you for your sacrifice."

The transmission ends. Khalil and Quinn look at each other and shake their heads in mutual understanding that this isn't their fight. Khalil, knowing what he knows now, has lost what little trust he had in the UF leadership on Titan. Kitta stands firm and struggles to hide her anxiety. She has no idea where Ezra and her father are, and much less is known of her father's ship and its capability to fend off an assault from underground. The two guards at the weapons depot shut and lock the depot, and promptly leave the Armory. The hundreds of people in the armory confer and debate with one another in a roaring commotion. They lack organization and lose their determination when Jameson Feiser's ominous silhouette isn't there to encourage or stimulate them. So much has happened to them in such a short time, and they have every reason to be apprehensive. Kitta senses the unease and anxiety of the people of First City, and sees the opportunity to sow seeds of dissent against Jameson Feiser. Luckily, she already stands with several of First City's young admins, who are well trusted and willing to help. It's time they know the truth.

SEVENTEEN

Home

POPP sits on the bridge of the *Comrade* with Linus Fogarty, and has ordered Houston Ives and Danny Jelani to regroup with the remaining personnel on the ship and lead its defense from the Hangar. The alarms ring in his ears. He hasn't heard them outside of drills in what feels like ages. Have they always been so loud during the drills? It doesn't matter. The mutant rats are flooding the underground levels of the ship, and Linus sits at a nearby terminal, doing his best to program the *Comrade*'s robotic interior defenses in the lower levels. The surveillance footage from below is haunting. Popp's soldiers are being hacked and slivered. The wild horde of rats rushes up the slopes and stairways of the ship, destroying every person, robot and android it confronts. The damage to the horde is little, and Popp watches as the individual camera feeds begin to blend together in the likeness of swarming, ravenous beasts.

Linus programs the doors to shut in the levels above the horde, at the Hangar. The lights flicker on the bridge of the *Comrade*, and Linus looks at Popp with fearful eyes and ghost white skin.

"An EMP?" Popp asks.

"Aye," Linus says. "I cannae tell where it's coming from. First I can think is an EMP may'been eaten by a rat, and they're triggering it from the City."

"How many more of those can we handle before it breaks through the dampener?"

Linus checks the *Comrade*'s EMP defense software. The defense AI catches the frequency of outside EMP charges attempting to shut down the ship, and immediately kills the ship's generators for several milliseconds, thus nullifying the attack.

"Not many," Linus says. "I've begun closing doors ahead of the rats, so —"

"You're what?! What about the people who are still down there?"

"After all the death we've seen, I don't —"

"You don't have to explain, it's alright," Popp says, realizing his ship could very well be lost if they don't block the upper levels. However, enough of the foreign EMP blasts could throw the ship into evacuation protocols and cause every interior door to open. "Get Rasputin online and see what he says."

"Ras, eh?"

"I don't like it either, but these AIs might be our only chance," Popp grumbles. The *Comrade*'s AI system contains several voices — some meant for interior navigation throughout the ship, others meant for administrative purposes such as defenses and piloting. Rasputin, or Ras, is the name of the *Comrade*'s AI voices combined into one personality, and is typically used only for emergency situations.

"Rasputin!" Linus shouts.

A multilayered, artificial voice shines through the speakers on the bridge.

"Captain Russo, Officer Fogarty. How can Lord Ras be of service?"

Popp looks at Linus, confused, "*Lord Ras?* What the hell is that?" He asks.

Linus shrugs, "The AIs are talking to our officers and employees daily. If they started calling him *Lord* Ras, then it likely adapted."

"So annoying. Ras, we're under attack. What's the best course of action when encountering hidden EMP charges?"

"I can see that we are under attack, and multiple foreign heat signatures have flooded the lower levels, and there are more foreign heat signatures outside the ship that have caused sur-face-level exterior damage."

Popp looks at Linus and rolls his eyes. To Popp, these AIs have always been a drag in combat situations. Ras continues.

"Before you summoned me, the employees in the lower levels informed me of quadruped robots. They are said to be disguised as organic, and I have deduced them as the most likely source of the EMP charges."

"Ras, how many more EMP charges can our deterrent handle? What's the best course of action against the threats in the lower levels?" Popp repeats.

"Running diagnosis. To address the androids and their EMP charges, I can change the frequency of our deterrents. Once I've finished shutting down the main computers on the Comrade, it will take several minutes to change the frequency of our backup computers, which will remain active so that I can carry out this task. The only calculated risk is a foreign EMP charge activating during these several minutes, so I can begin immediately after another EMP charge is activated. In the meantime — the extra organic signatures in the lower levels are using more oxygen than the ship can provide, and there is a strong enough

oxygen reading below the surface, so I've shut off the oxygen below and prioritized the upper levels."

"See? This is what I mean," Popp says to Linus, frustrated. "Ras, there are still *Comrade* employees down there, yes?"

"Yes, although casualties are climbing. Those accounted for have been alerted and given emergency power measures in the lower levels, though I'm reading critical damage to electronics and other machinery in the lower levels. Maintenance required."

"Okay, fine," Popp grunts.

Linus interjects, "Ras, what about the central levels? The hangar?"

"Central levels, including the hangar, are fully operational."

"But the defense generators are in the lower levels," Popp says.

"That is correct. While it remains operational during emergency measures, the defense generators below will need to be restarted manually."

"And the frequency change?"

"I can change it once you're ready. Again, the process will take a few minutes, and may compromise the central levels due to the organic threats."

"Ras — what needs to happen first is the young-uns and medical staff from central and upper levels need to be evacuated through the hangar," Linus insists and turns to Popp. "We have the vehicles, and they can blow right past those giants on the surface."

"I will alert those in the central levels, and evacuation will begin immediately." Ras pauses. *"Three."*

"Three what?"

"Three more foreign EMP charges can be activated within the

ship before all computers are rendered useless. After that — "

"Yes, yes. We know what happens," Popp interrupts.

"We have to go down there, sir," Linus says. "Even if we told somebody — Ives, or Danny — they wouldn't have the access levels needed to shut off the defense grid."

Popp sits and ponders. "Ras," he says, "is there a path we can coordinate for the evacuated? Where can they go?"

"I have calculated two options. I can program a path for the vehicles around First City's surface platform, and they can also be programmed to enter the platform upon it being opened, though I am unable to open it from here. The second option is the tunnels. The entirety of the organic threat is now inside the Comrade, *and the tunnels are empty. The vehicles will fit and be temporarily safe from the threats outside."*

"What do you think, sir?"

"I think both," Popp says. "If we have half of the vehicles running their path up top, then it will distract the giants outside while the other half evacuates into First City through the tunnels we used when we landed."

Linus smiles with approval, and stands to find a terminal. "I'll send Ives outside, and Danny into the tunnels," he says.

"Make sure Danny has the gear to cross that gap."

"Of course, of course. Good call, sir."

"Ras, one more thing," Popp says. "Activate our robots. Lower levels too," Popp says as he looks at Linus, who knows the robots on the *Comrade* are only for utilities, and not weaponized. "They can at least distract the rats from everybody else."

Linus nods, and sends the new orders to Ives and Danny. Ras alerts the employees and other evacuees of the new plan, designating their different paths.

Popp and Linus equip their weapons and breathing assistance from the bridge's wall armory and emergency kit, and leave the bridge. The quadruped and humanoid utility robots, as well as employees and medical staff from the upper levels, crowd the sloped hallways as they head downward toward the elevators. Drones float above their heads, and Popp wonders if Ezra's son, Ronan, is still watching them; why wouldn't he help them in such a dire time? They enter the closest elevator and descend toward the hangar level to rendezvous with Ives and Danny.

Ras chimes in on the speakers inside the elevator, *"Captain Russo, Officer Fogarty, if I may —"*

"What is it?"

Suddenly the lights flicker, and the elevator jumps, stopping for half of a second before continuing downward.

"Another EMP charge has just been activated. We can handle two more. I've called you because I can more effectively open the surface platform above First City. I would need to be transferred into one of the utility robots and taken into First City through the tunnels. The computer terminals in the Comrade's *hangar are perfectly capable of making the transfer. I can program a robot to meet you there."*

"Fine, do it," Popp says. "Tell Ives and Danny to meet us there too. But won't the ship need you, Ras? What about activating the EMP?"

"My first priority is protecting the people on the Comrade. *With them evacuated, and the soldiers in action, I will be of better use securing a destination for them. As for the EMP, I have programmed it to trigger automatically once you've shut off the*

defense grid and allowed the frequency to change."

"Okay. Thank you, Ras," Popp says, warming up to the ship's AI and its prioritization of the people.

The elevator stops at the central level. The high ceilings are swarming with drones, all following the robots and armed combatants to the elevators, then to the lower levels. The vast floor of the central level is crowded with the *Comrade's* employees and medical staff. They murmur and gossip as to what's happening both on the surface of Titan and in First City. Brothers and sisters, parents and their offspring say goodbye to one another as they enter the hangar and file into their separately assigned vehicles. Some of them panic as they search for loved ones they can only hope aren't trapped in the *Comrade's* lower levels. Popp and Linus make their way to the hangar's control center and are met by Ives, Danny and a quadruped robot.

"A *dog?* Ras — you sent us one of the dogs?" Popp asks.

"The humanoids are a larger target and are less mobile." Ras says.

Linus manually connects Ras to the closest computer terminal, and the transfer begins. Popp explains to Danny that Ras will follow him into the tunnels as the quadruped, and Ras' mission is to connect to First City's power grid, so the surface platform can be opened for Ives' party of evacuees.

"Lord Ras?" Danny asks. Popp doesn't answer, only nods.

The transfer completes and the quadruped squirms and finds its feet. It paces and looks around the hangar's control room before speaking from the quaduped's built-in speakers in a similar yet less complete voice.

"The transfer was a success. Captain Russo, Officer

Fogarty — the Comrade's *hangar doors will automatically open once you've opened the doors to the lower levels. I recommend we hurry.*"

Linus and Popp salute Ives and Danny and the hangar control room is abandoned. The vehicles within the hangar lie waiting, engines humming. Ives and Danny scurry off to their vehicles while Linus and Popp head for the lower levels.

The elevators are active, but the last thing they want is to find themselves cornered by rats when the elevator doors open. They reach the downward slope into the lower levels, and arrive at an emergency door between them and their descent. Linus fiddles with the controls beside the door, and the door slides apart, allowing them to pass. They hear the hangar doors activate and open behind them, and the many cars filing out of the hangar, and into the ship's airlocks.

Popp can only hope the AI's plan works. If Ras is lost, a new AI will take weeks to assimilate to the hardware of the ship, and months to be fully integrated with the staff and their records. He then shakes his head, disappointed in himself for pondering hypotheticals which may never happen. If Ras is lost before the surface platform is open, then his company could be cut in half by the mutant giants. All he can do now is trust in his assets, be they organic or artificial.

The lights flicker once again. This time, more persistently. Another EMP charge. The ship's power must be waning. The deterrent is supposed to be able to handle one more EMP charge, but the mechanical damage done by the rats and First City's drones may have exacerbated the power grid's integrity.

They pick up the pace in their steps, rifles drawn, and begin to hear the faint sounds of screaming rats, shouting soldiers and bullet ricochets. The power grid isn't far, but Linus barely healed from the last encounter with these rats, and if they're met again he will have no option but to face them head-on instead of running.

The floor levels out, and the walls quickly turn red, beginning in flecks, then in splashes and strokes of blood. The sharp scent of the blood and excrement permeates the air enough for Popp and Linus to equip their breathing assistance — tactical masks secured tightly to their mouths and nostrils. Popp and Linus step around the broken machinery of violently disassembled robots, and the incomplete corpses of half-eaten soldiers and perforated rats. The doorways stagger through the hallway ahead of them. The sounds of battle grow louder and more detailed. Guttural howls of human agony rip through the air past Popp and Linus as they near the door to the defense grid.

As they near the door, the lights vanish, and the halls turn black. Thundering mechanical moans echo throughout the ship as the machinery grinds to a halt. Popp and Linus activate the flashlights on their rifles to see that every door in the hallway has opened. Emergency lights are activated and the halls turn a dim red. Only seconds go by before they hear an uproar of screaming from employees and young trainees who were safe in their rooms, but are now exposed. Popp and Linus are too late, and a third EMP charge has been detonated, activating the emergency protocols onboard the *Comrade* and disabling the main power grid.

Three flashlights from the other end of the corridor dance their way toward Popp and Linus, held by the hands of panting and screaming employees sprinting for their lives. The lights from Popp's and Linus's guns don't shine far enough to see, but they watch as one by one the dancing lights begin to fall to the ground. The shrieking of the fallen combatants does little to drown the sound of flesh tearing and limbs popping away from their joints, and the last flashlight comes close enough for them to see a young man tackled by one of the beasts. The flashlight hits the ground so hard it breaks, and the young man cries for help as his armor is cracked like an eggshell, and his skin is stretched from his back and shoulders by razor teeth. Popp and Linus send scores of bullets into the monstrous rat until it falls dead atop the young man's corpse.

"Power grid is right here! I count two more rats!" Linus shouts.

They fire into the hallway at the two monsters remaining. One goes down with ease, but the other escapes the light and runs past as Popp and Linus reach the door to the defense grid. The rat, now behind them, lunges from the dark. Popp pivots to enter the room, and in one clean motion, the lunging rat removes Popp's right arm. It happens so quickly, Popp shakes and stumbles, taking a moment to register his missing limb. Linus leans from the door to pull Popp into the room. The rat slides in the pooling blood and cannot keep its balance, allowing Linus to begin hot-wiring the door's controls as Popp moans and crawls further into the dark room. Linus hears more rats coming from the dark halls, and abandons the control panel to manually pull the door to the defense grid shut.

"Son of a bitch!" Popp screams.

Popp has lost his weapon as well as his arm. Popp slows

his breathing; he bleeds profusely and attempts to avoid going into shock. Linus stands his own rifle against the wall near Popp, giving them enough light to see. Linus scours the dim room for a medical kit. He returns to Popp with a tourniquet, a cauterizing powder, and pain killers. He pushes the painkillers into Popp's mouth, and Popp swallows them dry. Linus then secures the tourniquet around the stub of Popp's remaining arm at the shoulder. The bleeding slows, allowing Linus to coat the bleeding trunk with the cauterizing powder. Popp groans and clenches his teeth as the salty chemical powder burns and scabs his wound instantly.

"No more bleeding," Linus says, "but your blood has been infected."

The rats can be heard outside rustling, eating and fighting with one another.

"So I'm going to die here anyway," Popp says. "You should've let me bleed out."

Linus turns from Popp, ignoring his cynicism, and searches the room for the emergency arms station. There he finds a pistol and several grenades — some lethal, and some stunning. He gathers the grenades, and waits for Popp to stand before handing him the pistol.

"I won't let you go down with this ship. The medical bays here are lost, but we can take the tunnels back into First City and cure your infection, as you did for me."

"We've failed, Linus. Our home is gone."

"We've done no such thing," Linus retorts. "The *Comrade* has not been lost, and we will return to it. The people of your company, of this ship, are still alive and need our help. They are our home. First City is still a dark mystery to us, but it's there, and Jameson Feiser still has to be stopped. We fail when we've failed our people and allow them to fall into Feiser's hands. I have stun grenades for the rats, and you can still walk. We're getting out of here."

EIGHTEEN

Old Age

An Open Letter by Ronan Pierce

TO the people of Sol, I offer this letter as an act of service. All I've known to do is serve, and I have served within the United Frontier for most of my life — a life defined by those before me. My grandfather, Bryndon Pierce, was Ambassador of our system, then of Titan, and this letter is my dedication to him, perhaps my final dedication, and I fear it comes as an admonition to the people of Sol more than anything else. My father, Ezra Pierce, gave me everything he could and enabled me to be successful as a programmer and technology specialist in Arcadia on Mars. However, by the time this letter is received, I fear I will be dead, and therefore it will be my right of passage. Too much has gone unanswered, and I hope to answer all of it now.

I begin with Jameson Feiser. He was Ambassador of Sol before my childhood, and was a hero to me in those times. He was the pioneer of the Jollitium magnet, and his discovery revolutionized commerce, machinery, weaponry, and travel throughout all of Sol. He was born of suspension, like many are, but in his case, he was born to no one. On the smoldering island moon of Io, in Jupiter's Jovian system, he was the only human asset assigned to a mining operation spearheaded by Ambassador Harlan Cain. It was in Jupiter's soft mantle he obtained the Jollitium magnets, and being a child, he decided to keep it a secret, *for he had no idea of its true power, until he was enabled by new UF leadership. It was far from the end of his story.*

Harlan Cain died a madman, consumed by his dream of discovery and having felt he failed in a way no person could ever have succeeded. His story, as well as Jameson Feiser's, has taught me things I could not have learned from my grandfather Bryndon.

Bryndon Pierce found Harlan Cain's expansive operations to be barbaric, and freed Jameson Feiser from his assignment on Io. Jameson Feiser would go on to start his own company, the famous FeiserCorp, and climb the ranks within UF while simultaneously changing the way humans lived and operated within Sol. My grandfather was Ambassador at this time, and his conservative agenda halted upstar expansion, focusing on prosperity within the Sol which had already been colonized. He was responsible for the synthetic soil initiative which not only saved the lives of those on Mars at the time, but allowed for others to migrate there from Earth, when the rapidly growing population gave way to shortages.

Bryndon then traveled to Titan with UF, FeiserCorp, The Lordes Company, and other privateers looking to claim land and prepare for an expedited colonization. One of these privateers was Melena Horn of E-Con, who rather than claiming land with the objective of contracting it, pioneered the communication infrastructure used on Titan to this day. It was during their trip to Titan that she fell in love with the captain of a UF-sanctioned orbital security company and Bryndon's best friend, Paulo Thiago Russo. Their time together ended abruptly, and they were stripped apart when Bryndon Pierce died tragically in a mining incident.

Bryndon's death had not happened, however, before Melena became pregnant with Captain Russo's child. Captain Russo was disgraced due to the orbital security's negligence in the matter of Bryndon's death, and Captain Russo traveled back to Earth with his most loyal employees. Their child grew for ten weeks before Melena placed it in embryonic suspension and sent it back to Earth with Captain Russo. Melena Horn was loved by all who knew her, and it was enough to get her elected as Titan's Ambassador when Bryndon passed.

The election was expedited after Bryndon's death, and Melena Horn was chosen by the electorate as Titan's next Ambassador. At this time, FeiserCorp had secretly taken its Jollitium experiments to the realm of pharmaceuticals. It saved Melena Horn's life when she became sick. The Jollitium medicine was in its early stages of development, and Ambassador Horn grew addicted. UF found out about Melena Horn's abuse of the Jollitium medicine she was given by Jameson Feiser, but she did not implicate him. She was quietly relieved of her position, and became the Ambassador of Mars.

Jameson Feiser was left unchallenged and his experiments unfettered when he became Titan's new Ambassador. The new Jollitium compound enhanced metabolism, accelerated growth, and allowed the human genome to be changed in ways never thought possible. The experiments on Titan gave him human subjects growing and mutating to heights of three meters with exponential strength and constitution. The experiments were far from perfect, however, and the giants produced by FeiserCorp would commonly suffer from rapid growths of cancer in the brain, causing pain and madness. They were weaponized and inhumanely utilized by FeiserCorp and Jameson Feiser's new UF.

Meanwhile, Melena Horn was acting Ambassador on Mars, working with her unknowing daughter as a Governance trainee. Kitta Russo had her father's name, and traveled to Mars to work as a teacher of children in Arcadia. Melena Horn watched over her, and enabled her to realize her potential as a leader within UF. It was on Mars where I met Kitta, and it wasn't long before we fell in love. I am forever in service to her, and I fear this letter may be the last she hears from me.

At the time of her death, Ambassador Horn spoke to Kitta and me personally within Arcadia's council chamber. She told us of the dangers posed by Jameson Feiser, who had faked his death when his secret experiments became an overwhelming priority. She told us of my father, Ezra Pierce, and his plan to stage a coup on Titan after discovering what the refined Jollitium could do to soil and its enhancement of plants and vegetation. Ambassador Horn's final orders were for Kitta to go to Titan, and not only help my father, but help UF avoid humiliation and dishonor.

With Ezra Pierce came Captain Russo and his orbital security company from Earth, and Doctor Jaco Delores followed. Ezra spoke with Delores briefly before their launch, and Delores promised his rendezvous on Titan, but never swore his allegiance to Ezra's cause. Jaco Delores's ideas were much larger, and his fealty was already bought by Jameson Feiser.

Jaco Delores plans to do something with the Jollitium compound that Jameson Feiser could not do, or refused to do — a vaccine to extend human life and enhance human metabolism. An all-encompassing, physical improvement without the mutations that Jameson Feiser had weaponized. Jaco Delores's satellite station in Saturn's inner orbit will undoubtedly bring the Jollitium right to our doorstep on Titan, whether he is friend or foe, and whether or not the end justifies his means. After all of our advancements in science over nearly a century, the Jollitium will be the true bringer of old age.

To Kitta—I'm sorry. In such a short time, we've shared so much, and I've been luckier than I can imagine anybody being to have you by my side. Your mother sent us to restore the United Frontier, and it now falls to you, whatever you choose to do. It was always meant for you, and I've been happy to be by your side. If I never see you again, don't think of it as the end of us. Think of it as the beginning of something bigger than both of us; something that we created together. I love you. I always will.

"You worm," Jameson Feiser says to Jaco Delores as he enters First City's upper medical lab. All the beds are empty.

Delores is getting dressed. He speaks in a raspy, damaged voice assisted by a voice box within the mechanical brace around his neck.

"Excuse me? What is it?"

"You mustn't have checked your inbox recently. Look at this," Feiser says as he hands Delores his tablet with Ronan Pierce's open letter, published by a red-level news outlet. Delores reads the letter; an exposure of his secrets, and a wedge between him and Jameson Feiser. Delores would like nothing more than to drive a laser light into Feiser's chest, as he did Ronan's, but their business is not finished. The unfortunate programmer played his final hand, but it may prove useful to Delores in the long run.

"It's a lie," Delores says. "He's trying to pit us against each other."

"*You* lie!" Feiser roars, his voice thundering in a way Delores has never heard. "You expect me to believe you over a dead man with nothing left to lose? One who rummaged through both our companies' private data? I should kill you where you stand." Feiser grabs Delores's neck brace and digs two fingers into the tight space between the brace and his healing neck.

"You wouldn't," Delores whimpers. "You need me."

Feiser throws Delores to the floor. The old man is stronger than Delores thought. He gasps and writhes on the floor, breathing heavily, but quickly finds his feet. The pain in his neck and upper chest is harrowing, and stalls his speech.

Feiser looks upon him with a smirk, and leans in to say, "Your usefulness to me hasn't run out yet. Once I meet with Ezra Pierce, I'm going to put an end to this myself, because you couldn't. What you think is yours, 'Jack,' is mine. Simple as that." Feiser storms from the room, leaving Delores to ponder his retribution. Feiser is now an enemy, and Ronan's letter will help with the funding from which Delores previously relied on FeiserCorp.

A few minutes pass before Spencer Gant stumbles into the room. His forehead is bruised and bleeding. "Sir! I'm sorry. It's Sam. We can't trust them."

"What happened to you?"

Spencer stammers, taken aback by the haunting sound of Delores' half whispering, half mechanical voice. It comes from both his mouth and torso, fitting for his general assertion, though Delores may not see the power in it yet.

"Sam struck me with your pistol," Spencer says. "I was out for ten minutes or so." Spencer notices Delores discomfortably adjusting his mechanical neck brace.

Delores continues to ponder the advantage Ronan's letter has given him. He feels gratitude toward the man — a man of the same age — whom he cut down. He wrote wisely, and made a fool of Jameson Feiser. The murderous guilt stirs, but Delores knows Ronan Pierce would not have survived the injury to his cybernetics. He had been lost already, and from the sound of his letter, he knew it as well. Delores then notices the empty medical bed where Sato Song lay, and wonders just how much more violence lies ahead.

"How are you doing? Surgery go alright?" Spencer asks after a pause.

"I'm fine. Did you see Ronan Pierce's letter?"

"I skimmed it until I saw your name. I read enough." Spencer knows better than to attempt prying into Delores's emotions. "Have you seen Kitta?"

"Not since the tactical briefing."

"I saw her running around with Sam and another First City scientist. I got a vitality reading. One lifeform."

"What are you saying?" Delores asks. "Suspension?"

"That's my guess. I thought she may have suspended the child on *Delores-I*, but I've spoken to Doctor Archer and she said nothing of it. It could have happened here."

"I need you to go back to the ship. Find Doctor Archer and confirm for yourself, and I'll check here. If it is with Archer, tell her to give it the same Jollitium vaccine compound my daughter's been getting."

"Your daughter?"

Delores sighs, because so much of him has already been exposed. He's never felt a greater trust in Spencer than in this moment. "I felt the most ethical way to put my vaccine to the truest of tests was to use a lab-grown subject with my own personal DNA signature," he says. "I'm certain it's going to work. She'll live over two centuries."

"You mean a clone?" Spencer asks timidly.

"You make it sound barbaric, but yes. She's a clone. Now get moving."

NINETEEN

Constellations

SERIOUSLY? How did you find that out? You must have some serious connections," Hassan Khalil says to Sam. Sam found Khalil and Quinn Peña in the hangar, and overheard them talking to others about Kitta. According to the young Admins and Officers of First City, she gave an enthralling speech before promising to end this fight without having to involve them. Now Sam, Quinn and Khalil sit in a boat, the lonely three, puttering southward across the hazy northwest reach of the methane lake Kraken Mare, just west of First City. Sam intercepted information regarding First City's mutinous mining vessels, UFS *Caelum* and *Pyxis*, and their rendezvous with The Lordes Company on Ceres. The vessels have reportedly returned to Titan, led by Patricia Lordes herself. The report included their landing coordinates on Titan, across the calm and thick Kraken Mare with First City as their destination.

"We're seeking an audience with The Lordes Company. To protect Kitta," Sam says.

"Well, we spent plenty of time talking to our friends and coworkers in First City, and they don't like what the Mayor — sorry, *Feiser* — has been doing," Quinn says, "and we have a few friends on *Caelum* and *Pyxis*." Khalil nods his head in agreement as Quinn rants. "It feels wrong; all of it. We're experiencing food shortages now, which we were assured wasn't possible! Nobody is explaining anything!"

"Hey, keep it down," Sam says as the mist begins to clear. The far shore of the lake is heavily occupied by persons clad in a mixture of armor styles. Some are dressed in the United Frontier-issued combat mesh, while some are dressed in privateer armor, clad with grenades, individual medical supplies and ornate armor plating. Behind them in the distance sit both UFS *Caelum* and UFS *Pyxis*, plus a third, unidentified carrier vessel adjacent to them, presumably owned by Patricia Lordes. The soldiers stand alert as they begin to notice the three strangers floating inbound. Sam signals them with wide arms and open hands.

"UFS *Pyxis* and *Caelum* — we request an audience with Patricia Lordes," Sam says on the open comms channel to the people at the shore. "There's information you deserve to know."

As they arrive at the shore, the three step onto the white, muddy ground. They find themselves surrounded by curious folk, some who are more clearly miners dressed in combat attire as they struggle to adjust, itching and squirming within their suits. Groups of three carry small boats and oars over their heads and prepare them at the shore.

An old man commands and directs other suited workers on a closed comms channel, unheard by Sam, Quinn and Khalil. As the old man nears, Quinn and Khalil recognize him as General Duval Kamasi, commander of UFS *Pyxis*. Kamasi notices the three newcomers and orders the armored onlookers back to work.

"Why are you here? I recognize you two," the rough, tan-skinned old man peers at Quinn and Khalil. He speaks with a deep, commanding voice. "But not you," the Major says, looking to Sam for a response.

"My name is Sam Levin, and I'm here with information for Patricia Lordes." Sam says, their makeup well-faded and unkempt at this point.

"She's busy," Major Kamasi says conclusively. "Whatever you tell me, I can relay to her. But this better be good."

Sam's knuckles turn white. Their hands begin to sweat within their suit. "I've brought these two distressed scientists with me from First City to help my case. Kitta Russo, the daughter of Paul Russo and late Ambassador Melena Horn, arrived in First City with Ezra Pierce, son of Bryndon Pierce. If you've read the open letter distributed by Ezra's son, Ronan Pierce, then you should know he is dead, murdered by those who work for Jameson Feiser." Sam refrains from using Jaco Delores's name.

"You should go back. I've heard enough."

"Major Kamasi, please do not take what I'm saying lightly. The people who remained in First City when *Caelum* and *Pyxis* left Titan — "

"I said I've heard enough! You two — you're staying with us," Major Kamasi shouts at Quinn and Khalil. He then glares at Sam. "I have to know we can trust you lot, and if all of this is true, then we share an enemy. Now go."

Sam nods to Major Kamasi, and bids Quinn and Khalil farewell before departing across the methane lake they came from.

Sam and Quinn spend the next few hours specifically assisting The Lordes Company's pirate soldiers, hoisting the freshly printed rowboats to the shore of Kraken Mare.

Quinn and Khalil are separated while they work, but respectively they each recognize certain people from First City, who denied Jameson Feiser's proposal to stay and fight. Despite their placement among The Lordes Company soldiers, Quinn and Khalil share stories of both Kitta Russo and the siege laid upon First City with the miners of UFS *Pixis* and *Caelum*. The tales of the mutated giants shock the mutineers of First City who have been ignorant of Feiser's Jollitium experiments.

They listen to the members of *Pyxis* and *Caelum* tell their stories of Ceres and the Pirate Queen Patricia Lordes: the brutal training which the pirate soldiers endure on Ceres, and the bleakness of the moon itself.

Word of Kitta Russo and her connection to the late Melena Horn as well as the family of Bryndon Pierce spreads quickly throughout the crews.

Quinn and Khalil meet again hours later when the rowboats are ready to shove off. They confirm with each other that neither has seen or heard from Patricia Lordes. They share a rowboat with General Duval Kamasi.

The constellations of rowboats slide across the northwest arm of the methane lake, and the crews of miners-turned-soldiers whisper and murmur to one another as they pass through the mist.

"You boys don't remember much of Melena Horn, or Bryndon Pierce, but they brought me here," Kamasi reminisces, "General Ren Tilson and I were as young as you back then, and they cared for us," he sighs. "We didn't know what to do when Bryndon Pierce's death was announced. It was like losing a father. He was a friend to all of us, and we felt lucky that Melena Horn took the reins." Kamasi laments at the memory of Bryndon's Pierce's sudden death. It becomes obvious to Quinn and Khalil that General Kamasi is mentally distressed reliving these memories. "… Back when UF had a heart. Melena Horn left a void in her wake. It wasn't long after she left that Feiser took over, and not long after that he manifested his phony death. The UF that loved left this place. I've never said the words out loud, and it hurts, boys. UF kills here. Boys like you. They've been turned into instruments of war."

Kamasi continues telling what little he knows of Feiser's experiments, and Khalil listens, heartbroken, while Quinn quietly censures himself. He knows well, more — and too much. Quinn had been involved in Feiser's genetic trials; witnessed the cancerous side effects take the subjects' minds and sent the enormous, uneducated, muscle-bound humans — some of them no older than ten years — to painful deaths. Quinn had only followed orders, but nonetheless abided, as an instrument himself, the deformation and dishonor of those who could have been his kin, but were instead domesticated like lab rats.

The ragtag armada of pirates and mutineers is nearly silent as they coast along the lake. It becomes obvious to Quinn that a nearby boat, full of Patricia Lordes' pirate soldiers, has been eavesdropping on their conversation. They must have found the channel that Kamasi, Quinn and Khalil have been using to communicate.

One of the female pirates speaks with a surly and flamboyant tone. "That's why we're here," the young pirate responds to General Kamasi, but is not looking at him directly — instead peering at Quinn and Khalil, who are weaker and less threatening than Kamasi. She then turns to several other surrounding boats and signals the comms channel which the other pirates can use to hear her. "We've been raiding the Mayor's United Frontier ships for years, and now we've hit the source! How's our new home look to you, friends?" The young pirate declares to her fellows sitting in the same boat. Several others cheer in response, and other boats who have tuned in to their comms channel cheer as well. "All the Jollitium we need to make more weapons, faster ships. It'll be a dream. These elitist pricks living here won't know what hit 'em now that their battle is fought, and what little warriors they may have left are licking their wounds."

"Quiet, scum," Kamasi grunts. "You look like you're awfully young, and probably just as naive. Let me guess — this is your first time off that little gray rock you call home? And what, you feel you've traded it for a better one?

"Let me be clear. This is not your new home. You don't want to live here. If the United Frontier inside the Belt found out Titan was overrun by the likes of you, it would be hell. They would sooner turn First City to dust and rebuild from scratch. *The Jollitium*," Kamasi scoffs. "You lot wouldn't even know what to do with it when you got it. And before you knew it, UF would be right on top of you in the form of a diplomat, but more likely a missile. Just one is all it would take."

The young pirate stays quiet until an elder female pirate chimes in. "Patricia Lordes will lay claim to this place. We do not fear UF," she says to the applause of other nearby pirates. UF has hurt you, I can see it in your eyes, old man. Try considering a better future for yourself. For your workers, your blood, if it will carry on. One not with a name you feel notalgia for, but with a name that can be feared. The Lordes Company strikes fear into the hearts of UF's commercial travelers, and rightfully so. They pray to UF to come save them," she says sarcastically while gesturing folded, praying hands and moaning her insincere parody of The Lordes Company's victims. "But the only thing they know after that is The Lordes Company."

"Shore!" A voice shouts from ahead on the open channel, turning every head in the flotilla.

Quinn and Khalil are disconcerted — embarrassed, even. The chill in their spines after hearing the pirates' incentives lingers, but still they feel safe, for it seems General Kamasi can be trusted, and the UF miners outnumber the Ceres Pirates. Quinn and Khalil silently lock eyes, mutually understanding their greatest priority — gaining support for Kitta Pierce as a potential leader for the United Frontier's future on Titan.

Kamasi stands in the rowboat and uses hand signals to further direct the boats around him into formation. From what Quinn and Khalil can see through the now thinning mist, they're near the center of the tens of boats. At the front of the group, they see the silhouette of Patricia Lordes standing in her own boat. The tiny reflections from her extravagant armor sparkle by the falling sun. She's surrounded by boats of people wearing similar armor — her own soldiers at the lead. Kamasi commands his UF miners in the center. Behind them, Major Ren Tilson directs boats of miners into formation in the same manner as Kamasi.

As the boats reach the muddy shore, Lordes' soldiers use

their multi-tools' lasers to cut holes in the bottom of each boat, then push them back into the lake to sink. One boat is instead dragged upon the dirt and flipped. Patricia Lordes climbs upon the overturned boat to address her horde of pirate soldiers, as well as the well-organized formations of UF miners behind them. The pirates laugh and cheer as Patricia mounts the boat, chanting "Lordes! Lordes!" and "Speech!" The UF miners remain silent. The pirate chants fade as Patricia Lordes raises her hands.

"No speech until victory, you animals." Patricia's voice is smooth, but it is loud within the helmets of the miners and soldiers. "My husband Andrew was on his way to Ambassadorship, but Jameson Feiser took it from both of us. My husband went mad and took his own life in shame. We are here to shut down United Frontier's operations on this moon and lay claim to Sol outside the Belt. We will march to the Great Door of First City and pry it open. We move forward!"

The decorated horde of pirates marches away from Kraken Mare, followed by the silent formation of UF miners. Quinn and Khalil look at each other with unease, but march near General Kamasi nonetheless. Kamasi looks at Quinn and Khalil and says, "Boys, on our way to First City, there's a secret passage alongside the Greenhouse plateau. Patricia Lordes and her pirates will surely find the Greenhouse entrance, so splitting from the group should put you ahead of us. Take the Greenhouse entrance inside. I'll try to stall this attack as long as I can."

TWENTY

Lord and Knight

TENS of vehicles carrying the youngest of the *Comrade*'s employees have left the hangar and entered the sub-surface tunnels, while a near equal number of vehicles carrying soldiers and adult employees circle First City's great surface platform. Danny operates the vehicle at the head of the group underground, and only the quadruped drone Ras shares the vehicle with him. The chasm has been traversed safely and now the vehicles move calmly through the quiet, ambient tunnels circumfluent with floating ice droplets.

The cars reach the main junction in the decrepit lower levels of First City.

Danny says to Ras, "You're sure the rats won't come back?"

"I'm confident the organic threat has left this place. Though inaudible to you and the other humans, there seems to be a high-frequency deterrent still active nearby. It's weakening now, but I'm sure it is what drove the rats into the Comrade *just hours ago. I've instructed the car at the rear of the convoy to set up a barrier as well."*

The young *Comrade* citizens and employees leave their vehicles and regroup in the junction littered with frosted bones and brown, crystallized blood. Some of them marvel at the outdated UF machinery and signage in the corners and along the walls. Danny opens the comms channel and speaks directly into their suits.

"Attention, Comrades. This is Daniel Jelani of Bone Squad. Many of you may realize by now that our beloved home has been compromised. Though it can be recovered, it will take time. Captain Russo and Officer Fogarty instructed me to bring you down here, and into First City, which is just above us. Lord Ras is with us, and his mission is to access First City's power grid and open the surface platform, so that the other vehicles and the rest of the survivors can find safe haven."

The young employees of the *Comrade* pet and coddle the quadruped robot carrying their beloved AI, whom they thought had been lost with the *Comrade*.

Danny continues, "I have been to this place once already, and though terrifying, I assure you, it is the safest place for us now. The floor above us has medical bays, and food dispensers for those in dire need. Do not be alarmed by what you may see up there, for this is a necessary step, and I applaud you and your calm and organization through all of this. Ras and I will be the first up the ladder, and those who feel they need medical attention or food rations should follow first with an able companion. The rest of you I encourage to remain here until I give the order to follow."

The people murmur amongst themselves through their individual proximity channels, but nobody argues Danny's plan. Some of the wounded and bandaged begin to follow Danny and Ras up the ladder and into First City's lower medical level. Those who are unable to climb the ladder are hoisted on shoulders and sometimes strapped to the backs of those with the strength to carry them. One by one they enter the lower medical level, and Lord Ras indicates to them the sources of food and medical supplies. Once the crowd settles, Danny finds the elevator and Ras follows.

"Hangar and Armory level," Lord Ras says.

"Can you get in touch with Officer Anand?"

"I've attempted to, but he hasn't responded. I do know that he is alive, but I would have to see him in close proximity to precisely read his condition."

Before the elevator reaches the Hangar, it stops at the Greenhouse level. Danny readies his rifle and stands firm. The door opens to Sam Levin wearing a dusty and muddied UF space suit with no helmet and a pistol on their side.

"This car's full," Danny says.

Sam analyzes Danny. He wears the distinguished pale-red armor of Popp's soldiers, and is followed by a peculiarly-behaving quadruped drone. Sam thinks quickly and knows only one thing to do.

"You have to help me," Sam says. "Are you with the Inquisition?"

"I suppose I am," Danny says. "Give me that pistol and get in."

Sam shakily hands Danny the pistol before entering the elevator. The door closes and they continue to rise toward the Hangar level.

"What are you doing here? And who's the dog?" Sam asks, acknowledging the strange nature of the drone's movements.

"I'll be asking the questions," Danny responds. "Who are you and where did you *just* come from?"

"Sam Levin is my name. I'm a journalist from Earth."

Ras interrupts, catching Sam by surprise. *"Sam arrived here on* Delores-I.*"*

Danny backs away from Sam and raises his weapon once more in their direction, prompting Sam to explain.

"I promise you," Sam says, raising frightened hands. "I have no allegiance to Jaco Delores or First City. I've spent the past few hours traveling to Kraken Mare where the Pirate Queen of Ceres, Patricia Lordes, has assembled an army that includes UF mutineers from First City. Combined, it's a greater force than any remaining here in First City. I know the mutineers are from First City, but the pirates from Ceres can't be trusted." Sam then looks at Ras with staunch curiosity.

"What's your mission? This is not a normal dog," Sam says.

"Ras here is going to open the surface platform so the people of the *Comrade* can find safe haven."

Sam doesn't immediately understand the nature of the quadruped drone, but asks, "The giant ship? Russo's ship? What happened?"

Danny shakes and hangs his head, disappointed, but curious as to how Sam knows Popp's name. Danny's silence is enough for Sam to understand his melancholy and change the subject.

"Well, I'm happy to help you however I can. I know enough about this place, and I'll do whatever I can to help Kitta Russo."

"Russo? Who's Kitta?" Danny piques his interest. Sam explains Kitta's covert involvement in Ezra Pierce's Inquisition and how they met Kitta on Delores's ship.

"It's also been made public that she's the daughter of Captain Russo and the late Melena Horn," Sam says.

"Lord Ras, you know anything about this?" Danny asks.

"I know very little of Captain Russo's social or personal life

outside the Comrade.*"* Ras responds. *"We're here,"* Ras says as the elevator door opens to the Hangar.

The circular surface platform is above them, and the hangar is a complex and multi-layered system of airlock chambers designed to allow many different types of vehicles. The layers are transparent, and the many ramps along the circumference allow for surface vehicles to safely enter. Large landing pads in the center are spacious enough for several carrier ships to dock.

The Hangar's control room is just ahead of them, and entirely visible from the outside. Danny can see there are no personnel, no android operators — only an empty control room. He turns to Sam before they reach the room and says, "Your mission is to protect Russo's daughter. That makes us allies." Danny hands the pistol back to Sam. "Go find her. I'll be fine here."

"Okay. Thank you. Good luck." Sam runs back to the elevator, pistol in hand.

Danny and Ras enter the control room, and Ras runs to the nearest terminal. Ras inserts a hard connection to the terminal, and begins opening the surface platform. Flashing lights dance to the sound of great warning sounds indicating the platform's opening sequence. The gears turn and the hydraulics press, tucking the platform sections into the walls and out of sight, leaving a giant hole in the surface of the moon, and allowing access to the *Comrade*'s refugees. The network of airlocks above Danny and Ras begin to fill with the *Comrade*'s surface vehicles.

"I've signaled those in the lower levels that the platform has been opened. I've also signaled Captain Russo and Officers

Anand and Fogarty the same." Ras says to Danny.

"Have you sent a command?"

"I'm waiting for your order. As of right now, while I cannot communicate with the Captain or his officers, you're in command."

"Send them to the —"

"I'm sorry to interrupt. I have just intercepted a message to Captain Russo. One word, reading 'Greenhouse.' It was sent to multiple people, but I'm unaware who else has received it or who sent it."

The elevator door opens and four UF guards sprint into the Hangar with rifles ready. Simultaneously, the *Comrade's* vehicles have left the airlocks to the floor of the Hangar and Popp's soldiers and workers begin to file out. The First City guards see Danny in the control room and run toward him. Danny readies his rifle and takes cover next to the door. He tells Ras to hide and wait for help from the soldiers and employees leaving the airlocks. Danny opens the door and opens fire on the guards. One guard is shot in the shoulder, hits the ground, and is dragged into cover by a fellow guard. All four guards are in cover and exchange fire with Danny. Danny hopes his fellow *Comrade* soldiers — though few — will hear the gunplay and assist him, but he's pinned down, and the guards draw near, taking cover behind various pallets of supplies and barrels of fuel. Danny sends a few more rounds blindly in the guards' direction. One of his bullets hits a barrel of fuel causing a loud, bright explosion.

Danny can't tell how many guards remain, and his ears ring from the explosion. He reaches for another clip to reload his rifle, and his side feels wet. The adrenaline masks the pain, but it's clear to Danny he's been wounded. Whether by a bullet or piece of shrapnel, he can't tell, but he's bleeding fast.

Danny listens, hearing possibly two guards approach the door, when a rain of bullets falls upon the guards. Bullets ricochet from the floor as the guards flail and fall dead near the entrance to the control room.

Danny hears his fellow Goons cheering and hollering as they dismount their vehicles and flood the Hangar's staging area. Danny's vision begins to blur and his hearing wavers. He hears Ras as the pitter-patter of the quadruped drone nears him.

"I've signaled for medical, Daniel. You're wounded."

"I'm dying, Lord Ras, but we did it."

"Yes, Daniel. We did it. The people of the Comrade *are safe."*

Sam sprints through the halls of First City. The halls are now peppered with the citizens of First City disobeying the stay-at-home order of their Mayor. Some of them are starving, seeking nourishment in a time of abandonment. Some are simply curious due to the commotion of the alarms and the opening of the surface platform. They mutter amongst themselves, asking questions. Sam receives an anonymous message: *Greenhouse.*

Sam remembers First City's admins, who could still be waiting in the Armory nearby. Sprinting past the elevator and toward the Armory, it doesn't take long for Sam to hear the commotion from the armed admins. They speak amongst themselves of the terrible things they've been forced to do, and some of them still wonder if it wasn't for a greater good, as Feiser's propaganda has taught them. Sam hears Kitta's name spoken several times among them upon entering the room.

Quinn bursts from the crowd and says, "Sam! What should we do? We're restless here. The Mayor hasn't told us anything, and the guards have been re-tasked since we heard the platform ringing open."

"Quinn? How did you get back? What about the Pirate Queen?"

"General Kamasi sent us on a shortcut. He's afraid of what Patricia Lordes might do when they get here."

"Everybody needs to go to the Greenhouse. Right now!" Sam yells so the whole group of admins can hear. Sam spares no time and sprints around the corner to call an elevator. Sam presses the call button, and the elevator immediately opens to Kitta. She's in tears. Sam enters the elevator and embraces her. "I'm sorry," Sam says.

"It's not your fault," she responds, bubbling. The elevator continues ascending.

"This is all happening so fast. Since Melena sent me to help — to help Ronan's father — I knew it would be a mess, but not like this. My son is still on Delores's ship, and I'm scared."

"I know you can trust Diana," Sam says. "Would you like to go check on it?"

"I can't be sure of anything anymore. I have to act *here*, and I have to act quickly. I forwarded that message to you, Doctor Pierce, and my father. It was sent to me anonymously, but I think it's Jameson Feiser. I have to speak with both of them. It's been too long." Kitta wipes her tears and looks at

Sam. "Thank you, Sam, for being there for me. You're the only person I can trust — not Doctor Pierce, or my father. I keep getting the feeling they represent what Melena Horn sent me here to fix. She knew they couldn't, or wouldn't; that they would fail somehow. I had no idea the measure of death here. The humane spirit of UF has been tarnished by these elders and their greed. I have to realize my purpose here — to bring about a time in which my son can thrive."

"It'll be a time in which we can all thrive, Kitta. What Ronan wrote was for all of Sol to see — and they've definitely seen it. When the time comes, the people will choose a new leader. And whether or not you're ready, it will be you."

Kitta embraces Sam once again. The tears wet Sam's shoulder. "Ronan. I don't think I'll ever see him again. Did you read his letter? I'm not ready. I'm more lost than I've ever been."

Sam holds her, and breathes slowly, attempting to calm her. Sam decides, for now, to omit Delores's part in Ronan's death. Kitta has been through much, and already has too many enemies more urgently in front of her.

"I did read the letter," Sam says. "He did the right thing, and he did it for you. I just ran into one of your father's soldiers. All dressed up in that red armor, the guy had a dog-drone with him. It spoke to me like a human."

"What were they doing?"

"Opening the big door up top."

Sam realizes as the words leave their mouth that opening First City's surface platform would allow Patricia Lordes' pirate horde and the UF mutineers she's leading to access the city unchallenged.

"There's something you should know," Sam says. "Patricia

Lordes came from Ceres, almost right behind us, and has an armada marching on the city right now. I really don't want to overwhelm you with this, but I would recommend you get to that Greenhouse as fast as you can. And I don't want to leave you right now, but I think I have to go back to that Hangar and make sure that platform is closed."

"Go ahead. I'll be fine. Thank you again." Kitta embraces Sam one more time before they both scurry off in different directions.

"Be careful!"

TWENTY ONE

Rendezvous Pt. 1

KITTA has found a quiet place in a nearby utility closet to weep. Ronan's letter crushes her. If what he's written is entirely true, as Kitta believes it is, then it makes sense. Melena's training, her patience, and her love were all preparing Kitta for when she would realize herself and choose to lead. If what he's written is as conclusive as it sounds, then the personal loss — both of mother and lover — is great, and now all of Sol will know. The exposure makes her feel lonelier than she's ever felt, but never more ready. Kitta has sent multiple messages to Ronan after reading his letter, but they haven't been received.

Quinn Peña and Hassan Khalil have already stirred dissent among the UF employees in First City, though Kitta still fears for them. It's a mystery what other tricks Jameson Feiser may have up his sleeve. It's also still unclear what Jaco Delores wants from all of this, but Kitta is certain he can't be trusted.

She dries her tears and bolts from the utility closet. Impatiently she checks her inbox in hope for a response from Ronan. Through the hallways she can't hold back her tears, and the air dries them as she runs past the onlookers lingering in the hallways and leaving their homes.

At the next corner, Kitta is met by a large, red-haired man in red armor, carrying an older, injured man wearing the same armor under his arm. The old man's head hangs toward the floor, and the larger man gasps. It's Linus Fogarty, carrying Popp under his arm, and he recognizes Kitta simply by her resemblance to both his captain and Melena Horn.

"Sir," Linus says.

Popp lifts his head and sees Kitta for the first time in over six years. He struggles to stand erect, and shrugs Linus's arm from his shoulders. He doesn't say a word. She looks just like Melena. Her long and dark hair, her sad, teal eyes and the large nose she inherited from him are unmistakable.

Kitta notices Popp's missing arm. She starts crying again and without saying a word she embraces Popp.

"I'm sorry, little one. For everything," Popp says.

Kitta doesn't say anything. She only sobs.

Popp can barely find the words to say. He sheds a tear himself, and succumbs to the overwhelming emotions of being reunited with his only blood family. "You left, but I was the one who abandoned you," he says. "I never knew you for real. Melena Horn must have taken good care of you."

"Ronan is dead," Kitta's speech is muffled against Popp's armor. "I haven't even seen Ezra Pierce since I've gotten here."

There is a long pause in their embrace. Kitta lifts her head and looks her father in the eyes.

"You're stronger than I could have ever made you," Popp says. "I was a terrible father."

"Melena taught me a lot," Kitta says, wiping her tears, "but I'm strong because of both of you. You were terrible," she smirks slightly through her sobbing, "but you're here now, and I need help."

"I'll do anything. Name it."

"We need to get to that Greenhouse, but not at the same time. Feiser sent me that message, I know it."

Popp admires her strategic thinking, but still fears for her.

"So you're going to be bait?"

"In a way, yes. I'm a political threat to him now and the control he has over this place. He wouldn't kill me."

"You should know, little one — he killed Bryndon Pierce for political reasons."

"It's a risk I'm willing to take."

Ezra Pierce, Advik Anand and Stella enter the office of the Greenhouse Annex, which sits on the Greenhouse's inner wall between the great garden and the treeline of the indoor forest. The windows of the annex are tinted, so they enter carefully. Advik and Stella check every corner of the large room with their rifles ready, and they find it empty. Only computer terminals and small soil plots for nutrient testing. Ezra has received the same message, *Greenhouse,* and waits patiently, finding the closest chair to the center of the room and closing his eyes.

"You said this message you received, it was sent to the Captain as well?" Stella asks, referring to Popp.

"Yes. He and his daughter will both be here."

"She is quite the celebrity now, from what I've heard."

"More politics, Stella. I won't hear of it. I'm here for the research owed to me — to Sol." Ezra's brow tightens, looking sharply at Stella, then Advik. "If Feiser killed my father, then his work against me is done, and I won't linger on it. I'm not afraid of a dead man. And my father — whether or not he felt me as his successor here on Titan failed. He was trusting, naive, arrogant. I won't make the same mistakes he made and fall into these traps so blatantly set by other arrogant men."

"I don't know you well, Mr. Pierce," Advik says, "but I can see now why you and the Captain get along so well."

"And how's that?" Ezra ignores that Advik isn't addressing him with the doctor prefix.

Advik hesitates.

"Speak plainly, Vik. You'd have to do something much more terrible than insult my pride to offend me."

"You're a cold man, Mr. Pierce. The Captain, he puts on a similar facade, but he feels deeply. I know this. I've seen it. If this stoicism you display is true, it provides balance, and I am thankful for it. I find it pragmatic. If your coldness is not true, then I pray you hold it only as long as you are with him, and us, and not a second longer. As I said, I am thankful, but to deny your feelings can be dangerous."

"I'm sure you know much more about danger than I do."

"What affects the mind, affects the body, Mr. Pierce. Your father taught me this."

"Did he? Well, you've got me beat," Ezra says with a surly tone. "He hardly taught me anything so emotionally profound."

"He said to all of us at the groundbreaking here, 'Let your minds be calm, and your hands true, for the future has no patience for imbalance. The future will not tolerate the body's intolerance of the mind, or vice versa.' I may be paraphrasing, but you understand."

"I do, Vik. I appreciate your honesty. You are a wise man. I hardly knew my father, and even less, longed for his *kingdom*, so to speak. You and Popp may have known him better than I ever did, which is why I'm glad you're with me. Despite my father's flaws, I'm aware he was a good man. My coldness has no place in politics or humanitarian causes."

"You call the captain 'Popp'?"

"Well, like I said before — after Bryndon passed, your Captain was my only connection to him. I first met him when I was a child, too young to care for the name Paulo Thiago Russo. Years before Bryndon passed, I called him Popp, and it stuck."

"Less cold than I may have assumed."

"Indeed."

Kitta arrives at the Greenhouse to see no personnel, but only a few automated robots tending to the oversized vegetation. She hears a rumbling from the hall behind her — heavy footsteps. She turns to see two large soldiers hustling toward her. She runs out into the open, down the main thoroughfare of the great garden. The large trees on the far side of the Greenhouse could provide better cover, but they're too far. In the center of the lower vegetation is a circular, red brick courtyard, surrounded by shrubbery three meters high. The courtyard tucked in the center of the shrubbery is bordered by four benches. Enormous elephant leaves provide shade from the bright, electric lighting and glimmering glacier above. The cover is not sufficient, and it's beginning to feel more and more like Kitta is walking into a trap.

"Doctor Pierce!" She shouts, and looks to the trees in the distance. She doesn't see Ezra.

She shouts again, and in the same second feels a pinch in her right buttock, from the direction of the pursuing guards.

Her vision begins to blur, but for a brief second she looks to the Greenhouse office annex at the end of the tree line and sees silhouettes beyond the tinted glass. She reaches down her backside to investigate and discovers she's been shot with a tranquilizer. Turning further to look at the pursuing guards, she sees a short, old man emerge from behind them and take the lead.

Kitta stumbles to one of the benches and sits. The old man stands over her — his short, wide shadow competing with the elephant leaves. His words are jumbled, but she remembers the low, rumbling sound of his voice from Melena's council chamber on Mars. His speech shakes her bones. Jameson Feiser has found her. Though she was expecting to meet him, she kicks herself for falling into such an easy trap. She remains conscious but cannot move. She wonders where her father and his friend are now, and how closely they followed. Whatever chemical circulates through her allows her to hear, but her sight has been compromised, and speaking is out of the question. A few more seconds pass in this state before she falls completely unconscious.

"Hey!" Ezra Pierce shouts as he paces swiftly from the Greenhouse office annex, unarmed, followed by an armed and ready Advik Anand. "Don't you hurt her!"

Jameson Feiser stands confident with his sickly, bloodshot eyes barely visible through the sagging skin below his brow. His robotic guards ready their weapons and face Ezra and Advik. Feiser controls their actions from his own Jym interface. "You act as if you have some sort of leverage here," he scoffs. "Though it is nice to finally meet you, Ezra. Let's keep this civil, shall we? The girl will be fine."

TWENTY TWO

The Ancients

KITTA sits on a bench outside a train station. She wears casual clothing—a loose, white button-up shirt with rolled sleeves and baggy, light blue denim pants. She doesn't wear her magnetic boots, but rather her brown leather slip-on shoes. It's an outfit she knows she hasn't worn in years. The gravity feels normal—like Earth. Memorial Station in Shanghai sits modestly before a port of high rockets and magnetic train rails stretching far in many directions. The memorial to the Last War is a functioning station, but no longer an orbital shipyard. The rockets that were kept there are tributes to the fallen heroes of the Last War, and a museum displaying the technology of the time. Kitta enters the station, and holds a ticket in her hand, reading, "United Frontier Scholastic Pass."

At age fourteen, Kitta is frightened, being truly alone for the first time. Though she always felt alone in her personal life, with her neglectful if not abusive father tormenting her, she feels vulnerable still.

The train moves fast. Very fast. The gravity begins to shift. The windows outside turn to darkness, and the greenery of Earth is no more. Dark, red rock and the occasional passing tunnel lights are all the windows yield until the familiar caves of Arcadia open to view. As the train arrives at the next station, a voice on the train's intercom says, "Welcome to

First Station!"

"Is this your stop?" a warm, familiar voice says to her as Kitta leaves her seat on the train. This young man's sarcasm isn't lost on her, knowing this is the last stop on the only train in Arcadia. She stands from her seat and says, "Yes," as she looks up at the tall, young man standing with her as the train empties. Faceless figures rush around them like a waterfall around rocks. The underground city on Mars is colder than Kitta was led to believe in school.

Her clothing hasn't changed, and she grows nervous knowing this place requires the United Frontier student jumpsuit, with magnetic boots. Now that she stands, the gravity doesn't feel different from Earth at all. This does not bother her, since she always hated the UF jumpsuits and their revealing nature.

"My name is Ronan," the young man says. "Are you new here as well?"

"I am. My name is Kitta."

"That's a beautiful name," he says. "You don't have a guardian?"

"Just my Scholastic Pass. What about you? How old are you?"

"Sixteen. I came with the new programmers, and I don't have a guardian either. You wanna team up?"

Kitta starts to cry, but doesn't know why. She feels safe again.

"Ronan, I'm so sorry," she says.

"Oh, everything's fine. My dad sent me."

As they begin leaving the train, the train becomes a hall-way, and the crowd of people around them blurs and fades away. The doors of the train become doors leading into class-rooms, and Ronan and Kitta now walk together through the hallways of the UF education center in Arcadia. Their surroundings look familiar, only slightly different. Older. Dirtier.

"So I was thinking — " Ronan says, "we've spent nearly two years together here now, and things are going well between us, yeah? I was thinking about after graduation — which isn't far off now — we'll be out of the dorms here and we'll be given places to live. If you'll be working with children, and I'll be programming, I could live close to the school."

Kitta knows Ronan is getting ready to ask if she wants to move in with him after they graduate from school. It's adorable to her how he dances around his question by stating obvious points, as if he thinks the question itself would catch her off guard.

"I like our place together," Kitta says. "And we were nice and close to the school, just like you said." Kitta realizes her response was somehow out of time. She and Ronan lived together for a couple of years after graduation, and while Ronan mostly worked from home, they lived close to the school where Kitta was teaching. They were happy, and Ronan was a supportive and loving partner. Now they walk through the halls of their old school as if the future from this point is changeable, but Kitta knows it isn't. She knows these are only memories, and she feels as if this is her only way of talking to Ronan, so she continues to play along and enjoy his company.

"Ronan, I'd be happy to live with you after graduation and start the next chapter of our life together," Kitta says. "You've been nothing but kind to me, and supportive," she starts to sob as she speaks to him, "and I don't know what I'm going to do without you. I don't know if I'll be strong enough to help the people of Sol without you by my side."

Ronan remains silent. The hallway becomes crowded with people. Kitta squints heavily and loses Ronan among the faceless figures. She searches for a brief second before recognizing Melena Horn standing in front of her at the doorway to a classroom.

"You must be Kitta Russo," Melena says to her. Her dark hair is long and relaxed around her shoulders, unlike Kitta's, but matches the color and natural waviness. Melena grabs Kitta's hand and gently pulls her into the classroom. Kitta, finding these moments familiar, but somehow more comfortable than memory, takes a seat while the small class of United Frontier students listens to the Ambassador's lecture.

"You are all here because you have proved your worth as leaders in your fields. This introduction to your new careers will begin by covering what we know about the Ancients and their purpose in Sol so many millions of years ago. You may have studied them at length on Earth, but I promise you, there is more to learn here, where they worked, and — "

Melena Horn is interrupted when Ronan Pierce enters the classroom in a hurry. Other teenagers in the classroom murmur, "That's Ronan Pierce." "Ronan Pierce is on Mars." Ronan finds an open desk next to Kitta and sits. He smiles at her before Melena continues.

"Welcome, Mr. Pierce. Don't think that your name gives you the right to be late to these lectures."

"I'm sorry, Ambassador… won't happen again," Ronan

responds bashfully.

Melena Horn continues her lecture, but Kitta is distracted by Ronan. His pale skin; his short, dark hair is thrown from his scalp as if it's trying to escape, or maybe he's just woken up. Being so tall, he struggles to adjust to the small desk. Kitta giggles at him, causing him to look over at her. He gives Kitta a playfully suspicious look before opening his tablet to take notes.

Ronan says to Kitta, "Is there anything I've missed?"

Kitta's eyes grow warm and soft. She knows he hasn't missed the lecture, but she breaks through the nostalgic scene she's found herself in.

"We have a baby," she says through her tears.

Ronan doesn't respond, but only stares at her with his longing, big and brown eyes.

"I've been in danger," she says, "but I've — "

"Please listen!" Melena Horn shouts. "Now, what little the Ancients left behind tells us that they came here for minerals: the iron, the ice, silicon, et cetera within the crust of Mars and other bodies in Sol. Now, theories — can anyone tell me why they didn't touch Earth?"

Kitta answers, "Because they knew better."

"Interesting answer, Miss Russo. Please explain."

"For a few reasons, they knew better than to land on Earth. I believe mostly that they didn't want to toy with the life that would come to it. They were advanced enough to know that leaving traces of themselves on Earth would alter our development, as well as our intentions."

"That is a common theory, and probably the most sound," Melena responds. "But you had another reason?"

"Just the dinosaurs being a nuisance, but the timing is unclear to me."

The classroom laughs and snickers at the thought of the Ancients battling dinosaurs on Earth.

"The time records we have show that there were, in fact, dinosaurs on Earth at the time of the Ancients' occupation of Sol. However, that theory is far more trivial than simply assuming that they, as you said, Kitta, were concerned with the trajectory of human development."

One of the classmates chimes in, "Could they have known a meteor would hit, then?"

"That is also a possibility — another of many theories, but a common one, nonetheless."

Kitta watches Ronan as he takes notes and listens to Melena Horn's lecture. Kitta ponders their child — the nameless being that shares their blood. It breaks her heart that Ronan will never meet him.

"Their artwork," Melena continues, "was carved into rock, and its interpretations by modern scientists and archeologists have been the greatest mystery they left us. We know why they were here, and we know what they were doing. The artwork is the only thing we have — the only hint — as to why they left."

Another student raises their hand, "Did they have a quota perhaps? Maybe they met it, and left."

"That theory was debunked when we discovered the graves and memorials to their dead. These ancients were ceremonial, like us, and wouldn't have created these elaborate monuments to their fallen only to abandon them within only a few generations.

"The two most famous drawings, which were found the most intact, show us two different things. The first drawing shows us two bodies orbiting one another. This particular drawing has been interpreted as a story of the beginning of our solar system. The theory of Jupiter's being a failed star is one that was debunked more than two hundred years ago, but these Ancients could have very well romanticized it in this artwork. The second, which is not only intriguing, but enlightening, is a drawing of one star in the center. This star, assumed to be Sol, is orbited by three other bodies. These three bodies are clearly receiving light from Sol, but one of them in particular appears to be broken — shattered. The condition of the drawing is a subject for debate, due to its age, and it's argued that the planet itself is not depicted as shattered, but the rock around the carving cracked and eroded, thus giving the illusion of a broken planetary body. However, revelationists and theists have their own theories involving late-stage solar flare activity which, in theory, could be devastating to planetary bodies in Sol's orbit. Something we are confident isn't possible in our lifetime, but nonetheless it could explain why the Ancients left Sol so abruptly."

Kitta is distracted once again by Ronan, who now frantically enters code into his tablet. He sweats and breathes heavily as Sato Song, whom Kitta didn't notice until now, leans into his shoulder and murmurs into his ear, smiling. Ronan wipes the sweat from his forehead and presses his thumb and fingers into his squinted eyes.

Kitta whispers loudly, "Sato!"

"That will be all for today," Melena declares from the head of the classroom.

The classroom starts to clear, but Ronan and Sato don't move, so Kitta stays. The faceless figures pass around and between them, and from the blurred periphery ahead Melena Horn emerges. She sits in a desk adjacent to Kitta, while Ronan remains buried in his tablet. Sato has disappeared.

"How are you finding Mars, Miss Russo?" Melena Horn asks.

Kitta stands from her desk and finds her footing. She begins walking toward the front of the classroom, past Melena. She sees her own name on the digital screen in front of her. Not her full name, just "Kitta." She knew she didn't want to be addressed by her last name when she became a teacher on Mars. It would only remind her of her father.

"The boots are strange," Kitta says without thought. The words are familiar, but foolish, knowing her clothes haven't changed. She turns and realizes that she now stands at the head of her own classroom. "But you'll need them in order to keep the strength in your young legs." Kitta turns, fully expecting to see her classroom on Mars, full of small children who were born on Mars and are now in the United Frontier's primary school program. Her clothes have finally changed to her teaching uniform.

"The Jollitium magnets, in their most raw form, are drawn to the core of any planetary body they're close to," Kitta continues, "and their gravitational strength is changeable. There will be lessons on it later, for this superconductor can be manipulated in so many ways, and has quickly become the most important element in all of Sol."

"Miss Kitta!" One child in front, named Rhubarb, shouts and raises her hand. "How long do we have to wear the boots?"

"Eight hours a day," Kitta responds. "The length of a daily shift. You can wear them longer if you'd like! I'm sure at least some of you have seen the little vests your parents had you wear when you were crawling, then eventually walking. They use the same magnets, and they help you to build strength. You might see Earth one day, and if you do, you'll need that strength for the stronger gravity there!"

"Miss Kitta!" Rhubarb shouts again with her hand raised to ask a question.

Before Kitta can call on her or Rhubarb can blurt her question out unprompted, the alarm for changeover in classes sounds, and Rhubarb shows a deep melancholy in her face. She begins to cry.

Kitta notices how Rhubarb attempts to hide her tears and heavy breathing from her classmates, and acts quickly.

"Okay everybody," she announces, "we'll learn about the history of Arcadia tomorrow, and we'll have a field trip to the surface next week to learn about the trade that keeps our city running. We'll get to see some trade ships coming and going."

The kids chatter with excitement and fade from the classroom, leaving Rhubarb alone at her desk. Her head is bent downward and she seems to have calmed her despair.

Kitta approaches Rhubarb and sits in the small desk next to her. As Kitta sits, Rhubarb grows larger, and Kitta finds herself looking up at this child who is now at least one meter taller than she is, sitting. Kitta doesn't question the strange physical shift before her, feeling familiar with the situation and her subconscious causing her to feel insecure.

"What's wrong, Rhuby?" She asks the large, crying child.

"My mommy and daddy talk about Earth. I want to go. I don't like it here. They've shown me pictures of when they were young, and Earth is so big. And Mars is so small."

Kitta's stomach sinks when she hears Rhubarb complain about her parents. Children are not supposed to be shown pictures or told too much about Earth at such a young age. It is considered a degree of child abuse to the United Froniter on Mars to make young children aware of the extravagance and beauty of Earth before they are ready to understand theirs and their family's purpose on Mars.

"Don't worry, Rhuby," Kitta says. "You may see Earth sooner than you think!"

"Have you been to Earth?"

"No," Kitta lies. She doesn't know how to treat this situation. If she reports that Rhubarb's parents have disclosed compromising details about Earth to their child, then it's a mystery to Kitta what the United Frontier would do. It would uproot their entire lives. But what about Rhubarb? She will only feel tortured being on Mars, and the risk of her doing something drastic — something potentially harmful to herself or others — is too great.

Kitta stands, regaining her normal size above little Rhubarb, and dismisses her from the classroom. She knows she doesn't have a choice but to report this to UF admins.

Kitta goes to her own desk to retrieve a tablet so she can contact an admin, and Melena Horn suddenly enters the room. She doesn't say anything. Kitta studies Melena Horn briefly. Melena looks different. She stares back into Kitta's eyes as if she's expecting a response.

"Have I failed?" Kitta asks. "That little girl and her parents were sent to Earth and removed from United Frontier employment. Her parents worked their whole lives and — "

"And they failed," Melena responds. "But you saved that child. It was how I knew you'd be great. You made the hard choice, and if you hadn't, someone would have been hurt. Parents fail all the time. I failed you in the greatest way."

"You were my greatest teacher," Kitta says.

"And if someone asked me who my greatest teacher was, I wouldn't have such a sure answer. It's probably the only thing I was ever unsure of. Every decision I made was without a second thought. When Paul took you to Earth, I knew I was failing you. I failed him too. Paul loved me and I abandoned him when he was cast out. When it happened, I knew what I had done was wrong, but I was needed here, too. I couldn't let Jameson Feiser take control of Titan — not after what the Jollitium did to me. It saved my life, but at a great cost. I failed Titan when I let the Jollitium consume me, and UF cast me out for it. You have not failed, Kitta, but you will. You will fail, it will make you stronger, and you will be better than I ever was."

"I don't know how I'm going to lead without you or Ronan with me."

"Ronan knew the risks, and he fought for you anyway. He will always be with you through your child. You need to find your child. Do not fail in the same way I did."

Kitta's watches as Melena Horn loses details in her appearance. Her garbs, face and hair slowly fade and disappear altogether. Kitta doesn't say a word. She doesn't know what to say. She's left alone in the classroom, and as the room changes around her, she smells a dewiness in the air. A bright light flickers slowly from overhead, and her surroundings are stripped away. It's dark between the infrequent flickers of light. She looks up and sees a giant leaf overhead, swaying in the breeze, and the light catches Kitta's eye as the leaf dances in and out.

Her eyes open.

TWENTY THREE

Rendezvous Pt. 2

KITTA lies on one of the benches in Titan's Greenhouse courtyard beneath the shade of enormous elephant leaves. She regained consciousness, but she can't move, and her rear feels sore from the contact point of Jameson Feiser's tranquilizer dart. She attempts to access her Jym interface, but it's hardly visible to her. Her cognition is strong enough to activate it, but her blurry vision compromises it. She feels nauseous. As of now, all she can do is listen.

"What's wrong with her?" Ezra Pierce asks.

"She's been tranquilized, but she can still hear us," Jameson Feiser says. "I want her to hear us. I almost did the same to you, but I figured we could be more diplomatic than these young guns. You have proven yourself to be quite unpredictable, Mr. Pierce, but if this girl is as unpredictable as your son, then I can no longer risk her meandering through my city."

"It's *Doctor* Pierce. And excuse me. *Your* city?"

"Yes, Doctor Pierce, *my* city. Look around you. I know your background, and I know that these plants — this food — it's a dream come true for a species on the brink of starvation. For someone of your status and field of expertise, self-indulgent, I'm sure."

"But you've faked the death toll, yes? So from where I'm standing, the cultivation is impressive, but how much of it is going to waste? Surely it's more than enough to feed the people here. Why fake a starvation crisis?"

"You're a fool! A fake death toll in the Yellow Sector media makes me — or *the Mayor of Titan*, rather — look like a hero to all the right people — the people with the money. You're asking yourself the wrong questions, Doctor."

Feiser tries to calm Ezra, and reaches for the sidearm on his hip. Ezra sees Feiser reaching for it, and tries to stop him. Ezra lunges toward Feiser, but Feiser thrusts a stiffened hand into Ezra's chest, knocking him back. Feiser then fires a tranquilizer into Ezra's shoulder. Ezra feels the same immediate effects as Kitta, but to a lesser degree. His vision remains intact, but his body is numbed and subdued. Jameson Feiser helps Ezra as he stumbles and gently collapses him into the courtyard bench across from Kitta's.

"I'll need you both to listen to me," Feiser says. He stands in the entryway to the covered courtyard, so that he can see outside the shrubbery. "Your condition is only temporary. I assume you've both read the young programmer's letter," he refers to Ronan. "So I suppose I'll be the one to confirm to you both — he's dead. All you've done by intruding here is slow down my operation, and gotten your own people killed. Jaco Delores works for me, and as young and foolish as he is, our goals are similar. Using the Jollitium compounds to create larger food is only a stepping stone to creating a better version of our species, and leaving our tormented, rotting past behind us.

"I'm truly sorry for your loss, and the boy didn't need to die. Ezra, if you blame yourself, you would be correct in doing so. Miss Russo, I don't know what you're doing here, or what good you thought you could do here, but I'll be placing you under arrest and sending you back to Mars to be stripped of your administrative status. My only advice to you, little girl, is to forget what your drunken mother told you, and be — "

Jameson Feiser is interrupted when he sees Stella emerge from a prone position in the shallow garden, just at the feet of Feiser's humanoid robot guards. Feiser recognizes her attire — the jewel and grenade-clad armor worn by the pirates on Ceres. Stella mounts the first guard and thrusts a dagger into the processing computer located on its back. She leaps from the now disabled guard, and rolls past the second, finding her feet behind it. As the second guard turns to find Stella, Jameson Feiser draws his pistol. Stella slaps a small, sticky-EMP charge on the chassis of the guard and orbits it, keeping it between her and Feiser and denying him his shot. The EMP charge activates, and the guard stands in place, disabled, but still erect between Stella and Feiser.

Feiser quickly accesses his Jym and releases more humanoid security drones from the nearby annex. Four more humanoid guards rush to Feiser's position, and ready their weapons in Stella's direction. Stella roars at Feiser and reaches for one of the larger grenades.

Stella stops when she hears Popp shout from behind her.

"Cool it!" Popp limps next to Linus with his remaining arm around Linus' shoulders. Linus has an arm hooked around Popp to help carry him. The infection from the rat bite has not been treated, and wreaks havoc on Popp's nervous system. Advik runs to Popp and Linus's position, just a few meters away from the courtyard. Stella backs away slowly, her rifle drawn and steadily aimed at Feiser.

"Sir, are you okay?" Advik asks frantically, noticing Popp's condition — the missing arm and the pale tint in his skin due to the infection. Popp doesn't speak, only nods.

"One of the rats got his arm on the *Comrade*. We were in medical when we received Ezra's message," Linus explains.

"The *Comrade*?" Advik asks. "What the hell happened?"

"The ship is lost, Vik. The rats were led there along with drones that had EMP charges large enough to take it offline completely."

Advik looks at the ground. After a pause he says, "What about the rest of the employees?"

Before Linus can answer, Jameson Feiser laughs loudly. Ezra and Kitta are slumped in the courtyard benches behind him with their eyes open. Popp grows angry at the sight of their condition. He recognizes Jameson Feiser, standing between them. A deeply hidden fear wriggles beneath the smug expression on Feiser's face. Popp knows his expressions too well. He swiftly draws his pistol and fires at Feiser, but the bullet ricochets past one of the newly-deployed humanoid guards, and barely misses him. Feiser lifts his pistol and aims it at the Inquisition leaders.

"Captain Russo, welcome back! I didn't think you'd be so excited to see me," Jameson Feiser jokes. "If you try that again my guards will cut you down where you stand."

"You've made your game known, James. Now you're weak."

"See, that's always been your problem, *Pauly*," Feiser sneers, recognizing that Popp is using his own words against him.

You make yourself known, you make yourself weak.

"Everything is a game to you," Feiser continues. "Such a

lack of understanding is what sent you away from here all those years ago."

As Feiser rants, Stella pulls one of the larger EMP grenades from her side and rolls it swiftly at the small formation of robots ahead. All four of them fall to the ground in a heap of deactivated machinery. Stella aims her rifle at Feiser once again and shouts, "Put the pistol down!" Stella notices Kitta squirming and struggling to keep her eyes open. "Put it on the bench behind you. Now!"

"Now, we were called here to talk," Feiser says in a much lighter, friendlier tone as he sets his pistol on the armrest of the same bench where Kitta is strewn. Kitta can see the pistol, but cannot move or reach it. "So, perhaps until Doctor Pierce is ready, *we* can talk. He and the girl can hear us just fine."

"Killing you is easier," Stella grunts.

"And what will that get you?" Feiser asks rhetorically. "You're outnumbered here. Your ship is inoperable. Think."

Suddenly, the door next to the Greenhouse's office annex opens again, this time to twenty humanoid robot soldiers, armed with rifles, marching on the Inquisition.

"If they don't stop, we will shoot you right now!" Stella screams.

Stella keeps her rifle steady. Advik joins Stella in aiming his rifle at Feiser.

Feiser accesses the Commands tool in his Jym and orders his humanoid robots to halt their position ten meters away. He then prepares to order his robot soldiers to fire upon the Inquisition if they fire any of their weapons, but suddenly Jaco Delores interrupts him, quickly entering the

Greenhouse with his two guards. Delores's pistol is drawn, along with his guards and their rifles, aiming at Popp as they approach from the Inquisition's rear.

"Tell them to stand down, Captain Russo," Delores says in his damaged voice. Advik spins to aim at Delores, and Delores and his guards stop and stand ready, aiming back at Advik.

Kitta is now able to keep her eyes open and access the interface of her Jym. She notices Ezra in a similar state of sedation on the adjacent bench, but his skin looks pale. She struggles to focus on him. His eyes are open and he's breathing, but he's been shot, caught in the path of Popp's ricochet.

Kitta's fingers start to tick as the tranquilizer begins to wear off.

Feiser's pistol sits on the armrest at the other end of the bench where Kitta sits, within Feiser's reach, and nearly within hers. As the others continue their stand-off, Kitta uses all her strength to drag her weight across the bench and closer to the gun. She knows she wouldn't have the strength to aim the pistol, but Feiser is equipped with the same Jym cybernetics, allowing Kitta to use the Augmented Reality tools of her Jym against him.

Ezra slides forward from his bench and falls to the bricks of the courtyard. He turns onto his belly and lifts himself up to a crawling position.

Feiser turns and notices Ezra's wound dripping blood onto the bricks of the courtyard. Ezra begins crawling slowly toward Kitta. Feiser accesses his own Jym software and calls for medical.

"Medical will be here in minutes," Feiser says. He then

looks at Popp. "You're impulsive, and dangerous. You always were. It's how you lost your position here on Titan and now, you've shot your dead friend's son."

The airlock at the south end of the Greenhouse suddenly chimes in its depressurization sequence. Loud hydraulics press and gears turn as the giant door opens. Patricia Lordes, General Duval Kamasi and General Ren Tilson are first through the enormous airlock doors and onto the entrance platform. Behind them march over two hundred soldiers, some of them dressed in UF mesh-armor and falling into formation, while the extravagantly-garbed pirate soldiers of Ceres stand scattered between them in no formation. All the weapons held between Feiser's drones and Popp's squad shift toward the large crowd of pirates and UF mutineers.

Stella smiles. "Mother!" She shouts to Patricia Lordes.

"Pirate trash!" Popp shouts, aiming his pistol at Stella's head. Stella lowers her rifle, letting it hang by the harness from her shoulders, and raises her hands. Advik stands firm with his rifle being the only one still pointed at Jameson Feiser.

Patricia looks at Popp with wide, curious eyes, noticing his missing arm. "Relax, dear," she shouts back to him, "we're only here to see our interests fulfilled." She turns to Jameson Feiser. "James, you small, small man," her tone shifts to her piercing sarcasm, "how have you been? Not dead, but you have gotten fatter."

"You should've stayed on the Belt where you belong, Lordes," Fieser responds. "I assume my men are with you?" Feiser uses his Jym to program the guards to fire upon any others who decide to fire first.

"Hardly!" General Kamasi shouts. Patricia Lordes' pirates follow his outburst with laughter. Generals Kamasi and Tilson's mutineers stand quietly and aim their rifles at the drones standing at the tree line. The pirates appear to be more relaxed, with rifles loosely in hand or hanging from their slings. They greatly outnumber everybody else in the Greenhouse.

Kitta's tranquilized state continues to fade, and Ezra Pierce persistently, painfully crawls toward her on his hands and knees while Jameson Feiser is distracted. Blood runs from his side and pools upon the bricks beneath him. His knees drag through it and smear it. He reaches Kitta's feet, and digs into his pocket, pulling his recording device and placing it at her feet. Kitta watches in disbelief. Tears run from her face and she cannot bring herself physically to reach the device at her feet, but she can cover it with her foot.

She is now close enough to reach the pistol Feiser set upon the bench, but is still too weak to aim it. She uses her Jym's Augmented Reality tool to copy the pistol's three-dimensional image, and quietly scoops the pistol from the armrest and onto the seat of the bench near her. The augmented image left on the armrest in the pistol's place is uncanny, and will look to Jameson Feiser as if it's still there. Kitta covers it by lying on top of it.

"Kitta," Ezra murmurs, choking on his words. He looks up at Kitta so that he can see her eyes. "Be what we couldn't."

Ezra collapses at Kitta's feet. Jameson Feiser hears Ezra's body thud against the bricks and turns to see Ezra's state. The trail of blood behind him is great, and he's lost too much to survive. Feiser notices Kitta lying on the bench, and assumes the non-lethal tranquilizer must have been strong enough to render her unconscious.

Popp shrugs away from Linus and approaches Feiser. "Let me see my daughter," he shouts.

Just then, Sam Levin sprints into the Greenhouse from First City's inner hallway, followed by Quinn Peña, Hassan Khalil, and nearly one hundred soldiers and employees from the *Comrade*. All of those who came from the surface, and many from the deep catacombs beneath First City.

The soldiers and employees from the *Comrade* are followed by all the young First City Admins from the Armory to whom Feiser gave weapons. They funnel into the Greenhouse and fall into a sloppy formation. Behind the soldiers, employees and Admins, a crowd of Titan's citizens — women, children and elderly — trickle hesitantly into the Greenhouse. Some of them gather and stand idly to watch the standoff while others scatter to eat and collect the abundant produce nearby.

Popp is happy to see the *Comrade*'s survivors at his back, but is greatly concerned with Kitta. He looks at Advik Anand and commands him to take the lead of the *Comrade*'s forces. Stella attempts to part from the group and head toward Patricia, but Linus stops her at gunpoint. Popp turns back to Jameson Feiser and approaches him. He steps around the pile of broken drones and Feiser shouts to him, "Don't you come any closer, Paul!" Feiser turns swiftly and reaches for the gun on the bench, but his hand passes right through the augmented image placed by Kitta. Popp draws his pistol and fires into Feiser's chest. Two bullets burrow into Jameson Feiser's chest before he falls to the ground. The drones at the tree line immediately open fire at Popp. Popp dives to the ground and takes cover behind the pile of disabled drones.

Bullets whiz closely past him, bouncing and ringing from the plastic and metal of the lifeless robots.

The soldiers of the *Comrade* open fire on the drones. Advik shifts his aim and fires at the drones as well as Stella, who uses her remaining EMP grenades. All twenty of the drones fall within seconds.

The pirates of Ceres and the First City mutineers take aim at the *Comrade*'s soldiers. The *Comrade*'s soldiers return their aim. Popp shouts as he shakily lifts himself from his cover, "Everyone stop!"

Sam runs to Popp and says, "Are you okay, sir?"

"I'd like my arm back, but I haven't been shot if that's what you mean."

Sam runs to Kitta. Kitta is now strong enough to retrieve Ezra's recording device from beneath her foot before Sam lifts her from the bench, pulling her arm over their shoulders. Sam sees the gun on the bench and moves to grab it.

"Don't," Kitta says. "I don't need it anymore."

Popp kneels beside Jameson Feiser, who breathes slowly. His bloodshot eyes have turned to red billiard balls bulging from their sockets. Popp looks upon him and sheds a tear. Popp presses against the wound on Feiser's chest with his finger. Feisers screams and wretches, spattering Popp's face with blood.

"Bryndon… Melena," Popp whispers, "my daughter."

Feiser's final breath leaves his mouth through gurgling blood.

Popp sighs, and looks at Kitta, who hangs from Sam's shoulders while the tranquilizer continues to wear away. They lock eyes for several seconds, and she looks away.

Instead of going to her, Popp backs away and moves to Ezra's body. He kneels beside him and checks his pulse. Nothing.

Medical personnel break through the crowd outside the Greenhouse Annex and tend to Ezra. They leave Jameson Feiser's body lying on the courtyard bricks, and cover Ezra's body before taking him away on a stretcher.

Patricia Lordes' pirate force still has to be addressed. "Comrades! Stand ready!" Popp shouts. His soldiers and the Ceres pirates hold their aim at one another, but the First City mutineers are unsure whether they would fire their weapons in the direction of their fellow citizens of First City. The armed admins and soldiers from First City also take aim at the Ceres pirates, but they too, are frightened.

"You're vastly outnumbered, dear," Patricia Lordes scoffs at Popp.

"That's the most embarrassing part on your account," Popp brags, but knows the Ceres pirates are greater warriors than any other group in the Greenhouse at this moment.

Kitta's consciousness is beginning to come back, but she feels drunk. She accesses her Jym and selects "Proximity," then "Intercom," allowing her to speak on all open channels and loudspeakers within First City. Everyone will hear.

"Stop!" she shouts. Everyone in the Greenhouse and across the entirety of First City stops to listen over the intercom system. "Everyone who came here over the past week has had their issues with the United Frontier, and some of you who've lived here didn't know the issue, but you knew something was wrong. Truth is, the United Frontier left this place a long time ago. My mother, Melena Horn, sent me here to restore it...to restore something I hardly knew, or appreciated. I grew up on

Earth with an abusive father who despised UF, and when I ran away from home as a teenager, I saw the UF as my escape from family, or at least the family I knew. Melena Horn knew me before I told her my name — my mother. I was welcomed on Mars with open arms. I had gained a few friends, and they were so dear to me. They're all gone now. Melena Horn; Ronan, my love; Sato Song is missing. My only family is gone, and I'm left here. Here is where I intend to remain. Ezra Pierce, son of Bryndon Pierce and father of Ronan Pierce is the man who initiated the Inquisition into Titan's affairs. He didn't ask for my help, but Melena did. She knew of the potential beyond the Belt, and that greed had taken hold of those in control of the United Frontier on Titan. The power found here should be treated responsibly, and shared by all. I do not wish to assert control of anything but my own destiny here, and whatever that may be, I know this much — it will be work. It will be difficult. It will be for the people, and it will work toward the betterment of all of Sol. I urge you to lower your weapons, and cast aside your grievances. Jameson Feiser is gone, and the United Frontier has a chance to be born anew. Please."

Generals Duval Kamasi and Ren Tilson look at each other; their soldiers all look to them for their command. Kamasi and Tilson fall to one knee, and their soldiers lower their weapons and follow suit. Popp turns to look at Linus and Advik, and takes a knee himself. Linus, Advik, and all of the *Comrade*'s soldiers and employees lower their weapons and fall to one knee. One by one, the admins and soldiers in First City take a knee, and the citizens around them do the same.

Patricia Lordes looks around at the masses, bewildered by the display of unity and knowledge that she would be outnumbered if she were to attack. Stella runs to her.

"There are too many," Stella says.

"I know, dear. Let's go home." Patricia signals her pirate horde to exit the Greenhouse. They walk slowly through the formation of kneeling UF mutineers and file into the Greenhouse airlock, bound for their ships. Patricia walks in the opposite direction, to Kitta.

Kitta studies Patricia Lordes as she approaches. Her armor is not only intimidating, but stylish. Her demeanor is undeniable, and Kitta knows exactly who she is without introduction. The Pirate Queen of Ceres. Denier of UF and ruler of her own people. If it can be done on Ceres, it can be done here.

Kitta says to her, "You have other plans?"

"I like you, dear. But we simply do not bow. We will recognize your *new UF* when it recognizes Ceres as a private entity and not something they can either regulate or destroy."

UF has taken much more from Kitta than it has given by now. Her education, her partnership with Ronan, and her relationship with Melena Horn all felt so meticulously planned, either by Kitta or by others she knew or cared about — but they're all gone now. Her child is all she has left. Her estranged father deserves to heal, but after all this time, she can't be sure of him. She is presented with a defining decision which will alter the future not only of UF, but herself, her child, and of Titan.

She speaks plainly. "UF is dead here. I'm making this my own."

Patricia turns and heads for the airlock. "I'll believe it when I see it, kid."

Curtains

OR five years now Kitta Russo has presided over operations upstar from the Asteroid Belt. She was offered the position of Titan's Ambassador and the United Frontier's youngest Ambassador in history, but turned it down. Her operation outside the Belt has been named Guild of the Horn, and has effectively replaced the United Frontier on Titan. Her son, Bryndon II, was given the surname Pierce, and lives a happy life in Titan's Child Science Program. His health and metabolism from Delores's Jollitium vaccine are setting new records in the biological field, and Kitta has approved the vaccine for use on Titan. The parents of First City are offered a choice to volunteer their children for the vaccine, and the volume of volunteers has created a long waiting list. The people of Titan are happy under Kitta Russo, and she and her child are a beacon of trust following the controversy surrounding the late Jameson Feiser's scandal involving the Jollitium, the vaccine, and its creator, Jaco Delores.

Jaco Delores's tethered space station in Saturn's inner orbit was completed. As he expected, the gas giant has become a second abundant source of Jollitium, boosting the economy of Titan and Sol's colonies on both sides of the Asteroid Belt. Populations continue to grow and the people of Sol prosper. Kitta ordered that neither Delores, Inc., which absorbed

FeiserCorp's assets, nor Guild of the Horn would be allowed a monopoly on the mining of Jollitium, allowing privateers, including the United Frontier, from across Sol to take part in the interplanetary commerce.

Jaco Delores was forced to resign in disgrace from his position as CEO of Delores, Inc., and Spencer Gant took his place. Delores has remained on Titan in prison, charged with interplanetary conspiracy against the United Frontier and embryonic crimes against Kitta Russo and her son. He continues to research and produce Jollitium compounds not only for humans, but also vegetation and livestock under not only the United Frontier, but also Delores Inc. in secret. He is not allowed to leave Titan, and is to remain there until his undetermined working sentence has been served. Spencer successfully smuggled his daughter back to Earth shortly after the events on Titan.

Kitta remains unaware that Delores fired the shot that killed Ronan. Sam Levin didn't have the courage to tell her, and the letter written by Ronan convinced everybody he had died, but to this day nobody knows the location of his body. Sam knew Jaco Delores had Sol in his best interest, and now he can no longer do harm while in servitude.

Sato Song remains missing as well. A funeral was held for Ronan in the months following Kitta's inauguration, and Sato's funeral was held months later when the search for him was finally called off.

After Jaco Delores's sentencing Kitta spared no time opening an investigation into anybody working directly with Jameson Feiser, including United Frontier Ambassador Jessica Barnes of Earth. The investigation was thwarted due to insufficient evidence, indicating to Kitta that the corruption of UF on Earth extends also to Adofo Manu, the new Ambassador of Mars. Kitta can only hope the fight against the greed of UF is a battle that can be won without bloodshed.

It was within Ezra Pierce's audio logs that he implicated Jessica Barnes as a conspirator. He recorded Jameson Feiser's confession in the Greenhouse, and Kitta's recording of Jaco Delores aboard his ship was enough evidence to charge Jaco Delores, but not enough to charge Jessica Barnes. Ezra's recordings were kept close to Kitta, for his last confession holds a special sentimental value.

"Ronan, if, or when you ever hear this, know that I'm sorry. I wish that I could go back, and be there with you on Mars. I wish I had the courage to leave UF on Earth when it was for you, and not for my own ego. You will do greater things than I ever could, and Kitta is lucky to have you on her side. She will be greater than both of us. In all of this mess I've created for you both, I hope that you can take away one thing, and that is a vision of hope for the United Frontier and, more importantly, for Sol: a vision that doesn't operate behind curtains, sow secrets, and perpetuate lies, fulfilling the comfort of only a certain few of Sol's citizens. I was privileged, and I knew nothing of the true darkness of the world. I'm hoping you only ever have to see the true suffering of Sol through the eyes of an ally; committed to, and equipped for real change. Be what we couldn't."

Popp left a message for Kitta upon his departure from Titan. "I'm sorry," it read simply. In response, Kitta granted him and his company commercial status outside the Belt, allowing Popp to fulfill his once dead dream of trafficking minerals throughout Sol, only not for UF, but as an Orbital Trade Captain for Guild of the Horn. He did as such, opening a new world of possibilities for him and his employees. The people of the *Comrade* live fulfilling and fruitful lives. Kitta has given her father permission to visit his and Ezra's grandson on Titan, when he's ready.

"I will do my best," Jaco Delores speaks to a run-of-the-mill tablet displaying an outdated, UF public records' picture of Patricia Lordes. He sits inside a medical wing, converted into a working prison cell, in the lower levels of First City.

"That's what the little Russo girl told me years ago. The only change we've seen here at the Belt was of our own making," Patricia Lordes scoffs. "It *is* what we asked her for, so tell me — based on what I've been seeing in the media — how are you in any position to help me?"

"Miss Lordes, my gilded cage allows me to continue my work, mass-producing my vaccine. My daughter and Kitta's son will each live two hundred years. It's how I'm going to earn my freedom."

"You're a fool if you think she's going to free you. Between the recordings she leaked of you, Ezra Pierce's recordings of James, and your trifling with her unborn son, you're going to die on that moon."

"Perhaps I will die on this moon," Jaco Delores retorts, "but I know how to continue my work from the shadows, and help us both. A partnership with you is how we get the power we want. Titan can be yours."

"I'm listening."

"I have loyalists here on Titan, and can ship your Jollitium. You continue to plunder whatever carriers you like, and all you have to do is give me information. I need you to monitor the traffic for me. You may never hear that I am missing.

"My daughter has been sent to Earth, but Spencer Gant will be with her. Whether she knows it or not, she will be drawn back to me, here. She is how the true power of this Jollitium will be realized. My time is limited, but hers…"

"Two hundred years, yeah. I remember. Are you done? I have work to do."

"Don't you forget what I said. When you get your first unmarked shipment, I'll be expecting information."

TO BE CONTINUED

Special Thanks:

Thomas Flowers

Andrea Maddox-Dallas

Chip Zempel

Elizabeth Zempel

James Vander Pluym

Kyle Braden

Tracy Riggs

Caroline Newman

Cyrus Fox

Claire Flowers

Karen Grahn

Barbara Flowers

Damian Redd

Travis Hiler

Jesse McKenzie

Geoffrey Alexander

Ian Stuart

Maureen Borkowski

Cregg Hancock

Rebecca Perez

Alexis Anderson

Jimmy King

Richard Zempel

Jordan Thomas

Garrett Calcaterra

Nikolaus Nagel

Katie Larsen

Jack Strader